The Settlers

A Novel by

Vilhelm Moberg

Translated from the Swedish by

Gustaf Lannestock

WARNER BOOKS

A Warner Communications Company

A special book and television presentation from

KCTSeattle

Copyright © 1978 by Mrs. Margareta Moberg.
English translation copyright © 1961, 1978 by Gustaf Lannestock.
The Settlers is translated from the Swedish book *Nybyggarna,*
copyright © 1956 by Vilhelm Moberg.

A special book and television presentation from
KCTSeattle
department of marketing and telecommunications
with the assistance of
BMR, 1668 Lombard Street, San Francisco, California 94123

Published by Warner Books, Inc. by arrangement with
Albert Bonniers Förlag, Stockholm.

International Standard Book Number: 0-446-38117-9

Warner Books, Inc., 666 Fifth Avenue, New York, NY 10103

W A Warner Communications Company

Printed in the United States of America

First Printing: October, 1983

10 9 8 7 6 5 4 3 2 1

ACKNOWLEDGMENT

To Professor Nils Sahlin of the Swedish-American Historical Society, Philadelphia, the author wishes to express his deep appreciation for invaluable help in obtaining documents about the Swedish emigrants, and for his personal kindness during the author's visits to the United States in 1950-1955.

AUTHOR'S NOTE

In the interests of fiction I have taken certain liberties with geography, time and distance in the passages describing the travels of Robert and Arvid.

V.M.

CONTENTS

The Settlers

PROLOGUE

THE LAND THEY CHANGED

A giant tree, uprooted by a storm, once fell across the path that ran along the shore of Ki-Chi-Saga, a lake in Chippewa Indian country, between the Mississippi and the St. Croix rivers. It was left where it had fallen, an obstacle to those who used the path. From then on they walked around the fallen tree (to the Indians it did not occur to chop it out of the way). Thus a new path was formed, making a wide curve around the tree. Instead of removing the log, the Indians moved the path.

The great tree lay there while the years went by and moss covered its bole. A generation of forest life passed, and the fallen tree began to rot. The path around it was by now well tramped, and no one remembered any longer that it had once run straight in this place. Over the years the Indians wasted a good deal of time taking the longer path; but to them time was there to be wasted.

One day a man of another race came walking along the path. He carried an ax on his shoulder and walked heavily, shod in boots made on another continent. With his ax he split the rotten trunk in a few places and rolled it aside. The obstacle was removed, the path was again straight and now ran its earlier, shorter course. And the man with the ax who couldn't waste his time on a longer road asked himself: Why had this tree been allowed to obstruct the path so long that it had had time to rot?

The tiller had come to the land of the nomads; the day he removed the tree from the Indian path at Lake Ki-Chi-Saga, two different ways of life met head on.

11

The era of the nomads was coming to an end in this part of the world. The people who had time to wait a generation until an obstacle in their path rotted away were doomed. The hunter who moved his fire and his tent according to the season and the migration of the game could count his days. In his place came the farmer, the permanent inhabitant, who built his fireplace of stone and timbered his house.

Through a treaty which the Indians were forced to accept, the land was opened for settling and claim taking. The hunters were turned back and their hunting grounds with the graves of their forefathers were taken over. Virgin soil, deep and fertile, was then transformed into fruitful fields. An immense country, until now lacking any order except that of nature, was divided, surveyed, registered, mapped and separated into counties, townships and sections. Millions of acres of wilderness were marked off on paper in square lots, each intended as a homestead for a settler.

The newcomers were farmers without soil who came to a land with soil but no farmers. They came from the Old World, where they had lived under governments they themselves had not elected. They came to the New World, leaving behind their rulers and overlords, poverty and suppression. They had left Germany because of revolution, Ireland because of potato blight, Sweden because of religious persecution. The immigrants were the disobedient sons and daughters of their homelands, and now they settled down on a land that as yet had little or no government.

The disobedient people from the Old World were young—young people in a young country. Three quarters of the settlers in Minnesota Territory were under thirty; they had no useless oldsters to support, were not held back by the authority of an older generation. For them life began anew; they depended entirely on themselves now. They broke many of the old customs, did their chores in their own ways and obeyed no will except their own. Here it was up to them to elect their own authority; in the wilderness they enjoyed in full measure the new freedom to disobey.

And here were no upper or lower classes; no one had inherited special privileges and rights, no one was by virtue of his birth superior or inferior. Each one was valued according to his ability, measured through his industry. The virgin forests fostered self-assurance and developed free men.

12

The immigrant did not wait while an obstacle in his path rotted down; he did not have time to take detours around a fallen tree. He had come to make a living for himself and his family, he must build a house and establish a home; he must build up a new society from its very foundation.

The first immigrants to take up claims were few and far apart. As yet they could not talk to each other across the fence — their houses lay miles apart. But from 1850 on, the influx into the Territory increased. They came in large groups, small groups, families, as friends or single individuals, and settled down along the shores of the heaven-blue waters that had given the territory its name: Minnesota.

Thus the nomad gave way to the tiller, the forest animals gave up their grazing to domesticated animals, the deer pastures were turned into tended fields, the tall trees were felled and made into lumber for the settlers' houses. The immigrants founded their new domain in a land without limitations, a land with room enough for everyone's dreams.

I

THE FOUNDATIONS

I

NEW AXES IN THE FOREST

- 1 -

One day in May, Karl Oskar Nilsson was out on his claim cutting fence posts. When the height of the sun told him it was noon, he stopped his work to go home for dinner.

He took off one of his wooden shoes and emptied out a few dried lumps of blue clay which had chafed his heel. On the shoe was a deep gash from his ax. What luck that he had worn wooden shoes today! In the morning, while felling the first linden tree, his ax had slipped and landed on the toe of his right shoe; if he had been wearing leather boots the ax would have split his foot. But his old long-legged boots — of finest leather, made by the village cobbler before he had left his Swedish home parish — had long been worn out and put away. After the many miles of tramping he had done in them during his three years in North America, they were now entirely gone. He had mended and patched them as best he could, but like nearly all their footgear and clothing from Sweden they were finally worn to shreds.

With his ax under his arm Karl Oskar Nilsson walked along the lake, on the path he himself had cleared, through groves of larch trees and elms, through thickets of maple and hazel bushes. It was pleasant along the path today, with the multitude of newly opened leaves and all the fresh greenery. Spring was early this year in the Territory. The wild cherry trees were already in full bloom and shone pleasantly white in the lush greenery. A mild rain in the night

15

had watered the earth and caused a fragrance to rise from grass and flowers. Between the tree trunks, Lake Ki-Chi-Saga's glittering surface could be seen all along the way.

In many places the greenery hung over the lake so heavily that no one could make out where the ground ended and the water began. Farther out the bay was full of birds — ducks, swans and wild geese. On the other shore rose a thick wall of tall elms; at first Karl Oskar had thought it was the opposite side of the lake, but when he had rowed over in his holed-out canoe he had discovered it was a wood-covered island, with still another great island beyond. Ki-Chi-Saga — in Chippewa the name meant "beautiful lake" — consisted of seven small lakes, connected by narrow channels. This was a lake landscape, a conglomeration of islets, peninsulas, points, inlets, bays, necks, headlands, isthmuses. Each islet, bay or tongue of land had another islet, bay or tongue of land behind it, and together they seemed to spread out like an inundated forest.

High above the shore rose the imposing sandstone cliff resembling an Indian's head, which was called the Indian. The cliff's red-brown face with its deep, black eyeholes was turned toward the lake, straining toward the east like a watchman over land and water.

A wide flock of doves came flying over the bay, like a darkening cloud. When they had passed, Karl Oskar stopped and listened. The whizzing sound of bird wings was followed by another sound: he could hear the ring of an ax.

That May day was clear and calm, and the sound carried far. He was accustomed to identifying sounds in the forest, and he was not mistaken, he could clearly hear the sound of a sharp ax striking a tree trunk. It came from the southeast and was quite close. Someone was felling a tree near the lake.

His eyebrows knitted. It was not an Indian at work — the Indians did not fell trees with an ax. It must be a white man; an intruder had come to his land. But he had his squatter's papers, and he had made two payments for his claim at the land office in Stillwater. His claim had been surveyed, it was number 35 of the section, and its borders were blazed. No one could push him out, no one could deny him his rights. Here in the forest he had up till now heard only his own ax ringing; he would permit no other ax here.

Karl Oskar turned and walked back on the path to locate the intruder. Last year, because of the Indians and also because he might encounter game, he had always carried his gun while working in the forest, and he often said that he did not feel fully clothed without it; but nowadays he frequently left it at home hanging on the wall, and this he had done today. Nor did he think he would need a firearm against the intruder. A man using a tool must be a peaceful man.

Karl Oskar walked toward the sound. The tree feller was farther away than he had anticipated; sounds could be heard a great distance on a calm day like this. The stranger with the ax was beyond his border. There was no intruder on his land.

But who was the woodsman, then? He had no close neighbors; it could not be anyone he knew. He climbed a steep cliff, and now he could see: the sounds came from a pine grove near a narrow channel of the lake. A man was cutting at a straight, tall pine, his broad felling ax glittering in the sun. The chips flew like white birds that might have been nesting in the trunk and then been frightened away by the blows.

Just as Karl Oskar approached, the tree fell with a thunderous crash, crushing the smaller trees near it. The undergrowth swayed from the force of the fall.

The tree cutter held his ax in his left hand while he wiped perspiration from his forehead with his right. He was a powerful man, dressed in a plaid flannel shirt, worn yellow leather breeches and short-legged boots. Judging by his clothes, he was an American. And he used the same kind of long-handled American felling ax with a thin, broad blade that Karl Oskar had recently got for himself.

Still apprehensive, the Swedish settler stopped a few paces from the stump of the pine. The stranger heard him and turned around. His face was lean and weather-beaten, with high cheekbones and deep hollows. Tufts of thin hair clung in sweat to his forehead; his chin was covered with a long brown beard. He eyed Karl Oskar from head to toe. He had the alert eyes of a man accustomed to danger.

Before Karl Oskar had time to prepare a greeting in English the stranger said, "You're Swedish, I take it?"

Karl Oskar stared back in silence; deep in this wilderness he had encountered a stranger who spoke to him in his native tongue.

17

Leaning his ax against the stump, the stranger offered Karl Oskar his hand. "I'm Petrus Olausson, from Alfta Parish in Helsingland. I'm a farmer."

Karl Oskar Nilsson gave his name in return, saying he was a farmer from Ljuder Parish in Småland.

"I knew you were a Swede!"

"How did you know?"

"By your feet." The Helsinge farmer smiled good-naturedly and pointed to Karl Oskar's footgear. "Your wooden shoes, man! Only Swedes wear wooden shoes." He grinned, showing long, broad teeth.

Karl Oskar knew that the Americans called the Swedish settlers the wooden-shoe people.

Petrus Olausson took off his hat and uncovered a bald spot on top of his head. He seemed about ten years older than Karl Oskar; he must be about forty. His clothes and his speech indicated he was no newcomer in America. He used the same mixed-up language as Anders Månsson of Taylors Falls, one of the first Swedes in the Territory.

"What kind of wood do you use for your shoes, Mr. Nilsson?"

Karl Oskar said that he used basswood, from the American linden tree. It was softer than Swedish linden wood and easy to work. But he had poor tools and was unable to make comfortable, light shoes. He looked at the newcomer's ax in the stump; it had an even broader and thinner blade than his own American felling ax.

"You'd work faster with American tools," said the owner of the ax. "The Yankees do everything more easily. Better take after them."

He took Karl Oskar for a newcomer here and looked disapprovingly at the ax he was carrying, a Swedish ax with a clumsy head and a thick edge. Karl Oskar explained that this was an old splitting ax he used for post making.

"So you're from Helsingland? You look like an American to me." He need not ask Petrus Olausson his errand here. No one felled trees for the fun of it; he had come to stay.

The two settlers sat down on the fallen tree to talk at ease. The sound of timber axes in the forest had brought together two men with the same interests and the same language — two Swedish farmers. They had met as strangers, but as soon as they had in-

18

spected each other's axes they felt they had known each other before and were now renewing the acquaintance.

Around them rose the great, ageless pines, and as far as the eye could see not a human habitation was in sight. It was unbroken, uninhabited land, these shores of Lake Ki-Chi-Saga.

"Good land," said the Helsinge farmer. "I plan to settle by this lake."

"You are welcome," said Karl Oskar, and he meant it. "Plenty of room, very few people so far."

"Yes, we needn't push for space."

Olausson pointed to a hut made of branches, about a gunshot's distance from where they sat; that was his shanty. He had begun felling timber for his cabin, and as soon as it was ready his wife and children would join him. He had come to America with his family in the company of the prophet Erik Janson; that was seven years ago, in 1846. They had been living in Illinois, but did not like it on the flat prairie. They wanted to live in wooded country, like their home province, Helsingland. Another farmer from Alfta, Johannes Nordberg, had been up looking over Minnesota, and he had come back and told them that the country here was rich farmland and suitable for settling. It was on his advice that Olausson had come here.

"Johannes told the truth," said his former neighbor. "This is a land of plenty."

"The St. Croix Valley is getting to be known," said Karl Oskar. "How did you happen to pick the claim next to mine?"

"I went to the land office and chose it from the map."

Petrus Olausson had picked a good place for himself; it had fine timber forest and rich grass meadows. He knew how to take up land; he had been in America twice as long as Karl Oskar, who felt almost like a newcomer now as he talked with the older and more experienced settler.

"I think my wife is cooking something. Would you like to eat with us?" Karl Oskar asked.

"How far is it?"

"Less than a mile. I have the northeast claim."

"All right. Might as well see your place."

From the top of a young pine dangled a piece of venison Olausson had intended to fry for his dinner, but it wasn't very warm today and the meat would keep till tomorrow. The settlers rose from the stump. Karl Oskar walked ahead to show the way.

"When did you come and settle here, Nilsson?"

Karl Oskar told him that next Midsummer Eve it would be three years since he and his family had landed in New York. They had arrived in the Territory on the last day of July, and in the same year, 1850, he had taken his claim here at the lake.

Without being conscious of it Karl Oskar walked today in longer strides than usual. He was bringing home news that would gladden Kristina: after three long years of isolation, they now had a neighbor.

-2-

They stopped where the path left the shore and turned up the hill to the log cabin. Olausson looked about in all directions: pine forest to the west, oaks, maples, elms and other leaf trees to the north and east, Lake Ki-Chi-Saga to the south. And at their feet lay a broad meadow, partly broken, and a tended field.

"A good spot, I must say! First come gets the best choice."

And Karl Oskar agreed; he had had good luck when he found this place. He called his settlement Duvemåla (dovecote), and it was a suitable name, he thought, for there were so many doves here that at times they obscured the sun.

The children playing outside the cabin had seen their father and came running toward him. They came in a line, according to age: Johan, the oldest, first; next Lill-Märta; after her, Harald; and last was little Dan, who often tripped on his small, unstable legs and so ran far behind his brothers and sister.

Karl Oskar picked up his youngest son and held him gently in his arms; it wasn't his oldest but rather his youngest child that he wanted to show to his visitor. Dan was two and a half and the only one born in America, the only one of his family who was a citizen of this country and almost the only native-born citizen among the Swedish settlers in the valley. He had been baptized Danjel, but had already lost half of his name; they called him Dan, a more suitable name for an American.

The Helsinge farmer patted the little American on the head. The boy, in fright, glared at the stranger.

"I'm Uncle Petrus, and you are Mr. Dan Nilsson. Isn't that right, boy? You were born here and you can become President of the United States. Neither your father nor I can be President, we're only immigrants."

Karl Oskar laughed. But his youngest son did not rejoice in the great future which opened for him; he began to cry loudly and clung to his father's neck with both arms.

"He's shy — hasn't seen any strangers," said Karl Oskar.

Johan felt neglected and pulled his father by the sleeve. "We saw a snake!"

"A great big one!" added Lill-Märta, all out of breath.

"A green-striped adder!"

"He crawled under the house!"

"Well, snake-critters will crawl out with the spring heat," said the visitor. "Better be careful."

Four-year-old Harald stood with his finger in his mouth and stared at the strange man who had come home with Father. Harald was running about half naked; the only garment on his little body was an outgrown shirt, so short that it reached only to his navel. Petrus Olausson quickly took his eyes from the child, as if embarrassed.

"Lost your pants, did you, little Harald?" asked the father.

"Mother has them. She's patching them."

"He tore a big hole in them," volunteered Johan.

Karl Oskar was still holding his youngest son on his right arm; he now picked up the half-clothed boy on his left. In that position some of the child's nakedness was covered. It seemed as if the sight of him had disturbed Petrus Olausson; he no longer looked like a mild "Uncle Petrus." Was he concerned about a four-year-old's bareness? The child could have gone entirely naked as far as Karl Oskar was concerned.

"The children grow awfully fast; they outgrow everything. Hard to keep their bottoms covered up."

Olausson stroked his long beard and said nothing. Karl Oskar felt ashamed before the visitor that his children were so ragged. All four wore outgrown, shabby garments, mostly patches on patches. After the long winter indoors they had been let out in the open again, and now one could see how badly off they were; the bright spring sun clearly showed everything that was ragged, torn, threadbare.

21

"I've seeded flax — last year, and this year too. The children will soon have something to cover them."

"Well, at least they won't be cold while summer lasts," commented Olausson as he threw a look at the father's own trousers, with patches all over.

Karl Oskar walked ahead to the cabin with two children in his arms and two at his heels. The door opened from the inside and Kristina's head, in a blue kerchief, appeared.

"You're late. I almost thought something had happened."

"Yes, Kristina," said Karl Oskar solemnly. "Something has happened — we have a neighbor now."

The Helsinge farmer stepped up and doffed his hat. "Here is your neighbor."

Taken aback, Kristina remained standing in the doorway. Then she dried her fingers quickly on her apron and took the guest's hand. He mentioned his name and his home parish in Sweden.

"Svensk!"

"Still for the most part a Swede, I admit. We'll be next-door neighbors, Mrs. Nilsson."

"What a surprise! What a great surprise!"

In her confusion Kristina forgot to ask the visitor to come in. When she finally did, she could not stop exclaiming. "A neighbor! What a welcome visitor!"

Petrus Olausson looked about the cabin with curious eyes, as if he had come to evaluate its contents.

"Did you make the furnishings yourself, Nilsson?"

"Yes. A little clumsy . . . "

"No, you're learning from the Americans. Very good! They do things handily."

Petrus Olausson praised the beds, which had been made of split scantlings, fastened to wall and floor. There was something authoritative in his speech and manners, and one could tell that he was a man accustomed to giving advice and commands. He was also the man of forty talking to the thirty-year-old, but more even than their difference in age was the fact that he had been in America four years longer than Karl Oskar.

The Swedish settler had invited a dinner guest without knowing what his wife, Kristina, had to put on the table. She apologized: She had nothing but plain fish soup, bread, milk and maple sirup

· - not much to offer a guest. Food was scarce now, for last year's crops were almost gone and this year's were still growing.

Karl Oskar remembered they had cooked the last of their potatoes only a few days earlier.

"We have a pork bone left," said Kristina. "I can make pea soup. But the peas take at least an hour to cook."

"Too long," said Karl Oskar. "We're hungry." But it annoyed him that they had nothing better than fish soup to offer their new neighbor on his first visit.

"I can add mashed turnips to the pork," said Kristina, thinking over what supplies they had. "We have turnips out in the cellar; they cook quickly."

Karl Oskar picked up a basket and went to get the turnips, accompanied by his guest.

Before Olausson he did not want to appear as an inexperienced settler; he wanted to show how well he had managed on his claim. He told him what he had done to protect the vegetables from spoiling, since he hadn't yet had time to build a stone cellar. For the turnips he had dug a ditch behind the cabin and covered it with straw and earth. Under this roof, about ten inches thick, the roots should be protected against the coldest winter.

But when they came to the spot, and Karl Oskar had cleared away the earth and the straw, an evil smell arose and filled him with apprehension. He stuck in his hand and felt for a turnip. His fingers touched something soft and slimy. When he withdrew his hand it was filled with a dark-brown, nasty-smelling mess.

"Damn it! The turnips are rotten."

Shamefacedly, Karl Oskar rose. The turnips they had intended to offer their guest for dinner need not be boiled; down there in the ditch they were mashed into a rotten mess.

"It's because of the early heat," said the guest.

"I forgot to make an air hole," explained Karl Oskar.

"Your covering is too thick," was Petrus Olausson's opinion. "Ten inches is too much — five inches would have been about right."

"Then the turnips would have frozen last winter."

"Not if you had covered the ditch right. You put on too much, Nilsson."

Karl Oskar's cheeks flushed. He knew a ten-inch cover was necessary to keep the frost out. But this spring it had become warm so suddenly that he hadn't had time to open an air hole.

They walked back to the cabin. Karl Oskar carried his empty basket, vexed and humiliated; what would they now offer their guest? But at the door a different cooking odor met them: Kristina had put the frying pan on the fire.

"I won't bother with turnips, I'll make pancakes instead, it won't take so long." She had flour, bacon grease, milk and sugar, and some of the cranberries she had preserved last year. Now they would have cranberries and pancakes for diner. "Please sit down, you menfolk. I'll serve you as I make them."

Karl Oskar's annoyance disappeared as he inhaled the smell of the frying pancakes. "You are a wizard, Kristina!"

She was piling the pancakes in a bowl, and even the Helsinge farmer looked pleased and appreciative.

Karl Oskar pulled up his chair and was about to sit down when Petrus Olausson, standing behind his chair, bent his head and spoke in a loud voice:

"We do sit down in Jesu's name,
We eat and drink upon God's work.
God to honor, us to aid,
We eat our food in Jesu's name."

Kristina, busy with her pancakes, repeated the prayer with him. She was deeply conscious of the fact that nowadays they almost always forgot to say grace. And, as parents, she and Karl Oskar ought to set a good and godly example for their children. The settlers had begun to forget their old Swedish table prayers; only Danjel Andreasson, her uncle, never missed saying grace. They acted like hogs rushing up to the trough to still their hunger. To forget the Giver of all good things in this way was un-Christian, beastly. But their new neighbor prayed over the food with a voice like a minister. He must be a religious man.

After a while Kristina also sat down at the table. She learned that their guest intended to settle in the neighborhood with his wife and three children.

"I had never thought anyone would want to live as far away as here," she said.

"Well, this is rich earth, and the lake has plenty of fish."

Karl Oskar was eager to confirm that the earth was indeed rewarding. Last year he had planted four bushels of potatoes and received forty-eight and a half bushels of yield — almost thirteen to one. And rye and barley gave good returns; the seeds were barely out of his hand before they began to swell and grow and shoot up blades in great abundance. One could spread sawdust on this earth and it would almost grow.

Kristina thought: However fine the earth was, it could never take the place of people. However great its yield, it did not help against loneliness.

"We are not only seeking our living in America," said Petrus Olausson. "We are seeking freedom in spritual things."

He explained that he and his wife had turned their backs on the false and dangerous Swedish church and had followed the Bible's clear words and truths. They had been so persecuted and plagued for this by the clergy and the authorities of their village that they had been forced to emigrate. They had followed Erik Janson of Biskopskulla and his group to Bishop Hill, Illinois, where they were to build the New Jerusalem on the prairie. But once in America, Janson had set himself even above God. After enduring Janson's tyranny for three years, Olausson had left the prophet of Bishop Hill and gone to Andover, where he joined a free Lutheran church.

Petrus Olausson helped himself to a few more pancakes.

"Have you left the Swedish state church, Nilsson?"

Karl Oskar explained that he and his family had emigrated of their own free will; they had not been banished, nor had they escaped as criminals. But an uncle of Kristina's and an unmarried woman in their group had been exiled by the court for heresy.

A scratching sound was heard at the window behind the guest's chair; Johan hung outside on the window sill and stared through the glass at the people eating inside. He had barely managed to climb so high, and his eyes grew large at the sight of the pancakes; his mouth moved as if he too were chewing. Lill-Märta's flaxen curls could be glimpsed below the window — she was not tall enough to look through.

"Our young ones smell the pancakes," said Karl Oskar.

"Only curious," said Kristina. "I just fed them." She shook her hand windowward: How could they be so rude, looking at a guest eating? The boy's face and the girl's curls disappeared immediately. Kristina looked uncomfortably at Olausson. Would he think her children didn't have enough to eat? But he must see by their bodies that they weren't starved. She herself never ate her fill until she knew they had had sufficient. Well, perhaps a few pancakes would be left which she could give them afterward.

Petrus Olausson now asked his host how they had managed to make a living and feed themselves on their claim for three years.

Karl Oskar replied that the first winter had been the hardest as they had not gathered any crops that year. But as soon as spring came and the lake broke up so they could fish, it was better. And during the summer they had picked wild berries and other fruit. That fall they had harvested their first crops, and there was so much that they had had all the potatoes and bread they needed for the second winter. As they gradually broke more land their worries about food dimished. During the second and third winters they had been bothered mostly by the cold; this cabin did not give sufficient protection. For the children's sake they had kept a fire going night and day through the coldest periods. The last winter had been so bad that the cabin had almost been turned over by a blizzard.

He had not figured on living in this log hut more than two or three winters; he had already laid out the sills for a more solid house. But he doubted the new house would be finished this summer. They would have to live in the cabin a fourth winter.

Kristina added: The weather was never moderate in this country, the summers were too warm, the winters too cold. In America the heat was hotter, the cold colder, the rain wetter, than in Sweden. And it was the same with the animals, big and little ones: the snakes were more poisonous, the rats more ferocious, the grasshoppers did more damage, the mosquitoes were bigger, than at home.

"The Indians are more dangerous than the animals," said Olausson.

Kristina thought the Indians around there had behaved very peacefully. During the winters they had come to warm themselves at the fire and she had given them food and treated them as friends. A few times there had been rumors of Indian attacks, and she was frightened, but nothing had happened here so far.

"The Chippewas are friendly," said their guest. "Some of the other tribes will steal and murder."

Kristina had finished eating. She was looking thoughtfully in front of her.

"We have forgotten to mention the worst we have gone through," she said. They had talked of weather and wild animals and Indians, but there was something else: the loneliness at Lake Ki-Chi-Saga. "I can't tell you how glad I am to have a neighbor at last!"

The words had escaped her full heart. She must tell her countryman how it felt to live alone for three long years: Months and months would pass without anyone coming to their land who spoke her mother tongue. Sometimes a hunter or a lumberman would stop by their cabin, but how much pleasure was there in a guest she couldn't speak to? With no one living nearby a person felt empty, depressed, completely lost. And that emptiness was worse than any outside pain. It grew greater with each sad, lonely day. She knew how it was after these years; she was speaking the truth when she said that human beings could not live without other human beings.

While talking, Kristina had avoided Karl Oskar's eyes. He looked at her in surprise. "I thought you had got used to living alone, Kristina."

"I don't think one ever gets used to it." She felt the tears in her eyes and turned her face away quickly.

Petrus Olausson had listened with great attention. Now he turned to Karl Oskar. "I'm sorry for Mrs. Nilsson."

She asked him not to call her Mrs. Nilsson — she was no American lady, only a simple Swedish farm wife. She wanted to be called Kristina; and couldn't she call him Uncle Petrus? Sitting here, talking Swedish with a Swede, she felt he was almost a relative.

"All right, call me Uncle! And now cheer up, Kristina. I'll be living next door."

She rose suddenly. "I completely forgot — I must put on the coffee!"

The Helsinge farmer also rose from the table, and again he said a prayer: "All praise to thee, O Lord, for food and drink."

Kristina, standing at the fireplace, with her hands folded around the coffee mill, repeated the prayer after him. To her it seemed like Sunday in the cabin today.

Karl Oskar was anxious to show his guest around his claim, but Kristina wanted to keep him inside with her. She had not been so talkative for a long time.

The Helsinge farmer told her that very soon more Swedes would come and settle here. Two families would arrive that spring; he knew them both. And in letters to his friends in Sweden he had described this valley and urged them to come. Soon it wouldn't be lonely here any more. This was wonderful news to Kristina, who had felt they would have to live alone forever at the Indian lake.

"How many Swedes are there in the valley?" asked Petrus Olausson.

"Eighteen, I think," Karl Oskar answered.

He counted in his mind: Their nearest neighbor over toward Taylors Falls, Kristina's uncle Danjel Andreasson, who lived at a place called New Kärragärde, was a widower with three children; and his neighbor was Jonas Petter Albrektsson, also a farmer from Ljuder who had arrived with their group. Jonas Petter had a woman from Dalecarlia called Swedish Anna keeping house for him. There were a few others. And they themselves were two grown people and four small children. Yes, there were about eighteen Swedish people in the St. Croix Valley.

"And now we three families will settle here," said the Helsinge farmer. "That makes more than thirty Swedes. We must start a congregation."

"What kind of congregation?" asked Karl Oskar.

"To build a house of God. In Andover we started a parish with only twenty-two members."

"A church parish?"

"Yes, we'll build a church."

"A church!" exclaimed Kristina, breathlessly.

"Only a little log temple, a house of plain wood."

It became silent in the cabin. Karl Oskar looked in surprise at his guest. The settlers out here had not yet had time to build decent houses for themselves and their livestock. How could they manage to build a church and pay for a minister?

"We mustn't strive so much with worldly things that we forget

28

eternity. Need of stables is no excuse for delay in building a house of God!" Petrus Olausson spoke in a severe preacher's voice.

He went on to tell them how America was full of false prophets who snared the settlers with false religions. He had observed, with great sorrow, some of his countrymen living a heathenish animal life, never using the Word. And some good Christian men from his home village in Sweden had gone to the gold fields in California; they sought riches instead of Gospel truths, they looked for lumps of gold instead of eternal life. But they had perished within a short time. Of twenty-eight gold seekers only four had returned, and of these only one had found enough gold for his future. Shouldn't this deter the worship of Mammon?

"I had a younger brother with me when we came here," said Karl Oskar. "Two years ago he and a friend took off for California."

"Have you heard from these foolish youngsters?"

"Only twice so far."

From a box in the Swedish chest back in the corner Karl Oskar took a sheet of paper and handed it to Olausson. "The second letter from my brother. It came a few days ago."

Petrus Olausson read the letter aloud.

On the road to California January 1853

Dear Brother Karl Oskar Nilsson,

How are you and Kristina and the children? I am well. Arvid and I are still on the journey to California. That road is long, you know, almost as long as the road back to Sweden. We have had many adventures. When I get back I will relate to you and Kristina everything I am now leaving out of my letter.

We are getting along well. We have had our troubles, but we shall make out all right in the gold land, be sure of that, Karl Oskar.

Don't worry about me. I will be back when I am a rich man, not before. Then I shall buy oxen for you and cows for Kristina. I suppose you are still poking in your fields.

Arvid sends greetings to his old master and all Swedes in that part. I greet Kristina and the children.

Your Brother,
Robert Nilsson

Kristina said, "Robert has not put down his address."

29

"He has no permanent address," Olausson answered. " 'On the road' means he is on his way. The gold diggers have to climb high mountains and cross wide deserts to reach California, and they need plenty of time for that road."

Karl Oskar looked at the corner of the room where his brother's old bed still stood. He repeated with great concern, "My brother has been gone more than two years now."

"He said he wouldn't be back without gold," reminded Kristina.

"Who knows if he is alive at this moment?" said Karl Oskar. Of twenty-eight gold seekers only four had survived. Couldn't he have prevented his brother from going on his dangerous journey?

He put the letter back in the Swedish chest. "Let's look at the livestock," he suggested.

While Kristina resumed her chores in the cabin the men went out to look over the frontier settlement. Karl Oskar wanted to show his neighbor what he had done during three years as a squatter.

To the north of the cabin he had started a stable, as yet only half finished. In it were a cow and a heifer, each in its stall. From a German in Taylors Falls they had bought a pregnant cow, and her calf had now grown into this heifer. The cow was called Lady — after the borrowed animal they had had the first winter — and the heifer was called Miss.

"When she has calved we'll have to call her Missus," said Karl Oskar, laughing.

In the sheep pen were two ewes with three lambs — already a little flock of five. Sheep were easy to take care of, and wool was always needed for clothing. Two pigs poked in the pigpen; of all the animals, pigs were the easiest to buy, and they fed in the forest as long as the ground was bare. Pork was indeed the cheapest food. One corner of the stable was left for a chicken coop, but the roosting perch was still unoccupied; a laying hen cost five dollars.

In the empty coop Karl Oskar kept his new American tools. He showed with pride the cradle, its five wooden fingers attached to the scythe handle, so much more efficient than the old Swedish scythes. Then the grub hoe with an ax on one edge and a hoe on the other — a very ingenious device. When clearing ground and removing roots, one need only turn this tool to switch from the one type of work to the other.

Then they walked out to inspect the meadow. "You've broken a sizable field," said Olausson.

"About ten acres. I plowed up most of it the first year."

By now he would have had three times as big a field if he had had a hundred dollars to buy a team of oxen. When he borrowed a team from the timber company he had to pay five dollars a day. He was short of cash — his greatest obstacle. Much of the field he had broken himself, with his grub hoe.

Karl Oskar showed Olausson his winter rye, lush and healthy. He had just sown the spring rye, and next to it was the field where he intended to plant potatoes. In the fall he would sow some wheat, that bread grain the Americans harvested in such quantities. He thought it would be fine to harvest his own wheat; in Sweden they had paid a great deal for the soft white flour and had used it only for holiday bread.

Olausson advised him to raise Indian corn, which could be used as food for both people and livestock. The corn gave a fiftyfold return down in Illinois.

"You must plant the corn on high ground. It needs dry earth," he said.

Karl Oskar now led his guest up the hill to a grove of tall trees. Shaded by some enormous sugar maples was the foundation for his new house.

"Here's where I'll build. I'll have a real house here."

It would be forty feet from gable to gable, he said, eighteen feet wide, with two stories. They would have four or five times as much space as they now had in the cabin. And this time he wouldn't build with fresh logs, as he had done the first time; those logs had dried out and left cracks that let in cold and wind. He had felled the timbers for his new house during the past two winters and had dressed the logs on all sides. They had dried out well. He had intended to build the house this summer, but he must first raise a threshing shed so that he needn't do his threshing down on the lake ice as he had done last winter. Next year his house would rise here, under the shady maples. And from the windows here on the south side he would be able to look out over his fields to the lake.

Karl Oskar became excited as he talked about the house which didn't yet exist, about the roof and walls not yet raised, about the view from windows not yet put in. The main room would be here, a bedroom in each gable, and here would be space for a large kitchen. Up there would be a second floor with two large or four small rooms, as yet he hadn't decided which.

Petrus Olausson had paced off the foundation. "Too much of a house! Remember what I tell you, Nilsson. You can't build so much." Kristina had told him this before, but a woman didn't understand much about building. When his new neighbor now raised the same objection, Karl Oskar began to wonder. Perhaps he had laid out too big a house, perhaps it would be too much for him.

Finally he showed his new neighbor something at the east gable of the future house. "Look there. See that plant? It is from Sweden."

In a litttle dug-up bed grew a small shrub, six or seven inches tall, tied to a stake. It had a few small dark-green leaves, and the earth around it was carefully tended.

Olausson bent down and felt the leaves. "An apple seedling, eh?"

"An Astrachan apple tree!"

"From Sweden? Well, well."

It was for his wife's sake that he had planted the seedling, said Karl Oskar. She longed for home at times and it gave her pleasure to have a growing plant from Sweden to tend and look after. He had written to her parents for seeds. They had arrived a year ago last fall, glued to a sheet of paper. And so he had planted them here, at a depth five times their own thickness, as they used to when planting trees at home. And this seedling had come up; it was growing slowly, but it was growing.

The men went back to the cabin. Kristina wanted to warm up whatever coffee was left in the pot, but Uncle Petrus couldn't stay away any longer from his timber felling.

He said that he had seen how much work they had done on their claim and that it was the beginning of a fine farm. As a fellow Christian, however, he wanted to add something before he left: Work alone was not enough. As neighbors they ought to get together and help instruct each other in religious matters.

"We'll see each other often, I hope. And my dear Swedish fellow Christians, don't so lose yourselves in worldly matters that you forget eternity."

— 4 —

When Karl Oskar and Kristina had gone to bed that evening they thought back on the day, which had been unlike all others on their claim.

"I think I like him," said Kristina.

"He seems a capable man with good ideas. But he wants to have you do things his way. He wants to correct others. I don't know that I like that."

"He meant well."

"I don't need a guardian — I'm old enough."

"Yes, of course, but we must try to get along with him and his family."

Later: "He must have thought we were heathens, not saying grace," Kristina murmured.

Karl Oskar yawned loudly. He turned over on his side to go to sleep. But when he had walked a good deal, as today, he felt the old injury to his left leg, and it took longer for sleep to come. Tonight the leg ached persistently.

Kristina was gathering her thoughts for her evening prayer. Petrus Olausson's words at his departure still rang in her ears. She brooded about them; they sounded like a warning from God Himself.

In this out-of-the-way place they neglected their spiritual needs. Someone coming from the outside, looking at them with a stranger's eyes, could see how things were with them. They neglected their souls and jeopardized their salvation. They were so busy gathering food for their table that they could not take even a moment to say grace. They lived the fleeting life of the moment and forgot the eternity that awaited them.

Kristina sinned every day, she reflected; in many ways she sinned. In Sweden she had once a month been relieved of this burden through the sacrament of Holy Communion. But now she had not been a guest at the Lord's table for three years. During this whole time she had not once cleansed herself in the Saviour's blood.

Outside, the crickets had started their never ceasing noise. The penetrating sound screeched like an ungreased wagon wheel revolving at a dizzying speed. Kristina often wondered what could make the poor creatures wail like this all the night through. And she would lie awake and listen to the sound until it echoed within herself; her own anxiety responded to the crickets' wailing.

"Karl Oskar," she said, "you have a good memory."

"Yes?" he said sleepily. "What about?"

"Do you recall when we last had communion?"

"The Sunday before we left home."

"That was three years ago in April. Three years since we last received absolution."

He turned to her in the dark, but he could not see her. "Are you lying there worrying about communion?" He sounded surprised.

"I'm worrying about our burden of sin. It has been gathering on our backs for a long time."

Karl Oskar replied that they lived in a wilderness without churches; therefore it could not be helped that they had been without the Sacrament for three years. God must know this and overlook it.

"We have buried ourselves in worldly doings," insisted his wife. "We live only in the flesh. We forget our souls — we forget death."

"I know I'll come to an end eventually. But one can't go around worrying about death all day long," Karl Oskar said.

No use to fret about it. All one could do was lie down and stop breathing when the time came, lie quietly on one's back and draw the last breath. So old people did; on their deathbeds they did not pay much attention to death, since it was inescapable. They usually thought more of their funerals. Death was the same for all, equally unmerciful to all, but funerals could be different, different splendor for different people. And those who had received little honor in life often wanted the grandest funerals.

"But there must be moments when you think of eternity, of what comes afterward, Karl Oskar."

What was the matter with Kristina this evening? Now he didn't know what to say. But it was true, he did forget his prayers. A settler with endless worries about keeping alive had little time to think of eternity.

Karl Oskar replied, with some hesitancy, that he didn't really understand eternity. His head couldn't grasp something that had neither beginning nor end. All he could wish was that God had given him a better mind.

Kristina reflected that Karl Oskar was unusually humble tonight. She often believed he trusted himself more than God.

"Karl Oskar — if you should die this very night, do you believe all would be well with you?"

It was a minute before he answered. "If I didn't think so, what could I do about it, Kristina?"

34

Now he was the questioner. And she had no reply.

"We must get some sleep," said Karl Oskar after a pause. "Tomorrow will bring new chores. We will be useless if we don't get some sleep."

He was right, it wouldn't help to lie awake. They needed strength for the morrow.

Kristina soon heard from her husband's deep breathing that he was asleep. But she lay awake a long time.

-5-

A thousand days and more had passed since Kristina had heard the ringing of church bells. That was in another world, in the Old World. In her parental home, in another Duvemåla, she had heard them from the distant church steeple. Every Saturday evening, with their clear tone, they rang in the holiday peace, every Sunday morning they vibrated over the village, calling the people together. And the villagers gathered on the church green and looked up and listened when the bells began to peal; the men lifted their hats, the women curtsied.

Here in the New World she had not yet heard the voice of God in the bells. Here Sunday was like a weekday, with all the sounds of a weekday. In North America too, churches had been built, but she lived so far from them that the sound of their bells did not reach her. Nor could she hear a servant of God speaking in her language from a pulpit, an organ's music, her fellow men's voices in prayer and singing.

But God had not forgotten her. Today she had heard His voice, she was convinced that He had sent her a message: She must not forget the immortal soul He had given her.

And so at last Kristina said her prayer. She prayed fervently for an answer to her question: What must they do, she and her husband, to save their souls? What must they do so as not to lose their eternal salvation in this un-Christian land where they had come to start life anew?

And she thanked God for the past day and the message He had brought her through a stranger — this day when Karl Oskar had heard a new ax ringing in the forest.

35

II

THE WHORE AND THE THIEF

- 1 -

It seemed to Kristina that the third winter would last forever. The cold returned and was unmercifully severe. The inside of their door bore a circle of rough nailheads, and they were always covered with hoar frost. The nailheads shining on the door like a wreath of white roses were the winter's mark of sovereignty over the people who lived here. The warming fire on the hearth had not strength enough to melt the frost on the door.

The dark-shining nailheads in the wood were the first visible sign of liberation; the cold had been forced back of the threshold. And what a joy it was to Kristina when she awakened one night and heard the sound of dripping water outside, melting snow running from the eaves. It ran and splashed the whole night through, and she could hardly go back to sleep in her joy. Spring had really come.

Since Ulrika of Västergöhl had moved to Stillwater as the wife of Mr. Henry O. Jackson, Baptist minister of the town, Kristina had had no intimate friends in the neighborhood. Ulrika's visits were infrequent, and Kristina was tied to her home by her children. She hesitated to undertake a visit to Ulrika; the road to Stillwater was long and difficult. In two years she had gone only once to see Ulrika in her new home. That had been on a winter day, and she had ridden with Uncle Danjel on his ox sled. In spite of all the clothing she had bundled around herself, she had felt as cold as if she had been sitting naked on the sled. They had brought along warm stones for their feet and had stopped several times on the way to rewarm them. But, even so, Kristina had had a frostbitten toe as a reminder of the visit to Stillwater.

During the past year, however, the lumber company had cut a new road all the way to Ki-Chi-Saga. Now the settlers could ride on the company's ox wagons. And so one day Kristina decided on the trip, partly to visit Ulrika, partly for necessary shopping. Her youngest child was now weaned — Karl Oskar could feed him, she would stay overnight with the Jacksons.

Thus, on a pleasantly mild spring day, Kristina set off to Still-

36

water. The sun had warmed the forest, which seemed friendly beside the newly cut road. And the company's ox wagon rolled along steadily on its heavy, ironbound wheels, very different from the settlers' primitive carts. Today Kristina traveled in comfort; the ride was a pleasure, not an ordeal.

The Baptist congregation in Stillwater had built a new house for their pastor next to the little white-timbered structure which served as their church. Ulrika saw Kristina through the window and came out to welcome her on the stoop. On her arm Kristina carried the covered splint basket which she had brought from Sweden.

"I can see you're in town on big business," said Ulrika. "But first you must have something to eat."

Pastor Jackson's house had one large and one smaller room, a good-sized kitchen with a storeroom and an ample cellar under the house. The large room was used only in the daytime; Ulrika sometimes called it the sitting room and sometimes the living room. The smaller room was called a bedroom and was used only for sleeping. Since Ulrika of Västergöhl had become Mrs. Henry O. Jackson, she lived like an upper-class woman. In the bedroom was the largest bed Kristina had ever seen, as wide as two ordinary beds put together, and over it was a thoughtful motto in gilt letters: "The Lord giveth us the strength."

Ulrika urged Kristina to sit down on the soft sofa of the living room. She wanted to show her something which she had acquired since Kristina's previous visit: a picture of Mr. and Mrs. Jackson as bride and groom. But it was not a painted picture of her and Henry, and that was the strange thing about it. It was like a miracle. They had stood in front of a machine, quite still for a few moments, while a man had gone to the other side of it with a cloth over his head and manipulated something. And then, by magic, their likenesses came out printed on a thick paper, as nice as any painted picture.

There they were, on the wall, the bridegroom in knee-length coat and narrow trousers and Ulrika in her white muslin bridal gown and plumed bonnet — her very first hat. Below the portrait of the couple a notice from the St. Paul *Pioneer* was glued.

BAPTIST CHURCH IS SCENE OF FIRST WEDDING
The first marriage in the history of the Stillwater Baptist

Church took place Saturday, when Miss Ulrika of Vastergohl became the bride of the Reverend Henry O. Jackson, minister of the Baptist Congregation. The bride belongs to the fine old family of Vastergohl in Sweden. . . .

Ulrika translated for Kristina: It said that she was the first bride in the Baptist church here. The man who wrote it had asked if she belonged to the nobility of Sweden; the Swedes he had met up to now in America had all been barons and counts. Ulrika, feeling that her ancestry was none of his business, had of course replied that she came from a family so old it could be traced back to the time when Father Adam and Mother Eve walked about naked in Paradise. So it was that the writing man had printed she was of a fine family.

Ulrika prepared dinner for Kristina and treated her to omelette, warm from the stove; it was made of ten fresh eggs which had been given to Henry for a sermon in Marine a few days before.

"Henry is serving as minister in Franconia today," said Mrs. Jackson. "He won't be back until late. You must spend the night with us."

"Come with me to the store first and help me shop," asked Kristina. "I can't talk to the clerks."

"I'll be glad to, of course. But you must speak to Americans so that you'll learn the language."

Kristina knew the meaning of a few English words, but never tried to say them. She felt as if she were play-acting, making a fool of herself, when she used English. Her tongue was not made for this strange language. And if she listened to others speaking it she got a headache; it did not suit her ears, either. Ulrika of Västergöhl, through her marriage to an American, had become so familiar with English that she could understand it well and also speak it easily.

"Let's go and get the shopping done with," said Ulrika.

Kristina rose and picked up her basket, while Ulrika went to the wall mirror in the living room to put on her bonnet. It was a beautiful bonnet indeed. In front was a large plume, as elegant as a soldier's plume at church parade; the top was bedecked with multi-colored feathers and flowers, and long red silk streamers dangled down the back. It was fastened under the chin with a broad green band tied in a large bow at the right ear. Kristina admired Ulrika's bonnet more each time she looked at it.

"In Sweden I had no right to wear a hat," said Mrs. Jackson. "But in America I've become a free person."

Kristina tied on the old worn black silk kerchief which her parents had given her as a bridal gift and which she had worn now for eight years. "Do you think I should lay aside my old kerchief and put on a hat too?"

"No! You don't need one. You were honestly married when you came here, but unmarried Ulrika needed one."

And so they were on their way to do Kristina's shopping at the store. They went along the street which followed the river. During the spring months the St. Croix was covered with floating timber, one log next to another all the way to the bend of the river. Stillwater smelled of pitch and fresh lumber. In some places on the town's main street the two women walked through sawdust up to their ankles. They met men in flaming red woolen shirts tucked into broad leather belts; Ulrika called them lumberjacks. Almost every male inhabitant of Stillwater had something to do with lumber.

And almost every second man they met doffed his hat courteously to Ulrika; she was the minister's wife and was well known in this town.

"Men in America are courteous," said Kristina.

"Here they respect women," replied Ulrika. "In Sweden a man uses a woman as a hired hand in the daytime and a mattress at night. In between she isn't worth a thing."

How had Ulrika herself been valued in the old country? Other women, married and unmarried, had spat at her. Yet the married men had come to her for their pleasure. They had used sweet words then. Then she was good enough. Good enough even for the churchwarden of Akerby. But in church on Sundays he did not recognize her. And he was one of those who had spoken against her participation in the sacraments. He was himself an adulterer, but in Sweden the Sixth Commandment applied to women only.

At Harrington's General Store, Kristina, with Ulrika as interpreter, bought so many things that her old basket overflowed. The two women carried it back between them, each holding one side. When they returned to the parsonage, Ulrika's daughter Elin was waiting for them on the stoop; she had brought a message for Pastor Jackson from her employer.

Kristina had not seen Elin for two years and was greatly impressed with the change in her. Though she was only nineteen, she looked and acted like a grown woman. She had a well-shaped body, and health shone on her fresh skin. She did not resemble her mother; she had black hair and dark eyes. She must take after her father, whoever he was; that secret Ulrika had never divulged. Elin had a position as an ordinary maid in town, yet here she was, dressed in the middle of the week and during working hours in a starched, Sunday-fine dress with large flowers. No one would have recognized the shy little girl who had been with them on the emigrant wagon to Karlshamn; then she had worn a discarded old skirt someone had given her, and she had carried a berry basket and had looked utterly forlorn. Today she looked like a daughter of the manor.

Kristina herself was wearing her best dress, and it had seemed good enough to her even though it was old and moth-eaten in places. At the sight of Ulrika's daughter, she felt she was covered with rags. She had put on her best, and Elin was in her working clothes, yet she felt poor in comparison with this servant girl. Many things were topsy-turvy in the New World. And Elin talked in English to her mother, which made Kristina feel awkward and pushed aside.

After Elin had left, Ulrika spoke of her daughter with great pride. Elin's employers had increased her wages to twelve dollars a month, and they kept a table that was better than holiday food in Sweden, where hired hands had to be satisfied with herring all year round. But still the girl caused her mother some concern. She was beautiful; men were after her, and Ulrika wasn't sure if they had marriage in mind. In Sweden a beautiful girl of poor parents was merely prey for lustful menfolk, and even here there was surely an occasional male animal out hunting. But this she had made up her mind to: her innocent child would not be prey for such a beast. Elin's virginity was not to be wasted in advance, like her own, without joy, but would be an honest man's reward in the bridal bed.

Ulrika now set the coffee table in the living room. They sat down on the sofa again under the picture of Mr. and Mrs. Jackson. Kristina kept looking at the groom. Pastor Jackson had been the first helpful person she had met in America. When they had arrived on the boat and were sitting by the river in a cold rain, their children crying, all of them wet through and hungry, it was Pastor Jackson who took charge and brought them to his home, prepared food, fed them, made up beds for the night and helped them continue their journey the following morning. And to think that one of the women in their group had become his wife!

"You have a kind and good husband, Ulrika."

"Yes, Henry is gentle. He never uses a woman for a slave."

"How could you and he understand each other in the beginning, before you talked English?"

"Well," said Ulrika, "a man and a woman always find a way if they like each other. We made signs and pointed and used our hands in the beginning."

"Ulrika," Kristina went on reflectively, "before your marriage I suppose you told your husband about your life in Sweden. Does he hold nothing against you?"

"No. And I hold nothing against him."

"Against him? Do you mean that he too . . . ?"

"Yes, he led a bad life. Sinful, like mine."

"I wouldn't have thought that," said Kristina, surprised.

Ulrika continued, "Henry was in prison in England. For stealing."

He had had the same unhappy childhood in England as she had had in Sweden. She had lost her parents at four, he at three. She was sold at auction to be brought up, Henry had been put in a foundling home. Her foster father had raped her and taught her whoring; in the orphanage Henry had learned to steal — he stole food to satisfy his hunger. At the age of fourteen he had escaped from the home and continued to steal his food until he was caught and put in prison for three years. When he was released he had signed up on a ship for America. In New York he had lived among thieves and prostitutes until he met a Baptist minister who converted him. He had been baptized and then had studied for the ministry. For fifteen years now he had been a pastor.

Kristina listened, confused and embarrassed.

"Henry is an old thief, I'm an old whore. We're two of a kind and very happy together."

Kristina thought Ulrika would feel hurt if she tried to excuse her and her husband. "All that is now past, all of it," she stammered.

"Yes, Henry and I have been immersed and live now in new bodies. We're forgiven by God. We're reborn. Our hearts are cleansed."

When she married Jackson, Ulrika said, no man had been in bed

41

with her for four long years. It was not easy for her to wait until after the wedding. But she wanted to show that she had conquered her old sins. Jackson had not tempted her, and in this way he had helped her to preserve her new, rebaptized body in innocence until the bridal ceremony was over.

When at last the time had come she had felt like a virgin. She couldn't quite explain it, but she almost felt like a girl again. And in her new body she really was a virgin, untouched by menfolk. She was still in her best years, newly married, and it had felt wonderful to be able, now that God had joined them together, to use her body for the purpose it had been created for.

Suddenly Ulrika leaped up, groaned and ran out of the room. When she returned a few minutes later she was wiping her mouth.

"What is the matter?" Kristina cried.

"It was only my priest," Ulrika said with a smile.

Kristina looked through the window, but could see no one outside. "Is Mr. Jackson coming?" she asked.

"No, not Henry. I meant the priest I'm going to bring into the world."

"What on earth are you talking about?"

Ulrika sat down again at the coffee table. "I'm in the family way, you see."

Ulrika used the English words — she said she thought they sounded finer, more elegant, than the Swedish phrase — and it was a few moments before Kristina understood. She went on to explain that she had decided long ago her first son should be a minister like his father. With a son in the pulpit she would be redeemed in the eyes of Dean Brusander at home — it was he who had excluded her from the congregation.

"That's wonderful!" said Kristina. "But you're late with your pregnancy. You're been married two years now."

"Yes, it's taken so long I was getting worried. I have borne four children in my life, but I was beginning to wonder. Having borne the others out of wedlock, I'm anxious to have a few real ones too."

Kristina sighed; the childbed Ulrika impatiently looked forward to she herself feared. Every month she waited nervously for proof that she was not pregnant. And her apprehension had increased since Dan stopped suckling; she thought she had noticed that suckling was a preventive.

Toward evening Pastor Jackson returned from his journey to

Franconia. He carried his bag of books and pamphlets and also a parcel which turned out to be five pounds of wheat flour and three pounds of fresh butter — his wages for the sermon. In the door he took his wife in his arms and patted her affectionately on the cheek with a big hairy hand.

"Ulrika, my dear, forgive me! I'm late. My dearest Ulrika — and we have a dear guest!"

The pastor offered a warm welcome to his wife's good friend. With blessinglike gestures he took Kristina's hands and smiled at her the same good, kind smile she remembered from the time he had taken care of the group of Swedish immigrants in Stillwater. The Jacksons spoke to each other in English, and Kristina felt outside again. But Pastor Jackson talked to her through his wife and asked her about things on the claim: how were the children, had they enough food, was there anything he could help them with? And she replied through Ulrika that all was well at home, that several new neighbors were moving in this summer. After a while it became rather tiresome to speak through a third person, and Kristina wished she could use the English language — if for no other reason, just to be able to talk to Pastor Jackson directly.

-2-

Ulrika made a bed on the living-room sofa, and Kristina, who was to leave early in the morning with the lumber company's ox wagon, spent the night there.

When she had eaten breakfast next day and thanked the Jacksons for their hospitality, Ulrika brought her a basket made of willow and quite new. A cloth had been spread over it.

"A small present from the two of us, Kristina!"

Behind Ulrika stood Pastor Jackson, nodding eagerly as if he understood the Swedish words.

Mysterious cackling and chirpings came from the basket. Kristina lifted a corner of the cloth and peeked. In the bottom of the basket sat a brown-and-white speckled hen, and tiny chicks poked their heads through the wings of the mother, their little beaks shining like pink flower buds.

Kristina cried out in joy, "Chickens! A hen!"

"Hope you like them. She has hatched twelve, a whole dozen."

Kristina almost wept with happiness. If there was anything she

43

had missed on the claim it was chickens. Now her throat was so full she couldn't say thank you the way she would have liked; she could only mumble.

Ulrika gave her a small bag of rice for chicken feed. "Be careful with the basket! The little ones are delicate."

Pastor Jackson then picked up the grocery basket and Ulrika the basket with the hen and the chicks, and both accompanied her to the lumber office at the end of the street. It was almost an hour before the wagon was loaded, but her friends remained with her until she could climb up and the driver was ready to start. After the wheels were rolling, Ulrika called to her once more: She must be careful there on the driver's seat with the newly hatched chicks.

During the whole journey back Kristina sat with the gift basket on her knee, holding it with both hands and listening in quiet joy to the hen's clucking and the peeps and chirps of the chicks. The sounds of the forest were drowned out for her by the wonderful song from the birds on her knee. A hen, chickens, eggs! An egg every Sunday, eggs for cooking during the week! Egg bouillon, egg milk, egg pancakes! This was what the chirp from the chickens meant: boiled eggs, fried eggs, eggs in omelettes, eggs in the pan, eggs, eggs, eggs!

Kristina thought gratefully of Ulrika and her husband all the way home. Mr. and Mrs. Jackson were the kindest people she knew. And both had come from such wretched lives in their homelands. They had turned into new beings out here — had become transformed in America.

Kristina now wondered if she herself hadn't changed. Didn't she judge people in a different way? In Sweden she had shared the common opinions, valuing those whom others valued and looking down on those whom others looked down on. At home a few people were thought to be better than the majority; it was the opinions of these few that one followed. But here she had not heard of any particular persons who were held up as examples; in this country, it seemed, no one cared what people thought or said about others. And here each must form his own opinions. She herself must decide, she alone must pass the judgments she considered right.

In this way she explained to herself the thoughts she had about her friends in Stillwater. She, Kristina, had visited in a home where the husband had been a thief and the wife a whore. But this married couple were her honest, devoted friends. Yes, outside her own family, her best friends in America were a former thief and a former whore.

III

NEW NEIGHBORS AND THOUGHTS OF THE OLD HOME

- 1 -

As soon as Petrus Olausson had raised his log house his wife and children arrived. His wife's name was Judit; she was a tall, rather lean woman with small, quick, sharp eyes, a strong nose and a severely compressed mouth which seemed distorted: the right corner was pulled up higher than the left. The couple had a girl fourteen years of age and twin boys of twelve.

Kristina felt a little shy with the neighbor woman the first time she went to call. Judit Olausson, in a black, tight-fitting dress with a starched lace collar up to her chin, did not seem like an ordinary settler's wife but rather like a matron on a well-to-do farm. There was something austere and commanding about her; Kristina did not feel on an equal footing with her neighbor. Judit Olausson was also fifteen years older than she.

Later in the spring two other families, from Småland, settled at Fish Lake on the east side of the valley. It was some distance from this lake to Ki-Chi-Saga, and the names of the newcomers were not known. But with the Olaussons' arrival Karl Oskar and Kristina at last had close neighbors. The settlers gave each other a hand from time to time; and Karl Oskar lent Olausson a few tools, although the newcomer had brought along more implements than Karl Oskar had owned at his settling.

- 2 -

Karl Oskar's remedy against his wife's homesickness had been to name the new home Duvemåla and plant an Astrachan apple tree from Sweden. Now Kristina could say: I live again at Duvemåla. And she was pleased with the little seedling which had grown from

45

the old tree at home. She looked after it constantly, tended it as if it were a delicate living being. But neither the name nor the seedling could divert her thoughts from her old home. On the contrary, they now returned more often to her native country.

This in the daytime. And even at night she would return, in her dreams. In her dreams she had moved back to Sweden, with husband and children. Happily back, she wondered over her foolishness in ever having left her beloved homeland. But in the morning she always awakened in America.

She tried persistently to suppress her longing for something she would never again have. She wanted to conquer her weakness and be as strong as Karl Oskar. She had her home here, she must make herself feel at home, become part of this country. But her heart would not obey her.

And spring in Minnesota, with its dark evenings, was her difficult season. How many times she wished that she could write a letter to her parents! But Swedish women were not taught to write. If she had insisted, when she was little, she might have learned. But how could she have known what was in store — that her life would be spent on another continent? Now she was separated from her dear ones, and not a word from her reached them, except through a third person. After Robert had left for California, Karl Oskar had written a few short letters for her to her parents. Robert had helped her express her thoughts, but Karl Oskar had difficulty in transferring her feeling into writing. It became almost word for word the same, letter after letter: She was well, all was well with them, her father and mother must not worry about their daughter, her daily thoughts were with them in dear old Duvemåla. These last were the truest words in the letters.

It was always her father who answered, as her mother too, being a woman, could not write, and he wrote equally short letters, using direct Biblical words: Their daughter must put her trust in the Lord, she must bring up her children in the Lord's ways with strict discipline, as she herself had been brought up in her home, she must obey the Ten Commandments and live irreproachably so that they might meet in heaven.

The final words were a repeated confirmation that she never again would see her parents and brothers and sisters on this earth. And she asked dejectedly: Why must the world be so immensely large? Why must the roads across it be so incomprehensibly long?

46

IV

GUESTS IN THEIR OWN HOUSE

-1-

Spring brought fine weather for the crops. It was dry during seeding and planting time, and when the fields were ready a generous rain fell for several days. It poured down in sheets from low-hanging clouds. The cabin's sod roof began to leak, and they brought out all available pots and pans to catch the dripping.

During one of the rainy nights Karl Oskar was awakened by his wife's touching his elbow. "Someone is knocking on the door!"

He sat up in bed and listened. Out there in the black night the rain was pouring down, beating against the window. It dripped from the ceiling and splashed in the vessels on the floor. But above the sounds of the rain rose a heavy banging on the door.

Karl Oskar pulled on his trousers and lit a candle. Who would come at this hour of the night? Someone must have lost his way and was seeking shelter from the rain.

Kristina too stepped out of bed and pulled on her petticoat. She whispered, "Ask who it is before you open!"

It might be one of the new neighbors in need of help. But they could expect unfriendly callers day or night and must not be taken unawares; their door was always well bolted at night.

Before Karl Oskar had time to ask, a man's voice was heard through the door: "I'm a lone wanderer. Please give me shelter, good people!"

Those words in Swedish were enough for Karl Oskar; he pushed back the heavy bolts.

A man in a long black coat and a black broad-brimmed hat stepped across the threshold, stumbling and unsteady on his legs. His clothes were covered with mud and soaked through with rain; water splashed in his boots with every step. As soon as he reached a chair he sank down on it, collapsing like an empty sack. He breathed heavily. "Much obliged. Thank you, my good Swedes."

Somewhat confused, Karl Oskar and Kristina eyed their unexpected night visitor, a thin young man with a pale narrow face and large blue eyes. He carried a handbag of shining black leather, and his muddy clothes were of fine quality. He had white, unused hands like those of a gentleman, not a trapper or a settler. Why was he wandering about in the wilderness in this ungodly weather?

The man removed his big hat, and the water ran from the brim; his hair too was thoroughly wet and clung to his skull. From his coat and trousers water ran onto the floor and formed puddles around his chair.

Kristina pulled on her night jacket. "You're out in bad weather," she said.

"Where do you come from?" asked Karl Oskar.

"I've walked from St. Paul." He panted for breath, exhausted. "I'm worn out."

"Make a fire so he can dry himself!" said Kristina.

Karl Oskar found dry kindling behind the chimney, and soon a great fire blazed on the hearth. Now that the room was lighted up he could see his night guest better. What he saw shocked him; there was blood on the man's forehead and neck.

"You're bleeding! Has someone attacked you?"

"I was asleep. They came at me — a whole swarm. They wounded me with their arrows."

"The redskins? Are they on the warpath?"

"No. It wasn't the Indians. I was attacked by mosquitoes."

The stranger pushed his chair to the fire and began to pull off his boots; the leather of one had burst and his big toe stuck through the hole.

"A swarm of mosquitoes made these wounds," he explained.

Kristina breathed more easily again; she was used to mosquitoes, and bad as they were she preferred them to Indians on the warpath. She took some of the barley porridge left from their own supper and put the kettle over the fire; she poured fresh milk into a bowl and laid out bread and sirup.

Their guest's appearance and speech indicated he was of the upper classes. Karl Oskar did not wish to seem suspicious, but he told the man his own name and the place in Sweden he came from, hoping the stranger would do the same. After all, this country attracted all kinds of people. Many criminals found their way here. And the stranger had arrived in the middle of the night, muddy, his clothes torn.

The man said, "My name is Erland Törner. I was born in Östergötland."

"Are you here to settle?"

"No. I am a minister in the Swedish church."

"A minister!"

The exclamation came from Kristina. She almost dropped the jar of maple sirup. "A minister from Sweden? Did I hear right?"

"Yes, I was sent by the church at home."

Kristina now spoke to the stranger with reverence in her voice. "When did you leave home, Mr. Pastor?"

"Half a year ago."

And it seemed he had sensed Karl Oskar's suspicion, for he searched in his bag and found a thick document. "I'm entirely unknown to you, my dear countrymen. Here are papers to prove what I say."

He handed the document to Karl Oskar, who read in it that their guest was Pastor Lars Paul Erland Törner, born at Västerstad, Östergötland, in the kingdom of Sweden, May 16, 1825. The pastor was two years younger than himself.

"We did not doubt you, Mr. Pastor," Karl Oskar assured him quickly.

"Mr. Pastor, you must change your wet clothes!" said Kristina.

The young minister now began to revive; he smiled at her. "Don't call me Mister, Mrs. Nilsson! Pastor is enough."

"And don't call me Mrs. — my name is Kristina. I'm not of the upper class."

"But in America all married women are called Mrs." This she must know, he added: There was no difference here between nobles and ordinary people, all were equal. That was why he liked it so much in this country; God had never created different classes, only people.

"Here, Pastor, are some dry clothes," said Karl Oskar.

He had found the suit the village tailor had made for him at the time of his emigration. He had now worn it for three years, both weekdays and Sundays; he no longer had any special Sunday clothes. Most of the settlers wore equally poor garments.

"If you can wear them — they're the best I have."

"Thank you, Mr. Nilsson. Any dry clothing is blessed clothing."

The young minister changed clothes in front of the fire, and his host hung up the drenched ones to dry. Karl Oskar had a full, strong body, and Pastor Törner was lean and spindly. Around his thin legs the trousers flapped, and his hands disappeared entirely in the long coat sleeves. To Kristina their guest looked like a scarecrow. It was almost a dishonor to the church to clothe a minister this way. She was tempted to laugh; she could not help visualizing this figure in the pulpit!

Kristina filled the washbowl now and handed it to the minister so that he might wash off the blood on his neck and forehead. And now that she knew his position she felt the food she offered him was too poor. Could one really treat a minister to warmed-up porridge?

She curtsied. Would the pastor partake of their simple supper?

"Mrs. Nilsson, you could not offer food to a more grateful being than myself!"

Pastor Törner sat down at the table and turned up Karl Oskar's right sleeve so that he could handle the spoon. Then he filled his plate to the brim with barley porridge. His hosts sat a few paces from the table; they wanted to be courteous. Kristina could not quite realize what was taking place in her home this night. A man of the church, who had stood in the pulpit in Sweden, who had officiated at baptisms, weddings, funerals and Holy Communion, had come to their house in the wilderness and now sat at their table, in Karl Oskar's clothes, and ate the remnants of their supper. It all seemed like a miracle.

"I got wet to the skin as I was crossing a creek," said the young minister.

"The streams are overflowing with all this rain," said Karl Oskar.

"I had lost my way, then I happened on a field and realized I must be near a settlement. God has led me to your hospitable home."

Karl Oskar was puzzling things out for himself. Three sorts of people emigrated from Sweden: the poor, those who preached religious opinions differing from the state church, and the criminals. A minister was never poor, and he preached the right religion. Why would a minister emigrate?

He dared a direct question: "Why did you come to America?"

"Because of the emigrants."

"Because of us?"

"Yes. I want to help look after the souls of my countrymen. That's why I left my homeland and resigned my position there." Pastor Törner had eaten with ravenous appetite and scraped up the last spoonfuls of porridge from his plate. He told them how, in his parish at home, he had preached against the so-called Church Resolution which decreed heavy punishment for those poor souls who — through negligence of the clergy — became ensnared in heresy. Fines, prison sentences, exile — these measures, he said, did not bring strayed souls back into the church. You could not force people into the right by severe civil laws, but only through Christ's Gospel. For sermons of this kind he had been rebuked by bishop and chapter. He had been permitted to resign, and when some farm families from his parish emigrated to America he had joined them as their pastor. He did not wish them or their fellow emigrants to become prey to the many false teachings that swept North America.

And he added, with a look at the sleeping children, "I was sent to prevent your children from growing up heathens in this foreign land."

He rose from the table. Kristina's eyes did not leave him. This thin, pale young man with little strength to endure physical tribulations had traveled the same long, hazardous road as they had. He had sought them out in their new settlement to help meet their spiritual needs.

He had come to the right place; he had himself said that God had shown him the way through the wilderness to their home. And now she realized even more fully the miracle that had taken place this evening.

-2-

Karl Oskar and Kristina got little sleep that night; they sat up and talked to the young minister.

"I was told in St. Paul that Swedes were living near this lake," he said.

"There are only a few of us so far," said Karl Oskar.

"I'll look up all of them."

"You say you resigned your position at home. Who is paying you now?"

51

"No one. Kind people feed and shelter me, as you're now doing."

Karl Oskar thought that since a minister spent much money on expensive schooling he ought to receive definite pay for pastoral duties.

"There's nothing stated about that in the Gospels. Paid positions for pastors are recent inventions."

Karl Oskar and Kristina thought their guest was a most unusual minister.

"Do people in these settlements remember the Ten Commandments? Have they God's Word with them here to read?" he asked.

From their Swedish chest Kristina brought the two books which, together with the almanac, had accompanied them from their home village: Karl Oskar's confirmation Bible and her confirmation psalmbook.

"I see that all is well in this house."

Pastor Törner had visited several Swedish settlements where God's Word was lacking. In one settlement of nine families on the Illinois prairie he had been unable to find more than two Bibles; all the settlers had been physically healthy and thriving, and although he had been pleased with their worldly success he had felt depressed by their spiritual poverty. He had encountered grown men and women who remembered no more than two or three of the Commandments. One poor old man, tottering on the edge of his grave, knew not one of the Commandments.

Kristina had long been sitting with a question on her lips, the question that was so important to her: "Could you, Mr. Pastor — would you be kind enough to give us Holy Communion? We have not enjoyed it for more than three years."

"With great pleasure, Mrs. Nilsson! But couldn't I hold communion for all the Swedes in this neighborhood at the same time? It would strengthen their spiritual solidarity."

"We live so far apart here," said Karl Oskar.

"And we have no church," added Kristina.

Pastor Törner smiled kindly and waved with Karl Oskar's long sleeves as if he were brushing away all their objections with the greatest of ease. He had held communion in dense forests, on the open prairie, in log cabins and kitchens, in sheds and stables and cellars, on ox wagons, on river boats — and a few times even in a church! What need had he, a poor servant of God, for a gilded pulpit and an expensively decorated altar, when the Founder of Christianity Himself had preached at a roadside, and His disciples from dim dungeons.

He looked about the room. "Could I be permitted to use this home for communion?"

Karl Oskar and Kristina at first looked perplexedly at each other, then answered, both at the same time: "Our home can be used, of course." "If our simple log cabin is good enough. Of course."

"Thank you! Then we will invite the people and set the Lord's table here in this house."

And the minister waved his long sleeves with increased liveliness. It was already decided, then!

But it was late, their guest was tired and needed rest. Kristina said she would make a bed for Johan and Harald on the floor and let the minister sleep in their bed.

"Don't awaken the boys for my sake, Mrs. Nilsson," he insisted. "Last night I slept under a pine tree. I'll sleep on the floor. As long as I'm under a roof."

But Kristina would not give in; they could not allow a man of the church to sleep on the floor as beggars and tramps did at home. It would be degrading to the church; they would commit a grave sin. No, their best bed, their own, must be given to the guest. And she spread a clean sheet on it. They would sleep on an old mattress cover; Karl Oskar took it out to the barn where he had some hay from last year, filled it, brought it back and laid it on the floor near the hearth.

Pastor Törner still protested, but finally he undressed and lay down in the settler couple's bed, where he fell into a deep sleep within a few minutes.

"Poor man," said Kristina. "He was completely worn out."

And so they themselves went to bed for a second time this night. They lay down on the hay sack, in the chimney corner, while the minister from Sweden snored heavily in their own bed. Karl Oskar was still wondering about him. He had given up a good position at home to wander through the wilderness without food or shelter. Otherwise his speech and behavior seemed to indicate that he had his senses intact.

Kristina felt a blessed assurance in her heart; a stranger had come to them in the night and promised her the Lord's Supper.

One night in early spring she had directed an anxious question to the Almighty: What should they do about their sins here in this isolated place?

Tonight she had been given an answer.

- 3 -

Before Pastor Törner awakened the following morning, Kristina had mended the torn places in his coat and a hole in his trousers. To have a minister walk about in ragged trousers was a disgrace to the church. Then she had brushed and cleaned the muddy clothes.

When the pastor awoke and put on his suit he hardly recognized it. He praised Kristina: "Give a woman a needle and thread and as much cloth as she needs and she can turn herself into a queen and her home into a palace!"

Kristina smiled; she was walking about in such old rags it would be a long time before she looked like a queen. But it was a shame if a woman with a needle and thread couldn't baste together a few holes in a garment.

After breakfast Pastor Törner made ready to continue on his way. He opened his black leather bag, which contained a flask of communion wine, a small sack of communion bread, a couple of white, newly starched minister's collars and a dozen small jars of a remedy for fever and chills. This was quinine, and the price for each jar was seventy-five cents. Another minister from Sweden, Pastor Hasselquist in Galesburg, Illinois, had come across the medicine and sent it along by Pastor Törner for those Swedish settlements where fevers and chills constantly plagued the people. Pastor Hasselquist had also hoped his colleague might earn a little by selling the medicine. But the settlers had little cash, and most of the time he had to leave the jars without payment. Many of them needed quinine for their bodies as much as they needed communion wine for their souls. Pastor Törner presented a jar of the remedy to Kristina as a small return for bed and board.

He promised to come back within a short time and set the date for the communion in their house. But first he wanted to call on the other Swedish settlers in the St. Croix Valley. Karl Oskar walked part way down the road with him to show him the route to their nearest neighbor, Petrus Olausson from Helsingland.

It had gradually stopped raining, and in the late morning the sun came out. Kristina picked up the mattress she and Karl Oskar had slept on; the cover seemed moist to her, perhaps it had got wet when Karl Oskar took it to fetch the hay, and she wanted to dry it. She carried the mattress to the barn and emptied out the hay near the door. She was barely through with this when she let out a piercing scream. While shaking the mattress cover, something that looked like a dry tree branch had fallen out. She saw now that it was a wriggling snake.

Karl Oskar was just returning from his walk when he heard his wife's cries. He ran to her as fast as he could.

"A snake! Karl Oskar! A snake!"

She pointed. "That thing! It was in the mattress—in the hay!"

Karl Oskar, standing beside her now, saw in the hay a snake extended to its full length. It was light gray with brown markings. The thick end of its tail showed it was a rattler. As he watched it coiled and raised its head.

The sight of the reptile had frightened Kristina so that she was unable to move. Karl Oskar grabbed her by the arm and pulled her away. "He might strike!"

As yet Karl Oskar had never killed a rattler. He had seen such snakes curled up in low places, but none had attacked him and he had not disturbed them. This one, however, must not escape; if it crawled under the barn they would live in constant fear.

Under the oak at the side of the barn was a pile of fence posts, and he grabbed one. Then he took down the scythe which hung in the tree; he held the scythe in front of him in his left hand and the post in his right. Thus armed he stole, bent forward, toward the reptile at the barn door.

"Karl Oskar! Don't go so close! Be careful!"

Karl Oskar was a few steps away when the snake again raised its head. Its tongue, shining as a flower pistil, flickered out of the jaws where death lurked. And now a rattling, buzzing sound was heard: the warning signal.

Karl Oskar made a jump at the same time as the reptile; he threw himself forward at the very last second, pressed the back of the scythe against the snake and pushed it to the ground. The rattler twisted and turned under the pressure, threw its head back and forth until the scythe steel tinkled. It rattled like the lid on a boiling pot. Now it raised its head against the barn sill,

55

and this gave Karl Oskar an opportunity to use his second imple-
ment. With a few heavy blows of the post he crushed the rattler's
head against the sill.

"The Lord is protecting you, Karl Oskar! You risked your life!"
Kristina stood behind him, the rake in her hand, her lips blue-
white, every limb trembling.

Karl Oskar lifted the snake with the point of the scythe; the
crushed head hung limp. Then he stretched the snake out on the
ground. The first rattler he had killed was also the biggest one he
had seen. It was over five feet long and had seven rattles. He had
heard that this kind of snake got its first rattle at the age of three
and from then on one each year; this one must be an old devil.

Kristina's voice almost failed her as she said, "The snake was in
the mattress I was emptying."

Karl Oskar looked at the cover she had thrown on the ground,
he looked at the rattler he had carried into their house with the
hay last night. When he filled the mattress, in the dark barn, if his
hands had happened to . . .

They both kept silence for several minutes. What was there to
say about this that had happened during the night? They had
shared their bed with one of the most poisonous snakes in North
America. They had slept their sweet sleep with death under them
in the bed.

"To think that we're all right . . . " said Karl Oskar in a low voice.

"Perhaps we're saved because we gave shelter to a man of the
church," Kristina answered.

- 4 -

Pastor Törner returned two weeks later. It was then decided
that he would come back to the settlement of Duvemåla the following Sunday and hold the first communion for Swedish settlers
in the St. Croix Valley.

Kristina at once began preparations. A great honor was to be
bestowed upon them; their home would be used as a temple. Their
table, which Karl Oskar had made of a rough oak log, would be
raised to the dignity of an altar. Their simple log cabin would be
turned into a holy room. In their own home Karl Oskar and she
would be the Lord's table guests.

56

She scrubbed the floor more carefully than ever before, she washed the furniture and polished her utensils. Against the ceiling beams and above the fireplace she placed maple and elm boughs; the rich, fresh leaves made the room look festive. She pasted gray wrapping paper over the roughest and ugliest parts of the log walls. She picked the most beautiful wildflowers she could find among the bushes; but she had no vase to put them in. Her eyes fell on the spittoon at the door; she washed it, filled it with flowers and put it on the shelf above their food table. No guest would recognize their old spittoon in this elevation, filled with flowers and decorated with greenery. When she had finished on Saturday evening, the room was fresh and green, like a summer pavilion.

Sunday dawned with clear skies. Kristina gave Karl Oskar a newly washed and ironed shirt, a bowl of lukewarm water and a wooden spoon filled with soft soap, and he went out into the yard to clean up. Of suitable communion clothes he had none; he must wear the same clothing he had long worn at work. Kristina herself had her black dress, which she had been so careful with that it still looked nice.

Pastor Törner arrived at the log cabin on foot, carrying his black leather bag with the sacred bread and the wine and a parcel containing his minister's surplice. It had become wrinkled in the bundle, so Kristina pressed it.

The communion guests began to arrive, and as they entered the cabin Pastor Törner wrote down their names in turn. Including Karl Oskar and Kristina, there were twelve communicants in all. All the Swedes in the valley who had received an invitation had come — all except one: Samuel Nöjd, the fur trapper in Taylors Falls. He had said that he did not wish to participate in any priest's foolery. He had hoped, out here, to be left in peace by those black-caped sorcerers who in Sweden had plagued him with their catechism.

Kristina was praised for having decorated the cabin so nicely; it was attractive and looked like a real church, her guests said. The table stood in the middle of the room, and Karl Oskar had put planks on sawhorses for people to sit on. When everyone was seated there was no place for him, so he went to the woodshed and brought in the chopping block for himself. The fresh planks smelled pungently of pine and pitch. On the table Kristina had spread her only linen cloth, ironed and shining white. There stood the pitcher with the communion wine, and one of Karl Oskar's big brännvin glasses which was to be used as a communion cup. On a small plate lay the communion bread, thin, flat, dry wafers.

Pastor Törner took his place at the end of the table, where the family Bible lay open. His cheeks were newly shaven and gleaming, his thick light hair was combed straight back. As he stood there in his newly ironed surplice and white collar it could hardly be imagined that this was the same man who only recently had sought shelter in the middle of the night, dripping like a wet dog, his clothes torn and muddy, his face bloody with mosquito bites.

The young minister said: There had been twelve communicants when Jesus gathered His apostles for the first Lord's Supper in Jerusalem, there were twelve here today when he would now distribute Christ's flesh and blood to his countrymen in the wilderness. In his wine flask on the table he had only a very little left of the precious sacrament, which therefore must be divided with great economy to make it enough for everyone. There would hardly be more than sip, a small teaspoon for each. Bread, however, he had in sufficiency.

As he began to read the text of the service, the participants sat stone-still. These settlers, who had attended services at home almost every Sunday, had not heard a sermon in years. And now they listened to God's Word again, in their native tongue, spoken by a minister, spoken well and beautifully. They listened, tense and still.

"I have chosen my text from the seventeenth chapter of the Acts. More than eighteen hundred years ago these words were spoken by St. Paul to the Greeks in Athens, but they have a meaning to the immigrant Swedes of Minnesota today: God has decided to what distances on the earth people shall travel and move their habitations. I speak to men and women who have traveled over one third of the earth's circumference, who have moved from one continent to another in order to found new homes. You, my countrymen gathered here, have participated in an emigration covering a greater distance than ever before in human history."

And his countrymen listened. It was a sermon all of them understood well; it was about themselves.

Kristina listened to the minister intently, but also with half an ear to the yard outside. If only the children didn't start crying or coming in to disturb them! They had been told to keep as quiet as mice. But through the open door she could hear the brood hen cackling persistently. What an awkward sound, coming like that between the words of a sermon!

"The Lord has decided where people shall live. To you emigrating Swedes He has indicated Minnesota. The brown-skinned sons of the wilderness have ruled this land for centuries. But the Almighty sweeps away one race from the surface of the earth and plants another. You are the new race to build the land. But it is your duty, my dear countrymen who were born in a Christian land and know the Ten Commandments, to treat these heathens as brethren. Indians too are our neighbors; they are not of the same color as we, but they have the same Creator. Be kind and patient with the vanishing race."

The hen outside cackled ever more lustily, but the minister continued his sermon without appearing in the least disturbed, and none of the other listeners paid any attention, either. Inside the cabin it was as still as if all had stopped breathing; no noise or sound in the whole world could disturb this settlers' service in Karl Oskar's and Kristina's home.

- 5 -

"Kneel and repeat after me the confession of your sins,"

Twelve people knelt around the table. Twelve had gathered around Jesus at the first Supper, and Pastor Törner had seen a deep significance in the fact that the number of guests here was the same as it had been at the institution of the Sacrament; Christ's church would be rebuilt here in the wilderness.

The minister read the confession. The kneeling men, women and children each spoke after him in his or her own way, some loudly and openly, some in low and mumbling voices. Children's voices repeated the words clearly, thick male voices halted and stammered:

"... and I have in all my days – from my childhood, even until this moment – many and bitter sins committed ... "

The communion guests knelt on the floor, their hands folded over their breasts, their heads bowed. Married couples knelt side by side, and children next to their parents. It was warm in the house and drops of perspiration came to foreheads and cheeks.

59

A breath of wind from the door felt blissfully cool. From outdoors no sounds were heard from the livestock. But in the midst of the confession, a child's laughter suddenly reached them from the yard.

"Thine Holy Words I have often neglected and avoided..."

Some were behind in their reading, and the young minister repeated the words, slowly, so that the stragglers would catch up.

One of the participants needed no one to read the words for him — Kristina's uncle, Danjel Andreasson. The confession was well known to him, word by word. At his last communion, in the old country, he himself had distributed the Holy Sacrament. That was at night, in his own home. Because he had been denied the sacrament by the clergy. And while he was thus occupied, a noise had been heard at the door. He had gone to open it, and in had come the dean and the sheriff, who had forcefully scattered the guests at the Lord's table. All had been fined or imprisoned, he himself exiled.

Danjel Andreasson was exiled from his homeland, but not from the Kingdom of God. Now he was here in the new land which the Lord had promised him. He heard a noise at the door, but it was open and he need not now fear; no worldly authority would interfere with their gathering. What he heard from the door was only the cool summer wind which blew over the grass and the trees. It was not a sheriff, not the hard, commanding voice of authority, silencing the voice of conscience in the name of the law, writing ordinances for people's souls. It was the Lord's own voice Danjel Andreasson heard in the sounds from outside — God's free wind, blowing hither and yon over the earth of his new homeland.

Kristina was kneeling to the left of her Uncle Danjel and to the right of her husband. Karl Oskar got mixed up in his confession, and Kristina herself found that in a few places she had forgotten the words. With tense breath and trembling lips she enumerated all the sins and transgressions she had committed.

"... I have been vain; I have sought the wicked, sinful world. I have been greedy, covetous, short in compassion, gluttonous..."

She was overwhelmed by the multitude of her wrongdoings, and repentance burned in her breast. Only through repentance could she become worthy of participation in this sacrament. And while she repeated the confession, and her lips moved, she prayed a wordless prayer within her: "O Lord, help me repent enough!"

Close to hers was Karl Oskar's bowed head; his face was hard and solemn, severe, closed. Had he repented enough, did he repent deeply enough now, was he worthy? She would have liked to whisper to him: You must not confess your sins with your lips only! You must not enumerate them as, at the end of each day, you reel off the chores you've performed. You must confess from your heart! You must be consumed with hunger for the bread, thirst for the wine, yearning for forgiveness! And I myself — do I repent sufficiently?

"My grievous and many sins press me hard and are like unto a burden too heavy..."

Kristina's legs began to tremble. Her knees shook against the floorboards. For a few moments she was on the verge of falling forward. Perhaps her heart's repentance was not complete? Perhaps she should bend still lower, feel greater humiliation, throw her face against the ground, lay herself at the Lord's feet?

The confession was over. The minister said, "Do you ask with a repentant heart for the forgiveness of your sins?"

Kristina's reply was a faint whisper only, barely audible to herself, but it was a whisper that shook her whole being: "Yes... yes..."

She leaned her forehead against the edge of the table so as not to fall. Her surroundings began to blur. She could hear the minister's voice, but not what he said. She heard psalm singing, but not the words of the psalm. She was alone in the world with her Saviour.

The words of the psalm completed the contrition. People around her cried; to the right and to the left of her they sobbed and wept. But she did not hear them, she was absorbed in her own tears, overwhelmed by her own weeping.

And so, dissolved in tears, kneeling as if separated from all other people, liberated from all earthly things, as if she were the only human being in the whole creation — thus Kristina, for the first time since her emigration, partook of the Lord's Holy Supper; she was a guest at His table in her own house.

Afterward she felt dazed and exhausted. But she was lighter of heart, more satisfied, than she had ever been since arriving in North America.

V

MAN AND WOMAN IN THE TERRITORY

- 1 -

About midsummer the little Swedish colony at Ki-Chi-Saga was increased by two new families. Lars Sjölin and his wife Ellida, a childless couple in their forties from Hassela, Helsingland, took land at the lakeside below Petrus Olausson's claim, and from Kettilstad in Östergötland came Algot Svensson and his wife, Manda, who settled on a piece of land to the west of Duvemåla. They were of about the same age as Karl Oskar and Kristina and had five small children. It was further known that several families from Småland were squatting along the southern shores of the lake and that still more Smålanders were on their way.

Immigrants from three Swedish provinces had now found new homes around the big Indian lake; Karl Oskar and Kristina had Helsingland neighbors to the southeast and Östergötland neighbors to the west. They speculated as to where people would come from to claim the piece of land to the north of them.

They became acquainted with their new neighbors from Östergötland at once; Algot Svensson was a kind, small man, rather taciturn, the type of settler who made little noise. His wife, Manda, on the contrary, was sociable, jolly, ever ready to talk. She related that she came from an old, well-to-do farm family which had rejected her for marrying the hired hand. Manda Svensson had brought with her from Sweden two loom reeds, one of which she now presented to Kristina. The winter before, Karl Oskar had with great difficulty made a primitive loom, but he had been unable to make the reed and there was no reedmaker among the settlers. Kristina almost jumped with joy at the gift. Through Ulrika's efforts she had last year obtained a spinning wheel from Stillwater; it had been made for her by the Norwegian, Thomassen, who was both shoemaker and spinning-wheel maker. She had already spun last year's flax, and with the blessed reed she could weave cloth for new clothing next winter; no one in the family had an unpatched garment to put on.

Hard winter work awaited Kristina, while Karl Oskar labored

62

most intensely during the warmer seasons. He was working on his threshing barn, which he hoped to have ready when the crops were ripe. The years before, when he had had to wait for ice to form his threshing floor, the rats, mice and other rodents had taken a sizable toll from his rye and barley. By putting up a threshing barn he would save many loaves for his family.

Now he split shakes for the barn roof, cut and worked the timbers for his new main house, dug on the foundation for his cellar, put up fences, mowed and dried grass and raked the hay into stacks. All these chores must be done before the crops were ripe, when harvesting would take all his time.

When he was preparing the ground for the winter wheat field his southeast neighbor came and filled his ears with praise of Indian corn. A word of advice from Petrus Olausson seemed like a command: Let the field lie fallow over the winter and plant corn the next spring.

Olausson had already planted this wonderful grain on his claim, he had begun banking the corn when it was an inch tall, and now it grew an inch a day in this heat. Corn would give up to seventy bushels an acre. But one must choose the right kind of seed, the big kind, which gave ten ears to each plant and three or four hundred kernels to each ear. Several thousand grains from one seed, many thousandfold! Because of sinful man, God had cursed the ground; but over one of the grains He had let flow His blessing — over Indian corn. And corn was the most healthy and most tasty of foods, for both men and animals; of corn, porridge and soup were cooked, pancakes were made, bread was baked, a potent drink brewed, sugar distilled; livestock and hogs were fattened on it. Corn bread was the most healthy ever eaten, it possessed a useful purgative power.

It was called "lazy man's grain" because the lazy Indians cultivated it in their small patches, letting their poor women tend it alone. Petrus Olausson said: The name "lazy man's grain" did not suit corn, since it did not grow by itself, like hair on a head, or nails on toes and fingers; it needed attention — weeding, hoeing, banking — but a well-cared-for field of corn was the most beautiful sight God had created on this earth.

Until Olausson raised corn none of the Swedes in the valley had tried it. They stuck to their old crops and were suspicious of new kinds. And what good could be expected from Indians? It would be like dealing with the Evil One directly. But after Karl Oskar had seen his neighbor's cornfield he decided to plant some himself next year. Why shouldn't a Christian Swede follow the heathens' example, if it was useful?

The hot Minnesota summers made the corn grow well, but the humid heat exhausted one's strength. In the evenings Karl Oskar fell asleep completely worn out. Settlers were said to grow used to the heat after a few years, but to him it was the same ordeal summer after summer. The heat sucked the sweat from his body, until he felt entirely dried out. The nights were the worst; the heat interfered with breathing and prevented sleep; hot, humid air made him feel as if wads of wet wool had been put into his mouth. The lungs worked slowly and laboriously and the heart felt like a heavy lump in the breast.

The cabin became unbearably sultry at night, and when Karl Oskar was unable to sleep he would walk outside and lie down on the ground. Here was no bedding but the cool grass, no cover but the dark night sky with the tiny star lights. Stretched out on this grass mattress, he would at last go to sleep, but would dream torturous choking dreams.

VI

STARKODDER THE OX

- 1 -

To plant and to seed, to harvest and to thresh, that was the order of things from spring to fall, the cycle of labor year in and year out.

Karl Oskar Nilsson had cut, harvested and threshed the third crop from his clearing. His old Swedish almanac had blank pages between the months, intended for a farmer's notations; on these he had written down his harvests in America:

Anno 1851 I harvested 18 bussels Rye, 11 bussels Barley and 32 bussels Potatoes, all ample measure;

Ditto 1852 harvested 24 bussels Rye, 16 and a half bussels Barley and 48 bussels Potatoes, ditto measure;

Now he continued on the same page, between the month of August and the month of September:

Ditto 1853 I harvested 38 bussels Rye, 26 bussels Barley and 69 bussels Potatoes, ditto measure.

He was getting along well on his claim; his third crop was more than double his first.

What he missed more than anything was a team. For three whole years he and Kristina had been their own beasts of burden. They had carried home all their necessities from Taylors Falls to Ki-Chi-Saga. They had lugged and carried and pulled until their backs were bent and their arms stretched beyond normal length. Out here they had assumed labors which in Sweden were relegated to animals.

There were two kinds of immigrants in the Territory: two-legged and four-legged, people and animals. The people were few, the animals fewer. But the latter were indispensable to the former. People must therefore import animals; cattle were driven in herds or freighted on the rivers from Illinois. Many of the animals died during the long and difficult transportation, and those that survived were so expensive on arrival in Minnesota that a squatter could not afford them. The price for a team was eighty, ninety or a hundred dollars, and so much money Karl Oskar had not held in his hand at one time since they settled here. What cash he received for unneeded hay or other crops had to be spent for groceries and tools. He must himself raise his cattle. Lady's and Miss's bull calves must grow into oxen.

But one day, on an errand to the lumber company in Taylors Falls, Karl Oskar learned that one of the company's oxen had broken both its front legs and they had been forced to slaughter it; now its mate was for sale. Karl Oskar looked over the beast and made an offer. He had come to collect twenty dollars for hay which he had sold the company; he would write a receipt for that money and pay ten dollars more for the ox if he might owe them this sum until next summer, when he would sell them more hay.

Thirty dollars was cheap for a thirteen-hand ox, but the company manager accepted even though he didn't receive the whole sum in cash. "I trust you, Mr. Nilsson," he said.

It was the first time in this country that Karl Oskar had been trusted for credit; when he asked for a few nails or a spool of thread, cash had always been required. Now that he had managed to remain on his claim for three years, perhaps the Americans at last realized that he intended to stay.

So Karl Oskar returned to Duvemåla the owner of a sturdy old ox. The beast had an enormous belly, its horns were thick and nicely curved, its coat was black with a white spot like a shining star in the middle of the forehead. A stone-hard enlargement on the neck, with the fur entirely worn off, told of the many heavy loads it had pulled; this yoke mark was the beast's letter of recommendation.

"That's a lordly ox!" exclaimed Kristina as Karl Oskar came leading the animal. It had a lumbering walk, but held its head proudly in the air. It was inded a lord among oxen.

From a thick oak log Karl Oskar sawed off four trundles – the wheels of a settler's wagon; he also made a single yoke for the ox's neck. At last he had his own wagon and his own beast to pull it. Up to now he had shared the lot of cotters and other poor people back in Sweden: they walked and carrried their burdens on their backs while the farmers loaded theirs onto wagons and rode snapping their whips self-confidently. Finally, after three years on his claim, he could ride his own ox wagon and feel like a farmer who owned something in America.

Petrus Olausson came and inspected his neighbor's new beast. "I too will buy an ox! Then we can team up and break land together."

A few days later Olausson came home with a thirteen-hand ox, entirely white, which he had bought in Stillwater. Karl Oskar measured the animal and said, "Our team is the strongest in the whole valley."

The two neighbors yoked the black and the white oxen together and helped each other break new fields during the fall. They plowed the same number of days on each claim. They used Olausson's plow, which had an iron bill and cut deeper then Karl Oskar's wooden plow; but however deep they plowed, the team was strong enough to manage.

Before the frost came and stopped their work, Karl Oskar had added five more acres to his field. Already he had more acres to seed than he had owned in Sweden.

The black ox became their most valued and best-liked animal. He was strong, good-natured, untiring. Standing there, sated with rich grass, chewing his cud, which dribbled down his chin tuft, he was a picture of true contentment. Heavy and immobile as a huge boulder, the black ox radiated security.

Karl Oskar named his beast Starkodder. It was a name he had taken from the saga of a brave Viking; Starkodder had been a hero with the strength of three men who was endowed by the god Odin with a life span of three ordinary humans. It was the hero's strength Karl Oskar had in mind when he named his ox.

He became their devoted helper — broke their land, pulled home their supplies and relieved them of much drudgery. They lifted their burdens and laid them all on his neck. And the old beast received everything patiently.

Starkodder seemed almost a sacrificial animal: he sacrificed himself for them.

-2-

Pastor Erland Törner had stayed with the Swedes in the St. Croix Valley and had conducted services throughtout the summer and fall. Now he was recalled to the Swedish settlement in Moline, Illinois. Newly arrived immigrants there had brought cholera with them, and it raged among the settlers. They urged him to return, for there were no ministers to conduct funeral rites.

When Kristina learned that Pastor Törner was going to move away, she decided to ask him to church her before he left. She regretted she had not asked him earlier to offer the special prayers said for a woman after childbirth. She ought not to have received the Holy Sacrament without first being purified.

She made her decision somewhat late; the following day she discovered she was pregnant again. No minister would church a woman in her condition. And now she was to bear a new child without being cleansed and blessed from the earlier birth.

Almost three years had passed since her previous pregnancy, and she had hoped that it was her last — that she might remain barren for the rest of her life. She had already given life to six children, four of whom were living. She would be twenty-eight next Michaelmas. The strain of so many pregnancies and the years'

67

labors had begun to leave their marks on her. Her blossoming youth was over, her rounded girlish cheeks gone. Recently she had lost a tooth for the first time, and as she held it in her palm she told Karl Oskar that this was the first sign of old age. He replied that they had gone through so much as emigrants that they were in reality older than those of equal age who had remained at home.

This would be her seventh child. And she felt depressed not only for her own sake, but for the children's sake; the more of them there were, the less each one could expect.

If she and her husband stayed apart, she need not become pregnant again. But the holy bonds of matrimony meant that a man and his wife should know each other bodily and beget children. God wanted them to enjoy each other in that way. And desire was so powerful with Karl Oskar and herself that they couldn't stay away from each other for very long. What took place between them took place according to the Almighty's will; through them He created new people. And now He had again created a life in her. What could she do about it? Nothing.

A pregnancy reminded a woman that God trusted her; it was a sign of His confidence in her, a blessing. Barrenness was a curse, a punishment. Thus Kristina was again a blessed woman. In her prayers she had never uttered her innermost wish. How could she ask to escape a blessing, pray for a curse?

Pastor Törner came to say good-by. He promised Kristina he would return next summer and help establish a Lutheran parish in the St. Croix Valley. He had become deeply attached to his countrymen here. In the meantime he asked them not to become confused by the disputes among the many religious groups in America. After all, a fight for men's souls was better than spiritual indifference.

The young pastor had received board and lodging among the Swedes in the valley, and they had also collected a little money for him: twenty dollars, a dollar or two from each homestead. Kristina watched him from the door as he departed. She had not told him that on his return next year there would be one more in the log cabin. She had figured out that her seventh child would be born in May.

November came and the oaks had lost their leaves. The wild geese had flown south; winter was near. But the weather was still mild and the ground bare.

Karl Oskar was preparing for a trip to Taylors Falls; he wanted to drive to the mill with some of the new crop before the first snow. He loaded the wagon the evening before: two sacks of rye, two sacks of barley; with two bushels to each sack it made as heavy a load as the ox could haul in the trundle cart on the bumpy forest road.

He arose before daylight and yoked up Starkodder; he wanted to start at the break of dawn to be back before dark. Johan, always awake early, wanted to ride with his father, who had once promised to take him along to Taylors Falls. But today the load was heavy, and Kristina felt the boy should stay at home; he would only get cold riding the long way there and back. It wasn't freezing yet, replied Karl Oskar, and when the boy kept on pleading he decided that it would be good for him to go; he would soon be eight and children ought to get around a little at that age.

Kristina wound her big woolen shawl around Johan to keep him warm on the cart. She lingered in the door and looked after them as the oxcart rolled away into the forest; Karl Oskar walked at the side, the reins in one hand, while he steadied the load with the other. Johan sat on top of the sacks and waved proudly to his mother; the gray shawl, covering everything but his face, made him look like a wizened old woman.

The oxcart rocked and bumped in the deep ruts. How easily it could turn over on the bumpy road, which was only wheel tracks. "Drive carefully, Karl Oskar! The boy might fall off!" Kristina called after them.

The cart with her husband and son disappeared from her view, enveloped by the gray mist of dawn. She sat down in front of the fire with her wool cards; she should card wool for days on end — all of them needed new stockings before the winter cold set in. The work made the hours fly. But she could not get the cart out of her mind. So many things could happen to Karl Oskar and Johan. Suppose they had to wait for their rye and barley to be ground;

then they wouldn't be home until after dark and could easily lose their way in the forest. The cart might turn over and pin Karl Oskar under the load, badly hurt and unable to move. Or Johan might fall off and break an arm or a leg.

In the late afternoon she began to listen toward the forest; wasn't it time for her to hear the heavy tramp of the ox and the rolling trundles? But there was no sound. At last she put her wool cards down. And when she went outside she understood: there was something else still that might have happened to Karl Oskar, something that had not occurred to her while she was carding — although she had been forewarned. She should have thought of it the previous evening, when the sun had set fiery red, red as a peony.

- 4 -

The forest held much for a child to see, and the road to Taylors Falls was all too short for Johan. From his high seat on the load he had a good view of all living and moving things. The flying squirrels, so much shyer than ordinary squirrels, fluttered among the branches at a distance, like enormous bats. The woodpecker hammered his arrow-sharp beak into a dry tree trunk until it echoed through the forest. At the approach of the noisy wagon large flocks of blackbirds lifted from the thickets, and the curious long ears of rabbits poked up from the grass in meadows and glades, their white tails bobbing up and down as they took off, their hind legs stretched behind them.

With a lumbering gait the black ox pulled his load. The oak trundles turned slowly over stumps, into and out of ruts, the axles well greased with bacon rind. It was the first time in America that Karl Oskar had driven a load with his own wagon and beast, and the first time he had been accompanied by his oldest son.

Johan had a mind ahead of his years. He had begun to help his father; he could look after the cows and the pigs when they were let out, he carried in water and wood, he was a willing helper as far as his strength went. In time he would be a great aid to Karl Oskar.

"If you're cold, come down and run beside the cart."

No, Johan wasn't cold. The weather was mild and he was warmed by his new experience. He was only sorry the road would

70

come to an end — and too soon did he see the water in the river; they had arrived.

An Irishman named Stephen Bolles had built a little mill near the rushing stream above Taylors Falls. The millstones were only eighteen inches in diameter; Bolles had no fine grind — his small stones could grind only rough flour. The mill was really a makeshift contraption, but it was their nearest one.

The miller looked out though the door of his dark mill like a dwarf, and Johan felt afraid of him. Stephen Bolles was a fat man with thick white hair hanging down to his shoulders like a horse's mane. His face was gray with white spots, like hardened, cracked clay. In the cracks, dirt and flour had gathered; it was a face that was never washed. In the midst of it his mouth opened like a hole, with one long black tooth.

Bolles spoke in short sentences and grunted like an Indian; Karl Oskar could not understand half of what he said. But the Irishman knew the errand of a man with sacks, and Karl Oskar knew the cost of grinding per bushel, so further conversation was unnecessary.

There was one load before them; Karl Oskar must wait an hour while the other settler's grind was finished. Then his own sacks would be poured between the grindstones. Meanwhile he and Johan ate from their lunch basket: bread, potato pancakes, fried pork. They drank milk from a bottle Kristina had tied in a woolen sock to keep it warm. During the meal they were watched by Bolles's granddaughter, a little girl with flaming hair. She talked to Johan, who didn't even try to understand what she was saying. Her forehead above her snub nose was covered with freckles; she was the troll child and her grandfather the old troll. Johan felt uneasy with them both.

The Irishman's ramshackle mill ground slowly, and it was one o'clock before Karl Oskar's grain had been turned into flour. During their waiting the weather had unexpectedly changed; the sun was no longer visible, the whole sky had clouded over, and suddenly the air felt much colder.

The old miller dumped the last sack onto the cart, squinted heavenward and grunted from his narrow lips, "Goin' to get snow. Pahaps a . . . "

The Swedish settler nodded good-by to the Irishman and made

71

haste to turn homeward. They needed four hours for the trip, and the day was far gone; he had no time to lose if he wanted to be back before dark. He urged Starkodder on. But the black ox moved his heavy body with the same slow speed as always, shuffled his hoofs in the same rhythm; this good beast was not to be ruffled by whip or urgings.

Johan had resumed his place on top of the sacks, but after a few miles he complained of being cold. Karl Oskar helped the boy down and had him walk beside the cart to keep warm. It had indeed turned cold; Karl Oskar buttoned up his heavy coat. Changes in weather took place so suddenly in the Territory; people said the temperature might fall from twenty above to twenty below within a few hours. And the Irish miller had croaked something about snow. Well, it was time, of course.

But there was another word in connection with snow, and that word Karl Oskar feared. Still, wasn't it too early for it, in the beginning of November? Yet anything might happen in this country if they were unlucky. A certain apprehension came over him and he peered at the clouds; they were thickening and dark above the treetops. And those trees, so immobile when they had come past a few hours ago, had now begun to sway.

But what he feared couldn't come on so suddenly; they would be sure to get home. Well, perhaps they had better take the road by Danjel's and Jonas Petter's settlements, at Lake Gennesaret, to be on the safe side. It was a little longer, a mile or so, but in New Kärragärde they would find shelter should the threatening storm break. Karl Oskar hesitated.

Johan was unable to keep warm even though he ran behind the cart and kept in constant motion.

"I'm cold, Father!"

"You should have stayed home, boy."

He wound the woolen shawl tighter around Johan's head and shoulders and taught him how to flail his arms against his body to keep warm. He put his own mittens on the boy's ice-cold hands — a child was more sensitive to cold weather than a grown person. For his son's sake Karl Oskar now decided to take the longer road through Danjel's claim and if necessary seek shelter there.

At the creek they left the old tracks and turned off toward New Kärragärde, barely two miles away. This stretch should take less than an hour, if he now could get his ox to move a little faster. He cut a juniper branch and struck Starkodder a few blows across the hind quarters. And the black ox hurried his pace a little, sniffing the air as if aware of an approaching crisis.

A raw fog was enveloping the wagon from all quarters. A penetrating wind had come up behind them from the northeast. It cut through their clothing and into their skin like a sharp knife. High in the air, above the trees, a dull roar was now heard; it sounded like waves breaking. The trees swayed like the masts of a ship. This was a sure sign.

"Father — I'm cold."

Karl Oskar looked skyward and discovered that he no longer could see the treetops through the fog. Snow was all right, but that other — no, he liked no part of it. It was a terrifying word in the Territory: *blizzard*. One's life was always in danger in a blizzard, even if one happened to be no more than five minutes from a house.

He urged the ox on, he yelled and hit and slapped the reins. The cart was moving forward; each time the wheels turned Karl Oskar could take a few steps, three long steps. They would reach shelter.

And then, like a hunting hawk, the blizzard dove down on the cart.

It began with whirling hail, biting like gravel. Then all at once the world around them was transformed into snow, a mass of hurling, whirling, whipping, piercing, smarting snow. If the onslaught had come from the opposite direction they would have been unable to go on; against such force their ox would have been unable to move. Now they were driven forward by the storm from behind.

Shivering and trembling, Johan clung to his father. "I'm so cold, Father."

The boy cried pitifully. Karl Oskar took the blanket which covered the sacks, wrapped it around him and put him back on top of the load. He reined in the ox for a moment; the boy had lost his wooden shoes in the snow and Karl Oskar must find them. It took some moments, the piercing snow hitting his eyeballs and blinding him.

Darkness fell over the forest, and the fierce wind blew through their clothing as though they were naked. Johan sat on the load, well bundled up, yet he whimpered with cold. Starkodder, in his thick hide, had the best protection against the blizzard.

On, on! They must reach Danjel's, they must find shelter. It could not be far now. Karl Oskar walked beside the wagon and held on to it as if he were afraid of losing it. Now and again he felt for Johan to make sure he was still there. Starkodder tramped steadily through the blizzard, pushing his big-bellied body strongly through the whirling snow masses. He was no longer black — his back was covered with snow and he looked like a moving snowdrift.

The snow lumped itself under Karl Oskar's clogs, clung like a freezing cover to his back, stuck to the trundle wheels in big clumps. The cart went more and more slowly as the drifts grew deeper. They must find shelter quickly; their lives were now in danger.

The roar of the blizzard rose and fell, it thundered in waves. Sharp cracking sounds were heard above the din: broken tree trunks crashing in the forest.

Karl Oskar's cheeks were stiff, frostbitten; he rubbed them with snow. How long could the boy hold out? He called cheeringly to Johan, who lay on the sacks like a bundle of clothes. The child's life was in danger; his resistance was not great.

Suddenly Karl Oskar's clog struck wood. Another step — yes, it was a plank. He recognized the place; they had reached the little brook. They were crossing the wooden bridge which Danjel and Jonas Petter had built over the brook Chidron. They were now in the hollow which the Biblically inclined Danjel had called Chidron's Valley. If he remembered right it was now only about half a mile to Danjel's cabin. If the ox didn't slow down they could make it in a quarter of an hour, surely in twenty minutes. Then they would be out of danger, sitting in the warmth of Danjel's cottage. He called to the boy that they would soon be at his great-uncle's.

But the trundles turned more and more grudgingly. Karl Oskar tied the reins around his waist and pushed from behind with all his strength. This would also warm him. And the trundles kept turning, still rolling, while each turn brought them a few steps closer to Danjel's house.

Suddenly a loud crash cut through the din of the blizzard, and the cart stopped with a jerk. Karl Oskar hit his ox with the reins, urging him on. But Starkodder stood still, the cart stood still. Karl Oskar walked alongside the ox, feeling his flanks. Why had he

74

come to a stop? He brushed the snow from his eyes and now he could see: A giant fir had fallen over the road, close to the ox, which now stood in a thicket of branches. Starkodder shook his head, twisted and pulled it to free his horns, which were caught in the fir's branches.

Further progress was cut off. With only a short distance left, they had been caught by the blizzard. Now they could move neither forward nor back.

Karl Oskar found his ax under the sacks, cut a few branches from the fallen tree and liberated the ox; he unyoked the beast and tied him with the reins to the cart. A faint sound was heard from Johan on the load. Karl Oskar climbed up and felt the bundled-up boy.

"Awfully cold, little one?"

He took the child in his arms, put his hand inside the bundle and felt the tiny limbs. Terror struck him.

"You're cold as an icicle!"

A faint voice came, "Are we home, Father?"

Karl Oskar began to rub the stiff limbs so violently that the boy cried out, "Stop! It hurts! Please!"

No part of the little body was frozen yet. But Johan was terribly sleepy and wanted to be left alone. It was a bad sign.

Karl Oskar Nilsson held his oldest son in his arms and tried to find protection behind the cart. He sat down in the snow, squatting against the sharp sweep of the storm. All around him was cold, whirling snow. He crept under the cart with the child; it did not help. Where could he hide Johan against the merciless cold? He himself was shivering and felt his limbs stiffen as soon as he stopped moving them; he had no warmth left for his son. What must he do to keep life in the little body?

Should he try to chop through the tree and clear the road? Then only a short distance and they would be at Danjel's. But he wouldn't have time; before he could cut halfway through that giant fir his son would be frozen to death. No, there was nothing he could do, nothing that would help. All he could do was pray to God. And sit under the cart and wait for the child in his arms to stiffen to a corpse.

At home Kristina was waiting with three more children, and one unborn life, while he was sitting under the mill cart, preparing himself for eternity. A tree had fallen and parted them forever; he had only driven to the mill, and he had failed to return. Was that the way his life would end?

No! He mustn't give up! He had never given up. He still had some fight left in him. And it wasn't the first time he had faced danger.

The ox Starkodder bellowed now and then between the gusts. He very seldom made any sound, but now he was frightened. Even a dumb animal could sense danger to life. Yet the beast would probably endure the longest of them, the ox would survive its owner and the owner's son.

Now that the branches of the fallen tree had swept the snow from Starkodder's back he was all black again. Only the white star on his forehead shone through the mist. Karl Oskar rose with the boy in his arms and walked toward his trusted beast of burden who bellowed helplessly against the roaring blizzard. A thought had come to him; there was still a chance.

Johan clung to his neck, his arms stiffening with the cold. The son was little, the ox big. The little one could find shelter with the big one, a human being with an animal. Starkodder was a good, reliable creature, but he was only an animal, and a new animal could be acquired in his place. No one could replace Johan once he had frozen to death. Karl Oskar had tools with him, the ax and the knife. It was still light enough for him to see. But he must hurry, it must be done quickly.

He had never been quicker in his motions than he was during the following few minutes. He bundled Johan in the shawl and the blanket and laid him in the snow under the cart. Then he led the ox a few paces away, to the side of the road. Starkodder followed him trustingly and stopped when he stopped. In the lee of a great tree trunk he came to a stop, gathered the reins and tied the ox, right foreleg to left hindleg, down low, near the hoofs. The ox stood still, patient, accommodating. Then Karl Oskar took his ax and walked up to the head of the beast.

His legs tied, Starkodder attempted a step toward his owner, sniffed the master's coat. Karl Oskar had raised his arm with the ax, but he let it drop again. The ox's mouth touched his sleeve, the animal's tongue licked it, as if expressing his devotion. Then Karl Oskar remembered the life he was trying to save. No time to lose.

With both hands firmly on the handle, he now raised the ax above his head, aimed at the little white star shining there between the ox's horns and let the blow fall murderously on the beast's forehead.

Starkodder staggered to his knees, his head against the ground, with a low bellow. The butcher hit again, in the same spot. Now the ox was down; from his throat came a sound of agony which for a few moments drowned out the blizzard's roar. After a third blow with the ax the bellowing died to a faint moaning sound. The ox's head was in the snow, but his body still rested on his hind legs; Karl Oskar pulled the reins he had fastened to the animal's legs, and Starkodder toppled over. But the four legs were still moving in the air.

Karl Oskar had never butchered an animal so big. He was unsure about the sticking point in the ox's neck. But then, with a firm hand, he pushed the knife in all the way to the handle. As he pulled it out he saw that he had hit the right spot; blood flowed in a heavy stream, as if he had pulled the plug from the bung hole of a barrel. The snow around the ox's head was stained dark red. Karl Oskar warmed his frozen hands in the steaming blood. He stood bent over the animal as long as the red stream flowed; soon it was only a trickle.

Its blood drained, life gone, the animal lay still at last. Karl Oskar picked up the reins again and managed with some difficulty to turn the heavy carcass over on its back. He quickly severed the ribs with his ax, put the ax handle into the hole and widened it enough to get his hands through. Then with his knife he opened the carcass from chest to tail and cut loose heart, lungs, kidneys, spleen, liver, bladder. A hot odor rose in his face. The butcher wiped the icicles from his eyelashes, and blood smeared his face. All of the entrails must be removed from the carcass to make sufficient room. Most difficult to handle was the large stomach sac, which flowed in all directions like an immense lump of dough, steam rising from it as from a caldron.

At last the carcass was clean. Karl Oskar had prepared a warm, safe room for his son.

He pulled Johan out from under the cart, carried him to the ox and placed him inside the carcass. There was plenty of room in there for the child, and the warm body would revive the boy. Then he folded the edge of the hide over the child. who was coming to life from the heat.

"Are we home, Father?"

"Yes. Go to sleep again, boy."

With the oxhide over him Johan thought he was at home in bed under the thick quilt; he went back to sleep contentedly. The father bundled the shawl around him as best he could. Then he picked up the reins and tied the carcass together, with only a small air hole above the child's mouth. Johan was as comfortable inside the carcass as if he had been sleeping in his own bed.

Karl Oskar's arms and legs were still shaking, but not from cold. His hands and clothing were covered with blood and entrail slime. But it was done; he had taken the only way out.

It was barely half a mile to Danjel's. Could he make it? Of course he could, even if he had to crawl on his hands and knees. It was entirely dark now, but he remembered the trees they had blazed for the road, and the wind would be at his back. He picked up his ax and began cutting a way through the thick fir which had stopped their progress. He was pleased to notice that he still had strength. He cut furiously. He would find his way through the blizzard, his bloody hands would find Danjel's door.

-5-

Yesterday she had seen the sun's blood-red globe; she knew it meant a storm. Why hadn't she remembered that before Karl Oskar left? Why hadn't she warned him? These were the questions Kristina put to herself when the blizzard broke just before dusk.

The afternoon was followed by the longest night she had ever waited through. She clung to a single *if:* If her husband had been warned about the impending blizzard, then he and her son might have remained at Taylors Falls. If not, they now lay frozen to death somewhere in the forest.

Life did not last long in a blizzard. Last winter at Marine a settler's wife had gone out to feed her chickens in a blizzard; she had never come back. After the storm was over she had been found, twenty paces from her door. An oxcart could be overtaken by a similar blizzard, stall in a drift and remain there, all life frozen to ice. The snow would cover and hide ox, cart and driver. Only after the first thaw in spring would they be found; the cold would have preserved their bodies and there would sit the driver, still upright on his load, the reins in his hands.

The blizzard had died down in the evening. After a night of

78

agony, in which Kristina did not sleep one moment, dawn finally came.

And in the morning she beheld through the window a strange procession approaching their house. There was Uncle Danjel with his ox team, but one more ox was with them: their own black ox, which lay on Danjel's wagon. His limbs dangled lifeless, his large head with the beautiful horns hung over the side of the wagon. Danjel walked beside it. Karl Oskar came behind, carrying some sort of bundle.

Kristina fumbled for something to hold on to; she recognized the shawl she had tucked around Johan yesterday morning. Her knees trembled as she walked to the door and opened it.

Karl Oskar stepped over the threshold and came slowly into the room. Silently he laid his burden on the bed nearest the door.

Kristina glimpsed the little head in the shawl. Her voice failed her and she barely whispered, "Is he dead?"

Relieved of his burden, Karl Oskar straightened up. "The boy is all right."

"But how — The blizzard . . . "

"It let up. But we decided to stay over with Danjel."

"Yesterday afternoon, when it began . . . last night . . . I thought . . . "

Her voice again failed her. She could not go on.

Karl Oskar had carefully washed away every sign of blood from his face, hands and clothing, so that his wife wouldn't be frightened, but now, as he unbundled the shawl, he discovered a large, liver-red spot on Johan's neck.

Kristina cried out.

Quickly he said, "Don't be afraid. It's only ox blood."

"Starkodder . . . ?"

"I had to kill him to save the boy."

It was not easy to explain why he had butchered his fine ox. Now that the storm was over he couldn't quite understand it himself.

"I put the boy in the ox's carcass while I went to Danjel's. Meanwhile the storm died down and we went back and found him asleep. Starkodder saved his life."

And so Karl Oskar was again without a beast of burden.

He kept the hide of the black ox to use for shoe leather, but sold the meat to German Fischer's inn at Taylors Falls for ten dollars, the sum he still owed for Starkodder. Kristina thought they should have kept some of the meat, but Karl Oskar said he couldn't eat it. The animal had assumed a truly sacrificial significance; not only had it given them its strength when alive, it had given its life to save their oldest son.

VII

ULRIKA IN HER GLORY

- 1 -

One Saturday afternoon, having fired the bake oven and raked out the embers, Kristina was just ready to put in the bread when she heard someone stamping off snow outside the door and an unexpected caller came in: Ulrika. Sledding was good along the timber roads, and she had ridden most of the way from Stillwater with her husband, who had been called to preach in St. Paul on Sunday.

"I took the opportunity to visit you!"

Kristina stood in front of the hot oven holding the rake and the ash broom. She was so glad to see Ulrika that she forgot to wipe the soot from the hand she offered her. She enjoyed no visitor more than her Ulrika. She had neighbors now, but it was difficult for her to feel intimate with them. Perhaps it was the long isolation that had made her feel shy and awkward in company; she never quite knew how to act with new people. And in order to be friendly with them, great efforts were demanded of her which she did not feel up to.

But when Ulrika visited her house all guards were down and all concerns forgotten, however inconvenient her arrival. Today, besides having the baking to do, she had to nurse Lill-Märta, who was in bed with a cold and a sore throat. Karl Oskar and Johan were down on the lake cutting holes in the ice for fishing.

The coffeepot was quickly set on the fire. But the rising bread must be put in while the oven was hot; as soon as Ulrika had removed her coat and shawl she took the dough ladle from Kristina's hands to help her. She stood right before the oven opening, even though Kristina warned her she might get soot on her fine clothing.

Mrs. Henry O. Jackson was in her last month of pregnancy and already thick around the waist and clumsy in her movements. But she handled the ladle firmly and within a short time had all the bread in the oven.

It had been an unlucky day for the children, Kristina said. Dan had crept too near the fire and burned himself on the forehead; she had melted sheep fat and put it on the burn. Barely had she attended to him when Harald, playing with a piece of firewood, had got a splinter under his fingernail and screamed until she got it out. The girl in bed was forever complaining of her throat and needed attention. All these things had more or less upset her household this morning.

But after a while Kristina had the coffee on the table and could sit down for a rest with her visitor.

"You're overloaded with work," said Ulrika sympathetically. "American women have it much easier. The men scrub the floor and wash the dishes for their wives."

Kristina said that when Karl Oskar came in from work in the evening he was so tired out that no one could ask him to wash up after supper.

"If he were an American he would offer to do it," insisted Ulrika. "He is still too Swedish!"

In Sweden men were ashamed to do women's chores, she continued. After eating, they just lolled about while the wives cleaned up and waited on them. Weekdays and Sundays alike. And many women in Sweden had to do the men's chores as well — carry in water and wood, thresh, plow, load manure. They were hardly better off than the animals. If they only knew how much easier their lives would be as wives to American men, the whole kingdom of Sweden would be without women in a few weeks.

Kristina noticed how her friend's pregnancy had advanced since their last meeting. "You too will soon have more to do, I can see."

"Sure enough!" Ulrika smiled. "My priest was made in March, I'll bear him before Christmas."

She had had such terrible nausea during this pregnancy, she was sure it would be a boy. A woman vomited more with a male child than with one of her own sex. This was only natural.

Kristina confided to her guest that she too was pregnant again. Ulrika looked at her compassionately. "I thought you looked a

81

little pale. But you have such a big household and so many to care for; you should really not have any children for a few years."

It was hard to look after babies here during the winter, Kristina admitted. But this child would be born in May, just the right time of year.

Mrs. Jackson looked about the cabin. "It won't be easy for you with five children in this little log hut."

"This is our last winter in the cabin; Karl Oskar has promised to have the new house ready by next fall." Kristina only worried because his plans called for so large a house she was afraid he wouldn't be able to get it up. It would have two stories, with rooms both upstairs and downstairs. Everything he undertook he wanted on a large scale. She could never persuade him to be moderate.

"But he is a wonderful man," said Ulrika with conviction. "He can use his hands and make anything." She added that she had heard what he had done in the blizzard. The Swedes in the valley had been talking about nothing else; Karl Oskar was said to be both able and ingenious.

"I'm only afraid it's going to his head," said Kristina.

It was true that Karl Oskar was fearless and undismayed and never gave up. But he *was* getting so that he thought he could help himself in any danger or trouble that he got into. He didn't realize that the saving of the boy was God's miracle. What would he have done if the blizzard hadn't gone down in the evening? The boy would have frozen to death inside the ox's belly. So Kristina had told Karl Oskar when he insisted that a person in danger had no time for prayers but must try everything he could to help himself.

"Well, at times I think the Lord wants people to help Him a little when He performs His miracles," said Ulrika. And Karl Oskar was a good man, no one could deny it. However, there was one activity he ought to curtail. If he rested occasionally from his male duties it would be good for his wife.

Again someone was stamping off snow outside, this time a man. Petrus Olausson entered the cabin. In his hand he held an enormous auger. He greeted Kristina by shaking her hand; then he looked questioningly at Ulrika. Kristina remembered her two guests had not met before.

"This is Ulrika from Stillwater, who has come for a visit."

Ulrika stood up, saying, "I'm Mrs. Henry Jackson, a good friend of Mrs. Nilsson. I gather you're one of the new neighbors?"

"That's right, Mrs. Jackson."

Petrus Olausson glanced at Ulrika and it seemed as though her pregnancy made him uncomfortable.

He turned to Kristina with his errand: Tomorrow, on the Lord's day, he had invited a few friends among the Swedes to spiritual talks in his house; he hoped Kristina and her husband would come.

Kristina would have liked to go, but as Ulrika intended to stay over Sunday she felt she could not leave her. She hesitated with her answer, putting a third cup on the table. "Sit down, Petrus. Have a cup of coffee with us."

Olausson sat down. While Kristina added more cookies to those already on a plate, he began to talk to Ulrika. The Swedes out here needed to gather for spiritual communion, he said. They could use his barn for services until they had built themselves a church. A formal service every Sunday and at least two sermons during the week were the minimum a good Lutheran needed; daily prayers at morning, noon and evening he took for granted, health permitting.

But Mrs. Henry O. Jackson shook her head. "It's unreasonable to have services so often. God doesn't expect it."

Petrus Olausson looked at her, flabbergasted.

Ulrika continued: She was sure God wanted moderation in devotion. A person should never exaggerate in spiritual matters. Her husband preached about ten sermons a week, at different places, and it was all he had the strength to do. His journeys over the rotten roads wore him out. And neither God nor congregations had any joy from a tired-out minister who came home so bedraggled that he was unable to undertake his evening prayer — or his manly duty to his wife.

Olausson's mouth had dropped open while Ulrika spoke. Now he said, "Are you married to a man of the church, Mrs. Jackson?"

"Yes, I am."

"Where does your husband preach?"

"He is serving as minister in the American Baptist church in Stillwater."

Petrus Olausson rose like a jack-in-the-box.

Kristina turned from the fire, the coffeepot in her hand. "Sit down, Petrus. I've just warmed the coffee."

"Thanks, I don't want any coffee today."

"Please, Petrus."

"I'll find Nilsson outside — I just wanted to return his auger." He nodded stiffly to Kristina, picked up his hat and without another look at Ulrika stamped out of the cabin.

Greatly disturbed, Kristina looked through the window after her neighbor. "What came over him?"

"Perhaps it was the looks of me he didn't like."

"Why?"

"Because I'm pregnant. But I told him I was married. I have every right to be pregnant!"

"Nonsense. He didn't run away because of that."

"I have known pious Lutheran men who detest a woman who dares show herself while in a blessed state. They consider her unclean — especially when she is big, like me."

Kristina could not accept such an explanation. Their neighbor was indeed pious and hard in his judgments, but he couldn't dislike a woman because she was pregnant. And she continued to worry about Olausson's strange behavior.

-2-

During a dark night in December, eight days before Christmas, Pastor Henry O. Jackson had to leave his bed to fetch Miss Cora Skalrud, the midwife. The baby was born before dawn. Miss Skalrud approached her duties with twenty-five years of experience. Mrs. Jackson was successfully delivered without other assistance.

The mother lay quietly in her bed while Miss Skalrud washed and cared for the newborn child. She was surprised that the mother had not immediately asked to know the sex of the child. Now she volunteered to Mrs. Jackson that she had given birth to a girl.

Ulrika raised herself quickly on her elbow. "What are you saying? Did I hear you right?"

"I said you have a lovely little girl."

"Do you mean that I . . . ?" The mother fell back on her pillow again. She lay silent; then she said, "Look again!"

The midwife felt hurt. Was this woman out of her mind? Why didn't she believe her? She replied gruffly that it was a girl she held in her arms.

Ulrika sat up in bed. "But you are short-sighted, Skalrud! And you are a stubborn woman because you are Norwegian! Give me the baby and let me look for myself." Without reply the midwife held the newborn child close to the mother's face and let the candle shine on the wriggling little body. Ulrika looked.

"Well, what do you say now?"

Ulrika said nothing. She had sunk down in her bed again. This child could not become a minister. No woman could be consecrated for pastoral duties.

Now, at the big Christmas party which Ulrika intended to give for her fellow immigrants, she would not be able to step forward and say to her guests: Look at this little one! He will be a man of the church. He will stand in a surplice before the altar. He will be as important a man as Dean Brusander back in Ljuder, Sweden. And she who carried this servant of the Lord in her womb for nine months is Ulrika of Västergöhl, the old parish whore from Ljuder, who at home was denied entry to the Lord's house. She is the one who stands before you now, in her glory — the mother of a priest!

That was what she had intended to say. But now she could not. And Ulrika realized she had not yet managed to shed her old sinful body; God looked upon her as unworthy of mothering a minister.

But that day would come, if she continued to improve herself. At the age of forty she had not many years to lose; she must make sure she became pregnant again as soon as possible.

VIII

"THOSE BAPTISTS!"

-1-

It was the fourth Christmas that Karl Oskar and Kristina had celebrated in the new country. They made things as Yulelike as possible, both indoors and out. At threshing time Karl Oskar had saved a dozen sheaves, which he now set up for the birds, in front of the window, where the yellow barley straw shone warmly against the tall white drifts. He made the children a little sled on which they could slide down the drifts as soon as the snow packed. The weather was mild this Christmas, their last in the log cabin.

Karl Oskar was in the habit of writing his parents twice a year, at Christmas and at Midsummer. Now he sat with pen and paper for several evenings after the holiday and worked on the letter to Sweden. His note last summer had been very brief; he wanted to make his winter message longer. But when he had written that all of them enjoyed good health, there didn't seem to be anything left to say. He worked laboriously trying to compose further sentences.

On the last day of the old year he received a letter from his sister Lydia, who had written in their father's place. Father's hand shook so, she wrote, that Nils Jakob's Son was afraid his letters from now on would be too poorly written for his son in America to read. But luckily she, Lydia, knew how to write and could report that both Father and Mother were well and active. She herself, during the past year, had married a farmer at Åkerby, so her name now was Lydia Karlsson. She had already borne a son, now six weeks old. She mentioned the names of a few parishioners who had died, whom Karl Oskar had known, and wrote that many farmers from Ljuder and neighboring villages had emigrated to North America, but she did not know where they had settled. Finally, she wondered what had happened to their brother Robert, from whom they had not heard for almost two years.

Karl Oskar could not allay her apprehensions concerning Robert, but only share them. Almost a year had passed since the last letter from his brother. And next spring three years would have passed since Robert started out on his journey with Arvid to the California gold fields.

What could Karl Oskar have done to stop him? He could not have denied his brother the right to decide things for himself. He could not have put him into a cage. Moreover, Robert would have escaped from the cage had he done so. Even as a small child he would run away; his parents had had to put a cowbell around his neck so that they could find him. The day he was to begin his first service as a hired hand in Sweden he had tried to run away, and later he had succeeded. Robert was the eternal escapist. If he once reached heaven he would try to escape there too, thought Karl Oskar. But why didn't he write more often?

"Robert won't come back until he has found gold," Kristina said.

"Then I'm afraid he'll never come back."

Karl Oskar had begun to fear that his younger brother was no longer alive.

-2-

Another new year came — 1854 — and again they were without a new almanac. However, for notations about crops, purchases, sales and other data to remember, they still had space in the old almanac.

With the new year came severe cold. Night and day they kept the fire burning. The hearth was the cabin's heart and center, the home's altar on which were sacrificed all the cords of firewood that had been cut during the summer and stacked to dry against the cabin wall. By the light of the fire they performed their chores, around the flames they gathered to warm their cold limbs.

Early one Sunday morning, shortly after New Year's, the Olaussons came unexpectedly to call. Karl Oskar had been in the woods looking for a pig which had broken out of its sty, and he had just returned. Neither he nor Kristina had as yet had time to think of their Sunday rest, and they had not yet cleaned up. They wondered at this early call from their neighbors; when spiritual gatherings were being held, the families did not meet until the afternoon of the Sabbath.

Kristina pulled forth chairs for the callers, who were dressed in their Sunday best. Petrus Olausson had put on a tie and trimmed his beard. Judit wore her best black dress with the white frill which buttoned all the way to her chin. Her black hair was combed slick and parted in the middle, displaying a white skin line like a straight white ribbon from her forehead to the top of her skull. On the back of her head she wore a black cap with white embroidery. Her powerful nose stuck out sharply, like a spy for her prying eyes. Her mouth was always tightly closed, the right corner always pulled up more than the left.

The couple's faces showed the severe Sabbath solemnity which Karl Oskar and Kristina recognized from previous Sundays, but also something new and ominous. What could their neighbors want so early on a Sunday morning? They sat stiffly and ceremoniously and twisted awkwardly on their chairs; they had not come just for the fun of it, so much was clear.

Karl Oskar finished telling about the escaped pig he had been hunting for over an hour. What luck the weather was so mild this morning! It was an important pig, a sow he intended to send to the boar for mating when her time came again.

Petrus Olausson barely listened. Then he said, "We have come to see you on a matter of great spiritual importance." He raised his chin with its newly trimmed beard and spoke as if he were reading aloud from the Bible. "We have come to open your eyes and to warn you, our beloved neighbors and fellow Christians!"

"To open your eyes indeed," interrupted his wife, and she adjusted her cap which had slid down over her left ear.

"It is the duty of a seeing person to warn the one who is blind," continued Olausson. "It is our duty as Christians to safeguard our neighbors' souls."

"Exactly so," echoed his wife. "We are here to fulfill our duty."

Karl Oskar and Kristina listened with increasing confusion. Their neighbors spoke as if the Almighty Himself had sent them here with the message that the day of doom would come on the morrow.

Petrus Olausson went on: "We have for a long time thought about this. We have hesitated, delayed. Now as Christians we can wait no longer."

"What's all this about?" exclaimed Kristina. "What in the world is going on?"

"I will tell you." Olausson rose and walked closer to her. "Some time ago I met in this house an unknown woman. A Swedish woman. You must recall our meeting? The woman had — "

"You said she made a fright of herself in a bonnet," interrupted his wife.

"It is so — she wore a bonnet on her head. A very expensive piece of headgear, full of vanity, and most outlandish. I have now learned who this woman is."

"You must mean Ulrika," said Kristina.

"That's her name," confirmed Judit, and she pulled up the right corner of her mouth still farther.

"But Ulrika didn't put on a bonnet from vanity — she is as good as any upper-class woman," said Kristina. "We're intimate friends!"

"Friends?" said her neighbor. "My poor woman, this 'friend' of yours is married to the Baptist minister in Stillwater!"

"She has gone over to her husband's religion and she has been rebaptized," added Judit.

"I know all that. It concerns no one but herself."

Olausson straightened up, to give greater weight to his words. "We must have no connection with lost souls! We must keep clear of sectarians. And that is why you must have nothing to do with this woman who is the wife of the Stillwater preacher."

Karl Oskar and Kristina stared at each other. At long last they were grasping their neighbors' errand.

"Look out for this Mrs. Jackson! Don't let that woman into your house! Don't ever open your door to her again!"

Karl Oskar snorted loudly. Petrus Olausson's advice seemed to him so outrageous that he felt inclined to laugh at it.

"With this Mrs. Jackson you admit the Evil One into your home," continued Olausson. "Without your being aware of it, she pours irreligious poison into your ears. Only out of Christian love do we wish to warn you. It concerns your soul!"

Olausson turned to Kristina, whose face had stiffened while she listened. Words stuck in her throat as she tried to answer.

"Uncle Petrus, do . . . do you know you're talking about my best friend in America?"

"Yes, I know. And because of this friendship the danger is so much greater for you."

"You're blinded," continued Olausson's wife. "Friendship blinds people."

Kristina's face had turned flaming red. What was this her neighbors asked of her? That she sacrifice her friendship for Ulrika and close her door to her! She remembered what Ulrika once had said to her: "I sold my body at times for a loaf of bread, but my friendship costs more than man or woman can pay. I don't bestow it on just anyone. But you have it, Kristina. You earned it that time when you shared your bread with me on the journey. You have received the most valuable possession I have to give to anyone, and you have it for all time." Now came these people and demanded that she repay good with evil and deny her friendship for Ulrika, that she betray her best friend!

Kristina had her own ideas about right and wrong, and never had anyone swayed her. Nor would Petrus Olausson and his wife. Not to the smallest degree.

And there stood Petrus, continuing in the patient voice of an

89

admonishing father, "Dearly beloved Kristina! These Baptists are false prophets, sent by the devil to spread dissension among us. You do not recognize them for what they are. You do not see the fiend in this Mrs. Jackson. Therefore, beloved Kristina, do not ever let her cross your threshold again. Will you promise this?" As he spoke he took Kristina by the arm.

"No!" she cried. "No! No! No! Never!"

And Kristina pulled away from him violently, as if he were unclean. Her explosion was so sudden that Olausson took a few steps backward. His wife jumped up from her chair.

"This is enough!" cried Kristina. "How dare you come to me and talk ill of Ulrika?"

"Poor child!" said Judit Olausson, and she shook her head so violently that her cap slid down over her right ear.

Olausson now turned to Karl Oskar. "You must corect your foolish wife, Nilsson! She acts as if she were already led astray. Help us bring her back to her senses!"

Karl Oskar looked steadily at his neighbor and raised his voice until Olausson drew back. "You leave Kristina alone! She can open her door to whomever she likes. And this I had intended to tell you before: I don't need a guardian! Nor does my wife! You hear?"

Kristina now stepped between the two men, her eyes aflame. "Let me have a word in this matter! Petrus, you come here and try to separate old friends. You insist I turn away the best friend I have. And *you* speak of dissension! Who is trying to start ill will and dissension? No one but you!"

Olausson tried to reply, but she would not permit it. "It's my turn to talk now! You slander Ulrika and accuse her of evil deeds. You denounce your fellow men. You've forgotten the Eighth Commandment, Christian that you call yourself! You bear false witness against your neighbor. You ought to be ashamed! Or haven't you any shame in your body — haven't you any decency, you evil old man?"

Petrus Olausson had remained immobile, listening. His eyes were riveted on Kristina; his look was one of sorrow rather than anger.

"Dear neighbors, I'm amazed and sorry. It is with sadness and pain that I hear — "

"Come, Petrus," said Judit Olausson, as she again adjusted her black cap with the embroidery. She took her husband by the arm. "This woman is possessed. Insulting us like that! Let's go."

"But our duty as fellow Christians . . . "

"You can see we're too late," said his wife.

"Dear Judit, it's never too late to lead a strayed soul back to the true — "

"But can't you hear? The sectarians already have snared her in their nets. Let's go home! Come, Petrus."

Judit walked toward the door. Petrus Olausson cleared his throat and turned once more to Kristina, lecturing her kindly. "Our Christian love for our neighbors brought us here today. We want to warn you; you reward us with insults. But I forgive you, Kristina. I overlook your words. For it is an evil spirit that speaks through your mouth."

"Keep quiet about your evil spirits! No one has led me astray. I intend to remain a Christian Lutheran as long as I live. But I won't betray my friends! Now you know!"

"You are a foolish woman. We must pray God to protect you. However, as Christians we must avoid this unclean house until it has been cleansed."

"Out with you!" shouted Kristina, trembling. "Out of my house, both of you! Not clean in here! That I'll never forget as long as I live!"

Her voice failed her at this.

- 3 -

The Olaussons had left. Karl Oskar and Kristina sat down to rest, as after some heavy chore.

"I lost my temper, but I don't regret it," said she.

Her voice still trembled. What did they take her for, this Olausson and his wife? A doll, without a mind of her own? A silly sheep letting herself be devoured by those Baptist wolves, Ulrika and her husband? But the neighbor's remark about her unclean house hurt her the most.

"Well, now they know how we feel," said Karl Oskar. "Let them be angry if they wish. But how stupid that we must quarrel with our neighbors because Ulrika jumped into the river and got herself baptized. It doesn't make sense."

Mrs. Jackson was not so essential a friend to him as she was to Kristina. The onetime parish whore had many characteristics still difficult for him to accept. But over the years he had learned to value her more. And regardless of who the person was, no outsider could dictate to him whom he could admit to his house and whom he must exclude.

After Kristina had calmed down a little she felt she must not be unjust toward her neighbors. The best intentions had caused them to call today. Uncle Petrus was honest in his concern for them; he had been sincere and fatherly.

But Karl Oskar replied: Why must people eternally worry about other people's souls? Olausson was a thrifty and capable settler, and his practical advice and examples were often worth following. A man like him was needed among the immigrants; he was interested in communal matters and got things started. The trouble was that he also tried to manage people, without being asked and against their will. The strange thing was that in Sweden he himself had been a dissenter.

"Yes," said Kristina. "How can he be so intolerant out here?"

Karl Oskar thought perhaps Petrus Olausson had become so warmly attached to religious freedom that he no longer allowed it for anyone but himself.

Well, the pleasant neighborliness with the Helsinge family seemed to be over. The Olaussons had been shown the door and were not likely to return. However, other neighbors had by now arrived, and more would come. The first settlers at Ki-Chi-Saga need no longer live as hermits. Nevertheless, said Karl Oskar, he would rather live without neighbors than have to fight with them.

For a long time Kristina kept thinking about their former friend Petrus. How could people who had sprung from the same Creator and belonged to the same race be so intolerant of each other? Here in these great wild forests a small group of people had settled; they came from the same country and spoke the same language; they were poor, dependent on themselves, and needed each other's company. They lived so far apart that the distance between their houses in itself separated them. Must they now also close their doors against each other because of different churches, different faiths? Must they separate even more — and because of religion? Because of Christ's Gospel, which preached that all people were brethren?

If any people in this world needed to live harmoniously it was the small group of Swedish settlers in the St. Croix Valley. Surely it was God's intention that they remain friends.

IX

HEMLANDET COMES TO THE IMMIGRANTS

- 1 -

Early one morning in the first week of May, Kristina's child was born — a girl. The evening before, she had sent a message to Ulrika, who had dispatched Miss Skalrud to aid her. The Norwegian midwife arrived a couple of hours too late, but remained for a few days while Kristina stayed in bed. Never before had she felt so weak and worn out after a birth.

Shortly before her delivery Pastor Erland Törner had returned from Illinois, and he had now resumed his pastoral duties in the St. Croix Valley, where he traveled from place to place among his countrymen as he had done the year before. He came on Sunday to Duvemåla and christened Karl Oskar's and Kristina's infant. The little girl was called Anna Eveline Ulrika. The first two names were after Kristina's own mother, Anna Evelina Andersdotter. But the girl was to be called by her third name, Ulrika.

In this way Kristina cleansed her home which the Olaussons considered befouled by Mrs. Henry O. Jackson of Stillwater. The neighbors had said: Do not open your door to this woman. Now she showed them where she stood; she welcomed an Ulrika who was to stay in the house permanently.

- 2 -

Great things were happening at Ki-Chi-Saga this year. During the spring and summer of 1854 the first great wave of Swedish immigrants washed over the St. Croix Valley. They came in large groups, by the hundreds, and the population of the valley was increased many times over.

All the claims suitable for farming around Ki-Chi-Saga — the fertile meadows along the lake slopes — were now taken. The newcomers put up their log cabins along bays and sounds, on every point and tongue of land. On the surveyor's map obtained from the land office the Chippewa word "Ki-Chi-Saga" was discarded for "Chisago Lake." And the thirty-six squares, or sections, around the lake which had been surveyed for settling were now referred to as Chisago Township. This in turn was part of a larger square, comprising thirty-six square miles. As each section was divided into four claims, the whole district contained 144 homesteads. There was still room for more settlers in Chisago Township.

So the Indian lake Ki-Chi-Saga had been renamed. The nomad people were pushed more and more away from the forests where they had hunted and the waters where they had fished. Their fires went out, their camping sites lay unoccupied the year round.

But on the western shore, high above Ki-Chi-Saga's surface, the Indian still held his watch, the red-brown sand cliff with its image of a savage still rose like an unconquerable bastion. The Indian's immense head was turned to the east, where the new settlers came from; with empty black eyes he watched day and night over his old hunting grounds and fishing waters. His eyes remained immobile, watching, and they seemed to mirror an inconsolable sorrow.

- 3 -

The only unclaimed quarter of Karl Oskar Nilsson's section, the northeast corner, was taken that spring by an immigrant from Småland. Their neighbor to the north was Johan Kron from Algutsboda, Kristina's home parish. Kron was the village soldier, but he had retired from the service and emigrated with his wife and eight children. So the last homestead suddenly had ten inhabitants. Section 35 of Chisago Township, where Karl Oskar had been the first settler, was now entirely claimed and occupied.

New axes ringing in the forest — no longer was that sound unfamiliar to Karl Oskar Nilsson. This spring when he walked over his land he could hear echoes in all directions. Who could have imagined that he would have so many followers from Sweden? It seemed as if the whole homeland was on its way out here. And in a way the homeland did come to the immigrants that spring — at least in the form of a newspaper.

Pastor Hasselquist in Galesburg, Illinois, had begun to print a

94

paper in Swedish, *Hemlandet, det Gamla och det Nya* (Homeland, the Old and the New), and he asked his colleague, Pastor Törner, to spread the word in the Swedish settlements. As Pastor Törner traveled about he took the names of people who wanted to subscribe to the paper. It would contain four pages of the most interesting news in both Sweden and America and would appear fortnightly. The price was only a dollar a year, but the publisher appealed to those who could afford it for an extra fifty cents, which he would need for the purchase of Swedish type.

Karl Oskar felt it would be worth a dollar—plus fifty cents for the Swedish type — to obtain news from Sweden twice a month. He could pick up his paper every second week in Mr. Abbott's store in Taylors Falls. Algot Svensson, his neighbor to the west, was also a subscriber, and they decided to take turns bringing back the paper so that they need not go to the post office more than once a month.

Hemlandet was soon received in the Nilsson home as a dear and welcome guest. Karl Oskar and Kristina discussed almost every word printed in it. After supper he would read to her while she finished her chores, and on Sunday afternoons they would sit down at the table with the paper spread before them and go through paragraph after paragraph systematically.

Through *Hemlandet* they were informed that a great war had broken out a few months earlier between Russia on one side and England and France on the other. It was assumed by the paper that Sweden would join in against Russia to retrieve Finland. But Kristina felt Sweden shouldn't bother with this; she had two brothers of military age and did not like to think of their participating in slaughter. Karl Oskar also hoped the old country would remain at peace. War was an amusement for lords and kings but no plaything for farmers who had more important things to do. All this warring would probably in the end destroy the Old World.

Another piece of news was that the Swedes were planning to build railroads. It was not easy to imagine that perhaps one day a train might come rolling down through Ljuder Parish. As yet, they and other emigrants to America were the only Swedes who had traveled by rail.

In almost every issue of the paper there was a description of some amazing new invention which the clever Americans had made: Pitt's threshing machine, which threshed a bushel of wheat in a minute; the reaper, which was constructed in such a way that it cut the crop with steel arms; the sewing machine, which could baste and sew when tapped by a human foot. From now on one could sew garments with one's feet instead of one's hands! Kristina had just finished her first weaving of last year's flax, and she could have used this apparatus now that she was ready to sew clothes for all of them.

But the strangest discovery was a new, secret power called electricity. It gave heat and light, it could be used to pull vehicles, it could heal sickness, like lameness, fever, epilepsy. Electricity returned hearing to deaf people, taught the mute to use their tongues. *Hemlandet* had a clarifying article about electricity:

> The cause of lightning is a peculiar power called electricity. Lightning emanates from clouds up in the sky which have become electric. How the clouds have become so is not known. But if a lightning cloud comes close to an object on earth, an electric spark passes with lightning and thunder from the cloud to the object, and then we say that lightning strikes. It is untrue that, as some people say, a wedge hits the earth when lightning flashes.

Lightning had once struck and burned a hay-filled barn belonging to Karl Oskar, and he therefore felt great respect for electricity.

In the paper's editorial about electricity the question was brought up as to whether or not Benjamin Franklin had broken God's ordinances by inventing the lightning rod. It was apparent that God now must cause hurricanes, floods and catastrophes of nature to destroy those people He originally had intended to kill by lightning. Mr. Franklin had thus interfered in the business of the Almighty and caused Him unnecessary trouble.

Pastor Hasselquist's paper fought for the Evangelical Lutheran religion, the world's only true religion, and condemned sectarianism. He praised the new law passed by the Swedish Riksdag, which condemned Baptists and set high fines for any layman distributing the Sacrament. Of sects in America, the Mormons were described as the worst. They preached the rawest gospel of the flesh since Mohammed had descended to hell. Utah, their place of habitation in the Union, had grown like a festering boil on the American nation. The Mormons had recently made a great conquest in Sweden: one hundred and fifty foolish young women had gone to Utah, where they had been divided ten to each man; in the new land they now satisfied men's carnal lusts.

Hemlandet's editor warned his countrymen not only against spiritual dangers but also against worldly perils, especially those connected with the confusing money matters of North America. Every issue had a column headed "Bank Swindles," enumerating the banks which had been started expressly to cheat people. It was useful for Swedes in the wilderness to know which bills were counterfeit or worth only half their face value.

Hemlandet was also useful to improve the knowledge of Swedish children; they used it in place of a primer. In *Hemlandet* Johan and Lill-Märta learned to recognize printed Swedish letters, both small ones and capitals. By and by they began to combine the letters into syllables and words.

-4-

"Inquiries" was the heading of one column in *Hemlandet;* readers used it to ask about relatives living in unknown places in America. Parents called for their children, brother sought sister, engaged couples who had lost touch with each other strove for connection. Many Swedes were wandering about in North America vainly looking for their relations, and "Inquiries" helped them. Kristina had seen this broad land during her journey, she knew how big it was — entirely too vast for a poor lost person. She suggested that Karl Oskar write an inquiry to *Hemlandet* asking about Robert, whom they hadn't heard from in so long. Karl Oskar now was almost sure his brother was dead. Moreover, he felt an inquiry in the little Swedish paper would be useless, since he doubted that it reached California. However, to please Kristina he sat down one evening and wrote an inquiry. With some changes in the spelling, the piece was printed:

BROTHER SOUGHT
Axel Robert Nilsson from Ljuder Parish, Sweden, who left for California in the spring of 1851, in the company of Arvid Pettersson from same parish, has not been heard from since

January, 1853. He is 21 years of age and tall. If anyone knows where Nilsson is, or has seen him, please notify his brother, Karl Oskar Nilsson, at the address of Taylors Falls Post Office, Minnesota Territory.

They waited a long time, but no answer came. Theirs was a message lost in the wilderness.

- 5 -

"Timberrim, timberram, timberammaram . . . "
On Ki-Chi-Saga's shores "The Timberman's Song" was heard again. This summer Karl Oskar Nilsson was building his third house in the new country.

His first one had been a simple shed made of boards nailed together; his second house was built of logs; but the third house would be constructed of hewn timbers — a real main house on a farmer's land. When Karl Oskar moved into a main house he would really feel like a farmer on his own land. Then he could stand erect; the well-timbered building would be the sign of his independence.

The board hut, the log cabin, the timbered main house — these are the three chapters in the story of a settler's progress.

In order to get the new house roofed this year, Karl Oskar had been forced to shorten his foundation by one third. He had had to give in to those who said he was attempting something too big; it irked him sorely. (This had happened to him before, with other projects.) Even with the smaller house he sometimes felt his strength was beginning to wane. Yet he was only in his thirty-first year, maturity was still between him and old age. He could build once more, he could raise a fourth house, the great big house he had promised his wife their first year out here. And he said to Kristina, "Next time! Wait till I build next time!"

Danjel and Jonas Petter were helping him. The walls grew a little bit each day, while Jonas Petter sang "The Timberman's Song." And the three axes fell heavily against the solid timbers, in rhythm to the song:

> *What's your daughter doing tonight?*
> *What's your daughter doing tonight?*
> *What's your timberman's daughter doing tonight?*

98

It was the log cabin's last summer as a home. One period was coming to an end in the lives of the immigrant family: their log-cabin days were ending.

X

A SEARCH IN THE FOREST

-1-

On the twenty-fourth day of May that year certain of the immigrants from Sweden met and formed the first Lutheran parish in the St. Croix Valley.

Fifty-eight adults were registered as members of the congregation, and forty children. Pastor Erland Törner was chosen as minister and Petrus Olausson as churchwarden. It was agreed to construct a church, but until it could be built a smaller building was to be erected and used for school, parish meeting hall and church.

In forming this new congregation, the Swedes in the St. Croix Valley were also laying the foundation of a new community. During the first years their great worry had been bodily needs; now they would make preparations for the filling of spiritual ones. They had missed the life of the old village, where the church and the church green provided a community center, a gathering place where both spiritual and worldly wants were satisfied. Now they would have a church and establish a real parish.

They would have to begin from the very beginning. They must elect a governing body for their parish and school, they must find a teacher for their children, they must establish a mediation board where disagreements could be argued in their own language, they must organize a district and elect representatives who could speak for them in the territorial government.

In their new situation there was no authority to oppress them, but they were also without aid from any authority. They alone were responsible for everything. A price was demanded for the liberty of the new country: much thought, a great deal of labor. From the irresponsible, responsibility was exacted; from the selfish, unified effort; from the arbitrary, willingness to listen to the opinions of others. In North America they were faced with the tests of all free citizens.

Through the new country's demands on the immigrants, powers within them would be developed which they had had no use for in the homeland. They changed America — and America changed them.

-2-

Four Swedish-born settlers in the St. Croix Valley met early one June morning and walked together through the wilderness. Their errand was to choose a place where their community could bury its dead. These four men had accepted the responsiblilty of selecting a cemetery site for the new congregation.

Once before they had walked in company through the forest. That time too they had been seekers of land. Then they had gone out to choose the ground where they would settle and live out the rest of their lives. Today they were selecting the ground where they were to be buried.

It was a calm bright morning; the St. Croix Valley spread out under a clear sky. A heavy dew had nourished the earth during the night; grass, herbs and leaves were still moist and gave out a fragrance as after rain. The fertile ground was beginning to warm itself in the sun. The oppressive summer heat had not yet come but the earth was already in the cycle of fertility; growth had begun, verdant and potent. The fields displayed their promise of crops in shoots and stalks, in buds and boughs.

The four men walked through groves of red oak and black oak, black and white walnut, elm, and linden trees. They penetrated thickets of raspberry and blackberry bushes. Here wild plum trees stood in full bloom, here grew black cherry, the biggest of all cherry trees, their smooth, even-thick trunks much taller than a man. Around them ripened the summer's wild splendor which would produce berries and fruit. Today the valley looked as if it would always bud and bloom and glitter.

The men walked silently and solemnly. Facing today's errand, they were more than ever reminded of the irrevocability of their emigration. In this country they would not only live out the rest of their lives but also remain when dead.

The trees thickened and rose taller and taller; they had reached the dense forest. They followed Indian paths which meandered around sand cliffs and over ravines. They crossed streams with water cascading from the rocks. They came to an open spot with a few mounds, overgrown with tall grass. These were Indian graves; the settlers had come upon one of the old burying places of the nomads.

But no Christian settler would wish to lie in earth tainted by heathens. The cemetery of the new parish must not be placed in the vicinity of these mounds. The searchers continued their walk, reached Ki-Chi-Saga and followed the shores of the lake in a wide arc around a bay. Now and then they stopped, exchanged a few words, deliberated: Wasn't this a suitable piece of ground? The cemetery site must be in beautiful surroundings where survivors could find comfort.

The four men wandered for hours. Finally they reached a promontory which cut into Lake Ki-Chi-Saga, and they stopped again.

The point comprised about five acres. On the lake side it ended in steep sand cliffs falling to the water. It was heavily wooded with silver maples. There was a clearing where sumac bloomed with its cheerful red blossoms, setting the clearing off like a room.

They remained for a long time on the point and examined it carefully. And they became more and more convinced they need seek no farther. This would make a resting place for human beings. And the four men sat down in the shade of a wide-spreading tree, leaning their backs against its trunk. The leaves of the maples glittered in the sun, the soft waves were heard below as they lapped against the cliff. They listened to the gentle wind and the water. This was a good resting place for both the living and the dead.

The men held a short deliberation and agreed: They would advise the new parish to have the ground on this beautiful point consecrated as a burying place for their dead. And after this last resting place had been chosen they sat for a while, their thoughts occupied. Who would be the first to have his grave here on this point? Who would first occupy his place under the silver maples? Would it be young or old, man or woman or child? Perhaps one of them, one of the four who today rested in the future parish cemetery, would be the first.

Four human beings sat at the destination of their life's journey. Wherever their steps led them in this world, to this place their wandering would finally take them. However much they strove, whatever they undertook, to this plot of ground they would eventually be carried. During their wandering today they had been reminded again of the old truth, the truth they felt in a shudder, deep in their souls: They were inexorably chained to the earth.

And when the seekers had rested, they rose and returned to the life which still remained to them.

XI

THE LETTER TO SWEDEN

New Duvemåla at Taylors Falls Post Ofis
in Minnesota, North America
Christmas Day, 1854

Dearly Beloved Parents,

That you are Well is my daily Wish.

I am writing to let you know that various things are well with us. We have Health and since last I wrote nothing of Importance has happened to us.

Last October we moved into our new Main House which has two Stories. It is built of Timbers which I roughhewed by hand on both sides. In this Building we have plenty of Room, it is warm, and lacks nothing.

My Situation in North America is improving. I have this Fall paid for my whole Land at the Land Office, 200 Dollar for 160 Acres. I have broken new Land three times as large as Korpamoen and fenced in about 300 yards, one yard equals 3 Swedish feet. I have four Cows in the Barn and 3 young Livestock in pens, I have cut a pair of Bull calves which I raise for Oxen. In America no one achieves comfort in one Day but we are satisfied with our Improvement.

We have now built a Schoolhouse in our Parish. Johan and Märta go to School and learn various Subjects from Books, English also. We pay for a Pastor in our Parish with 65 Dollar a Year and free firewood. Sometimes he travels to other Settlements and preaches. There is much Disagreement here about Religion. The Pastor cannot exclude anyone from the Parish or from the Sacrament, but two thirds of the Parishioners can discharge the Pastor from his Job.

We shall this Winter select a Swedish Justice of the Peace among us. But there is not much Authority here and I like that well. Here in America the Officials are appointed as Servants to attend to their Duties. When they do not attend to their Job other Officials are put in their Place. It is not like in Sweden. They have a perverted Government at home. Sweden has too many lazy Dogs to feed who who do not wish to work.

I think it is sad for you to sit alone. Is it cold in your room in Winter? Have you enough Wood for Fires? I wish I could send you some of the Wood we have here in abundance.

I got Apple seeds from Duvemåla which I planted and a sapling has grown up but it will take Time before the Tree has Fruit. Around the new House Kristina made a Flower bed and I have planted 5 Cherries and 12 Gooseberries and Wine Berries and some Strawberries which will bear next Summer.

It is Christmas Day today and I have taken the whole Day off to write to Sweden. I remember the Christmas Games at Home, but the joyful and happy Mind of a youth is no longer mine. It is hard to claim wild Land and I feel it in the Body although I am not yet old. I do not hop about on my Feet as lightly as in my Youth.

It would be a Joy to come Home to you once more in Life and sit down at the old Table and cut Slices off the Christmas Pig, like in my Childhood Days.

Many Days have now passed since I offered you my Hand in farewell and left a dear Childhood Home. I apologize if I have been slow in writing and write so seldom. I am thinking every Day I must write but always delay.

Immeasurable Seas separate us but Daily I have my dear Parents in my thought, and my Letters to Sweden shall not cease.

You are greeted heartily from your relations in a far-off land. Greetings also to my dear sister Lydia and ask her to write to her Brother in North America, if Father's Hands do tremble.

Your devoted Son,
Karl Oskar Nilsson

II

GOLD AND WATER

XII

A YOUTH WHO IS NOT YOUNG

-1-

Later, Karl Oskar Nilsson would often recall that June evening when he was going through his field hoeing corn and discovered a stranger approaching along the lake shore. A tall man with a rucksack on his back, he walked with a stoop, jerkily, and swung his arms as he climbed the road up to the old log cabin. Suddenly he stopped and looked at the new main house under the great sugar maples. Then he headed toward the maple grove, walking as if he had little command over his tall, loose body.

Karl Oskar leaned against his hoe and looked at the man. During their first years they had had barely one visitor a month; now some-one came almost every day. But this man was not one of their neighbors. And the stranger looked from one building to the other as if he had lost his way. When he saw Karl Oskar in the cornfield he turned and walked in his direction.

He was a young man, rather gaunt. Judging from his clothing he must be a fur trapper. He wore a broad hat, a black-and white-checkered coat and a hunting shirt of flaming red flannel. His trousers were made of deerskin, held up by a broad yellow leather belt; they fitted into high boots. He was terribly thin; his clothes hung on his body as if on a pole.

To Karl Oskar the stranger's walk reminded him of his brother Robert. But he was taller than Robert, and as the man now approached he could not discern any likeness to his brother. It must be someone who had lost his way and wanted to ask directions.

"Hello, Karl Oskar!"

The farmer stood openmouthed with the hoe in his hand. Before him stood a stranger, in strange clothing, with a strange face, who in a hoarse and cracked voice which he had never heard before called him by name.

"Don't you recognize your brother, Karl Oskar?"

Could someone be trying to impersonate the brother who had left for California four years before?

"I'm back from the California Trail!"

It was a light evening; Karl Oskar looked closer at the newcomer, looked him in the eye. And in the eyes he began to recognize him. But at first he felt rather than saw who it was. His younger brother, Robert, was standing before him.

Slowly, still almost hesitating, Karl Oskar put down his hoe and offered his hand. "Back at last. . . . Welcome, Robert!"

"Thanks, Karl Oskar. Didn't you recognize me?"

"Well, you've grown taller. And changed!"

It was the height that had confused him; Robert had grown several inches. And the clothes; he had left in his old Swedish wadmal, and now he returned dressed like an American trapper. But the greatest change was in his face. When Karl Oskar had last seen his brother's face it had been round and full, with all of a child's softness in its lines. Now the cheeks were caved in, the bones protruding under a yellowish complexion. Deep, dark-gray ditches had been dug under the eyes. And when Robert smiled there were black holes in his mouth from lost front teeth.

Robert had been eighteen when he set out. He was twenty-two now. He was still a youth, but he looked old.

"We thought you were dead."

"But I wrote, many times."

"Only two letters reached us."

"Well, some were lost, I suppose. The mails are often robbed out West."

Karl Oskar took hold of Robert by the shoulder, felt him as if wishing to convince himself that this was really his brother. "How did you get here?" he asked.

"I came up the river with the steamboat to St. Paul. Then I got a ride with an ox team. The last part I walked. You have roads through the forest now — " He was interrupted by a severe, hollow cough. "I caught a cold on the steamboat."

He turned and looked up at the new main house. "You've raised quite a house, Karl Oskar!"

"It isn't as big as I planned, but it will do."

"Two stories!"

Karl Oskar replied: He had not yet had time to finish the inside of the upper story. But downstairs they had one large room for daily use, a bedroom at the gable for the children and a good-sized kitchen. And he had built sturdy fireplaces so that they would be warm in winter.

Robert had only praise for the new house on the slope under the maples which gave shade in summer and protection in winter. And the maples were lush and looked well. When he compared the new house with the old log cabin he realized that things had improved for his brother while he had been away.

"Let's go home!" said Karl Oskar, and he picked up the hoe from among the furrows.

"I see you have started to plant Indian corn."

"This is the second year — it's well worth it. And I've sown wheat for three years now. Wheat and corn go best in Minnesota."

In a burst of brotherly affection Karl Oskar put his arm on Robert's shoulder while they walked up to the house. He had been almost sure that his brother was dead. Now joy at his return and bafflement at the change in him were mingled. Robert's thin body, his pale, unhealthy complexion, his voice which sounded so strangely hollow, his stiff motions — something of life itself was missing in Robert. And here he walked stooped beside him, like an old man. His brother was ten years younger than he, yet somehow he wasn't young any more. But what was the matter with him? Was he sick?

"I don't think Kristina will recognize you either, Robert."

They entered the new house through the kitchen door at the back. Kristina stood at the hearth tending the pot with the pea soup for their supper. After a momentary look of surprise and hesitation she did recognize him.

"Robert! Robert! Are you back!" Her exclamation was filled with joy. She threw her arms around her brother-in-law. Her throat choked with weeping, so moved was she. It was with difficulty that she found words to express her feelings.

107

"I've missed you terribly," she said. "But I've always felt you would come back."

"You recognized me sooner than Karl Oskar."

Robert unshouldered his rucksack and put it down on the floor.

"You are dressed like an American gentleman," continued Kristina. "And you have grown terribly tall – but so thin . . ."

The children had come into the kitchen. They were shy with the newcomer when he first approached them. Robert had been away so long they had forgotten him. Only Johan remembered. "You are the uncle who lived with us in the old house!"

"You've grown a lot, Johan. How old are you now?"

"Nine."

Robert picked up Dan and lifted him high into the air. "You were in swaddling clothes when I left."

"We have one more little one now," said Kristina. "A girl we call Ulrika – she's thirteen months old."

Robert picked up the girl too and tossed her in the air. The child had just started walking by herself and could cross the kitchen floor. But her uncle did not please her; she began to yell at the top of her voice and he had to put her down. Robert felt in his pocket and pulled out a bag of sweets, which he divided among the five children. After this they were no longer shy of the stranger, but jostled about him.

Karl Oskar sniffed the good smell from the pot on the fire. Pea soup with boiled pork was to him a delicious dish, and he knew his brother liked it. What luck Kristina had such a fine fare today; Robert looked as if he needed nourishing food.

"You've walked a long way. You must be hungry."

"I am thirsty, rather," said Robert. "Would you have some drinking water, Kristina?"

She handed him a quart measure she had filled from the wooden bucket on the floor against the chimney wall. He almost emptied it, with obvious enjoyment.

"Wonderful water! Did you find a spring?"

Karl Oskar replied that he had dug a well in the slope during the first year, but it gave brown, brackish water and in long droughts went dry. Then last summer he had found a spring in the oak stand behind the old cabin. It gave this clear, fresh water, the best drinking water one could wish. It was about a ten-minute walk to the spring, but well worth it.

Robert said, "Good water is worth any walk."

"Where is Arvid?" asked Kristina. "Did he come back with you?"

"No. Arvid didn't come back with me."

"But you were together?"

"Yes, we were together. But then we parted."

"Where is Arvid now?"

"He is out there. He stayed."

"Stayed?"

"You mean Arvid remained in the gold fields?" interrupted Karl Oskar in surprise.

"Yes, he remained. He is there."

"Oh!" said Kristina, and she looked questioningly at her brother-in-law.

"Yes, Arvid stayed behind."

Robert had made short and indifferent replies to the questions, as if they did not concern him.

Karl Oskar resumed: "I guess neither you nor Arvid had much luck? Or do you carry your gold with you in that sack?" He pointed to the rucksack his brother had put down on the floor; it was made of thick, excellent skin and looked new.

"Do you think I could carry the gold with me? I can see you have never been on the Trail!"

And Robert smiled his broad, toothless smile. So Karl Oskar thought that he would come with a sack of gold on his back when he returned? Gold was heavy, no one was able to carry it very far. And one could easily be attacked and robbed along the way. Oh, no! One put it in a bank for safekeeping.

Karl Oskar listened to his brother while he eyed Kristina. "Isn't supper ready?" he asked.

The peas were not sufficiently boiled yet, replied Kristina. But she could see that Robert was worn out from his journey — he could go into the gable room and lie down while she cooked. Karl Oskar showed his brother to the bedroom; he would have time to inspect their house later.

Karl Oskar returned to his wife in the kitchen. "I think something is wrong with him," he said.

"He may have some ailment; his hands feel hot."

"He said he had caught cold on the steamboat."

Kristina was taking plates from the open shelf, setting the table.

"But he seems to have had luck in the gold fields. Wasn't that what he said?"

"Yes, I think so."

"He talked as if he had put his gold in the bank. He may be rich."

"It sounded that way."

"You don't believe it?"

"Not a single word!" said Karl Oskar.

"He makes it all up, you think?"

"I know Robert by now. You remember his lies on the ship? Remember the dead Indian in the treetop?"

At their landing in New York Robert had spread a rumor that the captain was a slave trader and intended to sell them to the infidel Turks. It had caused great trouble. And during their first winter here Robert had found an Indian, dead and hung in a treetop, and said that the Indian had shot arrows at him.

"He has lied before, that's true," admitted Kristina.

"He is not going to fool me this time!" declared Karl Oskar with finality.

Kristina caught the sharp determination in his words. "Why should Robert come and lie to us again?"

"Perhaps he is ashamed to return empty-handed."

"But he has new clothes and a new rucksack."

"He may have worked for someone and earned a little."

But Kristina felt that Karl Oskar was too eager to suspect his brother, who had barely crossed their threshold. Why shouldn't they believe he had found gold?

Karl Oskar said that he did not intend to ask Robert if he had found any gold. Not even here in America did such great miracles happen. To him it was miracle enough that his brother had returned alive.

"I feel sorry for Robert," he added. "He must be ailing. But until he shows his gold I won't believe a word of it."

Robert's unexpected return had caused such great excitement that Kristina was confused with her chores and supper was late. But at last the family sat around the table in the kitchen, Robert between his brother and his sister-in-law. The children gaped at him.

Kristina looked more closely at Robert's face. "You must have had a hard time of it."

"Hunting gold is hard on one's health."

"Have you had any particular illness?"

"Everyone on the trail to California suffers from the gold sickness."

"We won't ask you anything about it tonight. You must be tired."

Kristina filled his plate brimful of pea soup. Now he must eat all he could and then get some sleep. She would put Harald's and Johan's bed in order for him; these two big boys could sleep on the floor for the time being.

"You are very kind, Kristina. Remember the food you prepared when I left? It lasted a long way on the journey. You've been kind to me in many ways."

"You're using a lot of English in your talk, Robert."

Yes, he said, during these years he had really learned to speak English and it was a great help for traveling in this country. But with his own people he would of course always use his mother tongue, except when he forgot himself.

Before Robert had had time to empty his soup plate Kristina refilled it. "Put on some weight now! You're only skin and bones."

But two plates were all Robert could manage. When they left the table he picked up the quart measure from the mantel shelf, filled it with spring water from the bucket and drank again. "Good water is wonderful. Better than anything in the world."

After supper Kristina sat down to nurse Ulrika. Then she put the child in her cradle; Karl Oskar had recently put rockers under it and was very proud of his handiwork. Robert inspected his brother's work. If he only had had such a cradle with him in the gold fields, he said. For gold had to be treated exactly like babies — put in cradles and rocked until sand and refuse and dirt were winnowed away and at last it lay clean and glittering in the bottom.

Kristina now forgot what she had promised and asked, "Where do they find the gold?"

"All over. In the most unusual places."

Gold was not only in the earth and the river sand and the rocks, explained Robert. For example, this had happened the first year he was in California:

Among his gang washing gold in a stream was a Negro. One evening when they had finished for the day and were on their way home the Negro suddenly became very ill. He had such an intense stomach ache that he lay on the ground and yelled. None of the others could understand what ailed him. There was nothing to be done for him; he was unable even to walk to his tent; they left him where he lay. The next morning when they came out he was still lying there on his stomach. But now he was quiet and yelled no more — he was dead.

Then one of the men guessed what had caused his stomach pains. He took his knife and cut into the Negro's body. When they opened it they saw the glitter of gold: nuggets and gold sand. The Negro had stolen the gold from his fellow gold washers, a pinch now and then, and had hidden the gold in a safe place — he had put it into his mouth and swallowed it. He had of course expected the gold to come out unspoiled when he went to the privy. But the nuggets had caused a stoppage that killed the poor fool.

And now his comrades took back the gold he had stolen from them; they cleaned it, and when they exchanged it for cash it turned out to be worth four thousand dollars. There were eight men left in the gang, so each got five hundred dollars, concluded Robert. He himself had been one of them.

Kristina had listened in horror to her brother-in-law. "How could they! How terrible!"

The kitchen door stood open because of the heat, and Karl Oskar was sitting on the threshold filing his wood saw; he could still see there in the lingering dusk.

"Did you hear that, Karl Oskar?"

Karl Oskar had heard every word, but he acted as if he hadn't been listening. He filed along at his saw, filed and kept silent.

Kristina now could not hold back any longer — she must know. "Robert, is it true — did you really find gold in California?"

"I am satisfied."

"Is it true? I mean . . . " She did not wish to hurt his feelings by sounding suspicious, and she searched for suitable words.

"You know why I left, Kristina," he replied. "And I wrote in my letters I would not come back until I was a rich man."

"And now you are rich?"

"I have done my last day's work and had my last master. I have plenty. There will be enough for all three of us."

Robert was standing close to the cradle and spoke rather uninterestedly, as if addressing himself to the child. Yet he said he was so rich that he had enough for himself, his brother, and his brother's wife! Kristina was rocking her child, but when she heard that her foot on the cradle rocker came to a stop.

"I have plenty, Kristina. Of that you can be sure."

Kristina sat in speechless confusion. Should she answer him: I don't believe you, you are not rich? But he spoke so calmly . . .

From the door the rasping of the file still came. Karl Oskar must have heard his brother: I am rich, I have enough for all three of us! But he remained silent and filed on.

Karl Oskar had heard, but he felt only sorrow for his brother. Robert had not learned anything from the fact that several times before he left he had been found out and proven to be a liar. Would it be right to pretend to believe him? Was it good for Robert? Wouldn't it be more merciful to him to speak out at once and stop his tall stories? Put an end to his lying once and for all?

The rasping from the saw came to an end. With his file in his hand Karl Oskar walked up to his younger brother. "Please, Robert, stop lying to us! I can't stand it any longer!"

Robert slowly turned his right ear toward him in order to hear better. His left ear must still be bad.

"You don't believe me, Karl Oskar?"

Robert's voice was short and acid. Kristina looked in dismay from the one brother to the other.

"You know you have brought back no gold. But no one holds it against you. We are glad you're back, glad you're alive!"

"You think I haven't anything? You think I lie?" Robert sounded deeply hurt. "All right! All right!" He turned quickly on his heel and walked through the door into the bedroom.

"You will only drive him away," said Kristina, reproaching Karl Oskar. "You could have waited, at least this first evening."

"I can't bear his nonsense! I had to talk honestly with my only brother."

But Robert returned in a moment with his new rucksack in his hand. His brother and sister-in-law looked puzzled as he put it down on the kitchen floor and unlaced its thick leather thongs. From the sack he pulled out a small leather bag which was badly worn and covered with grease spots. He poked his hand into the bag and pulled out a paper bundle. Without a word he handed

113

it to Karl Oskar. Then he stuck his hand into the bag again and pulled out a second bundle, which he laid on the knees of Kristina, who was still sitting at the cradle.

"These notes are for you. I have no gold in my sack. But these have the same value as gold."

Karl Oskar stared at his hand; it held a bundle of bills. Kristina looked down in her apron; on it lay a bundle of rustling paper money. Both of them were silent, dumfounded.

"I brought along a little cash for pocket money."

Robert leaned over the cradle and smiled at the child in it as he spoke casually to her parents. "It's your money. Take it and enjoy it."

Then he turned to Karl Oskar, as if he too were a small child in need of instruction. In order to make use of gold, he explained, it had to be turned into money. A bank in Bloomfield, Indiana, had changed his gold into circulation notes, taking one seventh of the gold value for its trouble. But at least he had his wealth in safekeeping.

"These few dollars are for you, Karl Oskar and Kristina."

Karl Oskar looked embarrassed, as if he had been fooled in some shameful way, as if his brother had cheated him with this gift.

The evening darkness was beginning to fill the kitchen. Karl Oskar lit a taper in the wooden candlestick on the mantel; then he took one note from his bundle and inspected it in the light. The paper was, and remained, money. He turned it. It was green on one side and black on the other; it had the colors he had always seen on American bills. And on both sides, in all four corners, was the figure 100. In eight places it was printed in clear numbers that the note was worth one hundred dollars. And in the center of the green side Karl Oskar could read in big black letters: "INDIANA STATE BANK, BLOOMFIELD, INDIANA."

At last he was able to open his mouth again, mumbling as if in his sleep, "If someone hasn't bewitched my eyes, this is a hundred-dollar bill."

And he began to look through the bundle which Robert had tossed to him like wastepaper. All the bills were of the same size, of the same color, green-black, with the same imprint; all had the number 100 on both sides, in eight places. They were wrinkled and dirty, but the value was the same. Each one was worth one hundred dollars.

114

Karl Oskar counted them slowly: there were twenty in the bundle. He counted them again, he wet his fingers and counted them a third time; they still amounted to twenty.

"You gave me five dollars when I left," said Robert. "I am paying you back with interest."

Kristina's hands had not yet touched the bundle in her lap; she only sat and stared at it as if it were a bird that suddenly had flown into the kitchen and perched on her knee. Now she handed the bills to Karl Oskar. He counted his wife's money also; the bills were exactly like the ones in his own bundle, and also twenty — they were and remained twenty.

"Four thousand dollars in cash . . . " He spoke as in a deep trance. "Four thousand in cash . . . "

And Robert called this pocket money. Karl Oskar Nilsson looked at his younger brother. He was deeply embarrassed.

Robert smiled. "You can see the money comes from the Indiana State Bank. Now do you think I'm lying?"

He told them that he had delivered four sacks of nuggets to the bank in Bloomfield. He had asked for smaller bills, fifty- and twenty-dollar ones, but the bank didn't have enough on hand to let him have all he wanted; they were printing new notes as fast as they could. A great many gold diggers had returned from California and turned in their sacks at the same bank. It would probably take a couple of months before all he had could be exchanged for ready cash.

"You mean you have more?" Karl Oskar's voice was thick.

"Of course! Much more."

Robert had given his brother and sister-in-law four thousand dollars in cash, and as yet they had not said one word of thanks. Karl Oskar and Kristina could not thank him, they could say nothing at all, because they were unable to grasp such a gift.

"Now go out and buy what you need, Kristina!"

She clasped Robert's hand with both her own, tears gushing. "You told the truth. You have had luck. You give us all this. God bless you, Robert!"

"Now don't let's talk of gold any more." He yawned with a broad grin and seemed thoroughly tired of the subject. "I can't tell you how tired I am of it. I've seen too much of the damned stuff!"

Kristina hastened to stand up. "I must make your bed. You are dead tired."

115

She had noticed him moving his hand to his left ear time and again; he had had an ache in that ear ever since his master had once boxed it hard.

"Does your ear still bother you?" she asked compassionately.

"Yes, it makes a terrible noise in there." And in a lower voice, as if wishing to share a confidence with Kristina, he said something strange she was to remember afterward: "My ear can talk. Do you understand? You should hear what it tells me during the night."

-2-

Robert had gone to bed. But Karl Oskar and Kristina sat up late on this strange, confusing evening.

Karl Oskar had spread the forty hundred-dollar bills before him; they covered most of the table. He sat and stared at this new table-cloth of green and black.

Four thousand American dollars were the same as fifteen thousand Swedish riksdaler. Before he emigrated he had sold his farm, Korpamoen, for fifteen hundred riksdaler. Ten times that sum now lay in front of him. On the table in his kitchen this evening was spread the value of ten farms. A fortune! The sum of money spread out under his eyes could change their whole life.

If only there wasn't something wrong with his sight! If these green-black papers on the table now were only what they were supposed to be. For he couldn't entirely believe — he wasn't quite convinced...

"I felt at once that Robert wasn't lying his time," said Kristina.

"We mustn't lose our heads. We can't be sure."

"Do you still doubt him?"

"The bills may be worthless."

"Do you think your brother is a counterfeiter?"

No, he didn't mean his brother had printed the bills himself. But there was so much confusion about money in America. Some states were flooded with bills entirely without value, printed by banks started only to swindle people. Robert's bills were well printed and consequently suspicious. Kristina and Karl Oskar must be cautious.

Kristina felt a hundred-dollar bill. "They're creased and crumpled — they look like good ones."

116

When she got the time she would iron out the big bills and remove grease spots and dirt. Such big bills ought to be clean and smooth. Then she was sure they would pass for their full value.

"I had better go to the bank in Stillwater and ask there," said Karl Oskar. "But I can't get away before Saturday. Then we'll know what Robert's money is worth."

"Do we dare to keep the money in the house until then?" asked Kristina. "It's only Monday."

Karl Oskar thought there would be no danger; no one would expect to find riches there.

With loving hands Kristina gathered the bills together into one big bundle, wrapped them in her silk kerchief and put them down at the bottom of her Swedish chest. It was the safest place she could think of. And yet it would be difficult for her to sleep tonight. What a worry, to have fifteen thousand riksdaler in cash in the house! They must be careful with the fire.

Karl Oskar went out to the barn to look after a sick calf; he should have done it earlier, but this evening he had forgotten both people and animals. He gave the calf some milk in a bucket and looked to see that the rest of the livestock was all right. One never knew — some animal might become tangled in its chain and choke itself. Never would he go to bed of an evening without first checking that all was well with the animals.

When he returned Kristina had already gone to bed. In this new house they had two beds at opposite walls of the big room, and sometimes slept apart. He started to undress, but felt it would take a long time before he could go to sleep tonight. His head buzzed with questions: What about this money? Was it real or not? And how had Robert got his hands on it? He couldn't have earned so much through work; had he actually found gold? In California, it was said, one might dig gold in the earth as easily as potatoes here in Minnesota. If one had luck. Luck! While he slaved away here on his claim, unable to save a cent of cash, Robert had dug up a few lumps of gold which had made him rich instantly, so rich that he would never need to do another day's work in his whole life. At least that was what he had said. Could it be the truth? It didn't seem right if it had happened that way. Karl Oskar had never believed in success except through honest work. Luck and good fortune could help for a while, but the only permanent re-

117

ward came from honest work. If Robert had told the truth, however, then he, Karl Oskar, had been wrong in his thinking.

He said good night to his wife, who still lay awake in her bed; but he had barely put his head against the pillow when a thought came which made him quickly sit up again. The paper — *Hemlandet!* He could find out right now!

Why hadn't he thought of it at once? Every week the Swedish paper listed banks that issued valueless money. Once recently he had counted twelve names in the column. Wasn't one of them an Indiana bank? Was it the Indiana State Bank of Bloomfield? He had saved every copy of *Hemlandet,* on a shelf in the cupboard within arm's reach of his bed.

He almost called out to Kristina: We needn't wait till I go to Stillwater on Saturday! We can know right away if we have become rich tonight — or if we are as poor as before.

But from his wife's even breathing he could hear she had gone to sleep. Then he mustn't disturb her. If she were to learn the truth, the truth as he suspected it to be, she would take the disappointment so hard that she wouldn't go to sleep again. Let her rest, let her be rich for one night. Tomorrow would be soon enough for her to learn, if it were so. But he himself must know the truth this evening.

Cautiously, silently, Karl Oskar rose from his bed. He lit a candle and stood in his nightshirt before the cupboard. He took from the shelf the accumulated copies of *Hemlandet,* every one of them, put them on the table, pulled up a chair and began to read.

The latest paper had come on Friday. He found the heading "Bank Swindles." In that column the Indiana State Bank was not listed. But in the adjoining column his eyes fell on a notice about counterfeit twenty-dollar gold pieces that the public was warned about; they were easy to recognize — a word above the head of the figure representing Liberty was missing on the false coin. But this did not concern him; it was not a question of stamped coins, it was bills.

Danjel Andreasson had once last year been cheated with a five-dollar coin from a hog buyer in St. Paul. It had been stamped "In God we trust," and that was why he had accepted it. Afterward he had been greatly disturbed that counterfeiters proclaimed faith in God. He had never thought that in America, the Lord's Promised Land, people would invoke God's name in their dishonesty.

Karl Oskar picked up the next copy of the paper. He went through issue after issue, reading all the lists of banks which cheated people. He found only two names of banks in Indiana. But the one which had printed Robert's bills, the Indiana State Bank of Bloomfield, he did not see.

With a deep sigh he blew out the candle. The bills must be real, then. Robert had probably told the truth for once.

When he crept into his bed for the second time, Kristina awoke. "Karl Oskar – are you asleep?"

She had been dreaming. She had dreamt that she washed and ironed hundred-dollar bills. She had moved the ironing board out into the barn and there she had ironed long green bills, so large they had hung to the ground. Karl Oskar too had been in her dream; he had the big shovel and shoveled money so fast that it flew all over the place and up against the roof of the barn. It seemed as if they had harvested a whole crop of hundred-dollar bills and now were about to thresh them, while she ironed and ironed as perspiration ran off her body.

"I was so glad when I awoke. For after all I had dreamt the truth!"

XIII

THE FIRST NIGHT – ROBERT REMEMBERS

-1-

What does Robert's injured ear tell him during the night?

His left ear buzzes and keeps him awake. As soon as he puts his head on the pillow in the evening it begins. It roars and thunders, it sings and rings, songs are heard, bells toll, shots are fired. The buzz and roar can be of such intensity that it sounds like a storm at sea. And in bed at night his heart moves up to his ear and throbs there. The heart has many beats in a minute, still more in an hour, and each beat feels to him like a wasp's sting, like a knife's jab.

His ear has been aching since that day in Sweden when he lay

119

on his back under the open sky and whistled and sang when he had been told to dig a ditch, and his master came and lifted the biggest fist ever seen and hit him hard on his left ear.

He emigrated to get away from masters, but his ear went with him with its buzzing turmoil. He ran away from service, he crossed the ocean, but the sound in the ear remained with him. It followed him on the road to California, and now it has come back with him. At night the ear tells him all it has recorded: people's voices and animals' cries, laughter and weeping, sounds of joy and pain, his own words and those of others — of his friend Arvid and other companions, talk, yells, swearing. He hears creaking wagon wheels, neighing horses, braying mules, the whipping wind, the pelting rain, the noisy great rivers, the sweeping storm over the prairie buffalo grass. It reproduces the echo of shots, drunken men's slobberings, voices in delirium. It recalls to him the days and nights of his four years on the road to California.

And so he lies awake and listens.

There you lie — and here I am. You'll never be rid of me!
Listen well to me now. How was it? Do you remember how it happened, that first summer?

-2-

In April they had started their journey.

On the paddle steamer from Stillwater they had traveled with the deck crew, employed as dishwashers. The pay agreed upon was free transportation to St. Louis. Together they had twenty-five dollars, well hidden in a skin pouch.

The last time they had traveled on the Mississippi they had gone upstream; now they traveled downstream on the same broad water. Last time the steamboat was called the *Red Wing,* this time it was the *New Orleans.* On the Mississippi, the world's greatest moving water, Robert had last time heard a song, a song about liberty and freedom: "We will be free as the wind of the earth and the waves on the sea . . . " Ever after he had been lured by that song and had trusted its promise.

But then he had been a free passenger above deck, now he was a dishwasher below deck. Arvid and he sat in a dark, dirty galley and peeled potatoes for the cook. Whole barrels full of potatoes were rolled up to them, and as soon as they saw the bottom of one barrel a new one appeared. They peeled potatoes, the cook boiled them, the passengers and the crew ate them. During the whole long, light spring day, as the *New Orleans* glided by the verdant river shores, Robert and Arvid sat in the same galley with the peelings wriggling like snakes about their feet. By evening the heap of peelings had reached their knees. At last they were liberated and could go up on deck. But they could not walk near where the paying passengers promenaded and viewed the wonders of the world's broadest river.

The boat went farther south, the days grew warmer, and it became oppressive in the galley where they sat with their busy knives. Arvid became depressed at peeling from morning to night, day after day, week after week, penned up in a dark corner on beautiful spring days. But Robert offered comfort. They must keep this in mind: They were on their way to California, they were peeling their way to the land of gold. When they returned they would ride as passengers on the upper deck and smoke cigars up there and look at the scenery. And they would have broad gold watch chains across their vests and heavy gold rings on every one of their fingers; every pocket of their clothing would be filled with rustling money.

Spring advanced and the *New Orleans* floated farther south on the river, and an ever hotter sun shone down on her deck. The Mississippi became wider, the shores more lush, the vegetation ever richer. And it grew ever hotter in the galley where two Swedish farm hands sat and peeled their way to California.

At last one day a bell rang and they heard the name they had been listening for every time the boat docked: St. Louis! They were liberated from their galley prison, they threw their peeling knives onto the deck with shouts of joy, picked up their rucksacks and ran down the gangplank.

They had traveled the first stretch of the road and it hadn't cost them a penny.

They were now in a place with crowds of people and jostling animals and vehicles on the streets. Stillwater was a river village on the St. Croix, St. Louis was a larger town on a larger river. It was the biggest city they had ever seen, except New York. But it

121

wasn't completed yet. Indeed, outside of New York they hadn't seen a town in America that *was* completed; all were abuilding, all were like a shell of a house not yet finished. In St. Louis timbers and boards were strewn over the streets, hammering and digging went on everywhere. People sat eating bread and fruit outside huts that were so primitive Robert and Arvid wondered if they were lived in.

In St. Louis the two boys got along better than on Broadway in New York last year. "I am a stranger here," Robert had told the people that time, but he had never been able to make anyone understand him. Now he could say almost anything he wanted in the American language, although maybe a little haltingly and not always according to his language books, and he understood most of what people said to him. It was not so with Arvid; he did not know many English words as yet, even though he usually pretended he understood everything. And Robert did not let on that he knew Arvid pretended. Arvid had never learned to read or write his own mother tongue; how, then, could he learn English?

From the pier they followed a broad street, perhaps the town's Broadway, although it wasn't half so wide as the street of that name in New York. But here too wonderful fruits were sold, many kinds whose names they did not know. At one stand they bought oranges, and against the tin wall of a shed nearby they sat down on some boxes to eat.

The sun felt good on their faces, they were sitting and eating juicy fruits, this was a fine place. But where was the road that led to the gold fields in California?

In Stillwater Robert had bought a map of the United States. Maps grew in number and size, for every year the Republic expanded night and day, throughout the week, the whole year round. Robert had therefore asked for the latest map which the President in Washington had issued as the official record for his country this year, 1851. He had paid one dollar and fifty cents for it — "Latest Edition, Completely Revised." But that sum he would get back with the first grain of gold he found on the California ground.

Arvid knew: If one had a map and a watch one could find any road in the world, however crookedly it ran, however rotten its condition. Robert had the map; he, Arvid, had the watch. He pulled it from his vest pocket, the nickel watch his father, Petter of

Kråkesjö, had given him as a parting gift. It was his paternal inheritance from Sweden. His father's labor had earned it for him; much sweat, many long days' toil, many evenings with a sore back had gone into it. It was not an old-fashioned unreliable spindle watch, it had cylinder works. Cylinder watches had more precise wheels — this watch kept time to the second.

And now they would make great use of the watch. If Robert's map showed the road they must take, then this watch would show the time it would take to walk it.

Robert spread his map of the United States over the empty boxes. He had not looked at it before, he had been unable to read it on board the steamboat. Now he inspected it carefully. And the longer he looked at it, the wider his eyes opened. Could it be right?

California, the new state of the Union, was that long, narrow strip of land near the Pacific Ocean. If they walked westward across the land from St. Louis, then they would reach the Pacific Ocean, and the sun, which set to the west, could all the time point out the way for them. But how far was it?

"Let me see . . ."

Robert used a pencil to measure as he figured the size of the United States. He measured crosswise, from east to west. From the east coast to St. Louis the distance was exactly the length of the pencil. But then it took two whole lengths of the pencil and still another half to reach the Pacific Ocean!

He measured with his pencil several times, but he couldn't make the distance an inch shorter. Last year they had traveled one month through the country, to Minnesota; this year, from Minnesota to Missouri; and they had not yet reached halfway through America! Not even one third!

At this discovery Robert grew very serious. With the aid of a pencil and a map on an empty box he had obtained his first general view of the New World. It made him dizzy. Arvid would be scared to death if he knew how great a distance they had left to go; Robert had better keep the discovery to himself.

He folded the map quickly and said truthfully, "We have a good part left. America is broad."

But where was the road to California? They must ask someone. Robert and Arvid resumed their wandering through the town.

Whom should they ask? Robert chose with great deliberation among the people they met on the street. Here came men riding sleek horses, dressed from head to foot in soft deerskin, with ten-inch-wide belts dangling revolvers and knives. But these riders sat so loftily on the horses, how could a walker stop them? Instead, Robert chose from the crowd on foot. He turned to more simply dressed people; he spoke to those who had neither revolvers nor knives in their belts. He felt in some way on equal footing with them.

The road to California? Some replied in many words, others in few, but all answered willingly and kindly. Some smiled, thinking perhaps the question was a joke, some looked serious, or surprised.

"To go to California is more complicated than you think." This was the general reply. And there was no definite information about the road; in this all agreed. When Robert had asked half a dozen people and added together their replies, he came to a definite conclusion: *No road had been built to California!*

Gold seekers found their way as best they could along different routes. People traveled in great groups, a thousand persons or more; the distance was over two thousand miles, and the crossing took four months—a whole summer. But there was no exact road to the gold fields.

No road. They must stay in this town for a while and think over their situation.

It was late in the afternoon, and they began to look for a cheap boardinghouse. In the outskirts of town they found a place where they could sleep for twenty-five cents apiece. They decided to stay there; cheaper lodgings they could hardly expect to find in a big town like St. Louis. Their host was a fat Irishman. He showed them their bunks: mattresses filled with rotten straw, spread on the floor; for cover there were torn horse blankets. Four men were to sleep on one mattress. Their sleeping companions had already gone to bed — two bearded horse grooms who slept with their boots on, even though a notice on the wall pleaded with gentlemen to please remove their boots before going to bed. The place smelled of manure, whether from the bedding or the guests.

Robert and Arvid reluctantly unstrapped their rucksacks. This was a poor lodging, but to their noses it was some reminder of home, since it had such a strong smell of stable; once they had lodged together in the stable room at Nybacken.

124

Their host was talkative, and when he heard that the Swedish boys were on their way to California he was immediately ready with good advice. He had a brother who had set out on the Trail last spring, so he could tell them all they needed to know: There *was* a route to the Far West; in fact, there were three routes: the Santa Fe Trail and the Oregon Trail, both of which started at Independence, and the Overland Trail, which branched off from the Oregon farther west and crossed the mountains to California. Most of the travelers to the gold fields used the last.

"You must go to Independence and join the gold army."

Robert had only casually looked at his map with its many Western states and territories, most of them without place names, it seemed. Now he asked how far it was to Independence. The Irishman said it was two hundred miles to the west. It was too late for them to join the caravan of gold seekers this summer, a whole month too late. It was May now, the wagon train to the West had left Independence in April. A new caravan would not leave until next spring. When the buffalo grass turned green next spring, then the gold seekers would gather again. Too late. They would lose a whole year.

Their host wished them good night and good sleep and left. They sat down on their mattress and opened their rucksacks, still full of the food Kristina had packed for them, took out bread and cured pork and ate. The food prevented Arvid from talking; for him to talk while eating would have been as sacrilegious as swearing in church. But Robert too sat silent now as he chewed.

While peeling potatoes on the boat they had figured that their twenty-five dollars would take care of their food and lodging for a month's travel from St. Louis to California. For they had hoped to reach the gold fields in a month, and once there they would have no further need for money. And now this — they couldn't get there for a whole year.

When Arvid had finished eating he took hold of the brass chain on his vest and pulled his watch from its pocket. He said: Whatever else happened on this journey, his cylinder watch he wouldn't sell. They might have to go without food, but his watch he wouldn't part with even if they starved. It was his inheritance and could not be touched. And Arvid's watch showed ten minutes after nine this May evening of 1851, in their manure-smelling lodging in the town of St. Louis, Missouri, where they had paid twenty-five cents apiece for sleeping accommodations. Gentlemen please take off their boots in bed!

Robert and Arvid, once having shared the same stable room, had sworn to stick together forever, never to separate. Now they crept under the same horse blanket. They were again a couple of farm hands. And incomprehensibly far away from the land of gold.

- 3 -

Later in the summer they got work on a farm near town; the owner wanted a potato cellar dug. Their pay was seventy-five cents a day plus board. In the farm kitchen they could eat as much meat and potatoes and beans as they wanted. But their room consisted of a ramshackle shed where they were worse housed than in the stable room in which they had lived in Sweden. However, there were no bedbugs in the walls as there had been at Nybacken, where each morning they had awakened with fresh bites on their necks. Perhaps this shed was so miserable that no vermin wanted to live there.

Arvid worried for fear they might be delayed so long that all the gold would be gone before they got there. Robert reassured him: In an American newspaper he had read that a very learned man, Mr. Horace Greeley, had said that California had at least two thousand million dollars' worth of gold. As yet only two hundred million had been dug up; there was still eighteen hundred million left. Did Arvid think that would not be enough for him? Did he want more than eighteen hundred million dollars?

When the potato cellar was finished they were put to work helping with the harvesting and the threshing; this kept them busy the whole fall, and when winter came they were put to wood cutting. Now the wages were lowered to fifty cents a day, but they could still eat as much meat and potatoes and beans as before. They might have liked their jobs if they had been better housed; when winter came, the sharp wind blew through the cracks of their shed and they had to creep close together at night to keep warm.

The cold increased, and Arvid began to complain: Why must they travel so far to sleep in this rotten shed? It had been warmer in the stable room at Nybacken. Had they emigrated to America in order to lie here and freeze at night? Robert said they must

126

be patient, just get through the winter. Every single ax cut brought them closer to the gold land. The younger boy usually found words that cheered the older one. And they continued to saw and split and stack wood in tall piles.

But one evening when they returned to their cold shed after a day of work, Arvid sank down on the bunk, his hands to his face. "I can't stand it any longer! I want to go home!"

He began to cry. He wanted to return to Minnesota, to his service with Danjel Andreasson, to the people from Sweden he knew. He had thought about it for a long while and had made his decision: He didn't want to go on to California. He didn't care for gold any more. He would just as soon be poor if only he could be with people he could talk to, whom he knew. He didn't want to work for an American farmer and live in this shed; it was better with his old Swedish master.

"But I can't find the way back — I can't ask in English. Won't you come with me, Robert?"

"No, Arvid, I won't return."

"But I can't go back alone. I can't manage. Please, Robert, come with me!"

"No — I want to see California."

His friend's weeping and pleading bothered Robert but did not change his mind. He would go on until he had found gold and could return as a rich man. And he reminded Arvid of their mutual promise, a promise for all times and all circumstances: *Whatever happened the two of them must stick together.* Didn't he remember the Sunday when they had made a bonfire at Lake Ki-Chi-Saga? They had been sitting there at the fire, warming their blue-frozen hands, and had sworn they would be comrades forever. Would Arvid now fail his comrade and his oath?

They talked about this until late that evening, until at last they agreed again and shook hands on it. When the prairie was green with next spring's grass they would continue west.

Yes, I heard it all. I heard you and Arvid, the two friends who would never part. You persuaded him to stick to his promise, to go with you to seek gold. You can never deny it. "Please, Robert," he pleaded like a little child . . .

127

XIV

WHILE THE RICHES LAY HIDDEN
IN THE HOUSE

-1-

Robert slept late in his room next morning, and no one disturbed him, since he was in need of rest. Karl Oskar had intended to do a day's work on the church building which had begun that spring, but as his brother had just come back he stayed home and did ordinary small chores. Kristina wanted to prepare good strengthening food for the returned one, and so she robbed the chicken nests of fresh eggs. For her brother-in-law's breakfast she also made dumplings, which she knew he liked.

Robert rose late and sat down alone at the kitchen table. After a while Karl Oskar came in. He had something to say which he should have said last night: Hearty thanks for the big bundle of bills — if now all this money was indeed meant as a gift! He had inspected the notes, both with candle flame and in daylight, and as far as he could see they were real, and current money; he would soon put them in the bank at Stillwater. But nowadays so many bills were worth only half their face value, or nothing, that he hoped Robert would understand why they had been doubtful at first. The main thing that troubled him now about this money, thought Karl Oskar, was the fact that he himself hadn't earned it, through his own work.

Robert mumbled something to the effect that he hoped his brother and sister-in-law would enjoy the gift. Apparently he didn't want to talk about it any further. He seemed to have little feeling for his fortune; last night he had handled the bills as if all he wanted was to get rid of them, the sooner the better.

They had many questions to ask Robert, they wanted to know all that had happened to him during his four-year absence. But concerning the money he discouraged their questions; perhaps he would tell them more once he was rested. Now he wanted to ask: What had happened here since he left?

Karl Oskar and Kristina described to him the activities around

128

the lake, the new houses that had been built, and told him the names of their neighbors, all new immigrants from Sweden. The population had increased so much they had now founded a Swedish congregation.

"We timbered up a schoolhouse last summer. Now we're hammering together a church," said Karl Oskar.

"Yes, at last," added Kristina. "They argued a whole year about its location!"

Well, each one of the settlers had wanted the church near his claim, said Karl Oskar. People had wanted it on both the north and the south, on the east and the west lake shore, in every imaginable place. Ten different sites had been under consideration. But at last they had been forced to agree; a site had been selected on the Helsinge farmer Lars Sjölin's claim, on a tongue of land across from Nordberg's Isle. It was really a good place for the church, as nearly as possible in the center of the Swedish settlement.

To build a church was a difficult and tiresome job, that they had learned. Everything was to be done voluntarily: each household was to cut, roughhew and deliver three loads of lumber, and each grown man was to give twelve days' labor. But no one could tell yet if this would be sufficient to complete the building. And many members were poor new settlers who had barely had time to raise a shelter over their own heads—each one must of course first of all see to his own needs. At least one thousand dollars in cash besides was needed to finish the church, and as yet they didn't know if they could scrape together this sum.

"They can't agree on anything, these people," said Kristina. "They quarrel constantly."

"They had no chance to decide anything back in Sweden, so now they make up for it in America," said Karl Oskar.

There had been great arguments about the little schoolhouse too before it was completed last fall. The parish elder, Petrus Olausson, had bullied them into building it on his land, half a mile from the church. The young pastor, Mr. Törner, had promised to act as teacher, and he kept school two months in spring and two months in autumn. During the winter there was no schooling—the children couldn't get out on the roads because of the cold and the snow, they might freeze to death in the drifts. Johan and Märta attended regularly, and Harald would begin this fall.

The children were curious about the stranger. Robert asked if

129

they learned in Swedish in school, and Johan reeled off some Swedish words, with derivations, repeating by heart. Märta too wanted to show what she had learned; she found a schoolbook and read the story about the shepherd who lied.

"A liar you cannot believe even when he tells the truth," she concluded her reading.

In a low voice Robert repeated the last sentence of the story, while his eyes sought his brother's. Karl Oskar quickly looked out through the window as if he hadn't heard.

Kristina hastened to say something. "The girl has a nice singing voice. Sing something for Robert, Märta."

Märta threw her flaxen braids back over her shoulders, stood wide-legged in the middle of the floor and sang in a clear, thin child voice:

> *"We go to school*
> *We stand in a row,*
> *Our hands are clean*
> *Our faces also.*
> *Now let us listen*
> *With open ear,*
> *What teacher says*
> *Let everyone hear.*
> *Knowledge is better*
> *Than silver and gold . . ."*

At these words Robert rose quickly from his chair; the spoon with dumplings in it fell from his hand and clattered to the floor. He had shied away as if the girl had struck him; he stared wide-eyed at her until she backed away, looking at him in fright.

Slowly he picked up the spoon from the floor. Then he sat down, silent and lost in thoughts. Karl Oskar and Kristina were puzzled by his behavior. The returned gold seeker seemed frightened at the mere mention of a word in a song — the word "gold."

-2-

In the afternoon they went out to inspect the farm. Karl Oskar and Kristina wanted to show Robert all they had tilled and planted and built while he was away. He showed great surprise at the

130

large field with sprouting corn, wheat, rye and oats on the slope where only four years ago nothing had grown but weeds. And such smooth, even fields! His brother had indeed worked hard.

"If the farmers at home could see these fields they would die of envy!"

The brothers walked side by side along the edge of the property. Robert noticed that Karl Oskar dragged his left leg. "What's the matter with you? You limp."

The older brother replied, somewhat embarrassed: It was only his old ailment in the left shinbone, an injury he had received when a couple of men had tried to rob him on their journey to Minnesota. It ached sometimes when he worked too hard, and perhaps he favored that leg while walking.

"You slave on your claim." Robert spoke seriously. Nothing in this world was worth aches and limps, he said, not even the good earth of Minnesota. He was a youth no longer. He had grown so old that he advised his older brother.

They looked at the fat, well-cared-for animals in the barn. All had been bred on the place except the cow, Lady. And this spring one of the heifers had taken the bull, so they would soon have five cows.

"I don't like to have any more to milk," said Kristina.

They went inside the deserted log cabin, which now was used as a tool shed and carpenter shop.

"Here is where I mend things," said Karl Oskar.

In the old log house he now spent rainy days at the workbench. The floor was strewn with shavings. On the wall deerskins and calfskins had been nailed up to dry. It looked like a junk shop. But here they had lived for four winters. When Robert compared the log cabin with the new house in the maple grove he could see how much things had improved for his brother's family in New Duvemåla.

But the most unusual thing they had acquired while Robert was gone Kristina showed him last: the small tree that grew at the east gable of the new main house. Could he guess what kind of tree it was? A little sapling, about five feet tall, its top reaching to Robert's chest. The tree had large, deep-green leaves, healthy branches and foliage. But he couldn't guess. Some kind of plum tree, perhaps?

"An apple tree from home!" said Kristina.

"Kristina's own tree," added Karl Oskar.

Robert lightly pinched a leaf of the sapling. He ought to have recognized an Astrachan tree from its wide, thick leaves with fuzzy undersides.

Kristina said that she thought it would take a few years more before the tree bore fruit, and no one could tell if it would have real Astrachan apples — those juicy, large apples, big as children's heads, with clear, transparent skin. Their neighbors, Algot and Manda Svensson, had said that crabapples might grow on trees planted this way from seeds.

Robert stroked the branches; the leaves felt soft to his touch. "It has come from the old country. It too has emigrated."

He felt nostalgia as he touched the tree, he felt a strange compassion for the little life, a desire to protect and guard it. As if it were a living being — as if four people instead of three were standing here at the gable, four immigrants. And when they walked on he turned around to look at it, as if afraid the delicate life might not be able to withstand the merciless winter cold here in North America.

-3-

Karl Oskar had put out the back copies of *Hemlandet* for his brother. Robert did not know that a Swedish paper was printed in America; in the part of the country where he had been he had met hardly any Swedes and he had never heard anyone talk of Sweden. Now he sat the whole evening and read the paper eagerly. Here he learned about the most important happenings in the world during the last year.

"I see women are allowed to write in the papers here," he said.

Following the example of American papers, *Hemlandet* had two articles by women. Male readers had sent in angry letters: writing by women was contrary to the Biblical and Lutheran spirit. The editor replied that when he received something worth while written by women he intended to print it. He wanted in this way to encourage females in learning, and he insisted he could still remain a good Lutheran.

"I believe he is right," said Kristina. "I can't think it's sinful to learn to write."

She felt that many Swedish immigrant women, like herself, felt sad because they could not write and were unable to communicate with their relatives at home.

"Everything is different here," said Robert. "You are a missus and Karl Oskar is a mister out here."

"Yes, I am now 'Mister' Nilsson!"

And Karl Oskar laughed heartily. If a farmer in Sweden were called "Mister" he would believe he was being made a fool of.

"You should know how respected your brother is in America," said Kristina to Robert. "He and Uncle Danjel were elected to the parish board."

"Are you a churchwarden, Karl Oskar?" exclaimed Robert.

"A churchwarden without a church as yet. Danjel and I are 'deacons'; we're chosen to run the parish."

"Deacons! That sounds almost like a dean or a bishop."

Kristina said: She remembered that time when Dean Brusander denied the Holy Sacrament to Uncle Danjel and refused to accept him as godfather for Harald when the boy was baptized. Suppose the dean now learned that Danjel and Karl Oskar ran the parish — that in America they could select and discharge ministers! Wasn't the world turned upside down out here?

That evening supper was late again because Kristina still had so much to talk about with Robert. She noticed his hearing had grown worse; she had to raise her voice in speaking to him. And she wondered again if he weren't sick in some way; he moved about so slowly and heavily, and even when he sat still and did not exert himself perspiration trickled down his forehead. He was very thirsty and walked often over to the bucket to drink. And as soon as supper was over he went to bed in the gable room.

Kristina looked after him as he closed the door. "Something is wrong with your brother."

"Yes. He's so quiet about his gold digging. And he hasn't said a word about Arvid."

Karl Oskar and Kristina remained sitting in the kitchen for a long time that evening, talking about something that had been in their heads all day long, something that had hardly left their thoughts for a minute—that something lying hidden in the bottom of the Swedish chest: the fortune that was secreted in their house.

XV

THE SECOND NIGHT—ROBERT REMEMBERS AGAIN

You're tired and want to sleep, but I will keep you awake. I am your faithful companion, I am the memories which refuse to leave you. You have an earache; you feel your heart's persistent pumping in your ear, a dull thudding. But there is nothing you can do about it. You were born with this body which has two ears, and one of them buzzes for you tonight. Three years ago you still had your health and lived with expectations which helped you to endure all trouble; you thought the only thing that mattered was to get to a certain place. Yes, I remember everything that happened during that spring...

- 1 -

The buffalo grass was again green on the prairie; the new shoots were three inches tall. Again there was fodder for the animals of the gold caravan. The buffalo grass nourished horses and oxen, mules and sheep — all the animals that carried California-bound travelers on their backs and sustained them with their meat. The grass was fresh and green for only one month of the year, but it remained nourishing to the animals all year round.

And toward the end of March two Swedish farm hands threw aside their axes, said good-by to their employer and made ready to continue their journey westward. This spring they would not be too late to join the gold army.

Every day great numbers of strangers arrived in St. Louis on their way to Independence and St. Joseph, the meeting places for gold seekers. Here they obtained part of their equipment — food, fodder, tools which could not be bought farther west. St. Louis was beginning to look like a great army camp bivouacking for a few days. On every open place in the town Robert and Arvid could see those strange vehicles, the Conestoga wagons, with their broad sideboards, heavy wheel rims, and canvas stretched above curved wooden bows. The boys looked with respect at the wheels which would turn over two thousand miles of prairies and plateaus, mountains and deserts, and at last sink down in the sand where the gold glittered.

The California-bound travelers rode in wagons or on horses or mules, and those who had neither vehicle nor animal must go by shank's mare — they must walk. But even for those walking, pack animals were necessary; one could not carry a heavy burden on a two-thousand-mile journey. Robert and Arvid counted their hoarded dollars and figured carefully. How ought they to travel?

And then one morning they were approached by a swarthy stranger, a man in a short red jacket with yellow stripes across the shoulders and chest, who carried a silver-ornamented Kentucky rifle. The man was not much taller than a young boy, but he wore the biggest hat they had ever seen on a human head — a brown hat with a band of silver-white string. They thought it funny to see such a short man with a hat brim almost half as wide as he was high. This peculiarly dressed stranger asked them if they were on their way to California.

"Yes, yes! We are hunting for gold!" Never before had Robert as quickly found an answer in English.

The little man smiled, exposing long white teeth. His complexion was yellow-brown, like honey. His strong, protruding nose reminded Robert of his brother Karl Oskar. His eyes were big and friendly.

He too was on his way to the gold fields. He would supply them with all they needed on the journey if they would keep him company and help him with his mules. Had they any experience in handling animals?

"We are used to farm work!" exclaimed Robert. "We can take care of cattle."

"Good! Let's go to a tavern for a beer."

They hung over the counter while exchanging information. Within the hour everything had been agreed upon: Robert and Arvid were employed for four months — the time allowed for the journey to California — to serve as mule drivers for the little man, who, they learned, was a Mexican named Mario Vallejos. English was not the native tongue of either Robert or Vallejos, yet they talked with ease to each other in this language. Vallejos had been born in Texas. A few years ago the Americans had come and taken his land, and now he wanted to get some of their California gold.

A few of his friends had agreed to meet in St. Joseph and start for California together. From St. Louis to St. Joseph the shortest distance was only about two hundred and fifty miles; this was the road they must first travel. Vallejos figured they could cover an average of twenty miles a day, so they would need about twelve or thirteen days for this distance.

The Mexican turned out to be the owner of eight mules. They were sturdy pack animals, each able to carry a three-hundred-pound load. Indian horses and Mexican mules were the toughest for both packing and riding, explained Vallejos. But his mules required constant attention — careful brushing and feeding and a friendly attitude.

Robert assured him that both he and his friend had always loved Mexican mules above all other animals on earth. No mules of any kind existed in their home country, but they had always looked forward to the pleasure of driving and combing and feeding these wise animals. In fact, this was the reason they had emigrated to North America.

Their new employer smiled and seemed pleased with his muleteers.

They helped him with the provisions for the journey, loading the packsaddles of the mules with flour, ham, beans, rice, coffee, dried fruit, sugar, salt, and water in canteens. Robert and Arvid were openmouthed at the sight of all the goods bought for the California journey, and Vallejos said he would buy still more when they arrived at St. Joseph. During the four months required for the journey each man would consume one hundred and fifty pounds of flour, fifty pounds of ham, fifty pounds of dried pork, thirty pounds of sugar, six pounds of coffee, one pound of tea, three pounds of salt, one bushel of dried fruit, twenty-five pounds of rice, twenty pounds of hardtack and half a bushel of beans.

It took more than a day to learn how to saddle a mule and pack it properly. The weight must be evenly distributed between the front and hind quarters and between the two sides. Balance was required lest the animal fall on its nose or sink down on its hind legs. The two Swedish farm hands had only harnessed horses and yoked oxen; to place several hundred pounds on a small mule was a much more complicated matter. Arvid reflected that in America a hired hand must be smarter than in Sweden.

At last one April morning at dawn the Mexican Mario Vallejos set out on his journey westward across the prairie, with his two young helpers and his eight mules. Two Swedish farm hands were on their way to join the gold caravan — the Train of the Hundred Thousand.

-2-

They traveled under the burning sun in the daytime and camped under the chilly starlight at night. They followed the footpaths of people and animals who had passed before them and had left, in soft places in the ground, the imprints of heel irons and boot soles, of hoofs and the broad wheel rims of the Conestoga wagons. But in sandy places the wind had obliterated all tracks, and on the plateaus and the hard ground tracks had never been left.

The little Mexican rode ahead on his dark-brown mule and located the trail. Following him were the two youths with the pack mules, each one carrying two hundred pounds for its owner. Robert and Arvid fed the mules crushed corn three times a day and watered them twice a day. They curried the animals and loaded them, followed them in daytime and guarded them at night.

The new muleteers learned that the longer a mule was scratched between the ears, the easier it was to handle. When the mules grew hungry they folded their ears back and brayed. It sounded as if they had attacks of hiccups. The muleteers thought at first that something was stuck in their throats, but by and by they understood that the creatures brayed when their stomachs were empty.

Vallejos considered Mexican mules the most suitable for the California journey, since they required less water than horses. And on the desert mules could smell water holes at a distance of two miles or more.

In St. Louis Robert and Arvid had begun to prepare themselves for washing gold. They had bought a pan each and filled it with water to see how much it would hold; each held almost a gallon. As they walked behind the mules they drummed with their fingers on the pans. They were ready. And they also knew how to dig.

The days were too warm and the nights too cold. At camp

137

in the evening they gathered dry grass and bushes and made a fire to keep warm. Each in turn stood watch and tended the fire. They slept stretched out on the ground with saddles as pillows. Arvid kept complaining of the weather in America; either it was too warm or too cold — why never right?

When the cold kept them both awake at night Robert cheered his friend by telling him what he knew about the gold land: In California the weather was perfect the year round, and so healthy that people lived to be a hundred years old. Old people only dried up a little more for each year in the good sun, until at last nothing was left but the skin, which finally blew away over the Pacific Ocean. Out there people didn't die in the same way as in other places. In California there were no sicknesses to kill people. Even suicides were impossible in that state. Californians aged two or three hundred years and tired of living would travel to some other state, where they immediately collapsed like empty sacks and died.

Vallejos had told them that in the Sacramento River nuggets had been found weighing as much as one hundred and fifty pounds, and worth fifty thousand dollars apiece.

"One single clump! Oh Lord, Lord!" exclaimed Arvid. And he had served as a farm hand in Sweden for ten dollars a year. If he found a single nugget he could buy Kråkesjö Manor, where his old father was a cotter.

Gold was the strength-giving word; dreaming of gold still held its power over them. But each evening when Arvid wound his watch and one more day had been added to the California journey he asked: They had been on their way a whole year now — how soon would they get there?

The Mexican was a good master. He didn't ask them to walk too far each day. And they could eat all they wanted; they gorged themselves on ham and dried pork. And Vallejos did his share of standing watch, looking after the fire for a few hours every third night. He could bear both heat and cold, it didn't bother him. He enumerated the dangers ahead: the fording of the rivers, the heat, the Indians, the wild animals. But of people he feared only one man: Yellow Jack. He explained who this was, but Robert was unable to follow his English and remained wondering about the dangerous Yellow Jack.

138

At the campfire Vallejos kept awake by singing, always the same song — droning it, like a bumblebee's buzzing in the grass:

> *"Oh, the good time has come at last,*
> *We need no more complain, sir!*
> *The rich can live in luxury*
> *And the poor can do the same, sir!*
> *For the good time has come at last,*
> *And as we are told, sir!*
> *We shall be rich at once now,*
> *With California gold, sir!"*

Robert listened night after night to the measureless dream song, the song of the yellow gold that would make him free. When at last he had reached the end of this road he would be free. He was a muleteer, he was still in service, but this service would be his last; the Mexican Mario Vallejos would be his last master in life.

- 3 -

On the ninth day after they had set out they saw for the first time the animal which had given its name to the tall grass on the prairie. At a distance was a herd of buffalo, a dark, closed circle moving across the plain. It looked as if the very ground were moving with the herd, and the heavy tramp of the animals sounded like a muffled thunderstorm when it first rises over the horizon.

Each time they passed running water — creeks or streams — the mules were allowed to drink all they wanted, but when they approached stagnant water Vallejos warned the muleteers sternly that such water holes were not to be trusted. The country grew more desolate and the ground more arid; they had reached a region with no streams, and they used the water in their canteens when they watered the animals.

Once they came upon a hollow where a broken pair of wheels lay; pieces of spokes and a broken wagon tongue were strewn about. The Mexican stopped his mule and nodded meaningfully

139

at the place, but said nothing. A few hundred yards farther on, a flat white stone had been raised on end in the ground. On it was an inscription in black letters:

Jack Maloney
Aged 18 years
Rest in peace Sweet Boy
For thy Troubles are over

Robert guessed the connection between the broken wheels and the little tombstone. He did not translate the inscription for Arvid. But it stuck in his thoughts for the rest of the day.

On the eleventh day their trail crossed a desolate sandy plain, with hills in the distance. The terrain was broken by boulders in strange shapes and by islands of stones in the sand. In the evening they made camp at a split rock in the center of the plain. It was Robert's turn to guard the fire. Later in the night a wind came up from the west and several times almost extinguished the fire. He moved the embers farther into the lee of the rock; here the fire burned well, and he dozed for a while, his head on a saddle.

Near dawn he got up and walked over to look at the mules. What he saw dumfounded him: There were only six animals. Two of the mules were gone. He hurried around the rock searching for them, but the two animals had vanished.

Arvid was the one who had tethered the mules last night when they camped. And Robert had warned him before that his knots in the halters were too loose.

He shook his comrade roughly by the shoulder, but spoke in a low voice so as not to waken their master, who slept only a few paces away. "You didn't tie those mules right! Two of them broke away!"

Arvid was wide awake as soon as he heard of Robert's discovery. He didn't try to deny it. He was the one who had tied the mules to some boulders; if they had got loose he was to blame.

Robert said that it didn't matter whose fault it was; both of them would suffer for this. If their boss should learn that the knots had been loose he would fire them on the spot. As long as they were with the Mexican they had all they needed for their journey; if they were separated from him they might never get to California. Therefore they must find the strayed mules and bring them back before he woke up. According to Arvid's watch it was four o'clock. As a rule they broke camp about seven; they had three hours in which to search.

"It's my fault!" wailed Arvid. "I was born with bad luck!"

"Don't lose your head. We'll find them."

The boys took off over the plain to search for the mules. Darkness still lay thick, and in the vague light a mule could not be seen at a distance of more than fifty feet. They shouted and called the mules by all the names Vallejos used: "Hekee! Hinni! Cheekte! Hekee!"

Every few minutes they stopped and listened hopefully for the familiar braying. But the strayed mules did not reply to their calls. They repeated the words without knowing the meaning: "Hinni! Cheekte!"

And no tracks were visible.

Mexican mules could smell fresh grass from a long way off. Robert remembered that yesterday afternoon they had passed a place between two ridges where he had seen green buffalo grass. Perhaps the mules had found their way back to this place? But it was several miles and he did not think he could find his way there.

They had begun by searching around the campsite and tramping the ground in ever widening circles. An hour passed; light came slowly to the plain. They stumbled onto a dried-out creek bed and followed its gently sloping path. Perhaps there was water farther down and the mules had smelled it? Water had once run here; there were tracks of animals, big and little ones, but they must have been made some time ago, since the tracks had already dried up. The creek wound its way in great curves, but everywhere it was equally dry.

It was now full daylight. The wind had increased and the dust blew in clouds about them. Arvid looked at his watch and exclaimed in terror, "It's already half past five! Shouldn't we go back?"

In order to reach camp for their usual hour of starting they must return at once. Vallejos was probably already up and about. What would he say when he missed both the mules and the muleteers? He might think they had stolen the animals and run away.

With heavy feet Robert and Arvid followed the dry creek back toward camp. The wind was increasing and they walked with eyes closed against the whirling dust.

141

"We must find the mules!" Robert repeated.

They were returning slowly, trying to follow their own tracks. Behind them the sun rose above the plain; the first rays felt pleasantly warm on their necks. But from the other direction came the wind, and it was slow walking against it.

The creek they followed grew narrower and shallower. Soon it branched out in still smaller furrows. Which one was the dry creek they had first encountered? They stopped and rubbed their smarting eyes. Where were their tracks?

They walked about for a while, searching in vain. From which direction had they come? The sun flooded down on the strange rock formations and the yellow-brown hills — but which rock sheltered their camp? They didn't know; they had lost their way. Robert and Arvid were lost on the wide plain.

-4-

They wandered without rest the whole day. When night fell and darkness enveloped them they lay down, dead tired, on the sandy ground.

They had left camp to look for the mules with nothing except the clothes they walked in. They had brought nothing to eat and nothing to drink. And they had wandered endless hours under the bright sun, through a desolate wilderness, until they were near exhaustion. They had tried to reach the mountains they saw against the horizon, but the mountains had remained as distant as ever.

They went to sleep, but woke up with limbs stiff and aching from the night cold. They opened their eyes toward the heavens; up there glittered the stars with a cold, bluish light, like icicles under an eave. They crept closer to each other, seeking warmth. As soon as the first light of morning broke over the plain they arose and resumed their wandering. They continued, hour after hour, through this region of emptiness and thirst. The wind stayed with them, dug itself into their bodies, whirled dust into nose and eyes, blew it into mouth and ears. The sand clawed and chafed, pierced and hurt; they smelled it, chewed it, tramped it, wallowed in dust. The dusty plain had moved inside them, into their intestines, it spread before them and consumed them.

There could be only one relief from this torture, one word of

142

five letters. A few times they thought they had found it. The ground under their feet sloped, and they looked into a hole. But it was too late: it *had been* a water hole. Now it was empty, dry and light gray, like ashes. After each such disappointment thirst gripped harder around their throats.

In the middle of the day when the sun was at its height the air over the plain felt hot, like burning embers in their lungs. They crept down into the shade behind a hill, panting and giddy. Low, thorny bushes grew around the hill. Everything growing in this region was thorny, prickly and without smell. In other places grass would have been growing — cool, friendly, soft. Here it was hard and sharp and piercing. Even the leaves of the flowering bushes were sharp and hostile. Everything that grew here plagued them, scratched and stung them.

What kind of evil country was this? wondered Arvid. He pulled out the leather pouch in which he kept his watch key. The watch must not be allowed to stop. He always wanted to know the time, even now when he was completely lost.

Arvid swallowed, and Robert swallowed, both of them kept swallowing all the time, without anything in their mouths to swallow. But all the time their thoughts were filled with the thing they would have liked to swallow.

Robert thought: If they only could find a buffalo cow; then he would milk her. Buffalo milk might not taste as fresh as water, but would surely slake the thirst. And buffalo milk was said to be nourishing. It would give them strength to continue. If they had luck enough to run across a cow that had lately calved, he said.

"Buffaloes are wild beasts," answered Arvid. "You couldn't milk them."

Robert stretched out full length against the hillside and immediately went to sleep. Then water came to him; in clear streams it flowed toward his face and he opened his mouth and drank. Spring-cool, refreshing water poured into his mouth, trickled down his throat. He opened his mouth wide. . . . He woke up. He was lying with his face against a boulder and found his tongue licking the dry stone as a cow licks a lump of salt.

He had drunk without anything to drink.

Arvid had pushed both his hands under a thorny bush and was digging a hole in the ground, poking, scratching. A spring

143

might exist anywhere, one never knew. If one only dug deep enough . . .

Robert sniffed the wind. "It smells of dead flesh near here."

"Yes, I smell it too."

"I wonder where . . ."

They arose and set out in the direction of the nauseating odor. Almost within a stone's throw lay the rotten carcass of a horse. They stopped a few steps from it and held their noses. Pieces of hide showed it had been dark brown. The flesh was partly eaten away; the ribs were scraped clean and looked like the peeled willow rushes of a wicker basket. The head had two deep black holes — the eyes had been picked out by carrion birds. The long horse teeth were exposed in a wide, eternal grin.

One hind leg had been torn off and skinned, and it lay some distance from the carcass. It was raised up in a last stiffened kick against the sky. Its steel horseshoe glittered like silver in the sun — it had been newly shod.

Only a few yards from the carcass lay the broken steering shaft of a Conestoga wagon, half buried in sand. One large wheel stood in dust up to the hub, as if it had suddenly been brought to a halt in its rolling.

Robert and Arvid felt sick. They were ready to turn when Arvid exclaimed, "Look! Oh, Jesus!"

He pointed. Something was sticking up in the sand just in front of his feet. Something white, only an inch or two long, spindly, like a skinned birch twig — and on its end was a human nail. It was a finger poking up from the ground in front of them. Arvid had almost stepped on it.

They ran away from the place, the smell of rotten flesh pursuing them.

For a while they went on in silence, the dust whirling around their feet. They did not go in any definite direction, they walked where it was easiest for their feet. They only wanted to get away from the place where . . .

Once Arvid stopped and mumbled hoarsely, "I almost stepped on . . ." He moved his hand to his cracked lips as if trying to help his mouth speak. "Robert! It was a finger . . . ."

And the finger in the sand had pointed right at them.

144

The sun was getting low, losing its power. It grew cooler; the shadows near the hills and boulders lengthened toward evening. They walked as if they were drunk, but their bodies were gripped in a vise of dryness and thirst.

Arvid stumbled into a hole and made no effort to get up; he had fallen head first and lay still. "I can't go on."

Robert sat down and took him by the shoulder, but felt dizziness come over him. The ground was wavering; he must sit until it stopped.

Arvid now rose to his knees and began to dig in the sand with his hands. He made a scoop of his fingers and dug holes a foot or more deep. Below the surface the ground was darker and felt cooler. Robert followed with his eyes, unable to understand. What was Arvid doing? The holes he dug were immediately filled up and obliterated. Yet Arvid continued without stopping, digging in the dust.

"It's all my fault. The mules ran away because my knots were too loose."

Dizziness and nausea for a moment so overwhelmed Robert that he did not know what Arvid was talking about. He understood their predicament, but couldn't understand how they had fallen into it. They were in a dust bowl; they wandered about in a desolate region where the ground, the hills, the boulders consisted of dust, small whirling hard grains. What were they looking for in this huge, empty space? Why had they come here? They were looking for one single thing, and they couldn't find it. They had reached a land of nothing, and it now closed in about them terrifyingly. It had caught them in its ravenous jaws. There they sat, like prisoners in a trap.

Arvid continued to scoop and scratch with his hands in the sand.

It wasn't gold he was digging for.

XVI

THE MISSING GOLD SEEKER

-1-

Wednesday morning Karl Oskar left at the usual hour for work on the church building. A few days earlier Kristina had dismantled her loom, and now she was busy cutting cloth for garments. As soon as Karl Oskar had gone she spread her linen over the table in the big room and began to measure, mark and baste. There were seven in the family who needed new clothes; she was no longer able to patch on the patches of the old. She had sat at the loom during the winter, now she was sitting at the sewing during the summer. She was not an expert seamstress, but the garments would do. The children were growing fast and she took ample measure so that they wouldn't outgrow their clothes too soon; there must be room for them to grow in.

When Robert had dressed and eaten his breakfast, he sat down near Kristina and watched her cutting and basting. He seemed to be willing to talk to her when they were alone; he was more reticent with Karl Oskar.

He said that from now on she wouldn't need to sew and struggle; she could buy dresses for herself of the finest cloth. She laughed in reply; the first things she intended to buy with her money were not silk and velvet to deck herself in. There were a thousand things she needed much more.

Because of Robert's unexpected return, she had almost forgotten her great new concern. For a few weeks now she had known she was again with child. And with this knowledge she had also learned that suckling did not prevent pregnancy, for she was still giving the breast to Ulrika, her last-born. This time the birth would take place in winter, the most inconvenient time of year. But after the happenings of Monday night she had nearly forgotten her new discomfort.

She threw a glance at the Swedish chest, as if wishing to assure herself that it still stood in its place. Riches had come to their

146

house, but for her nothing had changed from one day to the next. She still had her chores, which she couldn't suddenly run away from. But when she had had time to collect her thoughts about the immense bundles of large bills, she had begun to plan how best to use them. More than anything else she wanted help with her work, hired help to relieve her. The money would help her against the fatigue which at times almost crushed her. It was most unbearable at the beginning of a new pregnancy; she had to sit down and rest in the midst of a chore because everything turned black before her eyes.

She wanted to thank her brother-in-law for every blessed moment of rest his gift might bring her. "You are a generous and good human being, Robert."

"You have always been kind and good to me, Kristina."

"I guess board and room cost a lot back there in the gold fields?" she asked.

It was unbelievably expensive, replied Robert, turning his right, healthy ear toward her. A meal cost ten dollars, the poorest lodging fifteen dollars a night and a pair of trousers fifty dollars. All were out after gold and no one was willing to do ordinary chores. The Governor himself had to cook his own food and wash his dishes because his servants had fled to the gold fields. No one in California would work for anyone else, however high the pay. The gold diggers had to do everything for themselves. They couldn't get a shirt washed at any price; they sent their dirty laundry by ship across the Pacific Ocean to China. It was their only way to get something clean. The people of Asia washed for the people of America, the dirt of one continent was rinsed off in another.

"To think they freight dirty laundry to China! It sounds crazy!" Kristina cried. She added, "You must have had a hard time out there, Robert."

"Oh, Kristina! It's terrible on the trail. Life is worth nothing, nothing at all!"

Her hand around the cutting shears came to a standstill, she stopped her shears in the middle of the cloth. A quiver in his voice had startled her.

"Nothing? How is that possible?"

"Life has no greater value than a grain of sand. No one cares about his life. All they care for is gold. Didn't you know this, Kristina?"

147

"No."

"I'll tell you a story. . . ."

And he began: A man in one of the wash gangs suddenly died. He had been in good health in the morning when he walked down to the river. While he was cradling gold a fever suddenly overtook him and killed him, and when his gang returned home in the evening they were carrying his corpse. The next morning they dug a grave in the sand close to a rock and sent to the nearest camp for a minister. As a coffin they used an empty box which had contained smoked hams. The box was too short for the dead man, who had been tall, so they bent his knees. There was no lid for the coffin, but they covered the corpse with a red shirt.

When the box had been lowered into the grave the dead man's comrades gathered around the grave, took off their hats and bowed their heads. Everyone was silent. And the minister, who also was a gold digger, took out his Bible and began to read the service. But when he had read only one short verse he stopped. He stood and stared at the ground. He turned the pages of his book a little, but he didn't read any more. He just stood there and stared into the open grave. The men who had dug the grave for their dead comrade wondered what had got into the minister. They were all in a hurry, it was a warm day, they were thirsty and wanted to have something to drink as soon as possible.

But the minister never completed the service. He read no more. Suddenly he hurled the Bible away into some bushes, its leaves fluttering in the wind, and threw himself on the ground. With both hands he began to dig in the sand at the edge of the grave.

The men thought at first that he had had a sunstroke and lost his mind. But then they noticed he was picking up something and putting it into his pocket. And as soon as they realized what it was, they too became active. They all threw themselves into the grave, scratching and digging with their fingers as fast as they could. For they had discovered the same thing as the minister when he began reading over the corpse: nuggets were glittering down there.

Soon there was a great fight over the grave. The box with the corpse was trampled to bits, and the men used the pieces as weapons. Then they tore into each other with their fists, and finally knives and guns came out. It ended with the minister shot to death and one of the funeral guests pierced through the heart with a knife.

148

Several were badly wounded. The survivors made peace and divided the gold from the grave among them.

So it turned out to be three funerals instead of one. The old grave was turned into a gold mine, a great big one, and the three graves were dug some distance away. Now they had no minister to conduct services, since he had turned into a corpse, and there was no reading over the graves. Instead they fired four revolver shots; the survivors thus honored their dead comrades who had fallen in an honest fight for gold.

While Robert was telling the story Kristina had held her shears motionless. "What a terrible story!"

"Karl Oskar thinks I'm always lying," said Robert. "It's best to keep silent while he's around. But I know you believe me, Kristina."

She believed every word — while he talked. Only when he had finished did wonder and doubt cross her mind. "If this is the truth, then they live like wild beasts in California!"

"No one cares about his life. But all care about the gold."

"They're out of their minds if they value gold more than their lives."

Robert leaned toward her and spoke in a lowered voice, as if confiding a great secret to her. "The gold diggers are people who want to die."

Kristina forgot her sewing and looked into his wan face. The skin was so taut across his forehead and cheeks that it seemed as if the bones beneath tried to push through. "But you yourself? Did you go to California because you didn't wish to live? To kill yourself?"

"I meant the others. It was different with me. My real errand was not to dig gold."

And he looked beyond her, out through the window, at the tall maples outside, as he added emphatically, "I did care for life. But I didn't know this until afterward."

He then sat silent for a long while.

- 2 -

The intense heat had started in earnest that week. In Minnesota's oppressive summer air, chores were performed languidly; motion alone was an effort. Kristina was using her shears and her needle, the lightest tools a person could use, but she often dried her perspiring forehead with the corner of her apron. It was cellar-cool here inside, however, compared to the sweltering heat out in the sun.

The lake water was already tepid, and that morning Johan, Märta and Harald — the three children Kristina called "big" — had, after persistent begging, obtained their mother's permission to go bathing in the shallow inlet near their field. Kristina would have liked to cool her own body along with them, but she felt it could be dangerous to bathe in the lake while pregnant. She asked Robert to go with the children and see that they didn't wade too far out.

After the noon meal Robert said that he would like to wander through the forest; he wanted to see the Indian cliff where he had once gone hunting. Kristina warned him that a fatal accident had taken place below the Indian last spring. An American settler from Hay Lake had been found dead under a boulder which had fallen on him. The cliff was cracking, and rocks were falling in big piles all the time. It took only a small stone to kill a person, if it happened to hit the head; he must be careful and not go too near the Indian.

Robert smiled, exposing his gaping gums. He was not a settler, he had not stolen any land from the brown people; he didn't believe the Indian would fling any stones on an innocent person.

Kristina went into his room to make his bed while he was out. As she turned the pillow she made a discovery: Under it lay a watch, with a heavy brass chain coiled around it. She stared at it in disbelief. Robert had not displayed a watch since his return. As far as she knew he had never owned one. And if he did, then why didn't he wear it? It couldn't be a stolen watch, she felt sure. But why had he concealed it?

She noticed it was an old watch, scratched and badly worn. She put it to her ear; it had stopped. It had stopped at fifteen minutes after twelve, either at noon or in the night. The key to wind it was fastened to the chain. Perhaps the watch had stopped because it had not been wound, or perhaps the works were broken.

Kristina replaced her find under the pillow after she had made the bed, but her thoughts were occupied with it when she returned to her sewing.

She began basting a coat for Karl Oskar, but had barely taken twenty stitches when she saw an Indian approaching the house. At first she felt a sense of fear. Just now when no men folk were at home... The Indian came to the back of the house and into the kitchen, and then she recognized him — often these brown people were so much alike that she couldn't tell one from another. This was a very old Indian with thin hair, sunken cheeks, and skin wrinkled like cracks in dried clay. Last winter during the intense cold he had come several times; she had given him boiled milk. Each time he had sat long in the warmth of the fire. He spoke some kind of English, and Karl Oskar had understood that he had been converted to Christianity by missionaries who had preached among the Indians. He insisted he was a hundred and fifty years old, but Karl Oskar must have misunderstood him in this.

As soon as Kristina recognized the caller her fear vanished — this old Indian was not dangerous. He carried something which he handed her with a few grunts; it was a piece of meat, a large shoulder of venison. The Indian had brought her a gift! Surprised and pleased, she thanked him in Swedish: She had just been wondering what to have for supper — what a fine roast this would make!

The old man had carried the piece without any protection, and she soon discovered dark spots on the red meat: flies. That looked suspicious in this heat. She smelled it. The odor was also suspicious. In fact, the venison probably had turned bad and could not be used for food. But Kristina did not show any sign of this; she neither wanted nor dared to hurt the feelings of the Indian. His people did not discriminate between fresh and spoiled food; to an Indian stomach the meat was, of course, acceptable; the giver would undoubtedly have eaten it willingly. So she smiled at the old Indian, thanked him again and put away the venison as if it were a valuable gift. In return she gave him a fresh loaf of their new wheat bread, and he smiled back at her with his wrinkled mouth and uttered many grunts that sounded friendly and grateful.

After he had left, Kristina picked up the venison, carried it to the dunghill behind the stable and threw it as far as she could. What would the giver have said had he seen this? Probably the old man had carried his heavy burden a long way to her. And even though the gift was unusable, it strengthened Kristina in her belief that the brown people were not evil and heartless. She had

151

known it before: If one showed them kindness, they would do the same in return. They could be as grateful as white Christian people. Perhaps there was not too great a difference in the souls of whites and Indians. If the Indians were left in peace, they would leave the settlers in peace. But when they were taken advantage of they became violent and ferocious. They were beginning to suffer from starvation because their game was coming to an end. It was the white people who had hunted and killed almost all the game in the forest. The Indians would never of their own will have given up their hunting grounds, since they could not live without them.

As the afternoon wore on she waited for Robert to return from his walk in the forest. Karl Oskar came home from the church building at his usual hour, and she showed him what she had found under Robert's pillow.

The moment Karl Oskar saw the watch he exclaimed, "It's Arvid's!"

"Arvid's?"

"I recognize it."

He picked up the watch and looked closer. "I'm quite sure. It's the nickel-plated watch Arvid got from his father when he left Sweden. He showed it to me many times; he always bragged about its cylinder works."

Kristina had grabbed hold of her husband's arm. "Arvid's watch! Oh, dear Lord, what does it mean?"

Karl Oskar was weighing the watch in the palm of his hand. "It can only mean that Arvid is dead."

A man used his watch as long as he lived. It measured his allotted time. No one gave up his watch before his death.

This watch had cost ten riksdaler, twelve with the chain, Arvid had said that day when they all met and started on their America journey. It was the sum of money his father, Petter of Kråkesjö, had been able to save during his forty years as a cotter. It was Arvid's inheritance that Karl Oskar now held in his palm.

"Poor Arvid! I wonder how he came to his end."

"I'm afraid we'll never know — at least not from Robert."

"Why does he hide it?"

"Why does he hide everything from us? As yet he has said barely a word about himself. And no one knows when he lies or tells the truth."

Robert did tell stories, said Kristina, but she had never noticed that he invented them with evil intentions, in order to hurt someone or gain something for himself. He had never hurt anyone with his lies except himself.

"This is something he doesn't want known," said Karl Oskar. "But I'll show him the watch. He must tell us about Arvid!"

"But if you won't believe what he says . . ."

"He has lied too much to me! And now I'm beginning to wonder again. How about those — "

He cut the sentence off. But Kristina understood: those money bundles.

"I can't wait till Saturday!" exclaimed Karl Oskar. "I must know about those bills as soon as possible. Tomorrow is Thursday. I'll speak to Algot at the building — he and I will drive together to Stillwater on Friday."

"I don't believe Robert would deceive us about the money he has given us," said Kristina firmly. "You musn't suspect your brother of such evil."

"What can one believe after this? What can I think?" Karl Oskar put the nickel watch into his pocket.

Kristina was getting worried about Robert. But Karl Oskar felt his brother could take care of himself. He knew all the paths around there, and he had just returned from a much longer and more dangerous journey.

It got to be bedtime and Robert still hadn't shown up. Kristina pleaded with her husband, "Please go out and look for him."

By now Karl Oskar too was worried. He pulled on his boots. Yes, he would go out and look. But then at last heavy shuffling was heard and Robert stepped into the kitchen and sank down on the nearest chair. His boots were muddy and he dropped his hat on the floor; he looked completely exhausted and panted noisily.

"You're late," said Kristina. "Supper is cold."

But Robert shook his head; he didn't want any food. A mug of milk would be all he'd take tonight. His stomach was upset — he had vomited a couple of times out in the forest. It might be the heat; he was better now and would go to bed at once.

He was seized with a fit of coughing. When it let up he began to drink the milk in small swallows, while he talked:

He had been sitting resting below the Indian head, unable to tear himself away from the place. The cliff had changed since he saw it four years ago. Now the Indian had deep wrinkles in his forehead, his eye sockets had grown deeper and blacker, and all his teeth had fallen out and lay as heaps of stones below. Yes, like Robert himself, the Indian had lost teeth. And now, high on his rock looking out over all the new houses around the lake, he seemed profoundly sad. The Indian was mourning — mourning not one single person, but thousands of people, his people, all those who were driven away by the white settlers. The Indian's face was stricken with sorrow; when one's forehead cracked and one's eyes fell out and teeth dropped from one's jaws, all this in only four years, surely such a person has gone through deep sorrow.

Karl Oskar and Kristina listened in confusion to this speech about the sand cliff. It sounded almost as if Robert were talking about himself. He had deep furrows in his forehead, young as he was; his eyes protruded, their glitter gone; and he had lost his teeth.

"Great rocks have tumbled down."

They should go there to see for themselves that he told the truth. Big chunks, from the very eyes of the Indian, had fallen. Had anyone ever wept such tears? Tears of stone, enduring tears that would remain as long as the earth stood. Those tears were wept only during great weeping for a whole race that was being destroyed. A thousand years from now people would still see the enduring tears below the cliff of Ki-Chi-Saga's shore; the piles of stones would remain there as a memorial to the destruction of thousands of people.

When Robert had said all this to his brother and sister-in-law he went to his bed in the gable room.

Kristina asked: What had happened to Robert while he was away? In the morning too he had talked in riddles.

Karl Oskar still had Arvid's watch in his pocket; he had meant to pull it out this evening, but had forgotten about it while his brother talked of the Indian who had wept tears of stone. Now he must wait until morning for information about the watch's owner, the missing gold seeker.

XVII

THE THIRD NIGHT

It takes no longer to die than it takes to lift the hand and point a finger. I tried to buzz that fact into your head many times; you wouldn't believe how suddenly death can sweep a man off his feet and into his grave on the California Trail.

You noticed Kristina found the watch. Now they will want to know what happened to Arvid. But you have no reason to tell them, unless you want to.

You don't think you can sleep in peace tonight, do you? Listen now how your ear buzzes, like the wind that lured two muleteers to a dust bowl and thirst, like that treacherous wind on the plains that covered their tracks and prevented them from finding their way back.

Listen, gold seeker!

- 1 -

The sun's fire had burned out toward evening. Robert and Arvid continued their wandering. They must not stay in one place, they must always move on, forward. And they managed to keep going even though every step hurt. They stumbled across the plain, they held onto each other's arms for support. Two twisting bodies straggled along, held together in a firm grip; two bodies walked more steadily than one. Two youths walking arm in arm, like a couple in love, like a boy and a girl walking across the grass of a meadow on a cool June evening. For they were inseparable and would never part.

A few times they saw creatures moving over the plain: red-furred, sharp-nosed animals in small packs. They were the size of small dogs and moved as quickly and softly over the ground as the wind itself. They must be carrion animals, feeding on the dead horse.

Dusk was falling; no longer did they see the holes and crevices where they stepped. Arvid fell down. Robert lifted him under the arms and helped him to his feet again, even though he would

155

have preferred to stretch out and lie on the ground beside him.

As they walked on Arvid pulled out his watch; before it got too dark he wanted to know the time. And when parting from his father he had been instructed to keep the watch clean at all times. Now he was afraid sand might have got into his vest pocket when he fell. Arvid held the nickel watch against his swollen, cracked lips and blew on it as it dangled on its chain, blowing away the sand. Then he turned the lining of his pocket inside out and brushed it well with his fingers before he put the watch back.

Around them the cliffs and sand hills took on strange shapes as night fell. They seemed like monstrous creatures: a buffalo ox's spindly body, while a desert wolf with a thirty-foot tail opened its deep cliff jaws in front of them, and the wall of distant hills produced camels and dromedaries with humped backs and swaying necks.

The evening coolness had cleared Robert's head and he could again think clearly. He had thrown away his shoes, and the sand felt cooler when he walked barefoot. But inside he was filled with fire. His tongue had become a swollen, burning lump. There must be water somewhere, somewhere they must find it. It was still on the earth, it couldn't be gone, it couldn't have dried up everywhere. They must search on, they would find it at last.

-2-

Over the biggest dromedary's dark hump the moon rose. From the moon disk, three-quarters full, a pale, clear light was diffused over the sandy plain. Suddenly they found themselves in a hollow.

Arvid was the first to discover it: Something glittered in the moonlight at the bottom of the hollow. He saw it for only a second — then he let out a hoarse howl.

He pulled his hand violently from Robert's, rushed forward a few paces and threw himself headlong on the ground. Robert had seen nothing yet; he came stumbling behind, half asleep. What was the matter with Arvid? Was he seeing water again?

Arvid lay on his stomach, drinking from a small pool in the bottom of the deep hollow. It had been a big water hole, but had now narrowed to a small puddle. And Arvid was slurping and drinking. Robert not only saw the water, he could hear it from the noise his friend made in drinking. But when he came closer he could see in the clear moonlight that it was no fresh, gushing spring they had found. It was a mudhole with stagnant, dirty water. It did not look like anything to drink.

Nevertheless, he threw himself on his knees beside his comrade. And then such a nauseating odor filled his nostrils that he pulled back. The pool stank from something rotten, and his will to quench his thirst was checked by a feeling of nausea.

But Arvid was stretched out full length, his whole chin in the pool, like an animal that drinks by putting its snout in the water. He was lapping and drinking in long swallows, puffing, panting, snorting, drinking. He got water in his windpipe and coughed.

"It stinks like hell," mumbled Robert.

Arvid did not worry about that. He continued to drink, and at each swallow he let out a muffled groan of satisfaction.

Robert again bent down over the pool, driven by his almost insufferable thirst. His mouth touched the water; he must overcome the smell, he must drink — anyone as thirsty as he must drink anything, however nasty. In the moonlight it seemed as if the water was cleaner and clearer on the opposite side of the pool. He crawled on his knees away from Arvid to the other side. Here it did look less nauseating.

Beside him he saw a post driven into the ground, with a piece of board nailed to it. There were letters on the board, clumsily written in chalk. After one look at the board Robert was on his feet again.

LOOK AT THIS
Don't drink — The water is Poison — Death

The post with the narrow board across it rose beside the water hole like a cross on a grave. Robert looked at the wooden cross for one long, frightened second. Then he yelled, "Stop, Arvid! It's death!"

And then he remembered what the Mexican had said: The water holes along the trail were not to be trusted. Clearly, someone had drunk of this water before, discovered it was poisonous and put up the sign to warn others.

"For Christ's sake, stop drinking!" He grabbed his comrade by the shoulder to pull him from the water. But Arvid had already raised himself up on his knees. He had drunk a lot, he had satisfied his thirst. Water trickled in big drops from the corners of his mouth.

"Helluva dirty spring. Doesn't quench the thirst much."

"It's poisonous!"

Robert pointed to the sign where the warning could be read in large letters. But it meant nothing to Arvid.

"Arvid, you must vomit it up!"

"The hell I must."

"Don't you hear? The water is poisonous! You've drunk your death!"

"Oh, it couldn't be that bad."

Robert pulled Arvid away into a thicket of low bushes at the edge of the muddy pool. His friend must not be tempted to drink any more. "Puke, Arvid! Put your finger in your throat! Get rid of the water!"

But Arvid refused to think that he had drunk death. His belly was full of water, brimful, but he felt no discomfort. He refused to put his finger in his throat, he didn't want to vomit. All he wanted was to lie down and sleep. His stomach felt a little heavy after all the water, a rest would be good. And with a tired sigh of contentment he stretched out on his back under the bushes.

"Please, Arvid, listen to me! You must get rid of the water!" Robert tried to put his own fingers into Arvid's throat and make him vomit.

"Let me alone! I'm all right. Let me sleep now."

There was nothing more to be done. Arvid refused to move an inch. Why should he put his finger down his throat? He wasn't sick. All he wanted was sleep; it was the middle of the night and he was more tired than anyone on earth had ever been before.

Arvid pushed his head under some low branches, as if he wished to hide it. He went to sleep at once and snored noisily in deep breaths.

Suddenly it was very dark; a great cloud had crossed the moon and cut off its light. The contours of the landscape with its cliffs and boulders and sharp grass and bushes were enveloped in darkness. Somewhere under that black mantle lay the chewed-off horse shank with a new shoe, and near it a white finger pointing from the sand.

Robert sat beside his sleeping comrade, staring out into the desolate night. His vision could not penetrate far in this darkness. He could not see the pool, even though it must be less than thirty feet away. He could not see the wooden cross beside it. But it was there all right, the words remained where they had been chalked on the wood: "Look at this . . .Death." Death remained, it was quite near. It had only hidden itself. Perhaps it did so at times, to fool one. But it was there, and it stayed close to them.

Robert had two names for death, and they sounded very different to his ear. The Swedish word was hard and frightening and threatening: *"Döden!"* It would be the clarion call over earth on doomsday morning: *"Dö-ö-ö-den!"* The word echoed with fear, it was a sound without mercy, a wailing without comfort. But the English "death" — it sounded soft and peaceful, quiet and restful. It didn't call for an end to life in theatening tones. "Death" was soft-voiced, merciful, it approached silently, kindly. It brought comfort and compassion to a person at the end of his life. "Death" — it was a whisper in the ear, it didn't frighten or terrify, it said in the kindest of words how things stood, it said in all friendliness: *Now you will die.*

But it was only due to the softer word that the English death sounded kinder than the Swedish, and words were nothing but foolery. The English death lurking back there in the dark had no mercy either.

Arvid had drunk of death's water and now he slept and was satisfied. Robert had not drunk, he still had the thirst that consumed life in him. If he drank from the pool he would die. If he didn't drink, he would die.

He moved his swollen tongue; he said something to God. He wanted to tell the Lord of Life and Death that he did not wish to die. He wanted to explain: Life was dear in the moment it was to be taken away. Never was it dearer. Never had it been dearer to him than during this night in the wilderness. And how could his Creator demand of him that he, only in his twentieth year, must be consumed by unbearable thirst, his body to distintegrate until only the bones remained — like the rotting hind leg of the horse, helplessly kicking toward heaven? No, he wanted to keep that body intact, walk on his feet over ground that was covered with soft, fresh, green grass — and he wanted to drink of the clear, fresh, running water of earth!

159

Water, water! He must find it!

And Robert sank down against the body of his sleeping comrade. Confusion entered his thoughts, his head grew dizzy and he fell into a feverish sleep.

- 3 -

He was awakened by a groan. First he heard it from a great distance, then it came nearer, and at last it was close to his ear.

"O-o-oh — o-o-oh! My guts! They're killing me!"

Arvid was rolling over in the sand, pulling his knees against his chin, twisting himself into a bundle, stretching out again, throwing himself to and fro. He fumbled for Robert, got a viselike hold on his arm. Robert's hands found his and their fingers twisted together.

"It's killing me! It's tearing me to pieces! Help me, Robert! Please, help me! Help ... me ... "

Two great swollen eyes stared in the dark from Arvid's face. He held his hands against his stomach and rolled over again. Then, violently, he pulled away his hands and dug them into the sand, scratched wildly, kicked the sand with his feet until it whirled in a cloud around them. He was digging a hole where he lay, while his cries rose to a howling pitch.

"O-o-o-oh! O-o-oh! God ... help ... me ..."

It had already come — Arvid had death in him. He had unsuspectingly opened his mouth and in deep swallows brought it into his body. Now it tore at him and he cried out his pain as loudly as he could. Robert felt in the dark for his flailing hands. If he only had some medicine, a few drops to give Arvid, some salve to put on, any kind of help. But he had nothing.

"O-o-o-oh! Help me! Please! Help! O-o-o-oh!"

Arvid dug again, beat wildly about him, yelled until his voice and strength failed. As he weakened, his wail sank to a pitiful whine, a quiet whimper, a feeble sound like a bird's peep. At last he gave only a weak, low complaint. In his pain-ridden impotence he groped again for his friend's hands and crept close to him. They lay together. Robert could feel Arvid's burning breath in his face, his heart pumping like a smith's bellows.

"Don't leave me ... please."

They were two comrades lying together. They had come to-

160

gether from Sweden to North America, they had started out together on the road to California, they had traveled together thousands of miles, and now they were still together. They had sealed with a handshake their decision never to part.

"Don't leave me."

Arvid had once wanted to turn back, but he had kept his promise and stayed with his friend. And now he could trust Robert to stay with him. The two of them would never part. How many times had they repeated that? And it was said here again: "I won't leave you."

Arvid could trust him — they would never part. But as his cries gradually lessened there was nothing to keep Robert entirely awake. He slid into a sort of doze, between waking and sleeping; one moment he was asleep, the next he was awake. He felt Arvid's fingers fumbling for his and held onto them even harder. A cool wind swept over them. He moved closer to his comrade, who now lay almost silent; Arvid's breathing sounded choked.

It was still dark, and Robert did not notice when Arvid unhooked his watch chain and pulled the watch from his vest pocket. But his ear registered something he had heard in his sleep: "Take good care of it . . . good care . . . good . . ."

But now Robert wasn't listening, he was where he wished to be: He was thrown up high over mountains and deserts, up to the stars and the sky; there he met an immense river that flooded out of heaven. In that river he sank down, sank down to the bottom, to the bottom — and the bottom at last turned into the sand where he was lying. He lay there thrown down from heaven.

And then it was morning.

The sun stung his eyes and awakened him. He rubbed them, looked around, and then everything came back.

"Arvid!"

Arvid lay close to him, stretched out on his stomach. He lay on his face in the hole he had dug with his own hands. His hands lay palms upward, filled with sand. He did not move, he lay still, like the ground under him. His face was turned down, his nostrils in the sand. Robert stretched out his hand, felt his comrade's cheek and turned the face toward him. He saw two glassy eyes, their vision broken, yellow sand grains clinging to the eyeballs.

Robert called Arvid's name several times. But the body beside him did not reply.

161

In turning Arvid's face something had stuck to Robert's fingers; they were red, bloody. Arvid's chin was furrrowed with wide red streaks. He had vomited blood in great quantities. In the corners of his mouth it had coagulated into thick, blackened lumps, it had spread across his cheeks like blossoming flowers.

Everything came back to Robert without his understanding it. He called Arvid, he called louder but received no answer. He noticed that Arvid's fingers were bent to dig with; he lay there immobile, but it looked as if he wanted to dig his own grave. Or what was he digging for?

And over the golden-brown hills flared the sun's flame. A new morning had dawned in the land of dust and heat and thirst.

-4-

Robert's dizziness returned and he lost consciousness. He was again pleased as he heard the sound of running water; new rivers were streaming over him, and he lay down to drink. But into his mouth ran a hard, crunching water which hurt his swollen tongue, and he spit out the sand he had been chewing.

But Arvid had found a water hole and had hurried to drink. The hole stank but he drank and felt no discomfort from it and then lay down to sleep. He awakened and called and called, but he was still lying there. They were not separated.

They had set out together to look for gold, for they wanted to be rich and free. And there lay Arvid on his stomach. Help me, he had cried, and he had dug as if this would relieve him. He was digging for gold, but the only thing he dug up was potato peelings — whole piles of them, the whole heaving boat full of them. And their boss had been angry and called Arvid a son of a bitch. Lucky that he didn't understand English — it might have hurt his feelings. Arvid had once been accused of going after a heifer and had been given the nickname "the Bull of Nybacken." He had emigrated to get away from that name, he had traveled all the way here, to dig this hole where he now lay so quietly.

Beside his friend's arm Robert saw something that glittered. It wasn't gold, it was Arvid's watch, and it was only nickel-plated. The chain was brass. It was the chain that glittered. And Arvid was so careful with his watch. Why had he thrown it away like that? It could easily get sand in the works. He must retrieve it.

Robert stretched out his hand for the watch and held it to his ear. It had stopped. Sand must have got into the works; it had stopped a little after eleven, but now it was early in the morning.

So nice Arvid was still here, they weren't separated. Arvid lay still, he had covered his face with flowers. There lay two big roses right over his mouth, dark red now in the sun. Robert stared vacantly. Where had Arvid found those beautiful flowers on his face?

But Robert was still thirsty; he must drink, or he wouldn't reach California. He must get up and look for a water hole.

Oh! Back there a stream is bursting forth! A spring must suddenly have opened up. But the water is running in the other direction, it's running away from him; it's out of his reach. He must run to catch it! Water, water — now at last he had found it!

He yelled until he lost his breath, he cried out in wild joy, "Arvid! Arvid! Hurry! Come here and let's drink! Water! Come! Come!"

He staggered on wobbly legs. But Arvid remained still.

Robert ran after the water that streamed over the sand. It was a broad, gurgling stream; it ran faster, he followed, he ran as fast as he could, used all his strength. He was barefooted, but he didn't feel the sharp sand grinding against his sore feet as long as he saw the stream in front of him.

But it ran faster than he could. And all at once it was gone. He scanned the broad plain. Where was it? He stopped and stood there like a hunter who looks disappointedly after the escaping game.

Robert wandered about alone in the wilderness. Unmeasurable time elapsed. The world was a plain, a sun above it and a firebrand in his throat. He walked, he fell, he rose again. The sun burned and he crept into the shade under cliffs and boulders. He sat down to rest. But the stream came running by again in front of him. He rushed up and struggled after it until it was gone.

He chased many running streams which he never caught up with. He walked until the sand under his feet turned into grass. It felt different — softer. He tramped through short, withered grass, buffalo grass. He recognized it easily; their mules liked that kind of grass. And wasn't he looking for a pair of mules that had strayed? And hadn't he just heard their names called?

"Hekee! Hinni! Cheekte!"

163

He himself had called those names only a short while ago, when he and Arvid were looking for the strayed animals. It was someone else calling now. He had heard that same voice call animals before, and the animals had been dirty gray, as big as heifers, long-eared, spindly-legged. They had had coal-black eyes and braying voices. They had carried heavy packs, moved slowly on their thin legs, the sand whirling softly around their small hoofs as they crossed the plain. Mexican mules—that was what they were called.

"Hinni! Cheekte!"

Mexican . . . Now the call was clearer, sounded closer, and he recognized the voice. He had heard it sing by the campfire:

> *"Oh, the good time has come at last,*
> *We need no more complain, sir!"*

He tried to repeat the words and answer the singer, but his swollen tongue produced only a hoarse croaking. His reply did not reach far enough, did not reach his master — yes, it was he whose voice that was.

And the voice came closer. It was next to his ear. But in the same moment Robert slid away, fluttered out into the distance without being able to stop. Just as the familiar voice spoke into his ear, he floated all the way up into heaven, and all the stars glittered before him. Now he was so high above everything that he would never get down to earth again.

But up there in heaven stood a very little man in a red jacket and a broad hat, and he leaned over Robert, and he had black eyes, kind mule eyes, and a nose that was almost as big as Karl Oskar's. Judging by the nose it could be Karl Oskar, his brother. And he spoke like a brother:

"Poor boy! My muleteer. I've been looking for you."

And Robert was on earth again and lay on his back in the buffalo grass. He had fallen down from heaven and he held something in his arms, held it hard; with trembling hands he held on to a gourd.

"Oh, poor fellow. Just in time. My muleteer . . ."

Robert drank. He drank a water that stayed with him. It couldn't disappear, it was shut up in a bottle, in a gourd which he held in his hands — this water did not run away from him.

It's already growing toward morning and you are awake still, tossing your head back and forth on the pillow, trying to find a place which will silence me. Arvid is dead — "Help me, Robert, help me!" — but I'm your faithful comrade. You and Arvid had to part at last, but you and I will keep together. I shall never leave you.

Listen, gold seeker, where you toss on your bed I have preserved the sound of the wind over that dust plain. Can you hear how it whistles across those empty spaces in that country of dust and thirst? And the wind roars over the earth at will through the night! It quickly obliterates a wanderer's tracks and covers a wretched, naked, lone finger pointing accusingly from the sand.

XVIII

WILDCATS OF DIFFERENT BREEDS

-1-

On Thursday morning, as on every weekday morning, Karl Oskar was up and about before daylight. When he had dressed he walked over to the old Swedish chest against the wall and raised the lid. He picked up the two money bundles and held them in his hands for a few thoughful moments. He had picked them up and held them like this on two previous mornings, Tuesday and Wednesday. This was the third morning.

Cash — to him it was the most annoying word in the language of the foreign country. Cash — it was what he lacked. No cash, Mr. Nelson? You must pay cash, Mr. Nelson! How many times had he received that humiliating reply when he had asked for credit in a store? *No cash?* Those two words could be used to signify a settler's situation in Minnesota.

But here he was holding two bundles of crisp cash — four thousand American dollars, fifteen thousand Swedish riksdaler. These bundles would end all his worries about cash. Karl Oskar pinched the black-and-green bills. Were they worth their stated value? Could he trust the gift even though he could not trust the giver?

He must control his impatience for one day more. Tomorrow,

165

Friday, he would find out at the bank. Originally he had agreed with a neighbor to drive to Stillwater on Saturday, but after the discovery of Arvid's watch his suspicions had flared up again; by going to the bank on Friday he would cut down his uncertainty one day. Tomorrow he would know!

Meanwhile Kristina began to prepare breakfast. She had been thinking over what Robert had said to her yesterday, and it had become a still greater riddle. She had known her brother-in-law for ten years, but yesterday he had seemed a complete stranger. She wondered that Karl Oskar and he could be brothers. How could two people so different have had the same father and mother? As long as she had known them Karl Oskar had been the big brother and Robert the little brother, but there was a difference between them much greater than the ten years that separated them. Karl Oskar was like most of the hard-working, enterprising settlers out here, but Robert was not like anyone else she had ever known. There was something both stimulating and disconcerting about him; no one could guess one moment what he would do the next. And at times he acted as if he himself didn't know what he ought to be doing here on earth — as if it didn't matter at all what he did while his life flowed to its end.

Karl Oskar had often said that he regretted having brought his younger brother along to America; he fitted this country like a square peg in a round hole. He was too soft and lazy and lacked persistence, said the ten-years-older brother. And now Robert had become rich before anyone else from Ljuder! On Monday evening Robert had silenced Karl Oskar with the black pouch. As soon as he had showed his riches, the roles of the two brothers had been reversed. Now it was Robert who did the talking, now it was he who knew what was what. The younger had become more important than the older, and who could now say that Robert didn't fit in America?

But this new big brother who had returned from the land of gold had as yet not said twenty words about his riches. No one could complain that he bragged about them, no one could accuse him of big talk. And, like Karl Oskar, Kristina felt that there was something wrong and perhaps frightening about his silence.

Today Robert was up earlier than usual, and he came into the kitchen before Kristina had put the food on the table. His eyes were bloodshot, as if he hadn't slept. She had noticed that he slept badly; a few times at night she had heard him go to the kitchen for a drink. She put the food on the table and called Karl Oskar. He seemed surprised that his brother was already up; this was the first time since Robert's return that he had appeared at the breakfast table.

Robert's appetite was poor. He chewed slowly and had trouble in swallowing. Kristina urged him time and again to eat more; he ate less than the little boys, Johan and Harald, who had their breakfast standing up at the table — children were said to grow faster if they ate standing upright. For Robert's sake she had baked a big cornmeal-and-egg pancake, but he took only a small piece of it.

It was unusually quiet around the table in the kitchen this morning. But when they had finished Karl Oskar pulled the watch from his pocket and placed it beside Robert's plate.

"Why do you have Arvid's watch?"

Robert showed no surprise or confusion when he saw the watch. "I put it under my pillow. I noticed it was gone."

"Why do you hide the watch? Why don't you tell us the truth? Why don't you dare say that Arvid is dead?"

That was three questions at one time. But Robert only replied, "You have a right to ask, Karl Oskar. That you have."

He was interrupted by an attack of persistent, hollow coughing.

"The first evening you said Arvid had remained in the gold fields."

"Yes, I said he remained out there. He did." Robert had finished his coughing for this time.

"But you didn't say he was dead. That he had sacrificed his life."

"Who doesn't sacrifice his life on the Trail? Everyone does, one way or another."

"You talk in riddles! Tell us the truth straight out!"

Karl Oskar was growing impatient. But his younger brother remained sitting quite calmly at the table; he picked up the watch and coiled the broad brass chain slowly around his forefinger. Kristina rose and began to clear the table. Without interfering in the conversation between the two brothers she listened intently. She told the children to leave the kitchen.

167

Karl Oskar had asked but had received no clear replies. Robert twisted the chain of Arvid's watch still tighter around his finger until it remained there like a thick gold ring. He squeezed the watch in the palm of his hand. Kristina noticed that his elbows were beginning to tremble.

Robert's eyes looked so big and glassy today. She felt his forehead with her hand. "You're burning hot! You have a fever!"

She whispered to Karl Oskar not to cross-examine his brother in this way; they could see he was sick.

Her cautioning had an effect. Karl Oskar rose, and his next question came in a milder voice: "We are two brothers — why don't you confide in me?"

"The very first evening I came home you said to me, 'Stop lying!' I had just begun to confide in you then. But you didn't believe me. You said, 'I know you're back without a single nickel!' "

Robert had risen too, and he straightened his narrow, caved-in shoulders. They stood shoulder to shoulder, and with Robert straightened up he was two inches taller than Karl Oskar. Not even measured physically was Karl Oskar any longer the big brother. And his cheeks took on a slight touch of red as he remembered that Monday evening when his onetime younger brother had got the upper hand — "I brought along a little cash for pocket money."

"But couldn't we be honest with each other again? Why did you hide the watch? No one is going to think that you killed Arvid to take it from him."

Robert turned his face quickly toward Karl Oskar, and his reply came as a sudden thrust: "Maybe you're right! Perhaps I did kill Arvid! Perhaps it was my doing."

"Are you out of your senses?"

"He wanted to return once, but I — " Robert stopped suddenly. Then he said, panting, "I can't . . . Leave me alone. I'm not strong enough. Please, Karl Oskar, leave me in peace. Forgive me. . . . I can't stand it."

He rushed to the door and opened it with a heavy jerk at the handle. While they stood there, perplexed at his sudden outburst, he ran out of the kitchen as if he were pursued. They looked after him through the window. He had thrown himself face down on the ground near the newly planted gooseberry bushes and lay there immobile.

"Leave your brother alone," said Kristina. "You can't do anything else."

"No." Karl Oskar sighed irresolutely. "What else can one do? Nothing."

-2-

Karl Oskar left for his church building. A few moments later Robert came back in, and now he was like himself again. Today he wanted to visit the Indian, he said. And Kristina watched him walk off through the pine grove to the west.

She went to make up his bed in the gable room, and then it was that she discovered large dark-red spots on his pillowcase. They hadn't been there yesterday. The spots must be blood which had oozed from his sick ear during the night.

She had been wondering if Robert suffered from some consuming disease; he had a nasty cough, and sometimes he couldn't stand food. Such troubles were not caused by a bad ear. Did he perhaps have chest fever? When she was alone with him she would ask about this; he seemed to confide in her rather than in his brother. Now she felt that the red spots on the pillowcase had told more about him than he himself had done so far.

Kristina sat down to her sewing and pulled out the basting from a pair of trousers she had sewn for Johan. It was still early in the day, but the heat was already making her perspire. Each day was growing hotter. The bigger children had gone down to the lake again and must be splashing about in the inlet. Outside the chickens kept cackling; she now had a whole score of laying hens, all from eggs of the hen Ulrika had given her. The cow Miss had lately calved, but was not yet well and stood tethered down in the meadow.

Then the oppressive stillness of the summer day was broken by loud cries from the children. Kristina dropped Johan's trousers on the floor and was outside in a second.

Johan and Märta came from the lake carrying Harald between them. Harald's face was red and his eyes wild with fright. Kristina took the boy in her arms and carried him inside, putting him on the bed in the gable room. There was no use questioning him — he couldn't talk; he panted for breath and groaned and shivered.

169

His mother felt a sudden pressure across her chest. "What happened? Did Harald fall and hurt himself?"

"It was a wildcat! A great big wildcat!"

Johan and Märta were talking at the same time: While they had been out in the water Harald had crept in among the bushes on the shore. Suddenly he had come rushing back, yelling at the top of his voice, and they had heard a terrible growling and hissing — Harald had come across a big wildcat that was hiding in the thicket. They had seen it too, it was gray and had a thick short tail and thick legs. Its head was enormous, with long whiskers — like an ordinary cat, but much bigger.

Johan and Märta had been so scared when they saw it that they had yelled too, and with all three of them yelling the cat had been frightened and sneaked back into the bushes again. They rushed home, but had to carry Harald, who was so frightened he couldn't walk by himself.

Kristina pulled off the boy's clothes to see if the wildcat had hurt him, but could find no marks on the child's body. It must have been the scare that had affected him. But she felt he had been in grave danger; these big cats were said to kill children of his age. She had heard that wildcats came right into houses sometimes.

Kristina went to get some sweet milk from the spring where she kept it in a lowered bucket for coolness. Now she tried to make Harald drink.

"Dear boy, don't be afraid."

The child had lost his voice from fright, but by and by it returned. He stuttered a moment and then said, "The cat ... "

After a while he seemed all right again and could talk fairly well. But Kristina decided to keep him in bed for the rest of the day. She told the other children not to go back to the lake. The big wildcat might still be there lurking in those thick bushes that hung over the water.

- 3 -

Later Robert returned from his walk in the forest and lay on his back in the shade of the sugar maples outside the house. Kristina sat down on the stoop near him for a moment.

He had a book in his hand which he showed her; it was the

History of Nature he had brought with him from Sweden. He had left it here and had just found it among the discarded things in the old log house. The book was torn, the pages held together at the back by a few thin twisted threads.

"I just ran across an amusing chapter. Listen to this, Kristina." And Robert read aloud.

ABOUT GOLD AND GOLD COINS

Gold is always found as a metal, sometimes mixed with silver. It is found in mountains, imbedded in pyrites or quartz; but most of the gold is found in the earth, usually in fine grains. Then it is mixed with sand. Sometimes bigger clumps are found. Because the gold grains are so much heavier than the sand grains, one can wash away the sand with water which leaves only the gold; this is called "to wash gold."

Gold does not change either by air or by fire if it is pure; that is why gold is called a noble metal.

Pure gold is more than nineteen times heavier than water.

He looked up from the book. "Did you hear that, Kristina? A noble metal, nineteen times heavier than water. And worth more than human life! That isn't in the book, of course, but I'm going to write it there."

Kristina listened distractedly. At the moment it was hard for her to gather her thoughts about gold and gold washing. She was thinking of her boy Harald; she must go inside and see how he was.

"A wildcat almost scared the life out of Harald this morning, down at the lake. Why don't you take Karl Oskar's gun and shoot it?"

"Why should I kill a wildcat?" asked Robert, looking up from his *History of Nature*. "He has the same right to live as you and I."

"But it's a dangerous beast!"

"There are no beasts except people. White-skinned people."

"Now you're poking fun at me, Robert. I meant it seriously."

"I'm not fooling. I have never seen any beasts except people. The wildcat only eats his fill. But people rob everything they see. People are worse robbers than wild beasts."

"May God protect us if that is true!"

"It is true, Kristina. I know."

171

He had used a lot of English in his talk when he first returned, but after only a few days he spoke his native tongue as purely as before. His hearing, however, seemed to be growing worse; when Kristina spoke to him he always put his hand behind his right ear and turned it toward her. While they were alone now she must try to make Robert confide in her about his ailment.

"There was blood on the pillow from your bad ear last night."

"It's been out of use a long time. But it's a good sign when it bleeds — then the ache lessens."

"The spots looked horrible."

"I'm sorry, Kristina, if I damaged your pillowcase."

"I wasn't thinking of that! But I do feel sorry for you if your ear aches in the night." And Kristina shuddered to think that when the sick ear bled it stopped hurting.

She said that she and Karl Oskar were worried about him. They were afraid he had picked up some dangerous illness in the gold fields. Why didn't he tell her what was the matter with him? They must try to find a remedy.

He replied in a low voice: It was kind of her, but she mustn't worry about him. As soon as the buzzing stopped in his sick ear he would be well again. Sometimes when the ear kept quiet he immediately felt better.

"There is nothing the matter with me, nothing at all."

He sounded sure and full of confidence; he would soon get well again. He was lying on his back in the grass, holding the *History of Nature* above his face. Again he was reading the chapter "About Gold and Gold Coins."

"Did you hear, Kristina? Did you hear that gold is nineteen times heavier than water?"

"I heard you."

Now he lowered his voice, as if he wanted to confide a great secret to her and was afraid someone might be listening. "But it's only dead weight. Do you understand? The weight of the yellow gold is dead . . . dead . . . dead!"

From the gable room Harald was calling his mother. She rose from the stoop and walked away from Robert. But she turned twice and looked at him where he lay in the grass and held his old, torn book above his face.

His remarks about the chapter in the *History of Nature* had filled her with inexplicable anxiety and sadness.

XIX

THE FOURTH NIGHT

You push your head deep into the pillow tonight. Do you think you can shut me up in that way? Do you think you can choke me, get rid of me forever, by digging me down into the pillow?

- 1 -

"My poor boy! I take care of you. You get well."

Mario Vallejos had left his camp between the boulders and gone out to look for the lost ones from his caravan — two animals and two muleteers. Since none of his provisions were missing, he did not think the two boys had fled with the mules. Now, after two days' searching, he had found one of them, far gone from exposure and thirst. Vallejos had questioned him and learned that what he had assumed had happened. He never found his two strayed mules.

Robert was well taken care of by the Mexican, and within a few days he recovered enough to continue the journey. He still felt weak and was bothered by dizziness, but now he rode on one of the good Mexican mules instead of walking. The mule lent him its spindly legs and small, hardened hoofs. His own feet were worn down to bare flesh.

They covered a shorter distance each day than they had before, since six animals now must carry burdens previously distributed on eight. The pack mules had already thinned down during the trip from St. Louis. Their hindquarters grew more sinewy each day. And their owner said that on the California Trail the mules would eventually become so skinny that two animals were required to throw a shadow. Robert wondered what happened to people before they reached California. How many gold seekers would be needed to throw one shadow?

For more than a year now Robert had been on his journey to the land of gold, and as yet he was only at the start of the road. But in the grave where Arvid lay he had left something of himself. When he resumed his journey he felt empty inside. He rode his

173

mule and watched the accompanying shadow on the ground. He still had enough life in him to cast a shadow, something visible that moved along with him. But could he catch it with his hands? Was there any substance to it? What he saw was dark and thin and empty. But this nebulous something was to be his sole comrade from now on.

The Mexican talked to him about the land at the end of the journey. He sang of gold, dreamed of gold. He lived in the faith of gold. He feared none of the things they might encounter on the two thousand miles — not poisoned water holes nor wild beasts nor Indians. Only one name he still mentioned with fear: Yellow Jack.

Robert did not know what he meant, and Vallejos tried with gestures to explain. He held his hands to his head as if suffering tortures, he contorted his face, felt his back as if hit by a blow from a whip, opened his mouth and stuck out his tongue as if he wanted to spit it out: this was Yellow Jack! But Robert was unable to interpret the signs. Perhaps Yellow Jack was the name of terrible weather conditions they would meet in the desert regions farther west? When Vallejos described Yellow Jack by trembling in his whole body, Robert felt he was trying to indicate an earthquake in its upheaval.

Sometimes as they rode along Robert would stick his hand in his pocket and feel the nickel watch. It was as though he sought to touch the hand which for a thousand evenings had wound that watch. Now it had stopped; it remained stopped. But Arvid no longer needed to know when it was time to rise in the morning, when it was mealtime or time to go to bed at night. He had no more use for a watch; what good would it do when there was no more more time for him?

-2-

Twenty days out from St. Louis a train of two men and six mules arrived in St. Joseph. It was now the last week of April in the year 1852. It was the beginning of the long-journey season; the plains were green, and the army of gold seekers congregating at St. Joseph was ready to take off. During a few days the last preparations must be made for a life of travel during the next four

174

months. For the last time vehicles were tested, provision sacks inspected, test firings undertaken with guns and revolvers, and guides for the wagon trains were chosen.

In St. Joseph, Mario Vallejos had arranged to meet two friends from his own country who were to accompany him to California. He looked for them for several days among the hordes of people that filled the place, but he could not find them. He sat silent and sad in the tent until late in the night. At last he decided that the only explanation of their failure to show up was that they no longer were alive. And he said he was sure that Yellow Jack had killed them.

Vallejos and Robert had raised their tent in a hickory grove in a small valley; around them spread the immense camp of the gold seekers. It was a place of noise, of a thousand sounds, where commotion reigned. The camp seemed to Robert like a fair in his home country, a fair a thousand times enlarged that went on through day and night, a giant fair that would last four months without interruption. Drunken men shouted, angry women yelled, children cried, horses neighed, oxen bawled, cows lowed, sheep bleated, mules brayed; not for half an hour was there silence during the whole long twenty-four hours.

Robert kept to the tent most of the time and observed little of what took place around him. But one day as he was walking a short distance outside the camp he saw a group of men digging in the ground beneath some tall trees. He stopped to look. Were they already digging for gold? Couldn't they wait till they arrived? The men seemed in a great hurry, shoveling quantities of dirt from holes in the ground. But they didn't dig to get out something; instead, something was to be put into those holes. Behind them lay a row of bundles wrapped in blankets, six feet long. Robert easily recognized that measure: the height of a person.

The next day Robert's master entered the tent, fear in his eyes. Yellow Jack had come! Yellow Jack was in St. Joseph! Vallejos tried again to explain who and what Yellow Jack was, but he used so many incomprehensible words that Robert could understand only that Yellow Jack was not a person, nor an animal, nor one of the Lord's tempests, but an invisible murderer who had sneaked into the gold seekers' camp. It was because of him the men had been digging yesterday.

175

At last the day of breaking camp came, and on one of the first mornings of May the gold army moved out of St. Joseph. Mario Vallejos was excited and happy when he sat upon his mule. They should reach their destination in about four months. In September they would be in California.

They headed for Big Blue River. Their animals were rested, and the first day twenty miles were laid behind them. On the second day they were down to eighteen; the third and fourth days, the same distance. But after one week the caravan moved barely fifteen miles a day. The animals were getting tired, and a day of rest was decided upon. With the good speed of the first few days they could still hold a good average.

But at each camp, every evening a few corpses were buried. The men drew lots to decide who would dig the graves, and it sometimes happened that a man who helped dig one evening was buried the next.

After two weeks the first great obstacle was reached — Big Blue River. All belongings and all living beings who could not swim were taken across the broad river on floats left behind by gold seekers who had crossed this water before them. The crossing delayed them two days.

Now they were crossing Nebraska, the land of the big buffalo herds, the great plains. As they moved along under the open sky with its ever burning sun, and rested under the clear stars of the prairie, the train grew steadily smaller. The large gold-seeker army diminished as it encountered this immense expanse, and it crept along like a long worm over the ground.

On the fifth day after Big Blue River the plain was broken by a mountain range. That evening they reached Spring Creek, a recently established trading post, with plentiful, sparklingly clear water, and here they made camp to rest for a day.

The next morning when Robert rose to attend to the mules Vallejos remained in bed. His look struck fear into the muleteer. Vallejos held his head between his hands and said, "The Yellow Jack! Yellow Jack!"

After Robert had listened to him for a while and watched him, he knew what Yellow Jack was: a lurking, treacherous, contagious disease. It had been with them in St. Joseph, it had followed them when they broke camp, it had been in their train all the time, traveling with them across the prairie. It was because of this disease that the men each evening drew lots for gravedigging. And now Vallejos had been overtaken by the pursuer he had feared from the very beginning.

Yellow Jack was a fever. Mario Vallejos was on his way to California to seek the yellow gold, but he had found the yellow fever instead.

-3-

Close to the Indian trading post at Spring Creek a big tent had been raised, in which a great many people lay sick. It was a makeshift hospital. Vallejos was carried there, accompanied by the Swedish muleteer, who wished to remain with his sick master and care for him.

In this emergency hospital the victims of yellow fever lay on beds of dry prairie grass. They were looked after by an old woman, half Indian, with a red-brown face and white hair. The sick were not expected to get well; the nurse was only to look after them so that they would not be left to die alone.

Vallejos was often unconscious. In between, as his senses returned, he recognized his muleteer and said to him, "Leave me! He'll take you too. Get out! Hurry away! You're young. You still have your life. Leave me! Save yourself while you still have time!"

But Robert remained in the makeshift hospital. He made a bed next to Vallejos. He carried water from the clear stream and was always near when Vallejos wanted to quench his fever thirst. He brought his master water as the master once had brought him water.

After a day's rest at Spring Creek the gold caravan continued on its way. That morning Robert stood outside the hospital tent and saw the camp break up. All desire to go with the train had left him. The old nurse explained to him that yellow fever was terribly contagious. If he cared at all for his life he should leave. She could not understand why a healthy person would come into this tent of pestilence. She asked for his address so that she could notify his relatives of his death on the trail.

On the sixth day Mario Vallejos, born in Mexico, died during a fit of vomiting which choked off his breath. He passed away, steadfast in his faith of gold, aged thirty-two, mourned by his muleteer only.

That same day Robert Nilsson from Sweden became a rich man.

During the last day of his life the Mexican had been clear in his mind and had talked coherently. He unfastened a small pouch he had carried next to his body and handed it to Robert. The contents of this pouch, the mules, the provisions, all he owned, he now gave to his devoted muleteer. And a few hours later he died.

Robert dug a grave alone under some trees and put his master's body in an empty packing box which the nurse had used for dried foods. She was with him when he buried Vallejos. She sang a psalm in some Indian language, and Robert repeated a Swedish funeral psalm he remembered from childhood.

> "... and me in earth you offer
> a cold and narrow bed...."

Thus Indian singing and Swedish reading were performed over a dead Mexican.

It was several days after the funeral before Robert thought of looking at the contents of the small pouch with the letters "M.V." sewn on it. In it were gold and silver coins, in from five- to fifty-dollar denominations — a total of $3,150.

All of Vallejos' provisions and equipment Robert gave to the emergency hospital, and in return for this great gift the old Indian woman permitted him a corner of her own "bungalow" behind the hospital tent to sleep in. She told him he could stay as long as he wanted. He took his mules to an Irishman who supplied the trading post with buffalo meat. The man promised to slaughter the animals immediately; Robert had become attached to them and wanted to relieve them of further suffering on the trail. After this he had only the pouch left, but in it were gold and silver — three thousand one hundred and fifty dollars.

Robert now was free and independent, he had no animals to look after, no chores to perform for another, no master over him. He was alone, he was rich, and he had his life before him.

But his desire to live had not returned.

Robert remained in Spring Creek and sank down into a bottomless pit of fatigue and listlessness. The days passed by without his counting them or knowing their names. He heard people speak to him and he replied, but did not think of what words he used, or their meaning. Nothing of what took place in his surroundings concerned him. Days and nights followed each other, washed over him, all as similar as the waves of the sea.

Nothing hurt him any more, nothing pleased him particularly. He could not be happy, nor could he be sad. His body was given what it required by the old Indian woman, and it was satisfied. He had food and drink and a bed to sleep in, and he ate and drank and slept. What was there to do beyond this?

The stream that flowed through Spring Creek came from the mountains, and it had the cleanest, clearest water Robert had ever seen. It was so transparent it was invisible; if it hadn't been in motion a casual observer could not have seen it. The stream glittered with light even after dark. And Robert stood every evening at the edge of the creek and looked at the moving light. It seemed he had no strength to do anything.

Thus a summer ran by him; the prairie was now red with sunscorched grass. He saw people come to Spring Creek, rest for a day and a night, and move on. There were buffalo hunters, fur traders, settlers, land seekers, merchants, Indian agents, swindlers and cattle thieves, honest people and escaped murderers. What were they after, all these God-created creatures? They were on the same errand, all of them. All of them wanted to grab for themselves everything of value in this land — animals, the earth's growing plants and trees, minerals on the ground and below it. They rode, they walked, they endured hunger and thirst, they killed themselves and others. They were heroic. They were the resurrected Gospel martyrs; they were ready to die for their faith.

And few of the men Robert saw pass through Spring Creek that summer knew that it was water alone man could not be without.

During your stay in Spring Creek the summer of 1852 you thought you would never again have a master. You yourself had buried the last one, you alone had dug his grave and filled it with your own hands. You laid his body in a packing case and read a psalm over it. But you still had me. I am with you tonight, three years later.

179

XX

THE INVULNERABLE ONE

- 1 -

On Friday morning Karl Oskar rose before daybreak, greased his oak-wheel cart and made ready to drive to Stillwater. Already it was evident the day would be very hot. Since animals were much plagued by the heat and by mosquitoes, and since Karl Oskar felt his young ox team might be unruly in this heat, he wanted to get under way while the morning was still cool.

The evening before Kristina had gone through the two bundles of money, cleaning the bills and ironing out those that were wrinkled. A few grease spots she had been unable to remove, but on the whole the money now looked clean and neat. Karl Oskar pushed the two bundles down into the sheepskin pouch Kristina had sewn for him when they left Sweden.

While he was yoking the oxen Algot Svensson, his companion for the journey, arrived. He was always punctual. Today Karl Oskar was to be a witness for his neighbor at the land office, concerning Svensson's right to his claim in Section 35 of Chisago Township.

Before Karl Oskar stepped up on the cart he told his wife that today he was setting out on the most important errand he had undertaken so far in America. He felt almost the same anxious expectation as on that day when he had walked to her father's home in Duvemåla to ask for Kristina as bride; no one could tell in advance what the reply might be.

The cart trundles started their clumsy rolling down the road along the lake shore. The driver had put the sheepskin pouch under his shirt; the riches had left the house on the way to a better place of safekeeping.

- 2 -

That Friday turned out to be the summer's warmest day in the St. Croix Valley.

The heat bothered Kristina at her sewing, and she had to lie

180

down and rest for a moment now and then. She had a burning headache and she saw black every time she tried to thread the needle. The discomfort from her pregnancy increased with the hot weather; all smells became nauseating and as soon as she saw a blowfly light she wanted to vomit.

Robert had found a cool place to rest under the lush sugar maples near the house. He was not going to visit the Indian today; it was too hot in the forest. Kristina had noticed how tired and short of breath he was after his walks. She picked up her sewing and went outside to sit with him under the maples. The heat was not quite so oppressive here as inside the house.

Robert was reading the latest issue of *Hemlandet*. He had just discovered an advertisement:

HELP WANTED:
Youth for *Hemlandet's* Printing Office.
Applicant should be able to read Swedish; if he also can write, so much the better. If he has a good head, lack of knowledge can gradually be remedied.

"Do you think I should apply for the job, Kristina?"

"You with your riches needn't work any more!" And she reminded him: The very first evening he had said that he had done all the work he intended to do and had had his last master.

His sick ear was turned toward her; probably he didn't hear what she said; he was absorbed in his reading. She looked closely at his face: It was caved in, ravaged, wan. He must surely be suffering from a more severe ailment than his sick ear. She must ask him again.

"Have you never been to see a doctor, Robert?"

"Hadn't thought of it. I'm only twenty-two. Why should I go see a doctor? I'm supposed to be healthy."

"You may have caught something dangerous. I don't know — but it might lead to your death."

"Death?" Robert pulled up his upper lip in a great smile and exposed the broken teeth in the back of his mouth. He turned from the paper to his sister-in-law. "Kristina, you don't think I'm afraid of death?"

"All people fear death."

"Not I."

181

"You too — you are only bragging."

"No, I mean it. Death cannot really do anything to me. It cannot touch me."

"Stop! That's blasphemy." Kristina's body had straightened up with the last word. Now she fumbled with the needle so that it pierced her thumb instead of the cloth. "Do you mean you are above death? Above the Almighty?"

"All I said was, death cannot touch me." Robert threw down *Hemlandet* in the grass and leaned toward Kristina. "Nothing touches me any more. Neither good nor evil affects me. Do you know why?"

"No — you must explain, Robert!"

"I'll try. . . . "

His cough prevented him from continuing for several minutes. She sat in suspense, waiting for the explanation. And when Robert at last had finished coughing it came quite slowly and simply: "I have reconciled myself to my lot. That's all."

He had pulled up a few tall spears of grass, and he began chewing them as he went on: Looking back on his life, he understood everything that had happened to him. It was the way he was created that explained his life. If he had been an obedient and willing farm hand he would never have tried to steal rest periods while he dug ditches, and then he would not have been given a hard box on the ear by his first master, and then he would have escaped his earache. And if he had had the temperament of an obedient and satisfied farm hand he would never have emigrated. And even if he had emigrated, he would have remained with his brother Karl Oskar and worked on his claim in Minnesota and been satisfied with that life. Then he could have lived his whole life in one place, in constant peace of mind.

But the way he was born had prevented him. He couldn't stay in Sweden, he couldn't stay with his brother in America, he couldn't stay in any service. He had been given ideas about gold and riches and freedom, and he was forced to pursue them.

To him, as to everyone, a certain fate had been given which he couldn't escape, however he tried. At his creation it had taken charge of his body and soul! He had carried it through his whole life, in his head, in his mind, in his heart. He couldn't escape it any more than a person could tear out his heart and remain alive. There was therefore nothing for him to do except adjust himself to it. The most difficult thing in the world was adjustment — adjustment to oneself, adjustment to the person one could never escape. He had suffered for many years, intensely, patiently, but he had come through at last. He no longer fought his fate, he no longer was bitter about it. He had accepted it. And after that what more could happen to him? Because to his fate belonged also the end, death.

"Please understand me, Kristina," he said. "I'm not boasting, I'm full of humility instead. It's merely that I am reconciled."

Kristina remained silent. It was Robert's voice she had heard, but the words she herself had lived through and felt; they had sprung from her own heart. How many times hadn't she asked herself: Is everything that has happened to me decided by God in the beginning? When Robert talked about himself he had explained her own eternal questioning and pondering and wondering. Now for the first time she knew something about him — now, when she recognized herself in him. And one couldn't know a person before one discovered him in oneself, and oneself in him.

"Robert . . . " she stammered faintly. "Now I understand."

And that conversation would remain with Kristina forever after.

XXI

THE FIFTH NIGHT

You had intended to sit up and wait for Karl Oskar this evening; but he is delayed returning from Stillwater, you're tired and it's getting late. Go to bed! You'll see Karl Oskar in the morning.

I understand, you would have liked to speak with your brother tonight. He has looked so crushed since you opened your black pouch Monday night. This time for once he had nothing to say. But he has always been suspicious and he doesn't trust your gift.

Today, though, he'll learn he isn't cheated. And tomorrow he'll shake your hand and say: Forgive me, Robert! Forgive my mistrust! From now on I'll always trust you!

You wanted Karl Oskar to offer you his hand this evening. But you must wait till tomorrow. And now you want to sleep. I know, you have only one wish left: to sleep. And your intense weariness falls on your eyelids and closes them — but you don't go to sleep. You lie awake and call on sleep, the only good thing you have left in life, but it doesn't come. For with night and silence I come instead.

I'll keep sleep from your eyes a long time tonight. I have much to tell you, and you must stay awake and listen. I'll remind you of the ghost town on the sandy plain where you stayed so long. How long was it?

It began with a voice you thought you recognized. . . .

- 1 -

It happened in Spring Creek one day in September.

Robert was walking by the trading post, where ox teams rested and people always congregated. Several trains had just arrived from the prairie. He strolled idly among the vehicles and then suddenly heard a voice he thought he recognized. The speaker was just jumping off a big double-team wagon piled high with buffalo hides. A cloud of flies swarmed over the load, and the hides stank. Robert looked more closely at the red-faced man jumping off. He knew in advance that he would have the gold seeker's face, like all men passing through Spring Creek. But there was something more in this face, something he recognized: puffed-up, rosy cheeks, a flat nose, blood-streaked eyes under heavy lids. It was a gold seeker's face all right, but so ugly it was easily recognizable. And it was well known to him — it belonged to a countryman.

The man with the load of hides wore a flaming red shirt and light-yellow deerskin breeches with black fringes along the sides. But as Robert recognized his face he also remembered him in different attire: a light-brown, large-checked coat with matching trousers that fitted tightly around his legs, a voluminous handkerchief dangling from his hip pocket, and black patent-leather shoes. The man was standing on the deck of a sailing ship, leaning on the rail and spitting into the ocean while entertaining the other passengers with his stories. And in the crowd around him Robert had listened, too.

The American! The American on the *Charlotta!*

Robert recognized the voice he had heard tell so many stories

184

about the New World during their crossing to America. And the face — he had seen thousands of strangers but this face was not like any other, this one he knew.

He walked closer and asked in Swedish, "Aren't you Fredrik Mattsson?"

The man in the red woolen shirt turned and opened his mouth as if ready to swallow some of the fat flies that buzzed over his load of hides.

"God damn! A Swedish fellow!"

"You are Mattsson who crossed on the *Charlotta,* aren't you?"

"That's right! And I believe I've met you before, boy."

"On the ship."

"Oh yes, we traveled on the same ship. I remember you now. Well, well. What was your name?"

Robert told him his name, and Fredrik Mattsson shook his hand so hard that the finger joints snapped.

"Glad to meet you again, Robert Nelson. Not every day you meet a countryman in this territory."

The speaker was Fredrik Mattsson from Asarum Parish, province of Blekinge, Sweden, and he had been nicknamed "the American" on the *Charlotta.* When they landed in New York he had disappeared; none of the other passengers knew where he had gone. Robert had listened to his stories eagerly and often wondered what became of him. Now they had unexpectedly met again, deep in America, all the way out in Nebraska Territory.

Mattsson said that since landing in America he had never run across any of his many companions on the ship. And he was glad at last to have found a young friend from those days at sea.

"That old tub *Charlotta!* She must have sunk by this time."

"After the landing where did you go, Mr. Mattsson?" Robert felt he must call his older countryman Mister.

"Where did I go? I'll tell you, boy! But call me Fred. All my friends in America do. And I'll call you Bob. Now we can talk Swedish together!"

And Fredrik Mattsson from Asarum leaned against the tall wheel of the ox wagon and continued in the language he called his mother tongue, although Robert noticed that a great number of the words he used were English or the mixture of English and Swedish so common among his countrymen in America.

185

"I took a ship in New York, a clipper ship to California. She was a beautiful ship, loaded with gold seekers."

"The *Angelica?*" asked Robert.

"Oh, you noticed her too, boy!"

And Robert did indeed remember the sleek, copper-plated *Angelica* with her pennant fluttering in the wind: "Ho! Ho! Ho! For California!" How he had wished he could board that ship where the men danced and sang and had a good time! They were on their way to dig gold and become free.

"I took the *Angelica* to Frisco," explained Mattsson. "I stayed a year in the gold fields, but no luck for me. The best days in California are over. It's hell to live out there. No, sir, no digging for me! I've left gold behind forever. Last year I was traveling around and happened to come here to Nebraska. Now I live in Grand City. I have a bar and a hotel—the Grand Hotel in Grand City. Now you know, Bob."

The hotel owner from Grand City had been out on a business trip and was on his way home with a load of buffalo hides. He was in big business.

"What do you do around here, boy?"

Now it was Robert's turn to explain: He and a friend from the *Charlotta* had also started out to dig gold in California. They had taken a job with a Mexican to look after his mules. But his friend had died on the plains and the Mexican had died of yellow fever. He had been left behind in Spring Creek, where he had stayed alone through the summer. His dead employer had left him what he owned; Robert had enough to live on.

"You're lucky! Did you make any money?"

"I have enough."

"Good! Then you can live as a free gentleman in America."

Fredrik Mattsson stood in thought for a few moments. When he continued, his voice was even friendlier than before and he put his hand on Robert's shoulder. "I know what, my Swedish friend! Come with me to Grand City. Stay as my guest at Grand Hotel."

"Where is Grand City?"

"Fifty miles from here. Toward the east. You come with me. We Swedes should stick together. We'll have a good time."

Robert could live wherever he wanted. He didn't care where he went. So a few hours later he was traveling back across the

186

Nebraska plains. He had given up the West, he was traveling east now.

He had turned his back on the land of gold.

-2-

They drove for two whole days across the prairie. In the afternoon of the third day they came to a deep valley. They followed along its bottom and at dusk they arrived at Grand City.

The town had been founded a few years earlier by a group of Mormons. The Mormons had been chased out of Missouri, said Fred, and had sought freedom in Nebraska. Grand City had flourished, but soon trouble had arisen between the Mormons and new settlers of other sects. When the inhabitants began to shoot each other, the town had stopped growing. Last summer the Mormons had been chased out of Grand City too, and since then life had been calmer. Last winter a tornado had moved most of the houses far out on the prairie. Since then business hadn't been very good in Grand City.

As they came closer Robert saw that the town had been built in a gravel pit; the walls of the pit surrounded Grand City on all sides. The houses, all along one street, were of varying shapes and construction: some of stone, some like sheds, some just shanties of branches and twigs roofed with leaves and turf. And in many places the street had caved in; in one such hole lay a pile of boards that once must have been a house. Robert also noticed big caves in the gravel walls surrounding the town. Someone had been busy there. What kind of digging had taken place?

"The Mormons were always looking for their Bible," explained Fred.

Their first prophet, carpenter Smith, had found the Book of Mormon, written on plates of gold, while he was digging in a sand pit in Vermont. An angel had shown him where to look for the truth concerning the last revelation. Smith had been a capable man with a good head; too bad that he had been lynched in Illinois by people who were jealous of him. While the Mormons were in Grand City their local head had been given a revelation from an angel of God: The tablets Smith had found did not contain all the truth; several chapters of the Book of Mormon — indeed, the most impor-

187

tant chapters — were buried in the sand hills hereabouts. And on this prophet's instigation the Mormons had started to dig. They dug day and night, they poked through every hill near town. They sifted every grain of sand, but did not find a single written word. It had been a false angel, a lying angel, who had fooled the local prophet.

A cloud of dust enveloped the wagon as they drove their lazy team along the one street of the town. Robert looked at the sandpit walls. The upper layers hung far out beyond the lower ones; they might cave in at any time and bury the whole of Grand City.

One house in the center of the town had a sign painted on it in somewhat shaky letters, "Grand Hotel." It was built of stone, with a rather flat roof of bark, and was so low that it looked like a cellar house. The door had a sign in chalk: "If Anything Wanted Walk In!"

Mr. Fred Mattsson jumped down from the wagon; he welcomed his old friend and countryman, Bob Nelson, to the Grand Hotel in Grand City. He had all kinds of guest rooms for gentlemen; his was not only the biggest hotel in town, it was the only one.

It had been closed while the owner was away on business. He opened the door with some caution. The upper hinge was loose, and in spite of his caution the door fell on his boot as he stepped across the threshold. He kicked it aside.

They walked through a narrow hall which was pitch dark. The hall ended in a few stone steps leading up to a bare room: this was the Grand Hotel's best guest room, and here Bob Nelson could stay. Inside was a real bed, nailed together from heavy boards, with a mattress and fairly clean sheets, pillow and blanket. The only other furniture was a table and a chair at the window. The walls were decorated with buffalo horns; even this room indicated they were in buffalo country.

A room for a gentleman, said the host, a room for a man of means in America. Now Robert must rest while he went down and cooked for them. They would have their dinner in the main dining room. Unfortunately, the Grand Hotel was without personnel at the moment. Before he left on his business trip he had been forced to let his chef go — his last employee. The chef had been ordered not to get drunk until after dinner, but he had never obeyed. One day he had taken the wrong bottle and poured castor oil into the bean soup. The guests had all spent the night in the privy. In the morning they had moved out; they accused him, the owner, of trying to poison them and refused to pay their bills. That was why he had discharged the chef; that bean soup had cost him two hundred dollars.

About an hour later Robert came down to enjoy Fred's promised dinner. The "main dining room" was a widening in the hall with an iron stove in a corner. It had a long table at which twenty guests could sit down to a meal. Fred had fried buffalo steaks on the stove, and he served them with a red, peppery sauce; he called it "chili Colorado." The meat was good, but the sharp sauce stung Robert's tongue.

Fredrik Mattsson poured whiskey from a fat bottle and handed his guest a large tumbler of it. "Let's drink a Swedish *skål!* Good luck, boy!"

Robert was not accustomed to strong liquor. The whiskey scratched his throat and burned in his stomach afterward.

The hotel dining room had a closed-in, dank smell. Robert couldn't help saying that he felt as if he were sitting in a cellar.

"Yes, the Grand Hotel was built to be a potato cellar," said Fred proudly. And he related the whole story of his hotel.

When Grand City had been founded four years before, the first inhabitants had needed a place to store their potatoes and had built this house. But as the town grew and attracted cattle thieves, ruffians and murderers, it had become more important to have a safe place to put criminals. By and by they were hanged, of course, but that usually took a day or two and in the meantime the condemned men were kept in this jail. That was how the potato cellar had become a prison. In this very spot where they were sitting, many men had spent their last hours of life.

Then had come a time in Grand City's history when law and order had been set aside. For a year the jail had been abandoned because of the lack of officials.

After that came the church period of Grand City's history. The Mormons were followed by a group of Seventh-Day Adventists. The potato cellar was turned into a temple. Here the Seventh-Day Adventists had made themselves ready to ascend into heaven. The Last Judgment, it was decided, would occur on New Year's Eve 1850, and all the members of the congregation had gathered in here. They had sold their possessions and had dressed in white robes; they had done their earthly chores and were ready for the ascension. But then the last day had been postponed indefinitely, and since the Seventh-Day Adventists already had given away everything they owned on earth, without gaining admittance to heaven, some problems about money had arisen. The confusion increased when the pastor ran away with the wife of the church-warden. Now the Mormons took advantage of the other sect's predicament; they drove them out of the church and used the building themselves.

The host inhaled deeply, spat to the left and then to the right, and poured more whiskey before he continued:

This peaceful period had come to an end shortly after he arrived in the town.

There had already been a great lack of women in the West before the Mormons came with their polygamy. Now one man could take ten wives while a hundred men couldn't get a single woman. A small war broke out in Grand City. The Mormons used Colt revolvers which fired five shots without reloading, but some of the other men had Sam Colt's newest invention, which fired six shots. And with Colt's six-shooters they drove the whole Mormon group out of town.

After that the churches stood empty, and Fred had used the opportunity to take over the biggest building in town.

"I can thank Sam Colt's six-shooter, of course," he added. "Sam is the greatest living American. Do you know that he made his first revolver when he was fourteen? Think what the West would have been without him! It simply wouldn't have had any future at all if men had had to stop and reload at every shot."

Robert's head spun from the whiskey he had drunk; suddenly he felt drowsy, and he listened only vaguely to Fred.

But then a tornado had hit Grand City last year. Three fourths of the houses had blown away — thirty, forty miles out on the prairie. In many cases the inhabitants had sailed away with their houses. The town had again come to a standstill.

Robert was yawning; he was falling asleep in his chair. His host urged him to go to bed and rest for a while.

3

Robert slept a few hours and awakened with a burning thirst. He walked down the black cellar hall, felt his way along until he found a side door, which opened as soon as he touched the handle. He saw at once that he had come upon the bar. In front of a low wooden counter on a long bench sat a dozen or so men with their hats on. It smelled musty and sour, and the dirty floor had not been touched by broom or scrubbing brush in a long time.

"Hi, Bob! Welcome to my saloon!"

The host of the Grand Hotel now wore a big white apron which turned him into a bartender. He stood behind the counter and rinsed glasses in a bucket of water. The wall behind the counter had shelves with bottles and mugs, and the top shelf had a red painted sign, "Fred's Tavern."

It was strangely silent in the bar. The men sat immobile and did not offer to make room for the newcomer. Fred rolled up a chopping block and poured a glass of whiskey for Robert; then he started talking to him in Swedish.

The saloons Robert had seen before or passed by had always been noisy with the din of many voices, and he wondered why it was so silent in here. He looked at the customers. What was the matter with them? Presently, as his eyes became accustomed to the dim light, he saw that the men were asleep; they were drowsing, or unconscious. A few rested their heads on the counter and snored contentedly; some slept less heavily and winked and nodded now and then. Some stared glassy-eyed at the bottles on the shelves, as they might stare out across the plains when they had discovered something far away, some quarry that it was beyond their strength to reach.

Silence and drowsiness reigned in this saloon because the men at the counter were completely drunk.

"Time to stir up business!" Fred stooped under the counter and found a small hand spray which he filled from the wash bucket. Then he walked back and forth several times, spraying the befogged heads of his customers. "They need a shower once every hour."

The row of slumbering, dazed guests came to life again. They wiped their eyes, discovered their glasses were empty or gone and shouted for new drinks. The bartender put away his sprayer, its purpose accomplished, and attended to whiskey pouring instead. Business in Fred's Tavern had resumed its normal speed.

But after a while the owner again had time to speak to his new guest. "You mentioned a fellow who was with you — Arvid, did you say? And he kicked the bucket?"

"Yes. From thirst. He drank poisoned water, we couldn't find anything else."

"Last summer ten thousand people died from thirst on their way to California."

Robert said that he had never thought of it before — how impossible it was to get along without so simple a thing as water.

"In my hotel you needn't go thirsty! With Fred you won't miss a thing. You can have anything you wish to drink, my dear friend."

It had grown stuffy and close in the bar, and Robert felt sleepy. He rose and said he would go to bed.

Fred nodded. "Good night! Sleep tight! I must attend to my business." He looked annoyed at his customers and bent down for his spray can again.

- 4 -

Robert stayed on with his compatriot in Grand City. In the daytime he would wander about and look at the place. There were many remains of houses that once had stood along the street: foundation stones, heavy timbers, caved-in chimneys, an occasional iron stove — the heavy objects the tornado had been unable to carry out on the prairie when it struck the year before. Here were places where people had lived, Robert thought; the people themselves were dead or had moved away. Even the house rats were dead — furry, flat, dried-up rat carcasses lay strewn on the old sites like lost mittens. The town in the sand pit was a ghost town. It suited Robert to live here.

The guests at the Grand Hotel were travelers who passed through Grand City and needed a place to rest for a night. But for days on end Robert was the only guest in the house. After a few weeks he offered to pay for his lodging. He made the suggestion one day when only the two of them were eating in the main dining room. But Fredrik Mattsson threw up his hands — there was no hurry about that. Robert insisted he wanted to pay, he had plenty of money.

Fredrik Mattsson's bloodshot eyes fluttered about a moment, and he turned away as if suddenly embarrassed. He didn't want to snoop into other people's affairs, but would Robert feel hurt if he asked how much the Mexican had left him?

"Not at all, Fred. You are my friend — I'll show you."

He walked to his room and fetched the small pouch of soft black leather with the letters "M.V." embroidered on it. He had used only a little of the contents. He really ought to count how much he had left. He poured the gold and silver coins onto the table. Eagerly his host helped him count.

Robert still had almost three thousand dollars, two thousand in gold.

Fred threw up his hands. "My dear boy! Have you entirely lost your mind? How are you using your money? Do you just hide it away?"

Robert said he used the money as he needed it. What was wrong with that?

"My poor fellow Swede! It's criminal, that's all! You can double your money, many times! Has no one advised you about money?"

And Fredrik Mattsson's voice sounded truly sad when he heard how foolishly Robert had handled his fortune. To keep all that cash in a pouch! Money must be put into something to earn interest. Money must be kept alive, multiplied a hundredfold, a thousandfold, like seeds in the ground. If he had put this money into some business when he got it he would have had ten times as much by now. It was a crime to handle money this way. It was not only a crime aganst himself, it was a crime against humanity!

"Bob!" said Fred, and he patted Robert's hand in deep compassion. "Bob, you do need a good friend."

And in his solitude, after Arvid's death, Robert had often felt he did indeed need a friend.

Fred's eyes could not leave the piles before him on the table. At last a ray of light shot out of them. "I've got it — I know what to do, Bob! You and I should be partners."

Robert looked puzzled; he didn't understand. But Fred was jumping up and down with joy.

"Damn it! Why didn't I think of it before!"

"What do you mean? What should we do?"

193

"You put your capital into my hotel! You and I will be partners in my hotel!"

"Would this money be enough for that?"

"It will help in the business, and I'll pay good interest. You can't handle your money yourself, Bob!"

Robert knew he couldn't handle money, he had never had any to handle before. And he felt it could easily be stolen from the pouch; he had been thinking about finding a safer place.

Fred told him that he had been planning to expand his hotel business and could use some more capital. First of all they must find a staff of servants. Suppose Robert put some money in the hotel — say two thousand dollars, the rest he could keep for spending money; then he, Fred, would pay the highest interest ever paid in the New World — half the profits! They would share as brothers what they took in. Grand Hotel was already a fine business; it would be still better with more capital to modernize it. And since they were from the same homeland he felt they were practically relatives. With the two of them as partners they would have almost a family business.

Robert said, "You take care of my money! I hope it isn't too much trouble for you?"

"Hosannah!" exclaimed the host of the Grand Hotel. "From now on we'll do big business!"

-5-

The liveliest time of the week in Fred's Tavern was Saturday evening between eight and nine. At that hour the members of the Whiskey Club met, the largest and most important club in town. They met to drink Kentucky straight, and their bylaws stated they must meet for one hour, between eight and nine. During this hour they were allowed to, and had to, drink all the whiskey they could consume. The cost per member was one dollar and fifty cents. The one who consumed the greatest quantity during the evening hour need not pay the week's membership fee. The rush in the bar during this hour was enormous; Fred couldn't draw breath until the meeting was adjourned and the members had retired in more or less horizontal positions.

After the meeting of the Whiskey Club, Fred would devote Sunday to cleaning his saloon.

Even before Robert became a partner in the hotel business he had assisted Fred a little during the Saturday rush. He washed glasses, helped to serve and kept track of drinks consumed. During the hour of the club meeting the consumption of liquor was as great as during all the rest of the week. After Robert had become a partner he felt it his duty to assist the host whenever he could. He helped with the cooking, peeled potatoes, cut firewood, ran errands, swept up, and washed dishes; mostly he washed dishes.

Fred did not ask his partner to work. "You shouldn't work as dishwasher here, Bob. It's below your station."

But Robert said that he wanted to do his share. And since he was a partner in the business he felt a certain responsibility about the running of the hotel.

- 6 -

Robert stayed in the sand-pit ghost town for over two years.

During this time he felt each day that the pierced gravel walls might cave in and bury the town and its people. It seemed to him a miracle that they still stood. And he asked himself if he wasn't staying in Grand City only to see its burial. Perhaps there was a longing in him that the big cave-in might take place and end life for all of them.

After his experiences on the California Trail Robert felt that death was the only sure thing in this world, the only thing that really happened — and the only thing that could change anything for him. And he was separated from death only by a transparent film, thin and sensitive as the retina of the eye. He could see through it clearly, and he wondered constantly why it didn't burst. And because of that he lived a life of pretension; the day's events did not really concern him.

Fredrik Mattsson lived his life in great earnest, in a great hurry. He was involved in *big* business, bigger than before, whatever it was; his partner never asked. Robert was both hotel owner and hotel servant, and he did the heaviest chores. Fred intended to hire necessary personnel — he had already decided how many people they needed — but unfortunately he had not had the time to see to it as yet. His days were entirely taken up by other, more urgent activities. And since his partner had brought in new capital, the hotel was to be enlarged and improved.

One evening he asked, "Bob, can you hang paper?"

At first Robert did not understand what he meant.

Well, in the morning Fred would begin the great improvement: they would paper the hotel walls. Could Robert do this? Fred had come across a big pile of light-blue wallpaper rolls, very cheap. For several weeks Robert made paste and measured, cut and hung paper over the naked walls of the old potato celler. The work amused him, because he could see results: he changed something. He changed the color of the naked hotel walls from dark gray to light blue. He felt he made the days brighter for the strangers who would stay in the rooms.

But the hanging of the light-blue paper — at fifty cents a roll — was the only improvement undertaken at the Grand Hotel.

-7-

It was during Robert's third winter in the ghost town that his illness began.

It started as a persistent fatigue which did not disappear with rest, a hollow, empty cough, and sometimes a tearing pain in his stomach. He had no appetite, couldn't keep down the food he swallowed; he lost weight, grew wan. He stayed in bed for a while and felt a little better. For short periods he felt almost well. But the sickness came back. And then his teeth began to fall out. When he looked in a mirror he didn't recognize himself.

Fred would often say to him, "Your face is pale as hell, Bob."

By spring he no longer could assist his friend in running the hotel. And he had grown tired of the ghost town and wanted to get away from it as soon as he felt strong enough. He thought that perhaps it would be best for him to return to his brother in Minnesota.

Fred agreed enthusiastically. Since Robert didn't feel well he ought to be where he could get care and rest. And Fred added, "Bob, you needn't be a burden to your brother. I'll return the money you put into my hotel and I'll pay interest as well, the highest interest in North America!"

To the very last moment of Robert's stay the host of the Grand Hotel was helpful and generous to his friend and partner. He arranged for his trip home; an ox train would soon be due in Grand

City on its way east to St. Louis, and from St. Louis Robert could take the paddle steamer as soon as the northern Mississippi was open. Robert said that he remembered the way; it would be his third journey on the broad river.

"You must get yourself some decent clothes, Bob," suggested his friend. "You must return as a gentleman."

A few hundred dollars in silver were still left in Robert's black pouch, enough for his trip home, a suit of clothes and a new rucksack. Now anyone could see he was returning from the gold fields, said Fred.

And one day in April 1855 the younger partner in the Grand Hotel, Grand City, was ready to leave the business and the town. The ox train for St. Louis had arrived. The two friends stood at the counter in Fred's Tavern, and the one who would remain solemnly opened a bottle of Kentucky whiskey. With controlled emotion Fred said that they must drink the painful *skål* of farewell.

Now the moment had come for him to repay the two thousand dollars, with interest, as he had promised. "My dear friend! After two years your capital has doubled — you get one hundred per cent interest! Here is four thousand dollars."

Fredrik Mattsson put two heavy bundles of bills on the counter in front of his friend; he had of course changed Robert's gold into bills. This had to be done before money could circulate and grow. And he was paying back in bills. He looked at his countryman, as if to see his reaction.

"Have you ever seen or heard of wildcats out here?"

"Wildcats? Do you mean the animals?"

"No, I mean free money in America. What you see before you on the counter is four thousand dollars in wildcat money. You get your capital back in sound, free money!" This wildcat money, Fred said, would double again if handled wisely. In the right hands wildcats were as good as gold.

Robert was overcome by his friend's generosity. Was it right for him to accept these big bundles of money, four thousand dollars? He felt like a miser, a usurer. No, he couldn't accept all this money — he hadn't earned it.

But Fred forced him to accept it, he pushed the bundles into the black leather pouch. He knew how Robert felt, but after all, it was only his own money that had been doubled in two years by careful handling.

197

Robert thanked him. Instead of heavy gold he had now light, sound money in his bag, money with a name that suggested freedom, the freedom of animals in the forest. And in that very moment he decided how he would use this great sum of money.

Later, in the street outside the hotel, Fredrik Mattsson from Asarum, Sweden, waved a cheerful good-by to Robert Nilsson from the same country, as he left the Grand Hotel in Grand City on the ox wagon, with wildcat bills in his bag.

You're listening, but you haven't heard Karl Oskar return. You don't hear well; it's I who ruined your hearing.

It has been a long night for you — I have had much to tell, have tried not to forget anything of importance. But now my story nears its end.

It was during your last winter in the ghost town that I came back to you. Since then I've left you only for short intervals. I've buzzed and throbbed and banged and hammered so intensely that you have been forced to listen to me. And you can say what you wish, but you can thank me for the fact that you began to ponder your lot in life: I've kept you awake at night and given you time to think in peace when all is silent.

And at last you have returned and can play the gold seeker who struck it rich! The sound, free money in your pouch hadn't been touched when you returned. You decided not to spend a single dollar of it, for you wanted to give all your riches to Karl Oskar and Kristina.

Thus your trip has not been in vain, my dear gold seeker. Your money will help your brother and sister-in-law. Who would deserve the money more? Who could use it better? Who needs it more? Your brother is still young in years, but he has worked so hard that he already limps, though he won't admit it. When he has cleared one field he begins with another, and another, and another. And however big his fields he will never be satisfied. Yet he too, in the end, must be satisfied with a handful of earth — as much as the mouth of a dead man can hold.

And Kristina is not nearly so strong as your brother. She is only thirty, yet soon she will be bent and broken on this claim, if she doesn't have help. She has five children and will have more, she has her big household to care for, all the livestock, constant chores inside and outside. She is like a ship at sail: never entirely still, al-

*ways some little gust of wind that drives her on. You see how worn
out she is in the evenings. You can be pleased that your money
will help a little to ease her burden.*

*You returned one evening with riches to the home of Karl Oskar
and Kristina at Lake Ki-Chi-Saga. You've kept the promise you
gave them when you left four years ago. But it cost you mightily.*

XXII

WILDCAT RICHES

-1-

Karl Oskar had hoped to return from Stillwater before nightfall
on Friday. He was late; at bedtime he had not yet returned. Kristina put the children to bed, but she herself stayed up and kept
a fire going so that there would be a warm supper for her husband.

As yet she wasn't worried. Karl Oskar had been late on several
occasions before when going to Stillwater or Taylors Falls. On the
rough forest roads so much could happen to delay a ramshackle
oxcart. Their oxen were young and barely trained. And then there
was the heat and the swarms of mosquitoes. She felt sorry for Karl
Oskar, who must drive the team such a long way in this heat, when
even well-trained animals sometimes bolted because of the stinging insects.

Robert had gone to bed in the gable room at his usual time.
There was no need for him to stay up and wait for his brother. He
was sickly and needed his rest more than anyone else in the house.

A couple of long hours passed. Kristina waited. On the hearth
stood the pot with corn porridge she had cooked for supper —
now it was beginning to smell burnt. She must prepare something
else, something she could make ready quickly. She found some
eggs and poured water in a pot to boil them; then she cut a few
thick slices of pork. And she waited again.

She went outdoors and sat down on the oak bench near
the kitchen door, where it was cooler. The crickets squeaked and
wailed in the bushes and grass all around the house. She had become accustomed to this eternal din, but tonight she wished they
would keep quiet. Their noise prevented her from hearing the oxcart down the road.

199

It was almost midnight before Kristina heard the sound she had been waiting for. She went back into the kitchen and blew fire into the dying embers. The food would be ready as soon as Karl Oskar had unyoked the oxen and stabled them. After a few moments she heard his well-known footsteps outside the door. Only a few minutes more and the eggs would be boiled and the pork fried.

Karl Oskar came in. She greeted him with the words that many times before had met him when he returned. "You're late."

He flung his hat onto its accustomed nail on the wall, drew in his breath and told her that on the way home they had hit a stump in the road; the cart had turned over and broken its axle. They had borrowed tools, cut a tree and put in a new axle. This had delayed them several hours. His cart wasn't good enough for long trips.

She was just lifting the boiling pot off the fire, and she turned quickly around; his voice was strange to her. He spoke with effort, in short, stammmered words — she had never heard him talk like that before. What was the matter with him? The broken axle couldn't have affected him so seriously.

And Karl Oskar usually went directly to the table and sat down to eat when he came home hungry. This he didn't do tonight. He walked past her, into the big room, and she did not have time to look at his face. Wonderingly, she followed him. He had lighted a candle; his face was stern, his features frozen.

She had not intended to ask him anything before he had eaten, but now she couldn't wait. "What is it, Karl Oskar?"

Then she saw that he held something in his hands. With a sudden, angry thrust he threw it away — flung it all the way to the fireplace corner. Back there stood the old spittoon. What Karl Oskar had thrown away was a bundle of paper; it fluttered in the air as it passed her, and then in the spittoon in the corner lay a heap of green bills.

"We can throw those on the dunghill!"

"The money?"

"Wildcat money! Worthless!" Karl Oskar sat down on a chair heavily. " 'These bills ain't worth a plugged nickel,' the man at the bank said!" He tried to repeat what the man had said, the English expression that still rang in his ears.

At the bank in Stillwater, one clerk after another had come to look at the money. At last they had called out the director of the bank and he had inspected the bills at length. He was the one who had said, "Wildcat money! Good for nothing!"

The Indiana State Bank of Bloomfield which had issued the bills had long ago gone bankrupt. That was probably why its name hadn't been on the list in the Swedish newspaper. Bills on that bank were no longer in circulation in this part of the country, the banker had said, only far out in the wild West. And he had added: Even there it must be Swedish immigrants and other green-horns who were cheated with it.

He had said he felt sorry for Karl Oskar, and the clerks had said the same, but they couldn't accept his money. They had advised him never to accept bills unless he knew about the bank that issued them. And he had stood there like a fool when they handed the money back to him. He suspected the American bankers had had a good laugh at him, a trusting, ignorant Swedish settler.

Kristina stared at the fireplace corner, which was covered with the big bills, and tried to understand. How could the bills be false? Anyone in Sweden making false money was put into prison. Were such swindlers allowed to be loose in America? Had the banks themselves the right to cheat people?

Karl Oskar replied that as long as there was no order about money, anyone could start a bank and print bills. And wildcat money was a suitable name; the men who had printed these bills were the same as their namesake. They were as treacherous as the wild beasts lurking in the bushes.

Kristina sank down on a chair; she felt dazed and bewildered. Last Monday evening a fortune had come to their home. This was Friday, and it had come back to the house again. But now the money lay strewn like refuse in the spittoon in the corner. For it was a false fortune, wildcat riches.

An odor of burned pork came from the fire. She didn't recognize the smell. She had entirely forgotten that she had been preparing supper for Karl Oskar.

But he sniffed it. "Something is burning!"

He rushed to the kitchen and pulled the pan off the fire. Then he returned to her in the big room; he wasn't hungry tonight, any-way. He started walking back and forth across the floor, he pound-ed his fists against his chest — it was as if he wanted to punish himself for his foolishness.

"I had made up my mind I wouldn't let him fool me any more!

201

I had my doubts all the time! But he won — he made a fool of me."

"I can't believe Robert meant to cheat you when he gave us the money," said Kristina firmly.

"You still think well of him?" exclaimed Karl Oskar in a hardening voice. "Don't you know Robert by now?"

Kristina had just begun to know Robert by now. She had never thought of him as being evil or deceitful, and after her talk with him today under the sugar maples she was more sure than ever that he was not bad. Even though he sometimes lied, he was not a cheat. On the contrary, he himself was trusting and easily cheated. Wasn't it possible that *Robert* had been cheated by those bank men who had printed the bills?

"He must know they're useless!" said Karl Oskar. "He must have tried to use the same money himself. He found out the bills were useless and then thought they were good enough for us."

"No! I don't believe that of Robert."

"Of course — he felt ashamed to return empty-handed!" Karl Oskar looked toward the gable room. "I'm going to call him. Then you can hear what he has to say for himself."

"It's the middle of the night!" She took him by the arm. "He's sick. Leave him until tomorrow morning!"

"Well . . . "

Karl Oskar walked back and forth, flailing his long arms; bodily motion gave him some outlet for his anger. But Kristina sat crushed and silent, until the corners of her mouth began to twitch. "Is there anything one can trust here in America?"

"We mustn't take this too hard, Kristina." Karl Oskar lowered his voice, changed its tone completely. Looking at his wife, he could see that it was now time to talk differently. "No — no more crying about this! We aren't richer than before, but neither are we poorer. We haven't lost anything, not a single nickel. Nothing has changed for us."

He could also have said that in one way he almost felt satisfied: He had been right when he refused to believe in easy riches in America. For five years he had struggled and been hampered by his lack of cash — and the first time he had gone to a bank to put in some cash he had been told it was worthless! It was as though justice today had been meted out between the settler who improved his lot through honest labor and the good-for-nothing speculator who tried to get rich without work.

Kristina heard: As rich, as poor as before — no change. But for her something was changed. She had never for a moment doubted that their fortune was real, and she had already speculated on what the big bills would bring them. During these days and nights since Robert's return she had dreamed of a changed life on the claim. Stimulated by the thought of riches, she had already begun to live this new life. She had filled their bare rooms with new furniture, with new clothing of better cut and fit; she had traveled to her friend Mrs. Jackson in Stillwater on a new spring wagon, pulled by horses; she had engaged a servant to help in her chores — she had found aid for her great fatigue. She had bought thousands of things for the house and her dear ones during this wonderful June week when she had had her fortune for four days.

Yes, for Kristina something had changed. It was true, all they had gained out here in five years remained, they had not lost anything. Yet she felt as if this night she had suddenly become infinitely poorer.

- 2 -

Saturday morning Robert entered the kitchen as Kristina was busy starting the fire. His hair was ruffled and stood straight up, his cheeks were pale gray in the early morning light. He walked to the water bucket and took down the scoop from its nail on the wall. Just as he finished drinking Karl Oskar came in from his chores in the stable.

Karl Oskar took his brother by the arm. "Come, I want to show you something!"

They walked into the big room, Kristina behind them. Now it would come. She had been lying awake during the night, anxiously worrying about the morning meeting of the two brothers.

Karl Oskar pointed to the fireplace corner with the bills spread over the spittoon; they lay where he had flung them last night on his return. "There! You can take your money back! It might be useful when you go to the privy!"

He talked loudly, anger vibrating in his voice, but Robert did not seem to understand what he was driving at — he put his hand behind his healthy ear and turned it toward his brother to hear better.

"Keep your rubbish! I can get along without such trash!" Karl

Oskar stood straight and stern as he faced Robert. Now they had resumed the old order: Karl Oskar was again the big brother, scolding his little brother.

But Kristina could not see that Robert showed anything but puzzled surprise. "I don't understand, Karl Oskar."

He recognized his bills in the corner, all over the spittoon. Why were they there? Who had thrown them there? Wasn't his brother going to put them in the bank at Stillwater yesterday?

"Are you crazy, Karl Oskar? Why do you throw away all that money?"

"It's not worth a plugged nickel! All of it isn't worth one Swedish penny!"

"Not worth . . . ? No! You're crazy. Karl Oskar — it's impossible . . ."

Karl Oskar seldom grew angry, but when anger overtook him it came fast and furiously. His hands shook, he closed and opened his fists. He shouted with all his strength, "You liar! Why did I ever let you come with me to America! There isn't a decent bone in your body! You've poured lies on us all week long, but now at last it's finished! Finished, do you hear?"

Kristina stepped between the two brothers. "Stop shouting, Karl Oskar! You and your brother can at least talk to each other like civilized people."

Robert had several times tried to say something, but each time he had been interrupted by coughing. At last, in a weak, hoarse voice, he managed: "I always thought the money was good. I remember they called it wildcat money in English; that means free, sound money. And I told you the first evening — "

"I knew it!" interrupted Karl Oskar. "I knew you knew it all along!" He turned to Kristina. "There, you hear? He knew the money was no good! He admits it's wildcat money! He did it purposely — he wanted to fool us."

But the little brother was not listening to his big brother's accusation. He heard another voice saying: "Have you ever heard of wildcats? In the right hands they're as good as gold. Yes, wildcats are as good as gold."

Could it be that one Swede had cheated another Swede in America?

"Calm down, now!" Kristina pleaded with Karl Oskar.

"I — I didn't want to cheat anyone. Please, listen, Karl Oskar —"

"You're a hell of a brother! All my life I've had to feel ashamed of you — my own brother! Ashamed . . . ashamed!"

"But listen to me. I didn't think, I didn't know . . . "

"Shut up, I said! If you don't shut up, you damned liar, I'm going to shut your trap for you!"

It happened in a second. Karl Oskar's right fist shot out in a hard blow against his brother. It hit him on the mouth. Robert stumbled backward from the impact, against the wall.

"Have you become a wild beast yourself?" Kristina had grabbed hold of Karl Oskar's right arm with both her hands. Anger flamed up in her also and gave her strength. "Have you lost your mind?"

Karl Oskar tore himself free of her hold and walked back to the corner.

"Attack an invalid!" Kristina's lips were white with anger.

Aided by the wall, Robert had remained standing upright, but his legs still shook under him. In the very moment his brother's blow hit him he had been ready with his explanation: You must realize that I was cheated first — I never meant to cheat you, brother! But instead of his own voice all he heard now was his ear mocking him in a painful throbbing: *What did you bring home? Useless money! How about your health and your life? No riches and no life! What is there left for you?*

From the kitchen the children had been listening to the commotion, and the two smallest boys were yelling from fright. Kristina quickly closed the door. Karl Oskar remained in his corner, staring silently at the floor. His senses had returned; he stood with his head bent.

Kristina approached Robert. "Did he hurt you?"

"It's nothing." He turned to his older brother in the corner. "I am not lying. I didn't know. I had never tried to use the money. I had saved it for you and Kristina. I wanted to leave everything I owned to you and her."

Karl Oskar felt now that he had gone too far, that he had committed an outrage against his brother.

"Forgive me, Robert," he stammered.

"You had a right to hit me. It was my fault. I lived so long with that wildcat. I was blind."

"I blew up," said Karl Oskar. "Will you forgive me?" He had raised his head.

"I forgive you, of course. You're already forgiven! You're my only brother. I should have asked you to forgive me — but it's too late now. Everything is too late."

Robert sounded submissive, as if he had earned the blow, as if it were a well-deserved punishment. His legs felt steadier now; he walked slowly away, toward the gable room. Karl Oskar remained in his corner; it seemed the blow he had given his brother had dazed him instead.

When Robert came back from his room, he was wearing his boots, coat and hat. He moved quickly and resolutely.

"Where are you going?" asked Kristina, surprised.

He did not reply to her, but turned to Karl Oskar. "I'm off again. I don't want you to have to feel ashamed of your brother. Good-by! Forgive me the embarrassment I've caused you."

"Robert! Wait a minute!" Kristina grasped the back of his coat. "You can't leave again! You aren't well! You need care — "

"Good-by, Kristina. You've always been kind to me."

He walked toward the door, passing by the fireplace corner where the green-black bills lay scattered — wildcat money. When his eyes caught sight of them he stopped, as if a vision had appeared to him, revealing all, explaining all. He exclaimed, " 'As good as gold!' No — as false as gold! Bills or gold, all money is equally false. 'As good as gold!' As rotten, as deceitful, the root of all evil, that's what gold is. Now I can laugh at it all — ha, ha, ha!"

And as Robert hurried out through the door he laughed a high, piercing laugh that echoed through the house after him. His laughter frightened his brother and sister-in-law as much as a sudden attack on their home with shot and shell. They were utterly afraid. And they no longer tried to stop Robert.

They stood and looked through the window after him. He was already some distance from the house. He walked along the edge of the field, down the slope, toward the lake; he crossed the narrow creek and continued westward. He was headed for the forest. Once over the creek he would soon be swallowed up by the pines and the thickets.

"Hurry after him!" Kristina urged her husband suddenly. "Hurry as fast as you can. Don't let him get away!"

Karl Oskar replied that he knew his brother. Better leave him alone when he took off. Robert had always run away. He had fled many times in his life, but he had always come back. He was sure to return this time too.

Robert's tall, narrow body disappeared among the pines where the trunks glittered in the early-morning sun. He walked with hurried steps as far as they could see him.

XXIII

A STREAM THAT RUNS TOWARD GREATER WATERS

- 1 -

He walked without any definite course, around thickets, avoiding holes and stumps, choosing the easiest path. He made detours, walked sideways between tree trunks, around boulders and hills, across glades and clearings. He walked without knowing where he was going.

And the ear was with him on the walk. It buzzed and throbbed and ached.

It was a sizzling hot day. Tinder-dry branches cracked underfoot. No one cut or removed fallen timber from this wild forest; the dead trees stood where their roots held them and rotted above ground. In the clearings he waded through tall, coarse grass which crackled against his knees. And wherever he walked, mosquitoes in great clouds kept him company. One thick swarm circled his head and followed him faithfully, stinging angrily, humming steadily. They were wild beasts thirsting for his blood.

His legs grew tired during the walk, and he sat down on the ground to rest when he found a soft spot. But he took only short rests; soon he rose again and walked on — the pursuer inside his head forced him to move on. He must keep on the move, must get away. He must keep walking as long as he found ground to put his feet on.

He wandered about in the forest while the day passed. A dry branch knocked off his hat; he left it where it fell. The swarm of mosquitoes followed him and kept close to his head. He walked with a singing wreath of mosquitoes in his hair, he carried a crown of bloodsucking insects on his forehead. He walked through the forest crowned like a king.

In the afternoon the skies grew overcast; with the sun hidden it cooled off, and toward evening it began to rain. Soft drops wet

207

his skin, they fell faster and faster, and at last they drove away the mosquito wreath around his head. As dusk fell the rain increased. The drops no longer caressed Robert's skin; now they were sharp, whiplike. His trousers clung to his legs, water splashed in his boots. For a while he looked for shelter. Then he crept into a thicket of mountain ash. He tore leaves from the lush foliage and spread them on the ground; he would make a bed. He covered himself with a branch for a blanket and stretched out on the leaves.

Night fell over the forest. Here he was close to the wild animals, and his good ear registered the night sounds of living creatures: creeping, hissing, fluttering. A few times he heard persistent calls, perhaps Indians, perhaps birds. But his left ear heard only the usual sound, accompanied by pain. He picked up a few wet leaves and tried to press them into his ear. They felt soft and cool; they seemed to relieve the ache for a moment. He went to sleep, but woke up immediately. He pushed new leaves into the ear. Then he went to sleep again.

His night in the thicket passed in a continuous falling asleep and awakening. Both sleeping and waking, he heard his pursuer's voice: *I'm with you wherever you go! I'm inside your head and you can't get away from me! You can run away from other masters, but not from me!*

Day came with its light. A clear summer morning dawned over the wild forest. He rose from his bed of leaves and started to move, but he felt heavy weights in his limbs. He trembled and shivered; on this warm morning he felt cold inside.

He walked on, more slowly now, his steps unsteady, unsure. The oppressing heat returned, and the swarm of mosquitoes was back. Soon he again had the buzzing wreath around his head. He felt thirsty and began to look for water. His stomach was empty, but he felt no hunger.

Snails in great numbers had come out after last night's rain and they enlivened the ground with their beautiful houses; blue, yellow, red and brown — their shells were striped in all colors. But the rain had already been sucked up by the earth, and the creeks were empty. He must quench his thirst; he kept looking. In a clearing he found some wild strawberries and ate some of them. They tasted of summer at home in Sweden, when children remove their shoes and stockings and run barefoot; but they did not quench his thirst.

For some time he followed a winding deer path. He came to a bog with a narrow water hole in the center. But this was stagnant water and he dared not drink of it. In that hole lay fevers and ills and poison. Drinking water must be running water. The water in his dream was in motion, pouring forth, purling and swirling in freedom. Water must flow free as the river that ran to the sea.

He walked around the bog without attempting to drink, his feet sinking deep in the mud. He left clear tracks behind him. The Indians never left tracks when they passed through the forest. An Indian's foot moved lightly and quickly as a wing above the earth. Now he was back at a place where his boot tracks showed he had been shortly before.

He thought now and then: He had run away again. As soon as no one looked after him he ran away to the woods and hid. This he had done ever since he was a small child. Only this time no one had hung a bell around his neck, this time no one would find him. He would remain unreachable.

He saw a great body of water glitter blue among the pines; he was back at Ki-Chi-Saga. Many people had come to this lake, cutting the trees, timbering their houses. But in this particular spot the shore still lay wild and untouched as far as he could see. He walked slowly along the shore, looking down into the water, which clearly reflected the skies above him. He could see the reeds growing upside down, stretching their heads toward an open sky which undulated at the bottom. At one time he could see two skies, two heavens, the one above him and the one below in the water, and between them lay the earth on which he himself wandered about, lost.

Striking fins made circling ripples among some boulders; near the shore the lake bubbled with fish. If he had brought a fishing pole he would immediately have had a bite. And if he could have made a fire and had a pan . . . For a moment he thought about the taste of good fried fish; but he felt no real hunger.

On a flat stone in the sand lay a fish, washed up by the waves. Its whiskers indicated it was a catfish. But its skin was white; perhaps it had been lying here for a long time in the sun. Robert picked it up by the gills and held it to his nose; it had a nauseating smell, making him want to vomit. It was spoiled. With a jerk he threw it away, far out into the lake.

Weariness fell over his body, dulling his senses. The pursuer kept hammering and buzzing and hurting. It felt as if something had swelled up inside his head and wanted to get out; it knocked and thundered and pounded. *Open! Open! I want to get free!*

But his feet moved on, he wandered about, in circles, in wide arcs. And no bell around his neck tinkled to disclose his path.

-2-

It was late afternoon but the sun was still above the trees when he reached a small stream that wound its way among the thickets. The stream had shrunk in the summer heat, and clean-washed boulders rose from its bottom; but the water which flowed there was crystal clear, and the trees had helped to keep it cool.

Robert threw himself headlong on the ground and dipped his face in the brook. The water ran into his wide-open mouth; he swallowed, he panted, he drank. It gurgled in his throat. He drank for a long time. When he had quenched his thirst he sat down to rest near the stream, water still dripping from his chin. The foliage of trees and bushes formed a thick mantle over the brook. Close to him an elderbush spread its limbs over the water.

He gave in to his bodily weariness and sank down. While he watched the running steam, his mind cleared.

He had sat here once before. He had seen this narrow stream swell with the spring rains. It was the day he was on his way to his first job as a farm hand. But he had not wanted to work for anyone, so he had thrown his coat into the water and pretended to have drowned. He had escaped — but he had been caught later by his master. That had been his first attempt to become free.

Now he was back. He recognized the place, it was well known to him. Before his eyes he saw every detail: the smooth, shiny stones on the bottom, the lush vegetation on the banks and the fresh water with its bubbles glittering like water-lily pads. Everything he saw was the same.

He had come back to the mill brook.

He took off his boots and socks and dangled his bare feet in the stream; he always did this here when he was a young boy. The water bubbled between his burning toes. It cooled his legs mercifully. Everything felt good.

He had roamed widely, he had been in the Train of the Hundred

Thousand which was led by the Pillar of Gold, and he had almost perished in that evil place of sand and stone and thirst. He had lived years in a ghost town that was full of dead rats and desolate sites where people once had had homes. He had not thought he would ever return home again, he had not imagined he could return. But at last he had found his way back to Sweden. He recognized everything. Here he had rested the day he set out into the world. Now he had come home.

Now he needn't walk any farther, and that was well, he was so tired. He hadn't rested much for a long time. But here he could rest — he was at home.

What time of day was it? He had no watch, except the one that had stopped three years ago. He would have liked to know what time it was when he returned.

He lifted his feet from the water and stretched out full length on the ground below the wide elderbush. It was good to be home, to rest here by the brook and watch it through the foliage. And here he could go to sleep and dream again the water dream, the good dream.

- 3 -

Once he woke up and then he lay and listened, greatly surprised. His ear was silent, it didn't buzz any more. His left ear did not ache, did not buzz, did not throb. It gave no sound at all.

He lay quite still and listened intently, but could hear nothing. The world had grown completely silent. Then his left ear must have grown well. There was no pain. And he felt released and refreshed and deeply satisfied. His pursuer, his buzzing old ear, had at last left him in peace.

He was rid of his last master. He needn't run away any more. He was free.

He noticed it was evening, the day was over. Then he could just lie here and go to sleep again. Now that his sick ear was silent perhaps he could sleep the whole night through. And a drowsiness that was good, that was irresistible, soon closed his eyes.

All was silent in the world. The ear did not awaken him.

Close by the gold seeker's still body the stream in its course hurried on its way to mingle with greater waters.

4

A searching party found his tracks near the bog, and from there on they could follow them to the edge of the brook where he lay under the foliage. They thought he must have been dead for two days when they found him.

Karl Oskar Nilsson made the coffin for his brother. He was buried one evening on the point at Lake Ki-Chi-Saga where the Swedish settlement had consecrated a new cemetery. Karl Oskar put an oak cross on the grave and carved in the wood his brother's name and a line from a psalm he remembered:

Here Rests
AXEL ROBERT NILSSON
Born in Ljuder, Sweden, 1833
Died in Minnesota, North America, 1855
Let Me Have a Pleasing Sleep

His was the first grave to be dug in the cemetery on the point. Robert Nilsson was the first one of the Swedes in the St. Croix Valley to be buried under the silver maples.

III

BLESSED WOMAN

XXIV

THE QUEEN IN THE KITCHEN

-1-

Karl Oskar had caught sight of her in Newell's Hardware Store on Third Street between Jackson and Robert streets; he was walking by and she was displayed in the window. Her name, "The Prairie Queen," was lettered on her front. She was well polished, and her shiny iron surface caught the eye even at a distance. The Queen showed herself in all her glory to pedestrians, and many persons stopped to look at her. But the price asked for her was high: thirty-three dollars.

Karl Oskar had come to the pork market in St. Paul with four slaughtered hogs on his wagon. In Stillwater pork brought only four cents a pound, but in St. Paul he received six cents and thus it paid to drive the longer distance. The buyer had counted out forty dollars in silver; Karl Oskar could pay cash for the Prairie Queen and take her home with him on the wagon.

After a moment's hesitation he stepped inside Newell's Hardware Store and made the purchase.

The Queen arrived secretly at the New Duvemåla settlement. She came in a nailed box which Karl Oskar smuggled into the woodshed when no one was around. He put it in a corner and covered it with some old sacks; here the Queen was well hidden. It was early in December and the Prairie Queen was not to be moved from her hiding place until Christmas Eve. She was to be a Christmas present for Kristina.

Karl Oskar mused that the name Prairie Queen was an excellent one for a cookstove. The Prairie Queen, which had swallowed up almost all his income from the sale of four big hogs, was made of cast iron and came equipped with four utensils: a roaster, a kettle, a coffeepot and a frying pan; and the stove had the reputation of being the most convenient stove in the world.

When preparing food at a hearth, pots were placed on an iron trivet in the center of the fire. Only one pot at a time could be used, and care must be taken lest the pot turn over. All cooking had been done this way until now. But today in America stoves of iron could be bought, stoves that were not built into the hearth and anchored to the chimney but were movable like any other piece of furniture. Kristina had wondered what such a cooking machine would be like. Now she would find out for herself.

Karl Oskar let Johan and Harald in on the secret of the hidden box in the woodshed, and during the early morning of Christmas Eve, while Kristina was busy with the milking, the two boys helped their father carry the heavy iron object into the kitchen and place it on the old hearth. On top they put the four cooking utensils, each in its proper place on the lid of one of the four cook holes. Karl Oskar made a hole in the side of the chimney and pushed the iron pipe at the back of the stove into it. Finally he went over the whole stove with a rag and dusted and polished the cast iron until it glittered. The new stove lighted up the whole kitchen.

When Kristina returned from the barn she stopped and stared openmouthed. What in the world was that sitting back there? What had they put on her hearth? Her husband and sons stood silent, winking to each other as she kept asking.

"What in the world ... ? What is that in the fireplace?"

An important guest had come to their house this Christmas, explained Karl Oskar. A queen had come to them in their kitchen. She would always sit there on the hearth and would aid the mistress with her cooking.

Kristina walked closer to inspect the Prairie Queen. Her hands stroked the shiny iron, they took hold of the pot handles, lifted up the kettle and the coffeepot as if to feel how heavy they were. And now Kristina remembered the invention she had read about in the paper and understood the purpose of the new object in their kitchen.

"A new cookstove of iron!"

"Of cast iron," said Karl Oskar.

"Have you bought it?"

"Yes — it's bought and paid for. I'm not in the habit of stealing things."

"Oh, my, what a stove! How pretty it is!"

"The stove is a female, by the way. Called the Prairie Queen. The name is stamped on the front of her."

Kristina sat down on the pile of wood beside the stove, overwhelmed, as Karl Oskar described it with a pride that couldn't have been greater had he himself been the inventor. Into these holes with doors the wood was put. And here were the cook holes, with removable lids set into rims which also could be removed if greater heat was required under the pots and kettles. And that big door on the side was the baking oven, not for real baking, of course, but for smaller cakes. Food would cook much faster on this stove, since it preserved the heat.

"And all these cast-iron utensils come with her," he added. "Aren't they fine?"

"They are like the glory of heaven," Kristina said. "And the stove is a decoration for our home!"

She stood before the gleaming Prairie Queen admiring and respectful, like a dutiful subject before a royal personage. This queen had four crowns: kettle, roaster, coffeepot and frying pan. What woman could look at that glittering presence without being seized with the desire to use it?

"Can I light the stove?" she asked.

"She's connected, ready to go. You can begin cooking at once."

Karl Oskar had cut wood of the right size for the Prairie Queen's stomach. In no time he had a fire in her. It smoked a little, but he blamed this on the heavy fog that day; it kept the chimney from drawing properly.

The first meal Kristina prepared on the new stove was their Christmas Eve dinner, the most festive meal of the year. It was their third Christmas in the new house and their seventh in North America.

-2-

The children were allowed to eat as much as they could of the delicious Christmas food and then they went to sleep in the gable room, full and tired.

215

Since last Christmas a new life had come into the house; in February Kristina had borne a boy who had been christened Frank Aldo Hjalmar. They called him Frank; he was the first of the children to be given an American name. Of her surviving children Kristina had given birth to three in Sweden and three in America. One half of their children were Swedes, one half Americans; half of them represented the old country, half the new.

After her last confinement Kristina had been so weak physically that it took several months before she could fully resume her chores. And during the holiday preparations which were just over she had felt that her old strength had even yet not fully come back.

When the children were in bed this Christmas Eve, Karl Oskar read Kristina a few passages from the prayer book about Christ's birth, beginning as usual with Luther's words of greeting and rejoicing on the blessed day. By and by their talk turned to worldly things, and first of all to the new iron stove.

"Thirty-three dollars!" said Kristina. "What an expense!"

"The stove will aid you in your work," said Karl Oskar. "It's worth the price."

In a sudden burst of emotion Kristina put out her hand to him across the table. "Thank you, Karl Oskar!"

He had been thinking of her when he bought the Prairie Queen. This she had of course understood at once, but it was good to hear him say it. He never failed in his concern for her. It seldom took expression in words; he was shy and retiring in such matters. But they knew each other so well that speech between them was not required. What people said need not mean anything. What people *did* meant everything.

How much work and worry Karl Oskar had had in fattening those four hogs which had paid for the Prairie Queen! How many steps he had taken in order that she might have an iron stove. Nothing could have been more useful than this help in the kitchen. Yet she could not help feeling that he could have bought something they needed more for those thirty-three dollars. There were implements, invented here in America, that could have aided Karl Oskar in his work. Hadn't he several times spoken of a reaper and a threshing machine?

The reaper and the thresher were still too expensive for him, replied Karl Oskar. He would surely get himself both these ma-

216

chines by and by; he knew how many days' work they would save him in a year. But first he had been thinking of a horse. He couldn't raise a horse, since he didn't own a mare. He had had in mind to put aside this hog money for a horse; in fact, he had felt he almost had it by the halter chain. But just then he had caught sight of the Prairie Queen in the store window in St. Paul — and he had let go his hold of the horse.

"You need a little rest, Kristina. Things are too much for you."

Yes, she needed some rest. Her strength diminished and her chores increased. The older children were growing up and could begin to look after themselves, but new ones had arrived who required care in their stead. She always had three babies who depended on her, one in her arms and two hanging onto her skirt. And at fairly regular intervals she had to seek her bed of labor, from which she arose more tired each time. At intervals her body was turned into a supply house for a new life, her exhausted breasts were required to sustain a hungrily sucking mouth. Karl Oskar had known what he was doing a few years earlier when he had made a solid cradle of oak; that cradle did not often stand empty.

Karl Oskar himself pulled such a heavy load that he could not take on any of hers. His willingness to help was in itself a help, though. But she would never have managed without her comforting feeling of motherhood; she had carried them in her body, she had borne the children in pain, but when she had them around her, all healthy and without blemishes, chirruping like morning birds — in such moments she felt a joy so great that she wanted only to thank God for the lives He had created through her.

After a moment's silence she said, "I wonder how it is at home this evening."

"They must be on their way to early-morning Christmas service," said Karl Oskar. "The Swedish clocks are six hours ahead of us."

Kristina had thought often about this difference in time. It showed that Sweden and America were two entirely different worlds, with different hours. While it still was evening here, dawn broke at home. The two countries were given their days, their light and their dark, at different times.

For a few evenings before the holidays Karl Oskar had busied himself with the letter to Sweden. Tomorrow he would take enough time off to finish it. The most recent letter from his father had come during the fall. It had been short, yet difficult for Karl Oskar to read; the lines wriggled up and down like snakes, and in many places the letters ran into each other. His father, Nils Jakob's Son, wrote that his hands trembled more than ever.

It was in this letter that his father had replied to the news of his son Robert's death in America: "It was Sad for us Old ones to learn of our youngest Son's demise in youthful years. It was difficult for Robert to be satisfied with anything in this World. You wrote that your Brother traveled widely. Whither can Man flee where Death will not overtake him?"

The letter was barely ten sentences long, and Nils had written only these few words about Robert. It seemed as if his trembling hands had been unable to cope with his sorrow.

When Karl Oskar read the letter to Kristina, she told him what she had heard his father say that April morning when they left home and started their journey to the American ship: "I must go outside and behold my sons' funeral procession." The words touched Karl Oskar deeply — his father had felt his sons were dead to him while they still lived. Thus, when the message of Robert's death reached him he had already submitted to his loss.

The old parents did not know the circumstances of their youngest son's death. Karl Oskar had written only that Robert had died suddenly from an unknown sickness. Since then a new summer had come and gone; the silver maples had twice shed their leaves over the first grave of the new cemetery. And Robert was no longer alone in the Swedish burying plot at Chisago Lake.

Karl Oskar often thought to himself: You raised your hand against your brother the last time you saw him in life! Robert's assurance of forgiveness had been some comfort to him when they had found the body a few days later. But his brother's pardon was not sufficient; Karl Oskar could not forgive himself for what he had done. Kristina had never again mentioned this burst of temper, except to say on the day of Robert's funeral that it was something to learn from — people should always act toward one another as if each meeting were the last.

She had several times told her husband about the talk she had had with Robert under the sugar maples on the day Karl Oskar went to Stillwater; it had been her last time alone with her brother-in-law. Now she spoke of it again, and he wondered how she could remember what Robert had said so precisely after such a long time. She explained that his words had acquired a special meaning after he died, and she thought of them so often because he had spoken them when he had only a few days left to live.

"Do you suppose he knew he didn't have much time left?"

Karl Oskar had asked this question before, and she always answered the same way: She was sure that Robert knew he had not long to live. "I suspect he had consumption," she added now.

"Probably so."

"But Robert wasn't afraid of death. He was unreachable, he said."

"Unreachable? There he is, talking in riddles again."

"It's no riddle. I understand what he meant."

"You do?" Karl Oskar looked at his wife in surprise. "What do you suppose he meant?"

This time Kristina was somewhat slow in answering, and when she spoke her voice was tense and strained; she tried in vain to keep it from trembling.

"He was reconciled to his lot in life," she murmured. "We are not."

What was this all about? Karl Oskar asked himself. A few words spoken by Robert a year and a half ago had made such an impression on Kristina that she repeated them time and again. What did it mean? He now began to suspect that she was keeping something from him.

"What is it we must be reconciled to, Kristina?"

She averted her eyes, as if she felt she had said too much and was now regretting it.

"I don't want to talk about it tonight, Karl Oskar. It's very late, we should go to bed."

How deeply Robert's words about his fate had affected her she did not reveal even to Karl Oskar. They concerned her own life, the lot of the emigrant. And each new day posed this question to her: How would she manage *her* lot in life?

- 3 -

Beginning with Christmas Eve 1856 the settler wife had a good and faithful assistant in her kitchen. On the Prairie Queen she prepared and cooked the food for their large family in half the time it had previously taken her. After a few months with the new stove Kristina could not understand how she had managed her household without it for so many years. She loved her stove as if it were a living being. She dusted it every day and polished away spots and grease and soot. The Prairie Queen sat always shining clean, the first object a caller's eyes lighted on when entering the kitchen, and she always received her homage: What a beautiful stove!

The only name they used for it was the Queen: Have you fired the Queen? Has the Queen burned out? Did you empty the ashes of the Queen? The potato pot boils over on the Queen! Get some wood for the Queen! But Karl Oskar insisted that the truth be known in his house: "You, Kristina, *you* are the queen in our kitchen!"

To this she laughed heartily, her hands and face sooty. Pastor Törner had once said something similar when she mended his trousers; he had said that with thread and needle and nothing else she could turn herself into a queen and their house into a palace. Still, she had never before heard a man use such fair and poetic speech to his own wife.

But it was true that she reigned supreme inside their house. While Karl Oskar had his domain outside, Kristina kept things in order within, made new clothes for all of them, milked the cows, churned butter, made cheese, spun and spooled yarn, wove and sewed. She also, during some busy seasons, helped Karl Oskar in the field with sowing, mowing and harvesting.

And every day she fought fatigue. Every day there was some moment when she was tempted to give in and drop what she had in hand, when she wanted to lie down and do nothing except rest quietly. She would force herself to go on; it was her work, her responsibility, and no one else's.

She was not yet an old woman; at her age she had no right to be tired. Only after another twenty or thirty years as household ruler would she be permitted to abdicate.

XXV

THE YEAR '57

- 1 -

In seven years, seven hundred towns were surveyed and laid out in Minnesota Territory, and the number of inhabitants increased from six thousand to one hundred and fifty thousand. After the 1851 treaty with the Sioux the whole country west of the Mississippi lay open for settlers. Not all of them had come to Minnesota to farm. In the tillers' wake came the speculators who would gain riches from the earth without tilling it. To these, land was a commodity, to be bought one day and sold with profit the next. In their hands, land quickly rose in value. The price of a lot might double overnight. Claims were staked out with feverish haste. The money men grew rich, while the farmer remained poor.

Then came the year 'fifty-seven. It began with disturbing happenings in the East: New York banks closed. The disaster quickly spread westward; the Chicago banks toppled, and by the autumn of 1857 it had reached Minnesota. The banks in St. Paul and Stillwater shut their doors. People who had been rich in the morning were utterly poor before the sun set. People with no property except money were destitute. Paper bills no longer had any value. There was no gold and no acceptable currency. No one could buy without money, and no one could sell. Business came to a standstill.

What could money be used for when it was no longer trusted? What could money men do without money? The speculators' twilight was at hand; the great revolution in money swept them from the Territory. A horde of brokers and jobbers left Minnesota. In one year St. Paul's population dropped by four thousand. The men behind the plows remained in possession of the earth. It was they who would build the future state of Minnesota.

221

2

During 1855 and 1856 the weather had been favorable for crops, and the fields at New Duvemåla had brought good harvests. As soon as Karl Oskar had done his threshing in the fall he noted down in the old almanac the number of bushels. He saw that his crop in 1956 was half again as great as last year's, and his corn alone ten times as many bushels as his first year's crop. Now he was planting this Indian grain on one fourth of his fields; corn might give up to forty bushels per acre, and wheat was almost as generous in the deep soil.

But the following year, 1857, was to be one of adversity in more than financial ways. A severe spring drought had set in which lasted the better part of the summer. The corn was best able to withstand it; the other crops failed. Then, about harvest time, came the grasshoppers. There had been no such pests in Minnesota since 1849, but one day they appeared in immense swarms, consuming everything green in their path, leaving only the black earth behind them.

The legislature in St. Paul offered a bounty of five cents a bushel for grasshoppers. Johan and Märta earned two dollars each from catching them. And the Governor proclaimed a day of prayer in the churches against the plague. The authorities also urged people to observe a fast day, but few did this; the settlers felt they would probably have to starve enough during the winter after their crops had been eaten.

In Chisago Township the grasshoppers were less numerous than in other parts of the Territory, but Karl Oskar's crop was still only one quarter of the previous year's. Fortunately, having some left of the old harvest, his family could manage to get along through the winter.

And then, in the late fall of that miserable year, came the financial crash.

Karl Oskar had already learned once that money was sometimes nothing but paper. During 'fifty-seven many others were to share his bitter experience: they were fooled by currency the banks could not redeem. Few were the settlers who hadn't at one time or another been tricked into exchanging a load of grain or a fatted hog for worthless bills. Now the people's faith in paper money was completely gone.

The great money upheaval, while it lasted, certainly freed the country of the speculators; but the settlers had a difficult time for, since no one could buy, they were unable to sell their crops. For his grain and pork Karl Oskar would accept nothing but gold coins or good bills, and neither were available this fall. Thus he himself was without cash for the purchases he wanted to make. And when he occasionally could sell something for good money the price offered was pitifully low. Pork was down to two cents a pound; after fattening a hog for half a year, until it finally weighed two hundred pounds, he received only four dollars for his labor. Still, Karl Oskar grew neither poorer nor richer during 'fifty-seven. The banks might tumble, but he didn't have a penny in them. His fields lay where they had lain before. For months on end he didn't have a coin in the house to buy with, but his family had a roof over their heads, heat from their stove, bread, milk, butter, eggs, pork. Although money had disappeared, they had shelter and food.

Since Karl Oskar had got his own team he had every fall broken at least five new acres of the vast meadow below his house. By now he could look out on thirty tilled acres. Next spring he would seed four times as much land as he had owned in Sweden, and the earth here was three times as fertile as his old farm.

He liked to sit at the window and look out at his fields. This was the land he had changed. When he came the whole meadow had been covered with weeds and wild grass. Now it carried rye, wheat, oats, corn, potatoes, turnips. It was *his* hands that had held the plow handles when this fertile earth was wrested from the wilderness. The cultivation was his work and no one else's.

If he called the fields his own created work, Kristina would undoubtedly say that he was arrogant. A creator, to her, was one who could make something out of nothing, and only God could do that. Kristina was intimate with the Almighty and always trusted Him. But Karl Oskar could not be like her in this. Ever since the years of adversity at home he had been suspicious of God's help. No matter what a person did, he couldn't be sure of God's aid in his enterprise. He must trust himself and his own strength. Our Lord let the crops grow but what if one hadn't cleared the land, plowed and sown? Could it then be sinful arrogance to look out over fields and say: There is the creation of my own hands?

223

XXVI

THE LETTER FROM SWEDEN

Åkerby at Ljuder Parish
August 16 Anno 1857

Beloved Brother Karl Oskar Nilsson
The Lord's Peace and Blessing upon you.

I am about to write you a Message of Sorrow. Tears of Bereavement are falling as I pen these Lines: Our Father, Nils Jakob's Son, parted this Life the 4th inst. and he was brought to the Earth in the Parish Churchyard the 11th inst. His Life's Span amounted to Sixty-two Years and a few Months. He suffered a long Deathbed but did not complain. Our new pastor gave him the Sacrament three Days before he died, he managed to put himself in Order for the Pastor and combed his Hair himself.

It was our Father's wish to pass on and have Peace. He had some attacks of Fever and Dizziness toward the last and his Mind wandered. The last Night he mentioned you and Robert in North America, he heard your Wagon drive out of the Yard on your Journey to America and he rose from his Pillow and said, Now they are leaving. He said few Words in Life after that.

We must all one Day pale in Death. Our Strength will not suffice against it. But there is much to do when it is a Guest in the House. We are settling the Estate and I ask you to send me your Power of Attorney, then we need not have an auction after our Father. Send also an Attest that our Brother Robert is dead and then we won't need a Power of Attorney from him.

We are in good Health in our Family except that I have a Boil on a finger of my right Hand. I have a kind Husband, we have now 2 Sons and 1 Daughter. I have forgotten how many Children you have, Write and tell us. I suppose you have forgotten the People hereabouts. Dean Brusander is dead, he had a Stroke in the Sacristy Whitsuntide Morning. He asked about you a few Years ago when he baptized our oldest Boy.

Mother greets you as she can't write to you herself. Our Mother is getting old and worn out, When our Strength is gone all joy is over.

It is not easy to write down my Thoughts on Paper, I am poor in Composition. Don't forget us in your new Homeland.

God bless you, Brother, and I hope your Success continues.

Written down by your devoted Sister

Lydia Karlsson

XXVII

THE LETTER TO SWEDEN

New Duvemåla at Taylors Falls Post Ofis, North-America

October 3 Anno 1857

Beloved Sister Lydia Karlsson,

Your letter received, I could not help but shed a few Tears as I held it in my Hand and read that our Father had passed through the Valley of Death. I mourn him here, far from his bier.

I had hoped to see him once More, I had a good Father but was not always an obedient Son at Home. I feel though that Father forgave me my Emigration, I did the best for my Own, our Father couldn't think Anything else.

Now my Father is in that Land where I no longer can reach him. Peace over his Grave and Remains. Yes, Death mows with his sharp Scythe and makes no Exception among us. When he comes we must go with him, whether we want to or not. I am, however, glad that Father had one of his Children with him as a comfort on his Deathbed.

My kind Parents looked after me well when I grew up but out here in my new Land I have been of little Help or Comfort to them.

I enclose a Paper which assures you that you my beloved Sister Lydia Karlsson shall have my Inheritance after my demised Father Nils Jakob's Son. You shall have my Share for looking after our Mother as long as she is alive. I believe it cannot be a large sum of Money.

We have lately had some Trouble with Money Matters in

America but it is getting better. Many People have moved in from Sweden this last Summer and they are still coming daily. Even from Ljuder Parish people have come to this Valley. I see that the Dean is gone, how did he like it that his Parishioners followed me to North America? But he couldn't blame me, I like the land here but have never boasted in order to lure people here from Sweden. I urge no Man to emigrate; each One must do so at his own Risk.

The Number of our Children is 6 now, if I haven't written this before. Our Youngest is a robust Son we call Frank, it is an American name. He runs and plays on the floor. He was one Year old last February. Our Children have grown fast in their new Homeland.

I enclose my loving Greeting to our Mother. I know you take good Care of her. You are my beloved Sister and we must write each other more often. Before each Day reaches its End I always give some Thought here in America to my old Home.

Your devoted Brother
Karl Oskar Nilsson

XXVIII

KARL OSKAR'S FOLLOWERS

- 1 -

That fall brought endless rain. It began like a sudden shower, but lasted a week, two weeks. The rain did not fall in drops, it streamed down in sheets. Days on end it hung outside the window like a curtain. No settler had ever seen such a persistent rain in Minnesota. The autumn sowing was delayed and the rye did not begin to sprout until the winter frost had penetrated the ground.

On one of these long days, when the rain prevented all outside work, the Lutheran minister came to call. One memorable rainy night four years earlier Pastor Erland Törner had come to the settlement at Duvemåla for the first time. This time he came on a last visit — to say good-by.

There had long been rumors that he wanted to leave the St. Croix Valley, and now they were confirmed by his own words: He had accepted a call as pastor at the church in Rockford, a new town down in Illinois, where there was a sizable Swedish colony. He was going to be married, and this had influenced his decision to leave — she was a Swedish girl from Rockford and wanted to remain in her home town after her marriage.

The minister was no longer the pale, spindly young man who had warmed himself before the fire in their old log house, dressed like a scarecrow in Karl Oskar's clothes. He had put on weight and his body was firmer; his face was weather-beaten and his looks rugged. Now the young pastor could be taken for a settler. And his life was not unlike that of his fellow countrymen.

During the first two years they had gathered for services in the schoolhouse, and only last year had the new church been ready for use. Kristina almost never failed to attend services, and Pastor Törner's sermons had been a great comfort to her. This minister did not enter the pulpit like a stern judge; he was a mild Gospel preacher, on equal footing with the sinners. He was the only minister she could think of in their pulpit — he was The Minister. And now he would move away from them.

Yesterday Karl Oskar had shot a wild goose; she had plucked the white-breasted bird, drawn it and prepared it for the pot. She had thought of saving it for Sunday dinner, but then she knew that she must roast it today and invite Pastor Törner, since it would be her last opportunity to give him a meal.

She set the table in the large room, and her guest was asked to sit down on the sofa they had recently bought. Karl Oskar and she sat on either side of him. The children were not allowed to sit at table today; they would eat afterward in the kitchen.

"My first night in the St. Croix Valley I slept in your home," said Pastor Törner. "In your home I preached my first sermon in this valley, and here I gave the Lord's Holy Supper for the first time. Memories make you dear to me, my friends!"

He spoke his native tongue better than any other Swede she had met in America, thought Kristina. It was a balm just to listen to his voice. Most of the immigrants had begun to mix up the two languages dreadfully so that she could hardly understand them. Even Karl Oskar's language had changed; she noticed the mixture sooner than others because she herself never used English.

The children kept peeking in through the kitchen door while their parents sat eating with the minister. To the three oldest he had been their teacher, and they had great respect for him; they were always unusually silent and well-behaved as long as this caller was in the house.

In the beginning Paster Törner had acted as teacher of all the Swedish children, as well as minister to the congregation; but last year the parish had managed to get a teacher from Sweden, a Mr. Johnson — he was quite particular that they call him Mister. He was remunerated according to the number of children he taught, receiving one dollar a month for each child. A room had been prepared for him in the school building, and he was also given free firewood. The parish contributed ten bushels of rye flour a year, and thus he had his bread free.

Besides receiving instruction in the Lutheran religion, Swedish and English, the settlers' children were taught writing, arithmetic, history and geography. Johnson had proved to be competent; he had graduated from high institutions in Sweden. But after he had been here for a while it was discovered that he was given to drinking. According to the children he sometimes told funny stories instead of going on with the lesson. Once he had danced in school, jumped about and sung, and it had not been psalms he had sung, either. Some parents had become greatly disturbed and insisted that the parish must get rid of Mr. Johnson. Others said they would rather have a drunkard teacher than no teacher at all. At Karl Oskar's suggestion the parish council had deferred the question.

Now Karl Oskar asked Pastor Törner's opinion: "Should we keep the schoolmaster?"

Mr. Johnson did drink to excess, said the pastor, but he had implanted much knowledge in the children. The parish would probably not be able to find a teacher of his ability to replace him; the salary was not high enough to attract a graduate teacher from Sweden. As long as the teacher's drinking did not hurt the children, Pastor Törner thought they ought to keep him. Mr. Johnson was no longer a young man, and the pastor had spoken seriously to him, made him promise not to take any whiskey until after school hours. Then he would have a whole night to sober up before the next day of teaching. He hoped Mr. Johnson would keep his promise.

For his three children of school age — Johan, Märta and Harald — Karl Oskar paid the teacher three dollars a month. Next spring when Dan, the first American in their family, began school, he would have to pay four dollars a month.

Before Pastor Törner left he distributed gifts to the six children. Happiest of all was Harald, who received a Swedish book, *First Reader for Beginners,* which the pastor had sent for from the old country. The pastor had instructed Harald for a few months and he remembered what a good head the boy had.

"He reads Swedish like a minister!" said the mother proudly. "As soon as he has read a piece once he can repeat it by heart."

The father added: They had sent for *The Little Catechism* from *Hemlandet* and the boy had learned it by heart in a few evenings. And when he found anything printed in English he read it as well as an American.

Pastor Törner looked from Harald to Karl Oskar. "Of all your children, this one in particular takes after his father."

The settler smiled. "You mean he has my nose!"

Harald was the only one among the children who had inherited the big Nilsa-nose. But there was a belief in the family that its bearer would have luck in life. Perhaps a hundred years from now the big nose might decorate many American faces, and in that way the Nilsa family would set its mark on America.

-2-

The Swedes' new wooden church had been built in the spacious oak grove on the peninsula opposite Nordberg's Isle, a mile and a half from Karl Oskar's place. From the center of the roof a steeple had been raised thirty feet toward the sky. The builders had gone to a great deal of trouble with this spire, the timbers of which were carefully hewn and planed. Thirty feet might seem a pitiful attempt at a steeple, but none of the builders had raised a church before, and in any case it did point the way to the Lord's heaven. Although services were already being conducted in the church, it was far from finished inside. There were only a few pews, and most of the participants must stand during the sermon; church bell and organ were missing, too, because the parish was short of cash.

As a member of the parish council Karl Oskar had suggested the erection of a lightning rod to protect the new church; since it was built of wood, it could easily burn should lightning strike it. Petrus Olausson was immediately against Karl Oskar. To put up a lightning rod on the church would be to show distrust of God. A person who did not believe the Lord would be capable of averting lightning from His temple, and who preferred to trust a copper wire, could not be a good Christian. If they put up a lightning rod they would commit the grave sin of weak faith.

Karl Oskar replied: Was a person never to use protective measures? Then one couldn't use warm clothing against cold. Nor could a person swim to shore if he happened to fall into the lake. If this were the Lutheran religion, then he was not a true Lutheran.

"Yes, we know," agreed Olausson with sad finality. "You and your wife harbor sectarians and evil preachers in your house. The devil has put it into your head to use the lightning rod in an attempt to make us give up the true religion."

Olausson thus having raised a doubt in the minds of other council members concerning Karl Oskar's religion, one by one they refused to vote for his motion. Only Jonas Petter stood by him. Thus because Karl Oskar and Kristina still opened their door to the wife of the Baptist minister in Stillwater, no lightning rod was erected for the new church. The parish left it to the Lord to protect His temple against lightning.

- 3 -

The colony grew with each year's immigration. The newcomers were mostly relatives and friends of earlier arrivals, lured by descriptions of the fertile country. They would arrive during spring and summer, and their log cabins would be built by fall. They also came from other countries, although the majority were Swedes. In Chisago Township there were now five hundred.

On the peninsula opposite the island that had been named for the first land seeker at this lake a new town site had been surveyed and named Center City. This was a rather boastful name, but it was felt that the town would in time live up to it. It was in the center of the settlement and was planned to be the county seat of Chisago County.

A group of houses rose quickly in Center City. A few enterprising Swedes built a sawmill and a flour mill, both run with steam. The settlers need no longer drive long rough roads to have their timber sawed or their grain milled. An Irishman opened a lodging-house where travelers could sleep and obtain food, a German wagon maker built a shop with a lathe and other machinery. An American opened a tailor shop, a Norwegian blacksmith arrived with his tools. The Chisago people could now obtain clothing and tools near home.

And one day they heard that a young Swede had opened a general store in Center City.

The first time Karl Oskar went into the store, it was so new that shavings till lay in the corners. Counter and shelves had not yet been painted and there was a smell of pitch from new-sawed pine boards. From the ceiling hung a number of harnesses, lanterns, coils of rope and other objects, but most of the shelves were still bare.

Behind the counter stood a young man with a firm, narrow face and open light-blue eyes. His blond hair was cut short. Karl Oskar greeted the man in his native tongue — today he wouldn't have to use English to make his purchases — and was about to tell him who he was when the young man behind the counter said, "You must be Karl Oskar from Korpamoen."

If the ceiling had fallen on his head Karl Oskar could not have been more surprised. The new storekeeper not only used his own dialect, he also spoke to him as if his name had been in daily use at home.

"Why . . . yes! But how in the world . . . "

"I'm Klas Albert Persson from Ljuder. My father was Church-warden Per Persson of Åkerby."

"You must be his youngest boy."

"I am."

"Well!" Karl Oskar stared at the young man. "You certainly surprise me. I hadn't expected anyone from home to be the new store owner."

"I came to America three years ago," said Klas Albert. "I worked recently in a store in St. Paul."

Churchwarden's Klas Albert. Yes, Karl Oskar remembered the boy, who had been of confirmation age when he himself emigrated; now he appeared to be in his early twenties. He remembered the boy in Sweden and now he saw him as a grown man in America. In Klas Albert's growth he could measure the time he himself had been out here: enough for a boy to grow into manhood.

Many people were said to have come to America from Ljuder, but he had not met any of them. And now the first store in the new town of Center City in Chisago County was run by a son of Church-warden Per Persson of Åkerby. In some way the old and the new country had come closer through this meeting.

"I recognized you the moment you came in," said Klas Albert proudly.

"Hm. My nose, I guess." And Karl Oskar smiled broadly.

He talked for so long with the Åkerby churchwarden's son that he almost forgot he had come to do some shopping. Before he left he invited Klas Albert to his house next Sunday. It would be hard for Kristina to wait to meet him.

And the following Sunday, Klas Albert was greeted as a very welcome guest. Kristina began at once to question him about the home parish. She learned a great deal of news, and it was especially pleasing to her to talk with someone who had seen the home places more recently than she.

Klas Albert thought they had built a fine house to live in, and Karl Oskar took him on an inspection tour; he wanted to show his guest from Sweden how he had it in North America.

It was the nicest time of year, early summer; the green fields glittered with the new crops. Karl Oskar didn't want to boast of his farm, but Klas Albert could see he had over twenty-five acres. The fat oxen and the cows with their swollen udders wallowed in the meadow, healthy hogs filled their pen, thick-wooled sheep bleated contentedly. Barn, threshing shed and wagon shed were inspected, and American tools and implements were examined in detail. Then they looked at the huge sugar maples; every year Karl Oskar drilled holes in the trunks for sap which gave them all the sugar and sirup they needed. He asked the guest to taste the product. Didn't those blessed trees give them good sweetening?

The more Klas Albert saw, the more his respect grew for the farmer from Korpamoen. Time and again he asked: *When* had Karl Oskar done all this? *How* had he had time? The reply was short: He had not wasted a single working day.

Kristina showed the Astrachan apple tree, grown from a seed that had been sent from her Swedish home. The tree had shot up so fast it was now a head taller than she herself. Every fall she dug around her tree and covered the roots with an extra foot of soil to

232

protect them against the cold. Her tree was in its early youth; as yet it had had no blossoms.

When the inspection had been completed and they sat down at the dinner table, Klas Albert said, "Not one of the big farmers at home in Ljuder is as well off as you, Karl Oskar and Kristina."

He knew Karl Oskar was the first farmer in the home parish to sell his farm and emigrate to North America. Now he wanted to say how much he looked up to him and respected him for having taken this initiative. He always admired the first ones, those who dared something new, those who were courageous enough to move. Karl Oskar had indeed been bold in taking off for so distant a country.

"When I started to talk emigration, the whole parish felt insulted. People thought I should be punished for my arrogance."

"Now you can laugh at them," said Klas Albert.

"They poked fun at me and said my nose would be still longer when I came to America."

"Well, is it?"

Karl Oskar laughed. "It seems to be about the same, within a fraction of an inch."

"That I must write home!" said the young storekeeper.

They had so much to discuss that their guest remained until late in the evening. When he finally left, Karl Oskar said to Kristina with pride: Now Klas Albert would write home and tell them he had met the Korpamoen farmer in Minnesota. He would tell them about his situation over here. And what he wrote would be spread over the whole parish, and people would talk about them and about their fine home, New Duvemåla, on the beautiful lake. And how would those people feel who once had talked so badly about him because he left his old home? They were of course hoping to hear that he and his family lived in poverty in the new country. Instead, they would hear from the son of the churchwarden himself that he now had twenty-five acres of the most fertile land in America and harvested better crops than any farmer in the whole of Ljuder Parish.

"There'll be a great sickness in Ljuder for some time," predicted Karl Oskar. "People will be sick with envy!"

"I think you boasted a little too much," said Kristina.

"To point out the truth is not to boast."

233

XXIX

THE PRAYER OF A WOMAN BLESSED

- 1 -

Ulrika had given Kristina a mirror, which she had hung on the long wall above the sofa in the living room. In that position it could be seen from any place in the room and was convenient to look in. When Kristina sat on the sofa and turned her head she was confronted by her own face. A red rose had been painted on the glass in each of the four corners.

When Kristina was a girl she had often been told that she was beautiful. And perhaps it had been the truth, since so many had said it. But where now was the girl who so many times had blushed at compliments? Where now were her full cheeks with laughter's little soft dimples? What had become of her nicely rounded chin and her rosy color? What had happened to the lips once like wild strawberries?

The flower of her youth was passed and gone. The mirror showed her a face already marked by age. Every day she met the depressing sight of wrinkled cheeks, grayish skin, tired, fading eyes.

"How silly of me to put up the mirror!" she said to Karl Oskar. "I would know anyway that I look worse every day. And next to those four cheerful roses!"

"We must all age," was Karl Oskar's reply. "But the years are harder on emigrants; we grow old faster than others."

The years had set their mark on him too; he no longer moved about quickly and still complained of the ache in his left leg. But she had fared worse than he; the neighbor wives thought she was older than her husband, even though she was two years younger. It was the burden of childbearing that made the difference.

Frank, the youngest in her flock, had come as a birthday present — he was born on her thirty-first birthday, two years ago. She had been barely twenty when she had had her first child, Anna, who had died at an early age in Sweden. In the eleven years between her first and her latest she had gone through seven childbeds and borne eight children. During that time she had also gone through

234

their emigration to a new continent and the establishment of a new home. All those things were bound to leave their mark on her.

"I want to put away the mirror," she said. "Somewhere in a dark corner!"

"But it's a nice decoration," answered Karl Oskar. "And when Ulrika comes here she'll need it to look at herself."

"She doesn't age," said Kristina, with a trace of envy of her best friend.

"No. It is remarkable."

Kristina tried to tell herself that it was childish to regret that she no longer looked like a young girl. And deep in her heart she knew that her vexation was not primarily directed against her changed face. What she regretted was that her youthful years had run away from her while she was isolated in a wild and foreign country. Her youth was suddenly gone before she had had time to enjoy it.

She reflected that if at the age of nineteen she could have seen herself in labor seven times before age thirty-one, she would probably have said no to Karl Oskar's proposal and remained a spinster. Ulrika had given her a real scare by saying that she could go on bearing children until she was forty-six; she was only thirty-three now, so half her fertile years still lay ahead of her.

Frank was now two years old, and as yet no new life was in prospect. It was her highest hope that he might remain her youngest.

Kristina feared she could not survive another childbed.

-2-

That night Kristina dreamed that she gave birth to a child yet again.

It was a very short dream, but much happened in it. She was sitting in their new church and suddenly felt she was pregnant. She remembered it was her eighth time. The child seemed already well developed, and she could not understand why she hadn't felt her pregnancy before. When at the end of the service she was leaving the church, labor overtook her and she bore the child on the steps outside, in view of all the people. The child dropped naked on the top step and wailed loudly.

At this she awakened. Her shift was drenched through with cold perspiration, but a joyous relief filled her — only in her dream

235

had she been pregnant. Nevertheless, she decided she would talk about her worry with her uncle, Danjel Andreasson.

The next time she saw Danjel alone she asked, "Would I commit a grave sin if I prayed God to relieve me of further childbirths?"

Danjel was accustomed to his niece's talking intimately to him in matters she would not even mention to Karl Oskar, and he was not surprised at her question. He replied that the Almighty could see into the hearts of all His creatures. If she wanted to be relieved of bearing any more children, then this wish was already known to God. And it was assuredly permitted for each person to pray according to his understanding. If she was praying for something that was good for her, then the Lord would grant her prayer, otherwise not.

Kristina interpreted her uncle's opinion to mean that a woman's prayer for barrenness was not a sin against any of God's commandments. Of course, Danjel was only a poor sinner himself and could not with assurance tell her when she sinned and when she didn't. But if she had already transgressed with this wish in her heart, wasn't she courageous enough to do so also in prayer?

Thus it was that on a light, balmy July evening Kristina stole up the hill to a grove of oaks a short distance from the house. God saw her, and He would listen, but no one else must see or hear her. She felt she was on her way to a sacred meeting — which she was; tonight she was meeting God in His own beautiful oak temple.

Below a mighty tree she fell down on her knees to perform her secret errand. Her knees in the lush grass, her forehead against the oak trunk, Kristina prayed to Him Who had all power in heaven and on earth. She prayed for that which was good for her. A seven-times blessed woman prayed for barrenness for the rest of her life. She prayed the Lord to have mercy on her tired, worn-out body and not create any more lives in it.

"Dear, dear God, don't let me become pregnant again. I am unable to endure it. Think of me, dear God!"

The tall oak branches swayed above her head. The wind, rustling in their leaves, was the only sound heard in the grove up here tonight. The silence and the stillness aided in making her feel alone, alone with God. And after the prayer a great calm came over her. When she rose from her bent knees, she felt sure her prayer had been heard.

XXX

PARTNERS OF AMERICA

- 1 -

On May 11, 1858, a new star shone on the flag of the Republic — the thirty-second. On this day the United States Congress admitted a new state into the Union. The state was Minnesota.

There had been a long and bitter debate because the Southern slave states would not admit Minnesota unless Kansas too were admitted. But since the Kansas constitution permitted slavery it was not acceptable to the Northern states. Finally both territories were admitted.

The great news was dispatched by telegram to the Minnesota legislature. But the telegraph wires had been strung only as far as Prairie du Chien, Wisconsin, and from here the telegram had to be sent by steamer up the Mississippi. The new state was already two days old when the steamer arrived in St. Paul on the morning of May 13. The papers spread the happy message with the biggest headlines ever seen out there: "GLORIOUS NEWS!" "MINNESOTA A STATE!" "BRING OUT THE BIG GUN!" And half of the *Minnesota Pioneer* depicted a cannon being fired under a flag with thirty-two stars. "BRING OUT THE BIG GUN!" The letters above the cannon were so large the readers could almost hear the firing.

- 2 -

Even in the settlements at Chisago Lake the statehood news was celebrated noisily. No one there could really afford to waste ammunition, but this time everyone was generous with powder. Karl Oskar spent three shots from his old muzzle loader on the new state — they were the only shots he ever fired just for fun in America. His gun was old, but it had been made by the most famous gunsmith in Småland and it made more noise than any of the other guns in the district. And Karl Oskar himself said that since he had been the first one to settle at this lake he must fire a shot to be heard all the way to Washington, by the President himself!

Karl Oskar and his family received their citizenship papers that same spring. There were five of them to receive such papers — he, Kristina and the three children born in Sweden — and each paper cost a dollar. After leaving Sweden and having their names erased from the Ljuder Parish records they had not belonged anywhere; they had in a sense been vagrants in the world. Now they had printed papers to prove they had a new homeland.

"Are we no longer Swedish?" wondered Kristina.

"We were stricken from the records at home. We're American citizens now."

"In case of war between the two countries, would you fight against Sweden?"

He laughed. "I'd have to if I were asked."

Kristina felt it wasn't so easy to change a person. This paper couldn't transform her into an American even though it was large and thick and decorated with stamps and ornaments around her name. In this paper she was an American citizen — "Wife of Charles O. Nelson." But what did this new name mean to her? She was the same person she had been since her birth: Kristina Johansdotter of Duvemåla, Algutsboda Parish, Sweden. And however much her name was altered on American papers, she would continue to think as longingly as before of her old homeland.

But she had noticed that Karl Oskar had changed these last years. Not in clothing or external things, but in his speech and his way of thinking. He accepted the customs here, he felt that Americans were clever and industrious, he approved most of their ways and tried to ape them.

He himself testified to this change as he now asked his wife if he shouldn't use the name on the American citizenship paper and call himself Charles O. Nelson. What did she think?

"I don't like it!" said Kristina. "You may renounce Sweden, but if you change your Swedish name I'll laugh at you. For then it means you're getting uppity."

This was a clear reply and he said no more. Kristina was right, he thought. So he continued to write his name in the old way; he was still Karl Oskar Nilsson.

3

At this time there was talk about a lawyer down in Illinois whose name was Abraham Lincoln and who was at the helm of the new Republican Party. But the man was seldom referred to by his full name — he was called Old Abe, or Honest Abe. It was said of him that he was a homesteader's son and had been born on the floor of a log cabin in Kentucky. Honest Abe came from the deep forest, his ax under his arm; his strength, they heard, was fantastic: he could drive his ax deeper into the wood than any timberman ever before. In wrestling no one had been able to press Abe's shoulders to the floor; both as wrestler and as fighter he was unbeaten in all the states and territories of the Union. And the Creator had endowed him with spiritual gifts of the same immense proportions. He studied while he performed his daily labors; as a store clerk he read a book with one eye while he weighed up coffee and tea for his customers with the other. He had been called Old Abe ever since he was thirty, because of his great wisdom.

The homesteaders in Minnesota knew that Old Abe was capable of thinking for all of them. At last a great leader had been born to the men of the ax and the plow.

The stories about him changed and grew more amazing with the years. One day he had short-weighted someone by three ounces of tea, and he had ridden twenty miles to the customer's house with the small missing amount. Another time Honest Abe walked five miles to give ten cents back to a customer he had overcharged. Soon it was ten miles Abe had walked, and five cents; with the years the distance grew greater and the sum smaller. But when Honest Abe himself opened a shop he soon lost out — he couldn't lie and cheat and consequently had no success in business.

Now this remarkable man had become a lawyer in Springfield. It was a great distance to that town in Illinois, and to the settlers in Minnesota Old Abe seemed like the hero of some saga, good and strong and far away beyond the measure of ordinary human beings.

In the *Minnesota-Posten,* a new Swedish paper, Karl Oskar and Kristina saw a picture of him.

"His nose is almost as big as mine!"

"Not quite so bad."

"Well, it's more shapely, perhaps. I wonder if Abe's nose will give him luck."

"Why do they call him Honest Abe?" wondered Kristina. "It sounds as if honest men were rare in America."

The man in the picture with a nose almost as big as the Nilsanose wanted to liberate the three million slaves in the Southern states, those people who, like cattle, were listed among their owners' possessions and who were valued at three billion dollars. From a *Hemlandet* serial, "Fifty Years in Chains," Kristina knew of the cruel lot of the Negroes in the South. Southern marshals had been all the way up to Taylors Falls looking for escaped slaves, but people there had hidden them from the pursuers and helped them on their flight. Kristina had often hoped escaped Negroes would come to their house so that she could help them.

Karl Oskar cut out the picture of the man who wanted to abolish both masters and slaves.

Old Abe had said: In this country one man is as good as another, and sometimes better.

This wonderful expression the settlers often heard. It was a good slogan for free men in America, especially for those who handled ax and plow.

XXXI

IF GOD DOESN'T EXIST . . .

- 1 -

The fire burned and crackled on the hearth in the big room where the settler family sat within the circle of light this November evening. Each member had his or her chore to perform in the firelight. Kristina was carding wool for stocking yarn, while Märta, who had just learned to spin, picked up the wool wads as they came from her mother's carding combs. Johan sat like a man and read the new issue of *Hemlandet*, and Harald was spelling his way through a chapter in his *First Reader*. Dan was working on the runners for a sled he was building; with the aid of his father he hoped to have it ready for the first snow. Ulrika was dressing a doll given

240

to her by Mrs. Henry O. Jackson, whose name also was Ulrika; when the doll was dressed she removed all the garments and began to dress it again. Frank, the youngest in the family, had been in bed for a few days with a sore throat but was getting better.

The family father was missing in the firelight circle this evening. Karl Oskar had gone to St. Paul to look at horses; a drove had just arrived from Iowa. He would be away for the night and was not expected home until tomorrow evening. The children were in a great state of expectation at the prospect of Father's returning with a new horse.

Undisturbed by the din of loud child voices, Harald kept reading his lesson, the same piece over and over: "All things are made by God. He has made me. I am only a child, but I know I am more than a dog or a horse. What has a child above a dog or a horse? A horse or a dog can stand and walk as well as a child. Horses and dogs have sight, smell and taste, like me. But I have a soul. I can see my body. But my soul I can't see. My body will die. But my soul will never die. It ascends to God when my body dies."

Now and then a burned-out log broke and the pile of firewood caved in a little. The crackling from the fire, the screeching from Kristina's wool combs and the buzz from the spinning wheel mingled with the boy's prattling reading.

Harald went on: "God is your comfort in sorrow, He is your support in need, if you only pray . . . "

The words were like a sword in Kristina's heart: "If you only pray . . . " No, she didn't understand it, something was wrong. That evening last summer she had prayed under the big oaks on the hill, and after the prayer she had felt confident that she had been heard. This confidence had grown for four months. Now it was completely shattered; for two weeks she had known she was again with child.

Who could have prayed more fervently than she? But God had not heard her. He had remained deaf to her prayer. He had given her neither reply nor sign — unless her new pregnancy was the reply? During the very moment of prayer she had felt the Almighty's mild hand upon her forehead. But she had made a miserable mistake. He was unmoved, unresponsive.

She must go through it all again, all she had prayed to be relieved of: first to feel sick and miserable, then to carry the increased burden of her body and shuffle about on heavy feet, at last the terrifying labor, her spent strength and the great weakness and fatigue afterward. And just at that time the most would be required of her: getting up nights to give the breast to the baby, staying awake all hours when it was sick or fretted — constant care of the new life through day and night. And this time she met the pregnancy with less strength than at any of the other seven times. Her weariness was great when she went to bed in the evening, and it was almost as great when she arose in the morning.

She had waited as long as she could to tell Karl Oskar. No need to hurry with the information; she must be sure. And now she was sure. This morning before he left for St. Paul she had told him: It was time again for her; she must go through it again.

If he was disappointed he hadn't shown it. "Well, hmm, time again? Well, if we can feed six young ones I guess we can feed seven! As long as you can stand it." That was all he had said, and it was about what she had expected him to say.

"All things are made by God. . . . "

Now Kristina couldn't endure hearing Harald read the piece any more. There was one way to silence the studious youngster. It was the children's bedtime.

"Get to bed now! All of you!"

-2-

Kristina was unable to finish her prayer that evening.

She began several times. "Our Father in Heaven, let me this night rest within Thy protection." But after a few sentences the words choked in her throat, clung to her tongue. She stopped. She began again, but couldn't get any farther. She lay awake, her eyes wide open against the room's darkness.

The hours passed, it was close to midnight, and as yet she had not said her evening prayer.

What was the matter with her tonight? She wasn't worried because Karl Oskar was away and she was alone with the children — Karl Oskar had been away many nights during the last years and she wasn't afraid. What was it, then? She always said her evening prayer before she went to sleep. Now she couldn't go to sleep without doing it.

Something seemed to be stifling her breathing. She felt as if a pair of hands choked her; she must sit up and take a deep breath. Eased, she lay down. But after a while the sensation returned.

Finally she rose from her bed, put on a skirt and a jacket and stuck her feet into her soft deerskin moccasins. The choking in her throat was still there. She gasped for air like a fish on dry land. What had come over her tonight? She had never had these choking sensations before. It felt unbearably close in the house. She must go outside so that she could breathe better.

Cautiously, silently, she unlocked the front door and stepped out on the stoop. It was midnight and pitch dark. She seemed to have stuck her head into a flour sack. She could not see the sky, nor the moon, nor the stars. It was black at her feet, black above her head and black all around her. It was as dark as it could be on a November night in Minnesota.

It was cold, perhaps near freezing, but the cold felt fresh and dry; the clear night air released her throat, and she breathed more easily. She stepped down from the stoop and walked along the side of the building, her hands following the wall to guide her through the deep darkness. She stumbled a few times, but continued. At the back of the house her hands lost touch with the wall, but she walked on. She felt soft ground under her slippers; she was walking through her flower bed. Now her hands were in front of her, fumbling like a blind man's.

She walked a little farther, until her foot hit a large tree stump. She sat down on it, slumped over and shivered in the cold.

It was a silent night, without wind. Above her was no heaven, around her no earth. All she was aware of was emptiness and desolate silence. No leaves rustled in the trees, not a single crackling noise came from the stripped cornstalks in the field, not one complaint from the crickets. Sitting on the stump, enveloped in the night, her eyes could see nothing, her ears hear nothing.

She was in a black, empty hole. She was abandoned, alone in a desolate world.

And out here the same question assailed her. Why didn't God listen when I prayed to be spared another childbirth? Why didn't He listen, why didn't He grant my prayer? If God exists, why doesn't He hear my prayers?

If God exists! For the first time in her life Kristina caught herself putting an "if" before God.

What she had done shocked her. The Heavenly Father, did He

not exist? This thought had never entered her mind before. It would have seemed absurd, something one never even considered. But suddenly here she was thinking: *Suppose God didn't exist.*

That would be an answer to her questions, would explain everything. Then she need not anxiously ask herself why her prayer hadn't been granted. If God didn't exist, then He could not hear the prayers she addressed to Him. Then she had been praying all these years to a Heavenly Father Who wasn't in heaven.

The night air chilled her body and she shivered, her arms and legs trembling. She had come out without a shawl. But she did not go in, she was not aware of the cold. Tonight she was oblivious of her body. She knew only her disturbed soul.

What could she do if God didn't exist? In whom could she trust? Who would assist her? Who would protect her against danger? Who would in the future give her strength to take care of her home and her children? Who would help her endure life in this new country which to her always remained *away* from home, never home? And who would in the end receive her after death?

If God didn't exist...

No, she couldn't become reconciled to that. All the strength of her soul rose in defiance; the answer was unacceptable. She demanded of God that He exist. The Creator must assume the responsibility of looking after His creation, as a father was responsible for the children he begot.

Stiffly she folded her cold hands, clasping them tightly in prayer. She began in a low voice, haltingly. But after a few words a new life came to her tongue. Her voice grew strong, the words flowed from her mouth clear and sure. Her soul's need was the power driving her to prayer, and she was able to pray again:

"God, You must be! Listen to me, You must! Haven't You created me? Then You must not abandon me! Without You I would be a miserable creature, lost and alone in the world."

But when her voice had died down, silence again took over. Nothing more was heard, not even the faintest echo. No answer came; the night around her remained mute. The darkness around her remained silent, the desolation did not reply, nothing answered her.

She did not know how long she had been sitting on the stump behind the house when something startled her. She rose as if suddenly awakened from a deep sleep. She strained her ears and listened; she could hear something. A sound had reached her ears, a very faint sound, the first sound her ears had caught out here tonight. It did not come from the leaves rustling in the trees, nor from the dry cornstalks — it was the sound of a voice, however faint. And she felt in her heart that someone was calling her.

Did it come from up there? Was it God replying to her? Did He call her: Kristina! Kristina! I hear you!

But no sound came from above. And it wasn't her name she heard. Yet she did hear a voice and she felt that it called her. Someone near her was replying to her prayer of a moment ago. She was not alone in the world.

And then her ears discerned the sound very clearly. It came from inside the house, a child weeping, faintly, pitiably, and only one word was she able to understand: "Mother!" It was a single word, and it was uttered faintly, but it was enough for her. It was her boy Frank, who lay sick with his throat infection. He had awakened and missed his mother, and now he was calling for her.

A comforting calm descended on Kristina as she walked in to her child. Tonight she needed to go to a living creature who was more helpless than she.

XXXII

A PRAYER GRANTED

- 1 -

Spring had come earlier than in any other year since their settling in Minnesota. By March the powerful flow of sap in the sugar maples had risen, and Karl Oskar, pushing his auger deep into their trunks, received more sap then he had ever tapped before: a whole fifty gallons in this spring of 1859, he recorded in his almanac. And early in April the fields were dry enough for sowing.

And this spring Kristina's Astrachan apple tree bloomed.

She watered, weeded and fertilized her tree, but no matter what she did it grew too slowly for her. She wanted to see wider boughs, greater foliage, more height from year to year. She thought the severe winters were hard on the roots and delayed growth. Karl Oskar jokingly suggested she move the apple tree inside during the cold season. But now it had developed enough to bear fruit; suddenly it was covered with blossoms, beautiful white flowers with a faint pinkness.

And next fall they would for the first time gather in the precious crop of juicy apples, apples with so clear a skin you could almost mirror your face in them. Astrachan apples had a fragrance that filled the room; they were as pleasing to the eye and the nose as to the tongue.

But the tree blossomed for only a few days. Unexpectedly they had severe cold one night, and in the morning the ground was covered with frost. The apple blossoms hung limp and dead. With the first wind they flew away like a swarm of butterflies. The tree from Sweden had bloomed too early. But the tree itself remained, healthy and green, and it would grow and branch out and blossom again another spring.

Now it was time for Kristina's great spring washing, which she pounded and rinsed down at the lake shore. Her body felt stiff and clumsy even though she was only in the beginning of the sixth month of pregnancy. Her back ached from being on her knees at the washboard, and her scrubbing dragged on longer than usual. This spring washing was her heaviest chore of the year.

Toward the evening of the third day, as she was about to rinse the last few garments in the lake, a sudden pain cut through her back, so intensely that she had to sit down and rest on the beating board.

She thought she must have strained herself by lifting the heavy washtubs, and she hoped the pain would subside if she sat quietly for a few moments. But instead it grew in intensity and spread from the small of her back through her whole body. And then she began to recognize it; it was not the first time she had experienced it — it was the pain of labor.

Johan was fishing in the reeds a short distance from her. She called to the boy: He must go and fetch Father, who was sowing wheat in the field.

The pain forced Kristina to lie down on the steeply slanted washboard, which was far from comfortable. Lying there, she suffered a more severe pain than any she had ever felt in her life. Afterward she must have fainted.

Karl Oskar came running; he would help her get inside the house. She bent double when she tried to walk, her legs failing her. He carried her to her bed. Once there, she pulled off her clothes and discovered red runnels on the inside of her legs: bleeding had begun.

Karl Oskar hurried to his nearest neighbor, Algot Svensson, to fetch his wife Manda to come and help. Meanwhile Kristina had another severe bleeding. And before Karl Oskar returned with Manda she had borne a lifeless child.

-2-

Ulrika was sitting at Kristina's bedside. It was the day after her miscarriage; Mrs. Jackson had hurried to New Duvemåla as soon as the message reached her.

Kristina lay exhausted and weak. The bleedings had continued long after the stillbirth and had stopped only today. She felt as if she were torn to pieces inside. She had only one desire: to lie still in bed.

In Alex Turner's drugstore in Stillwater Ulrika had bought several kinds of medicines, pills and powders for her friend; she arranged the jars, bottles and boxes on the bedside table. She knew what was needed for a woman who had lost blood in a miscarriage. Here were the excellent Blood Pills; none other than the Governor's wife had written a testimonial to their excellence. And this was the Blood Rejuvenator discovered by a Swedish Methodist minister in Chicago; his pills were really miraculous. And then she had brought a bottle of medicine called Gift of Blood, which had been manufactured in Washington, the very capital of the country. She felt sure anything made there must be first-class, since undoubtedly the President himself would try the products of the capital.

Kristina was overwhelmed by her thoughtfulness and concern.

Tears of appreciation came to her eyes. "My dear Ulrika, you've gone to a lot of trouble for my sake."

"You never take care of yourself, Kristina. I've told you before, you have too much to do. You wear yourself to a frazzle!"

Now she must rest and gain strength, said Mrs. Jackson. Staying in bed was absolutely essential. And she mustn't do any heavy work for a long time. Ulrika would send over Miss Skalrud to take care of the household for a while. That Norwegian was a stubborn, bull-headed woman but very capable if you left her alone. "Skalrud helped me through my last childbed."

Last winter Ulrika had borne the third child of her marriage with Pastor Jackson. This time it was a son.

Kristina asked, "How is your baby?"

"My little minister! He's wonderful! He weighs twenty pounds, he's as fat as a bishop. Who knows, perhaps the Ljuder Parish whore has produced a bishop for America. Wouldn't that be something, Kristina?"

The Lord had finally heard Ulrika and given her a male child, whom the mother long in advance had dedicated to the church. Only now did she feel fully recompensed for having once been denied the Holy Sacrament in Ljuder and excluded from the Swedish church.

Before Ulrika left she spoke to Karl Oskar alone and gave him a warning: Undoubtedly Kristina's misfortune had been caused by her heavy work. Why couldn't he help her with the worst chores from now on? By now he ought to be Americanized enough to scrub the floor, milk the cows and wash dishes.

And Ulrika received from him this piece of information: It happened quite often that he milked the cows and washed the dishes. But he was still Swedish enough never to have scrubbed a floor. Perhaps he had better rid himself of this attitude too.

- 3 -

Kristina enjoyed eight days of bed rest while Miss Skalrud took charge of the house for her. Meanwhile Ulrika returned at intervals to see if she was following her advice and taking the blood-giving, blood-strengthening and blood-renewing pills, powders and medicines. But the rest itself was the best medicine.

When she got on her feet again, Kristina was still weak and

tired. She must do only lighter work for some time. Karl Oskar lugged in wood and water and milked the cows for her; she need not do any outside chores this spring. Märta, now twelve, was willing and a great help to her.

After some weeks Kristina felt fairly well again, but her spiritual welfare was more important to her. A life that had grown for more than twenty weeks inside her had suddenly left her body. The child in her dream, born on the church steps, had at least been alive, and its cries still echoed in her ears. Her stillborn child had been mute. Thus the dream had come true in one way, but not in the other; it was a half-true dream.

Karl Oskar had taken the child away, and she realized he must have buried it somewhere in the forest. Where was the . . . ? she had once asked. He did not tell her. And perhaps it was as well. She herself knew: *The child had been returned.*

One secret remained between God and her. She had prayed to be relieved of another birth, and she had been. This was the granting of her prayer. He had taken the child back. He had not dared trust it to her. For she had prayed to be relieved from fertility and wished for barrenness, she had rejected blessing and prayed to be cursed. Now it was clear to her: She had sinned with her prayer in the oak grove on the hill that evening last summer.

And a still worse sin had she committed in the night last fall: In a moment of great weakness her faith had faltered, until she had doubted that God existed. She had been given her reply. She had been rebuked: He had taken His creation away from her womb.

Thus Kristina had encountered the Heavenly Father in all His severity. She had received an answer, both to her prayer and to her questions of doubt. God had shown her that He existed, and He had shown it to her in a way that she never again need doubt.

Now there remained for her only to submit.

-4-

A SETTLER WIFE'S EVENING PRAYER

Tonight again I pray for forgiveness, as I did last night and the night before, and all evenings since I lost my child. I have confessed my sin and endure with patience my punishment, but soon I hope to feel that You have forgiven me a little. I want so to feel that You haven't turned Your face away from me. Otherwise my despair will be great. I have no one to turn to, no one but You. Karl Oskar is kind and thoughtful about me, but my husband can be my staff only in worldly matters. When I worry about my soul, then he cannot help me, no, no more than any other human being.

From now on I will patiently endure the life which You in Your grace and blessing give me. I will take care of the little ones with all the strength You give me. I shall try as well as I can to look after the other children You have given me. But You know how tired I grow at times; in the evenings I feel worn out, and in the mornings I wonder if I will be able to get up.

Sometimes I feel I would be glad to die, because then I would have the enduring rest which I long for. But I worry about leaving before my children can take care of themselves. Karl Oskar would be unable to handle the little ones alone, this You know. Ulrika is barely five years old and little Frank isn't three yet. Therefore I pray You, my Creator and Lord, let me live still a few years, at least five years more.

I think often about Robert, my brother-in-law. Like him, I cannot fight You any longer. Do with me as you wish. I am reconciled to everything. Like him I submit to my lot. But give me strength to last a few years more, dear God!

Bless and keep all of us who sleep under this roof and all the settlers who have come to this foreign land. Amen.

-5-

It was Kristina's habit at this time of the year to lie awake in the evening after she had gone to bed and peer out into the dark toward that land where the evenings in spring were light.

In her thoughts she traveled the path back, mile after mile, down the rivers, across the prairie, over the sea. But each time the way seemed longer. She never reached her goal, she spent all her time on the road. Each time she covered a shorter distance, while the land each time receded. And by and by, as the land of her childhood faded into the distance, it was transformed in her mind's eye.

As a small girl she had one day lost her doll, the first doll she had ever owned, a china doll in a blue flowered dress. It had fallen into the well at home in Duvemåla. She was inconsolable over her loss and cried and begged her father and brothers: Wouldn't they please get the doll out of the well for her? But the well was too deep.

Her doll had stayed at the bottom. On clear days she could look down and see the doll's dress, like a streak of bluing in the water. She would climb up on the well wall, until her parents had to forbid her to go near it. But whenever they were out of sight she would steal back to peek. She watched the rosy cheeks of the doll fade away and the dress disintegrate in the water. But her lost doll existed, and she knew where it was, though it was lost to her forever.

At the next fair her father had bought her a new and bigger doll, with a prettier dress, but it didn't help; her longing for the lost one was as great as ever. She talked only of her first doll, she put new dresses on it, enlarged it, made it into the most magnificent doll imaginable. At last it had become a doll no one had ever seen or ever would see.

It was the same with her native land. She had lost it in a well so deep that she could never retrieve it. The land was there, and she knew where it was; she had stood staring after it in the daytime, she had stretched her arms for it in her dreams at night. But she would never reach it, never get it back, never again see her beloved ones at home.

So she had done the same with her old homeland as she had with her doll. She made a special Sweden out of her longing, a Sweden she carried within herself, a homeland that was hers and no one else's. She built recklessly from anything she could get hold of: all her happy experiences in the home village, the good dreams she had dreamt while in this foreign land, happenings in Sweden she had heard others speak of, recollections from the Bible and the saga books. Of all this she wove a land that no one had ever seen and no one ever would see.

Kristina often told her children about her Sweden. The oldest had some faint memory of an earlier home far away, but to the other four Sweden was only the land where Father and Mother had been born and where their grandparents lived. The mother often told them of her own childhood, her sisters and playmates, of schooling and games, about the seasons, the first day of spring when she ran barefoot, the first wild strawberries in summer and the first apples that fell from the trees in fall, the winter's sleigh rides and the ice on the pond, about the Christmas-morning journey to the early service in the light of crackling pitch torches.

But her children listened to her as they listened to fairy tales. To them, Sweden was one of those wonderful countries in story

251

books, where only good things happen. One time little Ulrika asked her mother: Did Sweden exist in reality? Was it actually a country on earth? Or was it, like that country with the proud prince and the beautiful princess, somewhere east of the sun and west of the moon?

The mother replied that it did indeed exist and was on earth. Neither to herself nor to her children could she admit that she had described a country which no one would ever see.

XXXIII

RECONCILIATION

- 1 -

The whitewashed fireplace was trimmed with fresh leaves, and young birch boughs had been placed in each corner of the big room; outside, a birch had been raised on either side of the entrance. Above the door between the young trees hung a wreath of cornflowers, poppies, morning stars and bluebells. The path to the door had been well swept, and branches had been placed on either side to form a festive arch.

It was Midsummer Eve. Following the custom of the old country, they had tried to create a holiday atmosphere by decorating their home with young leaf trees and fresh summer blossoms. But they could not make it exactly the same — the northland's summer night was missing.

Today was a great day for them: their new Swedish almanac, printed by *Hemlandet,* was dated 1860. The brig *Charlotta* of Karlshamn had landed them in New York on Midsummer Eve 1850. Ten full years to the day had passed since they took their first steps on American soil.

And now Karl Oskar and Kristina went through in their memory the long time they had spent in their new homeland. They went through it all: their first shanty of boughs and twigs where the storm in the late fall had been so hard on them, the first long and severe winter when they often went without food; then came the first spring when Karl Oskar broke the first ground and planted the first crop. They recalled the first autumn they had had a harvest, the smallest ever but the most important of all. They had driven the first sacks to the mill and could bake the first bread from their own rye flour. It had been one of their greatest days in the new land when this bread was taken from the oven, steaming and warm — what a fragrance!

They remembered also the misery of the first summers' heat, and the intense cold of the winters in the log cabin — snow winters that never seemed to end. Their thoughts lingered on the good crops and the poor, on the births of their children, their baptisms, the first Sacrament in their house, the first service in the new church, Robert's return with the false riches, his death and funeral . . .

But most of the thousands of days encompassed by their ten years were lost to memory. Those were the quiet working days when nothing had happened, nothing except their hands' labor — the innumerable days which were only workdays, work from morning to night, and each day therefore confusingly like the next. Now these uncountable laboring days seemed like one day, one single long day of patient struggle. And it was of greater importance than any of the others, for during the course of that day they had started out, from the very beginning, for a second time in their lives, and for the second time built a home.

That Midsummer Eve when, tired and spent from the long voyage, they had walked down the gangplank in New York Harbor, was now removed to a distant past, incredibly long ago. The ten years of their lives that belonged to America had lengthened in their minds and seemed enormously long because they had been years of great changes.

Kristina looked down toward the lake, out over the water which glittered peacefully in the sunset.

"It has changed since we first came."

All around, the shores were now cultivated. On every surveyed claim stood a house; in every house lived a settler and his family. Karl Oskar gazed out over the slope where his fields now stretched; nearly all of the meadow had been turned into cultivated land, almost forty acres of it. But next to it was a piece of ground with heavy oaks where the topsoil was equally deep; before he was through he wanted to cultivate that piece too. It would entail heavier labor and take a longer time because of the big stumps.

253

"We have done a lot since we settled here, don't you think so, Kristina?"

"We are better off than I dared hope when we slept in that shanty the first fall."

Her remark made him appraise the sturdy walls of their house. But it was already almost six years old. Next time he built . . .

"Still, not everyone improves his lot here in America," added Kristina. She could have mentioned the names of two youths, members of their own group on the voyage, who had emigrated to find early graves in America.

Karl Oskar said: The success of an immigrant did not depend on the country alone, it depended as much on the man.

"At home the youngsters dance around the Maypole on Midsummer Eve," said Kristina. "All the old folk dances — I Weave You a Wreath, Find the Shepherd, Catch Your Partner."

"Well," said Karl Oskar. "I suppose everything there is as it used to be."

He could not imagine that any changes had taken place in his home village during the ten years since he had left it. In Sweden the people lived as they had always lived, performed their chores as their forebears had always performed them. In the America more new ideas were tried and greater changes took place in one year than during a hundred years in Sweden.

Karl Oskar could see his home village as it had been that April morning when they stepped onto the wagon to drive to Karlshamn, his father and mother standing side by side on the stoop, immobile as stone monuments, looking after the wagon with their sons driving through the gate, leaving their old home, their village where the family had lived through countless generations. The wagon swung out into the road, the team began a slow trot, he himself turned once more and saw his father leaning on his crutches, his mother beside him, tall, her back straight, perhaps straighter because of this farewell moment.

And that was how their son in America had seen his parents during the ten years his eyes never beheld them.

Father had been against Karl Oskar's great decision; he had never reconciled himself to his sons' emigration. Yet Karl Oskar believed that he had done right. How was it now, however, with Kristina? He had harbored through the years a question he had never managed to ask his wife. Perhaps he feared the answer.

Their emigration was from the very beginning his idea; it was he who had pushed it through. His wife had been against it, and only during the brutal famine winter when he had had to make a coffin for their oldest child had she changed her mind and said that she was ready to go with him. Since then it had often seemed to him that she had accompanied him regretfully. What did she think now, ten years later?

This memorable day might be the right moment to put the question to her.

"We did the right thing when we emigrated — don't you think so, Kristina?"

She turned her head and looked at her husband. Only vaguely did he distinguish her face in the dusk; he could not see any expression. She merely seemed surprised at his question, as if it had taken her unawares.

"We did neither right nor wrong. Our emigration was predestined. It was our fate."

"Do you mean that? Predestined? Our fate?" He in turn was surprised, perhaps even astonished.

"It was our lot. We need not ask about right or wrong."

"I only wondered if you hold me responsible."

"No person is responsible. There is only one Ruler."

And before he had time to say anything she went on: She still remembered very clearly the text Pastor Törner had chosen when he gave them the Sacrament in their old log house the first time. God had ordained how far and wide people must travel to find their homes on earth. He chose and decided the places for their settling. That was predestination.

But now Karl Oskar shook his head firmly. "I cannot believe that we don't decide things for ourselves."

In his wife's eyes he might be merely a blind tool of God's will, but in his own eyes Karl Oskar did not even have a partner in the emigration. He alone was the originator, the one responsible for the decision which had given them a new homeland and decided where their children, grandchildren and grandchildren's children would be born.

Karl Oskar had now reached his full manhood, but everything he had experienced strengthened him in the belief of his youth: It was given to man to decide for himself, to take care of his life and make of it what he could. Never must one give up in adversity and distress, always must one seek and try another way. This faith had never failed him, and he felt sure he would stay with it until the end of his days.

But after his wife's miscarriage the year before, he had noticed a great change in her. She often appeared absent-minded and pre-occupied; she was more closed up within herself than before. Yet at the same time she displayed a greater steadfastness of character, a more even temper and inner peace. Her old longing for her home-land, her worries and doubts, seemed to have diminished. And he had felt greatly relieved. Still, she had never said in any way that this was so.

Now he asked, "If I'm right, Kristina, I believe you don't long for the old country any more."

"No, I don't. It doesn't matter where a person lives in this life on earth. One corner of the world is as good as another. The on-ly thing that counts for me is the eternal life."

"Have you changed because it can't be otherwise?"

"I haven't changed. On the contrary. I have only accepted this worldly life — that's how I may *seem* to have changed."

Kristina's voice was not a voice of surrender, it was calm, firm, full of conviction. And Karl Oskar had a feeling he need not ask any more.

In the thickening dusk they could no longer discern the decora-tions or the festive arch which they had raised today. In their new homeland St. John's Eve was not light. Over the young settlement fell the cloak of darkness, and Ki-Chi-Saga's water turned black under the evening sky.

XXXIV

THE LETTER TO SWEDEN

New Duvemåla at Center City Post Ofis
in Minnesota State, North-America
Christmas Day Anno 1860

Dearly Beloved Sister Lydia Karlsson,
Hope you are well is our Wish to you. You must be waiting for a Letter from your Brother, I am slow in writing.

We are well in our Family up to date and all is well with us. Our Children have grown a lot and are well, Johan is our Hired

Hand and Märta our Maid. All the Boys are full of Life and Activity but that is their Age. Christmas has come again, I bought a Sewing Machine for Kristina, she was glad with this Christmas Present. She didn't like it here so well the first Years but now it is over. She planted a new Flower Bed in front of our House with many Swedish Flowers — Reginas, Yellow Striped Lilies, Brushblooms and poppies. Kristina's astrachan Tree has not yet had any Fruit because the Blooms have frozen two springs in a row. But the tree will undoubtedly give us Fruit in the Future.

You asked in your last Letter if I ever regretted my Emigration. I cannot say that I have. I won't boast but my Situation here is on a Level with the best Farmers at Home. Last Fall I harvested 125 Bushels Corn, 73 Bushels Wheat and 51 Bushels Rye, all heaped Measure. I have also bought a Horse.

I am master on my Claim and do not bow to anyone. But no lazy Fool will have Success in North-America. It takes a man's whole Life and daily Toil.

All the Land here in our Settlement around the big Lake is now taken. This Indian Water is commonly called Swede Lake. One Race leaves this World, another comes along.

I have this year served on the Jury in our Swedish district. I have long been a member of our Parish Council. You may tell people at home that your Brother in North-America has become both Churchwarden and Sheriff.

Last November 6 I voted for the first time for the Head of our new Country. I voted for Abe Lincoln for President of the United States. He was elected. Abe was born in a Log House exactly like the one I built the first Year I was here.

The Slave States want another President and there are rumors of a War to free the Slaves. We hope to be spared the Destruction and Devastation of our Country and I am sure Father Abe will find some Way to avoid War.

How is our old Mother, Greet her on behalf of her Son who lives in a distant Land in the far West.

Anno 1860 is nearing its End and we have also come one year closer to Eternity. To my dear Sister and all who still remember me in my old Village I send you Christmas Greetings and wish you Peace.

Written down by your devoted Brother
Karl Oskar Nilsson

257

ABOUT THE AUTHOR

CARL ARTUR VILHELM MOBERG *was born of peasant stock in the parish of Algutsboda, province of Småland, Sweden. He worked as a forester and a farm hand before becoming a journalist and then an author. He has published twenty novels and twenty-five plays, and his books have been translated into eighteen languages.*

ABOUT THE TRANSLATOR

GUSTAF LANNESTOCK *spent his boyhood on a Swedish farm not far from Moberg's home, was graduated from the University of Gothenburg and has lived in California since 1930.*